6.09.81

DAVID

all good things
should be for you.

Paul

Sabi H. Shabtai

 DELACORTE PRESS / NEW YORK

Published by
Delacorte Press
1 Dag Hammarskjold Plaza
New York, New York 10017

Manufactured in the United States of America

Fourth Printing—1980

Designed by MaryJane DiMassi

Library of Congress Cataloging in Publication Data

Shabtai, Sabi H
Five minutes to midnight.

I. Title.
PZ4.S5225Fi   [PS3569.H23]   813'.5'4   79-21897
ISBN 0-440-02569-9

*To Gay Yellen, without whom
this story might never have been told,
and to my parents for all their sacrifices*

While some of the events and characters depicted in this novel are totally fictional, the Doomsday Clock is anything but fiction and its hands still point to five minutes to midnight—

PART 1

CHAPTER ONE

HE moment he saw the lickspit grin on the manager's glistening rotund face, he was overcome by a strong urge to turn on his heel and flee. Driving there, he had toyed with the idea of using the blinding downpour as an excuse for not showing up. It was one of those hot, muggy Washington days which he had come to despise since he began dividing his time between D.C. and his post in Berkeley, and the closer he got to the bookstore, the more disgusted he felt.

Why, for Christ's sake, had he given in? How had he let anyone talk him into the autographing party? It was one thing agreeing to give up his pseudonym, his privacy; it was another to personally peddle his book like some cheap salesman, to prostitute his academic and professional stature by autographing trite inscriptions to people he neither knew nor cared to know. He felt more comfortable in the role of talk-show guest, helping promote the book on television or radio or giving newspaper interviews, where the selling was indirect, subtle. There it could be done with a modicum of intelligence and a veneer of respectability. He winced in anticipation of the condescending expressions on his colleagues' faces.

"We're *so* honored to have you here, Professor Sartain." The sweaty hand of the disagreeable young man was already pumping his. "Murphy, Roger Murphy. I'm the manager of the store. Really, it's *really* an honor to have you."

Too late now, Sartain thought. He had to go ahead with it; there was no way out. He forced a smile and hoped it looked pleasant. "It's my pleasure to be here, Mr. Murphy."

The store looked impressive by bookshop standards: large, tastefully appointed, and obviously well stocked. After a brief handshaking reception with some of the staff on the second-floor gallery, the professor was led to a podium on the ground level. A small gathering of people was already standing in front of it, some holding copies of his book with its unmistakable dark blue dust jacket.

The group was a mixed bag of late-afternoon browsers: some obvious bibliophiles, some casual autograph seekers whose favorite best sellers were those which had been personally inscribed by a visiting author, and others whose main purpose was to avoid the drenching downpour outside.

Murphy tested the microphone. Sartain felt relieved to finally be on the podium. This was definitely his territory. As Murphy introduced him, reading from the curriculum vitae the professor's impressive credentials, Sartain mused on the reasons why he always preferred facing an assembly of people from behind a podium, microphone in hand, to the personal, one-to-one contact with ordinary people as he had just so awkwardly endured on the second floor. Could he be guilty of the same contempt for the nonintelligentsia of which he so often accused his colleagues? He must talk it over with Linda, he decided, inwardly chuckling at the relish with which she always dissected his motives; laying bare his ego like the innards of an earthworm.

He only half heard Murphy's litany of his accomplishments. "Our distinguished guest . . . the author of . . . professor of political science . . . internationally known expert on guerrilla warfare and terrorism . . . fellow of the prestigious Harry S Truman Institute for International Affairs at . . . lecturer at the American University in Beirut and at . . . author of *The Rescue*, a novel about a daring commando raid . . . the real man behind the pen name . . ."

His thoughts were back with Linda in Tiburon when the sound of applause snapped him back. He took the microphone from Murphy.

Just as Sartain opened his mouth to begin, a flash of lightning and a crash of thunder interrupted. He used it to help break the ice.

"I promise to tell the truth, the whole truth, and nothing but, ladies and gentlemen," he began, rolling his eyes toward the skylight. "And owing to my penchant for long-winded dissertations, to which any of my students will attest, I suppose I'd best stick to a course of merely taking any questions you might have."

Sartain's bio placed his birthdate in 1925, but those in the audience who had expected a soft-bellied, myopic college professor were surprised to be confronting a ruggedly built individual. Sartain, with his trim torso and dark, full hair, looked more like an athlete than an academic. Most people's immediate impression was of a man of action rather than a university intellectual.

A tousle-headed, bearded young man in an orange Windbreaker, obviously a student, was the first person to raise his hand. "How long ago did you start writing *The Rescue*, Dr. Sartain and when did you complete it?"

"Oh, I started to write it . . . ," he paused, puffing on his pipe, reckoning aloud, "Now let's see. It was shortly before the La Guardia bombing, I remember that . . . I suppose it took roughly seven or eight months to complete. I completed writing it roughly two months prior to the Entebbe raid. Does that answer your question?"

The young man nodded.

Sartain took the next question from a man who looked every inch a Washington lawyer, from his executive all-weather coat to his hard-set features. When the man spoke, Sartain knew his impressions had been right.

"Your portrayal of the alleged events in Libya, which, I believe, is your fictional North African country, is remarkably similar to what has transpired in Entebbe, including, for example, your description of the segregation of the Jewish passengers from the others. How do you explain such precise foresightedness? Was it a coincidental fluke, clairvoyance, or, perhaps, complicity?"

The stern manner in which the innuendo was put forward elicited a few twitters from the crowd. Sartain could hardly conceal his own amusement.

"I'm sorry to disappoint you," the professor began, "but it is none of the above. It has more to do with my belief that those who study terrorism must train themselves to think like terrorists if they're not to misdiagnose the whole phenomenon. What I did was to apply this theory in the writing of my novel. To give you a broad illustration: frequently the objectives of terrorism are obscured by random attacks involving death and destruction which do not appear to benefit the terrorists' cause. Yet the objectives of terrorism are not at all those of conventional combat. To paraphrase one of my eminent colleagues," Sartain continued, "terrorism is publicity, is theater, and it aims at the demoralization of society with the hope that it will bring about total erosion of our trust in our democratic institutions. The terrorist thrives on our outrage, manipulates our emotions, and plays on our inner fears." He paused then, realizing he was getting carried away. His audience was silent.

Sartain managed a smile and in a much calmer tone continued. "You must understand," he addressed the lawyer, "that what happened in my book would have taken place sooner or later—in Uganda, Libya, Southern Yemen, or any other Third World dictatorship. That the actual hijacking took place shortly after *The Rescue* was published is only a matter of pure coincidence."

"Yes, but what about the Israeli—"

The professor indicated with his hand that he hadn't finished, that he was about to answer exactly what the man had in mind. "As for the Israeli response," he continued, "it's even simpler. I've been studying Israeli reaction to such acts for some time now. Knowing their attitude, knowing their capabilities, and being personally acquainted with some of the people involved, I was able to make a sound, educated guess as to how they would respond when faced with such contingencies. As it turned out," Sartain shrugged, "I was right on target."

The bookstore manager beamed. It was evident the professor was getting through to his steadily growing audience. Luckily the store was spacious. Murphy felt proud to be the manager of the largest bookstore in D.C.

Sartain looked at the pretty blond toward the back. This time her hand was up, waving at him, and she smiled broadly when he acknowledged her. She reminded him of someone he had once known.

"Ah've read your book, Dr. Sartain, and Ah found it extremely entertainin'," she drawled with a voice dripping Alabama honey. "Ah even recommended it to some of mah friends. It was so . . . gosh-awful realistic. Ah wondah if you personally have evah been hijacked?"

Murphy seized the microphone before Sartain could reply and interjected triumphantly (as though he had had something to do with it) that, indeed, the professor had also been consultant to several airlines on the handling and prevention of air piracy.

God save me from bubblebrains, Sartain silently wished, as Murphy's disclosure set the audience abuzz.

The attorney's hand went up again, and he demanded to know precisely what kind of things the professor had done and for which airlines exactly. Sartain barely managed to conceal his vexation with Murphy. Knowing that this was not what they wanted to hear, he explained that all he had done was to help formulate policies, draw guidelines, and suggest some preventive methods.

The tense student with the wild, curly hair, who had inched his way to the very front of the podium, pulled his fist from his Windbreaker's pocket, and shot it into the air. Before Sartain could beckon to anyone else, he was already asking his question. The challenge in his voice was unmistakable. "Don't you think, Professor, that it's very possible your book gave some ideas to the Entebbe hijackers?"

"If indeed this was the case," the professor was fully prepared for just such a question, "then the hijackers, my friend, were guilty of putting my book aside halfway through. On the other hand the Israelis apparently did not find me as tedious and managed to stay with the story to its conclusion." There was laughter, even some applause.

Murphy, consulting his watch, stepped in. "Two more questions," he announced with a grin. "We must sell books, you know."

Sartain winced as he accepted the mike again. The crowd had tripled since the session began. More people were coming into the store as the downpour slackened considerably. They were standing now shoulder to shoulder. Only very few had left. Murphy couldn't have been more satisfied.

Sartain pointed to a nondescript man in his late thirties whose only outstanding feature was his red hair. Concentrating more on the man's appearance than what he was saying, Sartain nearly missed the question.

"Sir, in *The Rescue* you wrote that Carlos, or the Jackal as you mostly referred to him, was the mastermind behind your fictional terrorist attack. You clearly suggested that even though he didn't personally appear in the actual skyjacking, he was the one who planned and oversaw it. It is common knowledge that Carlos is a real character, and so I'd like to know if you suspect that it was really he who masterminded the Entebbe hijacking, and if that is the case, do you fear he is contemplating revenge for the thwarting of his efforts as you hinted in the conclusion of your book?"

Realizing that the session was beginning to drag on, Sartain kept his reply simple. "The answer to both your questions are qualified 'yeses.' I don't mean to be abrupt, but time is running out."

"May I have the final question, please," a man's voice from the center of the crowd entreated. "It's an appropriate one."

Sartain agreed.

"Just briefly," the man proceeded, "are you planning to write another novel? And if so, could you tell us what it will be about?"

Sartain quickly responded that, indeed, he had already started to work on another novel. One in which Carlos, the Jackal, the world's archterrorist, will figure as the main adversary. Like *The Rescue* the new book will deal with transnational terrorism, but on a level far more ominous than skyjacking or conventional sabotage.

"I am convinced," Sartain drove his point, "that there is a much greater danger to the phenomenon of terrorism than what society has witnessed so far. And so this book will focus on what, I'm afraid, we will soon have to grapple with, namely, the specter of terrorism going nuclear."

Sartain knew he had touched a raw nerve, that he had laid open a deep, hidden anxiety. He couldn't tell, however, whether the silence that followed his last remarks was from shock, concern, fear, or anger . . . and whether it was directed against him or those faceless, dreaded terrorists. What response had he meant to evoke? He wasn't sure.

Sartain was relieved when the spell was broken by a stocky middle-aged man who asked in a heavy European accent, "Don't you tink, Mr. Professor, dat dis iss dangerous . . . dat dis iss giving dem . . . doze bandits . . . bad ideas . . . you know vat I mean?"

Sartain saw the nods of agreement ripple through the crowd. He knew that the man, in his inarticulate way, had spoken for many of them. He wanted to respond in a manner that . . .

Suddenly, as if to finally seal Sartain's dislike for him, Murphy stepped in and declared that there would be no more questions. "I would like to take this opportunity to thank the professor for . . ."

Sartain shunted the man aside and seized the microphone. "Look, I know we're running late," he apologized, "but this question deserves an answer, and I feel I must fully respond to it."

It was then that he saw him, standing apart, like a shadow from the past. His features were obscured by the distance. But Sartain's heart skipped in sudden recognition of the unmistakable face with those unforgettable horn-rims. The beard threw him off for a split second, but there was no question it was the man. Framed in the gray light of the street window, he seemed a specter from Sartain's past come to haunt his present.

He wondered how long Atkins had been standing there, but he was glad he had not noticed him before. It would have made him too self-conscious.

What a damn coincidence, he thought, or was it a coincidence? Of all the people he knew, Atkins was most probably the last person he ever expected to see there. The man represented another era, another time, another life—a decade that seemed like a century . . . He forced himself away from these thoughts and back to his audience.

"The danger is there, ladies and gentlemen, whether I write about it or not, and we cannot bury our heads in the sand and hope that it will go away." He had difficulty framing his thoughts with the presence of Atkins looming up from the back.

"We must be aware of the dangerous potentialities if we are to protect ourselves. The truth is that the public has precious few sources of information about the magnitude of the threat. I guarantee you that certain dangerous people are, even as we speak, aware of the possibilities of acquiring some nonconventional leverage and are plotting toward that end. And unless we publicize the danger before a catastrophe occurs . . ."

Sartain was doing his best to sound clear. He knew the subject was far too complex to explain briefly; he was afraid he was muddling it, particularly with Murphy conspicuously checking his watch every ten seconds and Atkins hovering back there. That's why he was writing a book about it, he justified to himself —the entire phenomenon was too immense for any other treatment.

"What I am trying to say is that the dangers involved in nuclear terrorism are not just physical, and by that I mean the loss of life and property. These we can overcome . . . the way we overcome natural disasters. What is threatened most, I believe, is our way of life, our democratic system, our survival as a free nation. Much will depend on how we react to this crisis, and how we react depends on how much we know . . ."

Damn it, Sartain thought, he sounded like some blithering Cassandra. He fought for control, for organization. He knew he had to try once more. He concentrated on fact and let emotion go.

"Let me give you a personal example. Back in nineteen seventy-four, when there was hardly any talk yet about the dangers of nuclear sabotage, I became concerned about the quality of the security at our nuclear installations. I decided to test one of them, the nuclear reactor at Dresden, Illinois, though security was negligent at all of them. I called up, using a fictitious name . . ." He paused and smiled.

"Anyway I told them that I was a student writing a term paper on the peaceful use of nuclear energy. Yes, that was all it took to gain entry, nothing more . . . I went there, announced myself, and was never questioned further. It didn't, for example, disturb anyone that perhaps I looked a bit too old to be a student. The main point is that I had a briefcase with me in which I had placed a large bottle filled with ordinary tap water but labeled nitroglycerin. In addition I had a hunting knife hidden in my jacket . . .

"Well, I'm sorry to disappoint you, but these two articles created no commotion whatsoever. Primarily because they were never discovered as no one bothered to search me at any time, not even when I started dropping some strange comments. Believe me if I tell you it was as easy walking into that nuclear plant as it was for you today to come to this store, disregarding the rain, of course . . ."

He let the laughter subside before he continued; now he felt he was getting to them again with his more personal approach. He glanced once more at the man by the window, wondering if Atkins realized he'd recognized him. "I reported the incident to the AEC, now the NRC, the Nuclear Regulatory Commission, and wrote about it in the *Bulletin of the Atomic Scientists.* As a result of this, and other more publicized warnings by people such as Mason Wildrich and Theodore Taylor, security in the last few years has increased substantially but, I regret to say, far from sufficiently. Much, much more attention should be given to this subject. The public at large should be aware of the very serious problems we face."

Sartain consulted his watch again. "Time really is running out. Let me just say that it is my conviction that publicity in this case will lead to increased public pressure, which, in turn, should hasten the introduction of better preventive measures and the development of more effective deterrents."

By now Murphy's impatience had manifested itself in beads of sweat on his forehead. Much as Sartain wouldn't have minded prolonging the man's discomfort, he thanked the crowd for its patience and announced that he was ready to autograph their copies of his book.

At least a dozen people had passed through the line before Atkins appeared before him. They stared at each other for a long moment, each noting the inevitable physical changes of the passage of time. Aside from the scruffy, grizzled beard that covered his face, his old boss hadn't changed much. Come to think of it, Sartain thought Atkins had always looked middle-aged.

"Good to see you, Fred." Sartain offered his hand.

Atkins didn't say anything. He just shook the hand and nodded, still gazing at him intently.

There was an awkward moment before Sartain took the two copies of *The Rescue* that Atkins gave him to sign. "You shouldn't have paid for these. I would very much have liked to give them to you as a gift." Sartain still couldn't shake the oddness of encountering him under these circumstances.

"Don't be silly, Sam," Atkins finally spoke in that familiar sonorous voice. "I appreciate the thought, but I won't have it. Anyway these aren't for me. They're for my kids. I read the book as soon as it came out, *before* Entebbe." He winked. "Incidentally you did a good job up there, Professor. I was rather impressed."

The people behind Atkins were getting impatient for their turn. Sartain opened the two books.

Atkins looked behind him at the line. "Sam, how much longer will you be here?"

Sartain handed him the inscribed books and checked his watch. "I suppose for another hour. I'd like to visit with you, it's been so long since—"

Atkins interrupted as the lady behind him gave him a noticeable nudge. "I would too, but I can't stay that long. How about dinner tonight? Or tomorrow night? Beverly and I would love to have you over. How about it?"

"I'm sorry, Fred, but I'm catching a plane tonight for San Francisco. I'll be staying there through the weekend, until next Tuesday." He hesitated, not quite sure he wanted to pursue the subject or ever see the man again. What the hell, he thought, it's only dinner.

"I'll take a rain check though, Fred. When I come back next week sometime, or the week after? Here's my number at home."

"No problem. It's a deal. Take care, Sam."

"You too, Fred."

The woman in line nearly shoved Atkins out of the way, and as Sartain mechanically signed an inscription in her book, he could not help but chuckle. If only these people knew that the bothersome squatty man who had held up the line had been his boss at the spy agency, the superspy agency, the NSA. There it was, the intrigue, the mystique, the undercover hero they all searched for . . . the true cloak-and-dagger connection in his life. There they were, in the presence of a superspy, a real superspy, more real than his novel's hero, and it all went by them so totally unperceived . . . as, of course, it should have. The irony of it all.

CHAPTER TWO

IT was midday, and traffic was heavy at the intersection of Ranke and Ausburger. Within view of Berlin's famous Kaiser Wilhelm Gedächtnis Kirche, its damaged steeple a reminder of the devastation of World War II, a voluptuous fräulein was helping an ancient woman make her way to the other side of the busy avenue. The girl had her mind on anything but the old war, or the old woman, and she had no way of knowing that grasping her arm was the gloved hand of the most wanted man in the world.

Dragging his feet slowly, bemoaning the misfortunes of old age, Carlos surreptitiously glanced at the appealing young blond. Would he, under normal circumstances, be able to add her to his long list of conquests? Had she ever heard of him? Would she be awed?

Ordinarily the native Venezuelan didn't go for Teutonic women. He found them lacking in élan, and even femininity, compared to his usual Latin or Oriental lovers. He didn't quite know why he was so attracted to this girl from the first moment he noticed her. He glanced at her again. There was no doubt: this young blond definitely appealed to him.

Perhaps it was the diaphanous dress she was wearing or the tickling chill breeze that pressed the voile against her body, outlining and accentuating every desirable curve. Perhaps it was the gaiety of her walk, the way she carried herself. Perhaps the oddity of the circumstances excited him, and yet perhaps, although he would never really admit it to himself, it was the fact that deep inside he knew he really had no chance with one of her breeding.

This brief, absurd encounter started his mind racing. Images of her reaching the height of her climax, wriggling, groaning, almost made him reel. He sharply shook his head as if to jar loose the rampant thoughts. What a dirty old woman I am, he smiled to himself.

In truth he had no need of assistance to cross the street, being a strong twenty-eight-year-old man. But he could never resist a flirtation, his Achilles' heel, not even while disguised as a crone.

The unsuspecting young woman helped him negotiate the curb, and he mumbled his thanks, staring downward at the hem of his skirts, not daring to look at her eyes lest his own give away the lusty prince under the frog's skin.

Carlos strolled on in the direction of the Kurfürstendamm, that bustling aorta of Berlin which at dusk would turn into a river of animated light. He halted occasionally, pretending to window-shop but in actuality to catch his reflection in the store windows. As an artist pauses from time to time to admire his creation, Carlos silently applauded himself. His disguise was perfect.

The ankle-length faded and frayed indigo dress had a matching loose-fitting top which suited the costume to his needs. The jacket had relatively large pockets and long sleeves, wide enough to conceal his muscular arms. Over this he had a long black woolen shawl, the kind worn often in rural Germany, ideal for camouflaging his unfeminine shoulders. On top of his gray-haired wig he had tied a viridian scarf which covered both sides of his expertly made-up face and shadowed his thick neck. He was wearing large, cheap tinted glasses and tattered blue gloves of some indistinguishable material. In his right hand he clutched a large canvas bag.

In addition to being windy and overcast, the day was also unusually cold for July. Most Berliners, and many of the tourists, found it too chilly for their summer wear, but Carlos thanked his good fortune that the weather had provided him with a reason to don several layers of clothing.

He walked haltingly, with stooped head and shoulders, not only to convey the impression of age but also to make himself appear shorter. He was not a tall man, only five feet seven, by German standards rather short. But the "master of disguise," as he was often referred to, was not letting any detail escape him. Neither the recent plastic surgery that removed his jowls nor his sizable weight loss caused him to relax his efforts to remain incognito. After Entebbe, and with the big one ahead, he was taking no chances. There was only one person who knew what he looked like at that moment—himself—and that suited him fine. Thus he shuffled on.

While Carlos was indulging in his latest camouflage, Ahmad Azzawi was landing at Flughafen Tegel, Berlin's modern international airport, with an important message for him. A smallish swarthy man with a penchant for green suits and magenta shirts, Ahmad was, by profession, a vocational schoolteacher in Lebanon. The Kuwaiti passport in his jacket, though, proclaimed him to be Hassan Tayeh Khafari, a merchant. To his comrades he was a veteran feisty freedom fighter and loyal revolutionary.

Ahmad was on the last leg of a thirty-six-hour journey, and as he looked out over the rooftops of Berlin, his lifeless expression mirrored the aching in his cramped body.

Last March Ahmad had turned forty-two, but the trip from Mogadishu, Somalia, made him feel eighty-four. He was thinking that perhaps it was time his eldest son, Ibrahim, should prepare to take his place at the forefront of the revolution. Yet he was loathe to make still another sacrifice to the cause. It was time for other Palestinian families to do their share; he had done enough for both himself and his sons. But these were heretical thoughts, and he discarded them immediately. It disturbed him that there might be a certain erosion of his commitment. Palestine and world revolution were still his first priorities, he reassured himself. He was just weary, and after Entebbe who could really blame him if his spirit was somewhat shaken?

As the Air France Caravelle touched down, the anticipation of spending the night in a comfortable bed nearly made him swoon. Making one last swing toward the terminal, the plane trundled forward a few feet, then halted. The noisy engines whined a bit longer, then died.

Ahmad twisted and stretched and slowly rose to join the queue of passengers lining the aisle. Except for an overzealous search through his valise, customs went quite smoothly for the veteran terrorist. Now all that remained was to find a taxi, deliver his missive, and fall into a blissful sleep. "Vierzehn Jungfernheide Strasse," he commanded the cabdriver as they pulled away.

If Ahmad had been less exhausted, he surely would have noticed the gracious Frenchman and his two companions from the plane enter the taxi behind his. Surely he would have been alarmed when their cab seemed to follow, turn for turn, the route his was taking.

In the second taxi the three agents from the Direction de la Surveillance du Territoire (DST), the French equivalent of the American FBI, were tailing Azzawi in hopes that he would lead them to the man they really were after—the man who on June 27 of the previous year killed two of their colleagues and seriously wounded their beloved section commander, Commissaire Principal Jean Herranz. The incident had devastated their ranks, and the men had sworn that nothing would prevent them from redeeming *l'honneur* of their unit, not even the regulation requiring them to obtain clearance before boarding an international flight in pursuit of a suspect. Without such clearance, without informing the appropriate German authorities of their arrival, they were clearly in violation of several international codes. But, when they had spotted Azzawi in transit at Orly Airport they knew they could not let the trail go cold; there was no time to secure clearances. And informing the Germans was out of the question. This had become on that bloody June 27 a private matter between them and Carlos, the Jackal.

The events of that bloody June night in Paris were also indirectly responsible for Ahmad's traveling in that taxi, a year later, toward his appointed meeting with Carlos. On that night the Jackal had not only wrought havoc within the ranks of the DST but also had killed Ahmad's predecessor, an Arab by the name of Michel Wahab Moukarbel.

Moukarbel was then the liaison between Dr. George Habash, the head of the radical Popular Front of the Liberation of Palestine, and the Jackal. In addition, like his successor Azzawi later, he was also the PFLP's paymaster in Europe. No one ever found out what exactly went wrong. Why had Moukarbel been picked up by DST agents on a return trip from Beirut? He had just delivered to Carlos coded instructions from Habash and some ten thousand francs. There was nothing on him to implicate him. No one within the PFLP ranks ever learned what had transpired during Moukarbel's interrogation by the DST, and Carlos had been totally unaware of the fact that Moukarbel was arrested only a few hours after they had met.

What was known was that on June 27, thirteen days after his apprehension, Moukarbel led Commissaire Principal Herranz and two other DST agents to the Latin Quarter apartment of Nancy Sanchez, one of Carlos's girl friends and a Venezuelan like him.

Herranz and one of the two agents mounted the stairs and walked into a noisy farewell party. Nancy was leaving for Venezuela, and Carlos, who was in a particularly merry mood, was singing bawdy songs and playing a guitar. At a pointed question by the commissaire, the Jackal stopped his singing. "I do not know anyone by the name of Mouka . . . Moukarbel, or whatever . . . ," he shrugged drunkenly. "You must be mistaking me for someone else; Carlos is a very common name around here, you know."

Herranz motioned to his subordinate, who left and shortly reappeared with the second agent and Moukarbel in tow. Moukarbel seemed stunned to see Carlos, but the latter maintained his cool facade. "Is this the man with the funny name?" he asked, eyeing Moukarbel like a curiosity at a freak show. "Never seen him before," he slurred.

Moukarbel tried at that point to say something to the Jackal in Arabic. He wanted to let him know that he hadn't really compromised him, that he had taken the DST agents to Nancy's apartment to get them off his back, that he didn't expect Carlos to be there, that this way Nancy would have been able to warn Carlos . . . But Commissaire Herranz silenced him before he had a chance to utter more than a few words.

Since Carlos continued to insist that he didn't know Moukarbel, the commissaire produced his trump card, a photograph of the Jackal and Moukarbel conferring a couple of weeks earlier in a small café on rue de Babylon. He shoved it up to Carlos's nose. The Venezuelan, however, only shrugged again, raising his wineglass in a mock toast to the commissaire's cleverness. "Tricky photography, no doubt, *mon Général*," he taunted as he winked at the rest of the people in the room. They all burst out laughing.

Herranz lost patience. "Get your passport!" he snapped angrily. Carlos acquiesced without argument. He rose tipsily, and teetering around, reached for the coat hanging behind him. But when he swiveled back, there was no passport in his hand, only a high-velocity Czech M52 automatic, blazing away.

Herranz was the fortunate one: he took the bullet in his throat. Later Carlos would complain that it had been the first shot, and he wasn't fully sober. The other two agents, however, were pierced dead between the eyes. Moukarbel, to whom the Jackal turned last, had enough time to shriek a bloodcurdling "*La!*" ("no" in Arabic) before the fourth bullet struck him at the back of his gaping mouth.

Before Carlos dashed out, the petrified guests watched as he sauntered over to Moukarbel's still twitching body, looked at the death throes in disgust, and squeezed his fifth shot, muttering in Spanish: "Dirty Arab!"

When Ahmad Azzawi was selected two months later to replace the dead Moukarbel, he was assured during the briefing that Carlos denied having called the dying Moukarbel a "dirty Arab." Carlos had claimed, he was told, that he called him, "a dirty traitor." Though Palestinian on his father's side and Iraqi on his mother's, Azzawi really didn't much care what Carlos had called his predecessor. But on that taxi ride from Tegel Airport to his destination, he was somewhat uneasy over his upcoming encounter with the Jackal.

Ahmad had just left Dr. Wadi Haddad in Mogadishu. It was from there that the PFLP chief of operations had directed the holding action at Entebbe. Ahmad was one of the few who knew that Carlos had initially planned the skyjacking of the French airbus in Athens. Haddad, however, had insisted on taking over once the plane landed in Uganda. The Palestinians had been taking a beating in the Lebanese civil war, and Haddad wanted the hijack to look more like a Palestinian operation. The publicity would boost the morale of the Palestinians entrenched in the hills of Lebanon and skyrocket their prestige throughout the Arab world. This time Haddad didn't want the Venezuelan archterrorist and his multinational group to claim all the glory. He wanted to try for it himself. Carlos reluctantly agreed. But the glory never came.

Ahmad, who had accompanied Haddad on his secret meeting with Idi Amin in Kampala, knew that had the operations chief heeded Carlos's advice, the Entebbe debacle would have been the terrorists' greatest victory. From the outset the Jackal had urged Haddad to execute a few passengers to demonstrate their resolve against any delaying tactics. Carlos had also strongly protested the decision to release all but the Jewish passengers. His war was not only against Jews or Israelis, and this slipup proved to be the most costly of all. It allowed Israeli intelligence officers in Paris the opportunity to grill the freed hostages on the terrorists' security arrangements at Entebbe airport.

Carlos's wrath over this grand-scale botching was no secret to Azzawi, who knew that the Jackal had counted on the operation to secure certain imprisoned comrades. And now, as he stared out the cab window at the street scenes passing by, Ahmad knew the message he carried would incur yet another onslaught of that fabulous fury. Ahmad had been in the trenches too long to be unnerved by displays of temper, even of the Jackal's magnitude, but his energy and spirit were at an ebb, and he was in no condition to withstand the abusive ravings to which he knew he would be subjected. He had no particular love for this role of fall guy for Haddad, of go-between for two revolutionary prima donnas. He sighed audibly as the taxi rounded the final corner.

An hour earlier Carlos had arrived at 14 Jungfernheide, a blank, whitewashed tenement above a small bakery. He checked the tarnished pendant watch pinned to the bosom of his dress. It was five after two P.M. In his stooped, haggard approach he had carefully cased the street up and down for signs of surveillance or ambush. With his animal namesake, the Jackal shared a taste for carnage as well as a keen sense of danger that seldom failed him. One more careful check, and the old frau disappeared inside.

Carlos pulled his ponderous, ancient peasant-woman's frame step by halting step up to the second floor. He rang the bell at apartment 2B. No answer. Unperturbed, he knocked three times, paused, knocked twice again. Still no answer. He cursed quietly. Rummaging blindly through the canvas bag, he found the key, unlocked the door, and swung it wide.

A rush of stale air escaped from the darkened rooms as though it had been pent up, decaying, for months. Carlos's batlike sonar told him the place was empty, so he entered and locked the door behind him. Away from public view he strode to the windows, cracked them open, and eased the shades to allow some light. Methodically he checked each room and its furnishings including the kitchen refrigerator. Satisfied that the house was safe, he relaxed on the sofa, browsing through an old *Der Spiegel* while he awaited Ahmad Azzawi.

At three o'clock P.M. the doorbell rang. Carlos, still on the sofa, raised his head and quietly watched the door. There came three knocks, a short pause, and then two more. In character he slowly lifted himself off the sofa. The old lady edged slowly to the door and opened it.

Ahmad Azzawi, expecting Carlos, if anyone, to answer, jumped at the sight of the ancient crone. He stood there, key in hand, blankly staring at the ugly woman. "Excuse me," he said in German, "but . . ."

"*Ist nichts, ist nichts*. It's all right," Carlos responded in an effeminate falsetto, smiling kindly and waving him in. "*Bitte, bitte*, please come in."

Ahmad hesitantly took a few steps over the threshold. "Who are you?" he demanded to know, cursing himself for not having removed his Walther automatic from the double-bottomed suitcase.

"I'm your grandmother, stupid," Carlos said mockingly, reverting to his normal voice. He was pleased that the Arab had failed to recognize him.

Relieved, Ahmad sank into the armchair by the window. "It's unbelievable," he admired, looking Carlos over. "You've outdone yourself. I'm willing to bet that no one, not even your own mother, or Fusako, would be able to recognize you. It's absolutely amazing. It's a masterpiece, a work of art . . ."

Carlos cut off the traditional Arab penchant for long-winded adulation. "Where do you come from?" he asked tersely.

"From the airport, directly from the airport," Ahmad responded in a more composed manner.

"I know that," Carlos said impatiently. "But where did you fly in from? You didn't fly directly from Mogadishu, did you?"

"No, there was no direct flight. I flew from Mogadishu to Cairo and from there to Paris . . ."

"Paris?" Carlos interjected. "Why Paris? I thought I made it clear that . . ."

"I know, I know," Ahmad dared for once to interrupt. "I had to deliver something for Haddad. It was urgent, and it was important that I deliver it personally."

Ahmad could tell that Carlos was upset by something, but it was hard to read, especially through his disguise, the degree of his irritation.

"Any problems in Paris?" the Jackal snapped.

"No, all went smoothly."

"Any problems here?"

"No, not really."

"What do you mean, 'not really'?"

"Oh, nothing," Ahmad said, yawning. He eyed the beds in the next room with a desperate yearning. "Really, nothing much . . . it's just that the customs agent got curious when he saw my Kuwaiti passport. He raked through my suitcase quite thoroughly, and for a minute I was sure he would find my gun. I guess they've all got the jitters nowadays. They don't trust anyone who carries an Arab passport. We are all terrorists, you know . . ."

"Are you sure no one followed you here?" Carlos asked, ignoring the Arab's pleasantry.

"I'm positive. I double-checked." Ahmad knew very well that he was lying, but could he confess that he had been so exhausted that his usual caution was usurped by a blind desire to reach his destination, deliver his message, then fall into bed and sleep for days? He diverted the conversation, complimenting Carlos again on the perfect disguise. "Wadi will be totally impressed when I tell him about it." He was canny enough to know that this last remark would please Carlos.

"How is Haddad?" The Venezuelan's true concern for his comrade was as masked as his real appearance.

"Well, what can I say?" Azzawi began slowly, searching for the right words to describe Haddad's state after the Entebbe embarrassment. "I think he managed to get over his initial shock. He is regaining his confidence, already talking about the retaliation he's planning. But frankly I could see that he took it hard. He'll get over it though. You know Haddad." Ahmad's eyes again flickered yearningly toward the bedroom. He hoped Carlos would suggest soon that he get some rest.

"What retaliations are you talking about?" The crone's body

jerked erect in the chair. His fiery gaze riveted the Arab's eyes. Ahmad's tired back stiffened in defense of the impending trouble. "What is he up to now?" Carlos growled. "I want no more half-assed adventures. Not while I'm working on the big one. I thought we agreed on that. What the hell is going on?"

Ahmad, forewarned by Haddad to anticipate Carlos's fury, tried to mollify him. "Haddad wouldn't interfere with your plans, Carlos. He assured me he would wait at least until the jailbreak. But in the meantime we, too, need to regain our pride." He wanted to explain about the humiliation the Palestinians had suffered, particularly the PFLP, about the vital need to avenge the disaster at Entebbe, the need to do it soon, before they became a laughingstock throughout the Arab world. Their enemies within the Palestinian movement were already capitalizing on the debacle. The PFLP could lose their financial backers if they didn't act soon. All this and more he wanted to say, but he knew that any explanation would only further enrage the Jackal. Anyway he carried a letter from Haddad that would explain the situation. He could give it and the money to Carlos and then collapse on the beckoning mattress.

Ahmad removed his shoe and started working on the heel, which after a few seconds came loose. Inside was a bundle of thousand-mark notes. "This is what you requested for the operation," he said as he handed it over to Carlos, hoping to placate him, "and here is the letter."

Carlos took the money, counted it quickly, and pocketed it. He seemed far more interested in the coded message that Ahmad brought him, a folded piece of paper, six by five inches. It contained two dozen lines of uninterrupted English letters:

cdlerfoienoeiojwopuetdgvxmslduyuejfnslsogjsldjklvnidoavaa
rirlgjieotdncslfoturhdnslwoejgntkfkdlosskfjgjgflfnvksorutyw
hmaxvcvkfuhgnfkdodjebrieowplskdjwuqryhdnejkkdjghteiwo
wbvdhskfirejenfkdoejrhtddbshskwowklsenfowuslffgtrqfqjfjk
jofuhoytiensddoerttkgjhmbnfowuwqfahdkfgefktutoyhmhjds
vsfeuotpylgmvldjfhdgswterudndjfidfkgjhyochedffgtjyjuliokk
dgsfeetdbdjrirkdlfuggkejdjdyridjqasd

Carlos took the pad and pen that Azzawi proffered and began to break the lines of letters into groups of five letters each. The first line broke out:

cdler foien oeioj wopue tdgvxm slduy uejfn slsog jsldj

He completed the groupings, then pulled from the canvas bag a paperback copy of Frederick Forsyth's best-seller, *The Day of the Jackal*.

Ahmad couldn't help but smile as he recalled the origin of Carlos's most famous nickname. Shortly after the shooting of the three DST agents in Paris a cache of arms was discovered in the London apartment of one of Carlos's girl friends, a Basque woman by the name of Angela Otaola. Besides many guns, grenades, slabs of dynamite, plastic explosive, gelignite, and a number of forged passports all bearing Carlos's face with several different identities, Scotland Yard turned up a number of books. One of the books was an underlined copy of Forsyth's novel, the story of a professional assassin, a master of disguise, who is hired to kill Charles de Gaulle. Hours after, the news of the find appeared on the pages of the *Guardian*, the press was full of headlines about the hunt for the new "Jackal."

Ahmad also remembered the night in Vienna when Carlos boasted to him that, unlike his fictional precursor, he would have succeeded in assassinating the carefully guarded French president. As if to prove a point, two days later Carlos successfully pulled one of the most daring operations in the annals of international terrorism, the raid on the OPEC headquarters in Vienna and the kidnapping of, among others, eleven oil ministers.

Carlos interrupted Ahmad's thoughts. "Okay, I'm ready. Give me the year."

"Nineteen eighty-four," Ahmad responded.

A smile broke across the Jackal's face. "Very clever." He nodded his head, pleased. "Have you read it?"

"Read what?"

"The book, stupid."

"The book? What book? You mean *The Day of the Jackal*?"

"Never mind," Carlos retorted with unmasked disgust. He often wondered why he had to work with these oafish fellahin.

Carlos rapidly computed in his mind: one, nine, eight, four, came to twenty-two. He multiplied by four (two plus two); that gave him eighty-eight. It was quite simple once you knew the code. He opened the book to page eighty-eight, counted twenty-two words from the beginning of the page, and began to break the next few sentences into groupings of five letters each. These

24
SABI H. SHABTAI

he inserted directly below the five letter groupings in Haddad's message. This task completed, he began to decipher. The process was like second nature to him by now. Those months of training in Cuba and Russia gave him the facility to execute the code by memory. C and D is Y, D and L is O, L and R is U, E and X is A, and so on. He chanted the three-letter groupings under his breath.

Carlos hadn't finished a half-dozen groupings when the doorbell shattered the silence in the apartment. He glanced at Ahmad, who was staring at the door, transfixed. Carlos motioned to him to remain silent. Quickly, silently, he removed the papers from the table and concealed them in his bag. Then, eerily, came the agreed signal: three knocks, a pause, and two knocks. Carlos frowned.

"When is Fusako scheduled to arrive?" he breathed.

"Not until tomorrow," Ahmad whispered back, frightened.

"That's what I thought," Carlos said.

The knocks were repeated: one, two, three . . . pause . . . one, two.

Carlos motioned Ahmad into the bedroom and quickly arranged his costume. Once again an old woman, he waddled to the door and eased it open, peering around it timidly. He was almost knocked to the floor by the two men who barged in, guns drawn.

The first mistake the DST agents made was to have let emotion interfere with their professional work. They had acted impulsively, ignoring regulations and formalities, failing to report their arrival in Berlin to the Germans. The first mistake led to the second: under the circumstances they had created for themselves, there was no time for effective surveillance. Protective measures were thrown to the wind.

But it was the third mistake that proved to be fatal: they ignored the old frau. They took her for what she seemed to be: a crippled, harmless old woman, whom they had pushed to the sofa, ordering her to stay put. Their mind was on Ahmad Azzawi and whoever else might have been in that hideout with him.

One of the two agents covered Ahmad, ordering him out of the bedroom. The other kicked open the bathroom door. The crone remained on the sofa, obediently quiet.

There was a soft, muffled "phut," and then quickly another "phut," like children's firecrackers going off in the distance. It was the last thing the Frenchmen heard before they each collapsed to the floor, astonished eyes wide with disbelief, their Colts still clenched in their fists. They never even saw the silencer-fitted Vzor automatic with which the old frau, still seated on the sofa, killed them both.

Ahmad froze, trying to comprehend what he had just witnessed. But Carlos was quickly on his feet. In no time he slammed the front door shut and rushed to the windows. Hidden from the street by the shutters, he carefully scanned the backyard and that part of the street which could be observed from the apartment. He ignored the men on the floor; he knew that the bullets were lodged deep in their crania. Later he would take the time to rejoice, to savor his new accomplishment as a marksman.

Carlos saw no suspicious movement outside, yet he failed to notice the third DST agent who was covering the back entrance of the building. The Jackal returned to the door and placed his ear against it. The stairway was soundless. Brow furrowed in concentration, he listened for a few seconds more before he relaxed and turned to Ahmad, who had sunk to the sofa in relief. "*Allah Akbar!* God is Great!" he was chanting.

"Do you recognize these two?" Carlos asked sternly as he bent over the bodies, carefully searching and emptying their pockets with his gloved hands.

"No, I've never seen them before," Ahmad replied, feeling somewhat queasy as he forced himself to look at the dead men's contorted and bloody faces.

"Are you sure? They must have picked up the signal when they heard you knocking."

"Of course I'm sure." Ahmad looked at Carlos, puzzled. He felt beads of sweat trickling down from his armpits. "That was some shooting," he ventured hesitantly, trying to change the subject. "I knew you were a crack shot, Carlos, but this . . . it's amazing, just totally unbelievable."

Carlos ignored the adulation. In the inside pockets of the dead men he had just discovered, in addition to their passports and identity cards, Air France ticket stubs. He turned to Ahmad, showing him the stubs. Ahmad withered under Carlos's icy gaze.

"They are DST agents," Carlos said, his voice like cold steel. He had suspected all along—by the way they dressed, by the guns they used, by the way they acted—that they were French operatives. His analytical mind had already connected the chain of events that led them to the apartment, even before he started to frisk their bodies, before he found the incriminating ticket stubs. "They followed you here all the way from Paris. They were on your flight . . . and you assured me no one was on your tail . . . that you double-checked . . ." He mocked Ahmad's Arabic accent, not disguising his disgust for the veteran guerrilla's ineptitude.

The ashen Azzawi felt fear creeping over him all at once: the cold sweat at the back of his neck, the racing of his heart, the shaking of his knees, the stone chill in the pit of his stomach. He couldn't help but remember Moukarbel's fate. Stuttering, he vainly tried to explain that he had taken every precaution, that he just couldn't understand, that it had never happened to him before. Pleading, he rose from the sofa, but Carlos sharply ordered him to remain seated. Ahmad cowered into the cushions.

Carlos removed a pistol from one of the dead Frenchmen's fists. He was grateful that they had decided to use silencers on their Colts. It would help him work out his plan.

With Ahmad watching him, spellbound, Carlos crouched behind the Frenchman's body. He eyeballed the angle and distance between him and Ahmad. "Move slightly to the left," he ordered the terror-stricken Arab. Ahmad obediently hitched himself sideways to exactly where Carlos himself had been sitting when he shot the Frenchman.

"What are you going to do?" Ahmad whined, trembling.

"Just do as I tell you!" Carlos snapped.

Still crouching behind the body, Carlos held the Colt just above the dead Frenchman's right hand and aimed it at Ahmad's chest.

The Arab jerked back in fear. "Carlos, please no!!" he pleaded. "I didn't . . ."

"I told you to sit still," Carlos hissed, still aiming the gun at his petrified target, shifting his position slightly. "You have not only endangered me, you have endangered the whole operation, the whole organization. You've become a liability. I'm sorry but I'll have to . . ." He stopped suddenly, remembering something. "Where is your gun?" he asked.

Ahmad, speechless with fear, motioned toward his suitcase. Carlos walked over to the case, and with Ahmad's shaky instructions, removed the Walther from its secret compartment. As he returned to his emplacement, however, he noticed the opened window. Turning to shut it, he suddenly spotted the third DST agent in the backyard.

Ahmad, who had already considered himself a dead man, regained some hope when Carlos beckoned to him to join him at the window.

"Do you recognize the man hiding near the big crate down there? Was he on the flight with the other two? Now don't lie to me," Carlos whispered ominously. "If you want to save your life, if you ever want to see your family again, you better tell me the truth."

Ahmad examined the man down below. His mind flashed back, remembering now the three Frenchmen sitting a few rows behind him. Of course! The ones who were playing rummy throughout the flight. And this was the one who had so politely let him cut in line. He had taken them for ordinary businessmen. The other two, the dead ones, were slim and tall, and that chubby one, he was sitting between them. Now he remembered seeing them again at the terminal, behind him, but he hardly paid any attention to them. What a fool he was!

"They were on the flight," Ahmad said flatly, "all three of them."

Carlos shook his head, smiling cruelly. "Now, are you sure? Are you sure there were only three?"

Ahmad nodded timidly. As far as he could tell, there were only three. He didn't remember seeing them talking to anyone else, he said, and he didn't recall anyone approaching them. Of course, he admitted, he could be mistaken. Obviously he hadn't paid much attention to them or the whole thing wouldn't have happened.

"*Alors, bien, mon ami,*" Carlos said, smirking, somewhat more relaxed. "You've earned your chance . . . you may still live. Now go over and sit on the sofa, just where you were seated before."

"But—"

"Go! Do as I tell you!"

Antoine was getting restless. Seven minutes had passed since his partners had gone upstairs. Jacques had told him to wait five or ten minutes before checking with them. Now what was he supposed to do? Wait five, or ten, minutes? He wished Jacques had been more explicit. He decided to wait the full ten minutes, particularly since he wasn't exactly sure what he should do. Maybe they would come back by then, and he wouldn't have to do anything.

Carlos stuck Ahmad's Walther automatic between the folds of his dress and placed the Colt back in the Frenchman's hand. He handed his own Mauser automatic to the puzzled Ahmad. Az-zawi held it limply in his hand, watching Carlos's every move for a sign of what was to happen. He couldn't fathom Carlos's motives. Why had Carlos given him his gun and taken Ahmad's own Walther? Something was deadly wrong, but he felt totally helpless, as if under a hypnotic spell.

Carlos resumed his crouch behind the body of the dead Frenchman. In an eerie, offhand tone, he said, "You are going to die like a hero, Ahmad, like a revolutionary hero . . . taking with you two imperialist agents. Your family and friends will be very proud of you."

Ahmad couldn't believe his ears. "But . . . but . . ." He shook his head, lifting his hands. "But you said . . ."

"I told you I would give you a chance to save your life," Carlos broke in. "Well I'm giving it to you. By now you should have been a dead man . . . like them." He nodded toward the bodies. "But all you have to do to save your life is shoot me with the gun in your hand, before I have a chance to draw. You obviously have a great advantage over me, my friend, but it's only fair . . . because I am the better shot. Besides you probably will die anyway, if not from a bullet, then from the fear that is paralyzing you." He smiled as he said it, and it wasn't even a cruel smile. He was enjoying himself.

Ahmad again tried to beg reprieve. "I served you . . . In Vienna we . . ."

Carlos cut him short again. "I appreciate everything you've done for me in the past, but when I say 'fire!' you'd better pull that trigger, or you're a dead man." Once again an ugly smile crossed the crone's face as Carlos toyed with the poor man. "Believe me," he said, "it won't hurt. The very moment you feel the pain, you'll be dead. Now, shoot!"

Ahmad had enough time to raise his arm and attempt to aim, but he hesitated for a split second too long, and before he could squeeze the trigger, he was hit by three bullets from the Frenchman's gun.

Carlos wondered later if Ahmad had realized before he died that Carlos never went for his own gun. That would have defeated the whole purpose of the staged gun battle. Carlos had reached instead for the dead man's hand. He raised it, still clenching the Colt, to aim. Pressing the Frenchman's index finger with his own, he squeezed the trigger. He had counted on Ahmad's incapacitating fear to give the extra precious time he needed to execute the intricate maneuver. It was nevertheless an amazing feat, and Carlos gloated over his newest accomplishment. The Jackal had once again outdone himself. He only wished someone had been there to witness it.

He rose and surveyed the scene. It was perfect. Ahmad, he mused, would enter the annals of the Palestinian revolution as a great hero. And for a while, at least, no one would know about his own presence in Berlin. That was vital for the success of his mission. What a pity, he thought, that his best performance yet would go unheralded. But, he consoled himself, let's see their faces when the big one takes place.

Antoine was worried. It had been more than ten minutes since he saw his friends go into the building after the Arab. He began to question the wisdom of the whole operation, and he felt very isolated in this foreign country, not knowing exactly what to do. Well, he thought, he better do something.

Antoine had started toward the front entrance, weighing the alternatives, when he ran into an old lady coming out of the building, carrying a canvas bag in her hand.

She grinned at him and greeted him with a broad, *"Guten Tag!"*

He smiled back politely. *"Guten Tag!"* he replied, the only German he knew. What he didn't know, however, was that for him, unlike his unfortunate friends, it was a good day indeed. He was lucky to be alive.

As the taxi driver helped him into the cab, Carlos was suddenly overcome by a strong sense of déjà vu. Once again they were dead, and he was alive. It gave him a tremendous feeling of vitality, of power, of immense elation. His libido heightened, his manhood swelled, throbbing in sudden desire. He needed to chuck his crone's disguise, now, as soon as possible. He felt restless in those clothes. He wanted to be Ilich again, and he ached for the touch of a woman's body. He remembered the blond, but more than anything else he wanted to be with Fusako, the one woman with whom he could share not only the joys of carnal love but also the intimate pleasures of cunning and brutal murder.

CHAPTER THREE

FEARING capture, a mouse confronted by a snake may throw itself into the open jaws of its predator rather than test escape. Truly unsettling behavior, considering the experts' claim that the instinct to survive is the supreme impulse. There are those, of course, who would argue in favor of the serpent: that survival is relative to that stomach which suffers greater hunger pangs. Still it is a questionable prologue to the death-wish theory and says little for modern man who seems to have ascended at last to the stature of a helpless rodent in these all too civilized times.

These were the thoughts grinding uncomfortably in the mind of the deputy director of coordination as his wife dropped him off at the security gate to the CIA compound. Beyond this point only specially classified persons were permitted to pass. It was another lovely morning in Langley, Virginia; only it was Saturday.

"Couldn't they let us know in advance they'll be needing you on weekends?" she asked, fighting a yawn. "I wouldn't have left my car in the shop."

"I'm sorry, Bev," Fred Atkins said. "I had a feeling Colton'd be calling me in this morning. I guess I should've mentioned it to you." He looked across the front seat at his sleepy wife. Half her collar was stuffed inside out, and her shoelaces were untied. She had thrown herself together hurriedly after the phone call woke them. "What makes you put up with an incorrigible old man like me, anyway?" He smiled at her as he pulled his briefcase from the back seat.

"Oh, Fred!" she murmured, embarrassed, and pinched his arm. "Fred," she said and then paused to look at him, "what does

Colton want with you today?" She knew her husband suspected what it was about, and suddenly felt a discomforting wave of premonition shake the sleep out of her. "What's going on, Fred?"

Fred sat back and looked at the middle-aged woman whom he had loved and with whom he had shared nearly half his life. She had been the most loyal and understanding friend he had ever had. And now he could see that she was anxious and upset.

"It's nothing at all, Bev," he answered. He leaned toward her and held her soft face in his hand. "If I'm guessing right, they'll be offering me another post or an additional assignment, that's all." They looked at each other silently before he added reassuringly, "I believe it will be here."

He said it because he knew she was hoping they would not be going abroad again. But he also knew that if they were, she would accept it as she always had before, without a note of complaint. Indeed he couldn't help but reflect that the life of a spook was anything but easy on the other half. No wonder the Agency was plagued with so many broken marriages.

"All right," she said with a smile that was meant to convince him. And then one gentle kiss, making sure his whiskers didn't brush too hard against her tender cheeks, and Fred slipped across the vinyl seat and out of the car.

Atkins barely glanced at the thirty-one stars carved into the main marble hall; they represented the CIA officers who had died in the line of duty. He had known only a few of them personally. The star for Dick Welch, his close friend, the Athens's chief of station who was assassinated only a few months before by unidentified terrorists, hadn't been added yet.

But as he stood blowing his nose in the elevator, on his way up to the director's office, he felt a slight queasiness rising in his stomach. On his climb toward the apex of the intelligence business, he had made many friends and several enemies. But even his enemies knew him to be a man who was very good at pulling factions together. It was no coincidence that he was given the job he now held. He had always treated his subordinates with unusual dignity and care, and they in turn respected, and were loyal to him. It was his higher-ups, however, who felt at times threatened by this outspoken man who had made it so quickly to the top cluster of one intelligence establishment and then another. While they listened closely to what he had to say, they also watched him guardedly.

Fred acknowledged this petty jealousy, but he never permitted it to deter or influence him. Fred had never allowed himself to shy away from new responsibilities, not even with his advanced age. Somehow he would get used to the ulcer.

At the seventh, and top floor, the elevator came quietly to a stop. Atkins stepped out and walked slowly down the corridor, past his own office to the thick oak door at the end. Here he knocked lightly and entered without waiting for an answer. The secretary of the director of the Central Intelligence Agency was seated at her desk blowing at a cup of steaming coffee.

"Morning, Edna," Fred said as he folded away his handkerchief.

"Good morning, Mr. Atkins. Mr. Colton's expecting you."

"Good morning, sir," Atkins said, pulling out a chair before the director's desk.

"Good morning, Fred. I'm sorry to get you up and out on a Saturday morning, but"—he motioned with the cigarette in his hand toward the white telephone—"he's leaving this afternoon for Camp David and would like to know something by then."

Fred's eyes shifted from his boss to the white telephone and then to the desk plaque which read: BE BRIEF, BE BLUNT, BE GONE. He said nothing.

"Well, Fred," the director cleared his throat and took a last puff on his cigarette before he put it out. "With this Entebbe business things have begun to move rather rapidly. And then this . . ." He handed Atkins one of the pink-sheet reports in front of him.

Atkins glanced over it quickly and then looked up at his boss. Was this what he had dragged him out of bed for? To discuss a shoot-out between two French DST agents and some Arab in Berlin? And why would the White House be interested in that?

"I don't understand," Atkins said.

"It's simple," the director said. "It's the French and the Germans who have been dragging their heels on the issue of creating an international committee to coordinate our efforts against terrorism, but now that things seemed to have gotten out of hand . . . Well you know what I mean."

Atkins half nodded, trying to follow Colton's line of thought.

"Of course, not that our own boss"—he glanced again at the white telephone "was so eager himself at first. But Entebbe convinced him, and the rest of them, that we better start doing something—"

"You mean they've at long last witnessed what standing up to terrorists can accomplish?" Fred asked before Colton had a chance to finish his sentence and in the rhetorical tone that some of his superiors, including the director, found so irritating.

Colton studied him for a long moment. It was not exactly what the director meant to say. "Yes and no," he continued finally. "After all, we've been in the process of putting this thing together for some time now, ever since the foul-up in Munich. You know that I and my predecessors have been conferring with the other intelligence chiefs on this issue for some time now."

Atkins knew of course that the heads of the Western intelligence services conferred once every six months on problems relating to terrorism, among other things. But he also knew that little more than the mere sharing of information took place in these high-level meetings and that they had done almost nothing to douse the many brush fires of terrorism the world had seen since the bloody massacre at the 1972 Munich Olympics.

"We're slow learners out of fear," he muttered to himself, "and have been jumping into the mouths of serpents ever since the first snake lied to Eve."

"What was that?" the director questioned.

"Oh, nothing," Atkins smiled awkwardly. "Just a small prayer."

"I see," Colton said dryly. He had never really quite understood the man in front of him, even though he had learned to respect him. He shuffled some papers uncomfortably, and, leaning over his desk, continued. "We've finally got something going, and we're calling it the Counterterrorism Coordinating Committee, or the 'Triple C,' if you prefer."

All these years Atkins had prayed for the creation of an international organization which could effectively fight back. "I'm delighted to hear that, sir."

The director continued matter-of-factly. "The committee will include representatives from the United States, Canada, and from most of the European members of NATO. In addition Japan and Israel have also been asked to join and have already agreed."

"You said most of the European members of NATO?"

"Well, Portugal, Iceland, and Luxemburg will not send any permanent representatives, for obvious reasons. But they'll be covered."

"I see," Atkins said. "It makes sense."

"Now the reason I've gotten you out of bed like this, Fred, is to find out whether you'd be willing to run it. Apparently some people, particularly some of our foreign colleagues who have worked with you in the past, think you're the only one who can handle all these folks in one room."

Atkins could tell by Colton's use of "some people" that the director himself might not have been one of those who had recommended him initially for the job. But he was still proud of this new offer.

"It's not going to be an easy task, you know, considering the politics involved," continued Colton. "After all, that's the reason it never got off the ground before. I know I don't have to spell out the details of this thing to you. Most of the world is running on Arab oil. The touchiest problem will be working so closely with Israeli intelligence. You understand that."

"I do," Atkins said. "But I can't see how we can do without them. They are the real pros today, whether we like it or not. They've proved it more than once, and personally, I've nothing but admiration for the way they pulled that thing off at Entebbe."

"Yes, of course, but—"

"I do understand you, sir," Atkins interrupted. "We'll just have to learn to work around it. Won't we?"

The director nodded in response. "Well, what it comes down to, Fred, is that finally the good guys have decided to get as organized as the bad guys. A Counterterrorism Coordinating Committee versus Terror International. The kind of operations the sons of bitches have been pulling off couldn't have been done without a damned tight organization. We know that. The Triple C, we hope, will even the odds. We've got to, in this age of nuclear proliferation."

Atkins couldn't agree more. The subject had long been a cause célèbre with him. Reminded of Sartain, he blurted, "We can't just sit here in this day and age of nuclear proliferation and wait until the bastards make their move. We must go after them and preempt their plans before they have a chance to act."

"That, Fred, is what we hope the Triple C can do," Colton said. He took a fresh pack of cigarettes from his top drawer and peeled off the cellophane as he spoke. "But I don't want you to get the wrong idea about what you're getting into. You'll be the chief coordinator, not the head of the committee. As I said before, it's not going to be easy keeping everyone in the room together. Because of shortsighted nationalistic or economic reasons this committee's going to be constantly on the verge of exploding into a hundred little pieces, each looking out for number one. In the final analysis you're going to have to rely on persuasion. And you're going to have to do a damn good job of it. It won't be within your power to give binding orders. But I'm sure you'll be convincing. That is, if you want the job."

Fred remained silent. A United Nations of intelligence establishments . . . A sure ulcer.

"I think you'd be surprised," Colton added with a note of encouragement, "to find out how many of your colleagues share your own views on the situation about what has to be done. Most of these people will cooperate. They'll cooperate because they're damn scared that some madman will one day get his hands on something they know they can't keep under tight enough lock and key."

"Then," Fred sighed, "there shouldn't be any problem."

The director smiled ironically. "Unfortunately it's not as simple as that. It's their duly elected political bosses you'll have to watch out for. But, after all, Fred, that's what democracy is all about, isn't it?" Atkins failed to respond.

"It was late last night that I got the final go-ahead from the President," Colton continued. "It's taken this long for all the countries to agree to participate. So? Can I tell him you'll accept the post?"

"I'll accept it."

"Good," Colton replied as he reached for the white telephone.

"There's just one thing," Fred added. Colton's hand froze midway.

"What?" the director asked, looking at the clock on his desk.

"I want a free hand in recruiting some people from outside the intelligence community."

"Who did you have in mind?" asked the director.

"No one in particular," Atkins lied.

"Well you'll have to clear them with me first," Colton said.

"Sure," Fred said.

"And, of course, the Committee will have to approve them," he quickly added.

"That's understood," Atkins answered.

"All right then," the director said. He lifted the telephone receiver.

CHAPTER FOUR

"WELL," she responded, brushing aside a lock of golden hair, stretching her slim, sleek body as she turned lazily to face the sun. "I guess it must be the Gemini in you again."

She lay back with her head cradled in her hands, her full, firm white breasts resting gently on her rib cage. Her eyes were shut as she let the sun's rays and the soft afternoon breeze caress her face and bare flesh. "Why should it surprise you?" she murmured, letting a smile cross her lips. "You know you have a dual personality, to say the least."

Sartain was lying on his side, cheek propped against fist, examining her with one eye, reflecting on how she fit so perfectly into the panorama: the sparkling blue bay with its magnificent white city and the graceful orange-red bridge whose perfect contours traced the sensuous curves of her body.

"I thought, for once, this was going to be a serious discussion," he protested, trying in vain to add a sober note to his tone, "and here you are again with your silly Zodiac interpretations."

"Oh," Linda gently chided him. "Is the ultraintellectual professor beneath indulging in some pedestrian pseudologic?" She loved to play games with him. She knew that he really didn't mind being made fun of by her. He enjoyed the teasing as much as she did. She knew it made him feel younger. It was part of why he loved her.

She pressed her point. "Well, isn't it?" She turned her head toward him, her eyes squinting against the sun. "You obviously have a great deal of sympathy for the masses, for the ordinary people. You empathize with their daily suffering, and yet you loathe them for their lack of imagination and sophistication.

"Do you want me to be serious?" she asked mischievously. "I don't believe you ever really walked away from the ivory tower. I think part of you at least is still very much there, even though the other part will very much deny it."

Linda quickly rolled outside his reach, away from the chastising twig he held in his hand. It came to her that she never loved him more than in those moments when she managed to bring out the playful child in him.

"You see," she laughed, "it's exactly the way you treat me. One moment you make love to me, passionately, desperately, and the next you come after me with a stick in your hand. Now do you call this consistent behavior? You know what I call it?" she giggled. "I call it Gemini!"

She threw herself back against the warm grass, her nude body convulsed with laughter. Sartain watched her, trying hard to fight his growing desire. She was tantalizing him, and he knew it. But he wouldn't give in, not yet.

"Come here!" he said with a commanding finger, pretending still to be angry. She cautiously approached, but not before she had put on her blouse, which unbuttoned made her even more seductive. When she neared, contrite, he grabbed her roughly to him, but then pressed her tenderly against his body, his lips searching hers.

They fell gently to the blanket spread in the small, secluded glade which they had discovered only a few weeks before on one of their hiking trips to Angel Island. The grassy clearing was boarded on three sides by oak, madrone, and eucalyptus with thick brush underneath. On the southern side the silent bay offered a magnificent panorama of San Francisco itself. They were somewhere off the trail between Perles Beach and Battery Drew, some fifteen minutes by bicycle—the only mode of transportation allowed on the uninhabited island—from the picturesque Ayala Cove, where they had disembarked by ferry from Tiburon that morning.

It was one of those perfectly warm cloudless days when even the ubiquitous westerly wind gentled to a soft breeze. They had spent the morning riding around the island, visiting the vacated army sites, feeding the free-roaming deer, and then just before midday they had reached their sheltered spot to picnic.

Linda suddenly pushed herself away. "You know something?"

she said with that cunning smile which told him she was up to something.

"What?"

"I betcha Carlos is a Gemini."

"Wrong!"

"Are you sure? He reads like one." She referred to the first two chapters of Sartain's new manuscript which he had let her read the day before. A journalist and herself a student of social science, she frequently proofread his work for him, and he often solicited her comments. It was a new thing to him, this intellectual rapport, something which he had never really shared with Jane, his late wife, nor with anyone else.

"Yes, I'm sure. I don't know much about sun signs, but I do know when he was born, and he's definitely not a Gemini."

"When was he born?"

"October, nineteen forty-nine."

"When in October?" She knew he had a phenomenal memory.

"Well, let's see . . . October . . . October twelfth, which makes him . . ."

"A Libra!" she interrupted cheerfully. "I knew it."

"Sure," he said mockingly, putting on his shirt as the sun slid under some low clouds.

"Well, I suspected so," she said ignoring his sarcasm. "And it absolutely makes sense. I should have known. He doesn't have a dual personality. He has an ever-changing one. He's a chameleon."

"Now, c'mon," Sartain protested, having realized that Linda was taking the subject too seriously. "For an intelligent person like you to dwell on this . . . astrological nonsense. Ever since you worked on that article, I swear . . ."

"Now, you c'mon, Sam. You know I'm not a great believer in this stuff. All I'm suggesting is that there may be something to it. I don't exactly know what, or how, but it has helped me draw quick, rough portraits of people. And besides it's kind of fun, and what's wrong with that?"

Sartain didn't respond. Only the barking of the seals on the rocks below and the scolding of the sea gulls interrupted the silence. In the distance they could hear a child calling for his mother. Sartain gazed at her, reflecting on how much indeed the woman, whom he had met so accidentally, and so unexpectedly, had changed his attitude toward so many things. In a sense she had restored his youth, the youth so abruptly stolen from him by his tour of duty in the Pacific and later the Korean War. He thought how ironic it was that they were lying only a few hundred yards from East Garrison where twenty-one-year-old Lieutenant Samuel H. Sartain had received his discharge papers at the end of the war.

"Well then, Sphinx," Linda picked up the conversation again, "how about sinking to my level and allowing me to tell you a few things about Libras, which may, or may not, help you in comprehending Carlos? How about it?"

"On one condition," he eyed her sternly. "That while you're talking, you'll give me a back rub. Then you can tell me all you want about Libras, Geminis, or for that matter, about any sign you care to discuss. How about it?" he asked, removing his shirt again.

"You should have been an extortionist," Linda said, already straddling the small of his back, beginning to knead. Actually she didn't mind the back rubs he always conned her into, though each time she protested with vigor. She loved to leisurely study his body.

His back was broad at the shoulders and narrowed classically to the buttocks. Even at his age it was a beautiful body, though the once rock-hard muscles had mellowed to a firm softness. She loved his body, not only because it was pleasing to look at but because it represented familiar comfort to her, like her parents' house once had. There was a solidness in it that paralleled the strength of his mind, and these two things made him irresistible to her.

"The first thing you should know about Libras," she said, scooting down to his rump so she could massage his lower back, "is that they are consistently inconsistent. They can be good-natured one minute and sulky or quarrelsome the next. They are usually highly intelligent but also tend to be incredibly gullible at times. They are frequently restless, and yet they don't like to be rushed. Actually they're very much like their sign, the scales. Sometimes they're very up, sometimes very down, and sometimes at perfect equilibrium."

Sartain was only half listening to Linda's exposition. His mind was gone, his senses had taken over. He was truly enjoying the sun, the fresh air, the smell of the eucalyptus. With each soft pressure of Linda's hands he felt closer and closer to nature, almost melting into it. If there was heaven, this was it. The wine they had with lunch began to affect him. Carlos, terrorism, and any of the other world problems which usually occupied his mind seemed remote and unreal.

"Well, what do you think, Sam?" Linda's voice brought him back to reality.

"Ummm," he mumbled, stretching his back. He must have begun to doze.

She stopped rubbing. "Are you even listening to me?" He could feel her back stiffen.

"Sure. You just eloquently pinpointed Carlos's character by saying he could be this, that, or the other."

"But . . ."

She sounded hurt. He was not keeping his end of the bargain, playing the game.

"Okay," he tried to mollify her, picking it up again. "Inconsistency can be an important trait too. And, curiously enough, people who have known Carlos have offered widely differing interpretations of his character. If it makes you feel better, many of the intelligence services, including the Israelis, have thought at one time or another that there is more than one Carlos."

"Now, while you rub the back of my legs, you can tell me about the physical characteristics of Libras, or doesn't the Zodiac cover that?"

"As a matter of fact, smart ass," she said, giving his bottom a sharp slap, "people who were born under the same sign do share some physical characteristics. For example you look like a typical Gemini—ugly!"

"First you make me listen to this pseudoscientific nonsense, then you beat me and call me names," Sartain complained, turning to face her. "I don't have to put up with this, you know."

"I don't have to rub your legs either," she grinned down at him.

He turned on his stomach again. "And you have the nerve to call *me* the extortionist."

"There is no such a thing as a typical Libra feature," Linda became serious again, working down his thighs, "unless it's the Venus dimple. Libras' features are almost always even and well balanced. They're pleasing, and the dimples are always there.

There are usually a couple in the cheeks and one in the chin. If they're not in the face, you might want to check to see if the knees are dimpled."

"I hope Carlos wears shorts." The professor's body was shaking with laughter. He was fully enjoying the topic now. He didn't know whether it was the wine or just the conversation, but yet in the back of his mind he remembered that in some of the pictures he had of Carlos, the man definitely had dimples. "What else?" he asked more soberly.

"Well, most Libras are full of curves rather than angles. Their hair is often curly. They are not necessarily fat, although the tendency to be plump is definitely there. Still they can fool you. They can go on a diet and before you know it cut quite a trim figure."

"Very clever," Sartain said. "And I almost fell for it. You have been looking at Carlos's photographs, and now you—"

"No, Sam. I swear. I can easily prove it to you. Check any book about the Zodiac and find out for yourself. I told you, it boggles my mind sometimes. I never believed in it myself until I did the article and started thinking that there must be something to it. It works just too many times to be a coincidence." She shrugged, "What can I tell you?"

Sartain adamantly refused to take the discussion seriously. A skeptic by nature, an atheist by conviction, he wouldn't listen to anything that smacked of the occult, of the spiritual. To him astrology was just another aspect of humankind's vain attempt to make order out of chaos.

"Tell me about the Libra's love life," he said as he reached for her.

"Okay, I will, but don't laugh when I tell you something else first. Libras in general hate bloodshed."

"Well, that's definitely Carlos," he said sarcastically. "Now I've no choice but to admit that your theories make a lot of sense. We all know what a pussy cat he is." He grinned, triumphant. He was glad he could so easily refute her theory.

"All right, all right," Linda admitted. "I knew I shouldn't have mentioned it, but I'm not trying to win a point. I'm just trying to be helpful. I'm just . . . I just think it's something worth looking into." There was frustration in her tone of voice. "Perhaps he's reacting to something . . . perhaps to something back in his childhood. I think it wouldn't hurt to find out what he was like as a teen-ager, back in Venezuela. How did he react then to the sight of blood? Seriously I think there may be something to it."

Sartain cast a doubtful look at her, but he remained silent; the idea had registered. He recalled something about Carlos's high-school days that caught; he decided to ignore it.

"Their love life," he demanded.

"Well," she said, baiting him again, "like the Gemini, the Libra man is fickle, and tends to involve himself with a number of women. He is generally a successful and well-accomplished lover, particularly when it comes to romance, which, it is claimed, he invented."

Her description, Sartain noted again, wasn't far from what he knew about Carlos. Linda could see by his expression that something had clicked. "Am I getting to you, just a little, Sam?"

"Well," he admitted reluctantly, "there might be something in all that mumbo jumbo. I don't know what," he grinned, "but something."

"Now you want to tell me," she grabbed for the upper hand, still needling him, "that the CIA, or the FBI, or for that matter, the NSA, when they do a profile on a criminal or a terrorist or whoever they're after . . . You want to tell me that they don't check his chart?"

Sartain felt queer when she mentioned the NSA. He hadn't told her that he had seen Fred Atkins. It was the only thing he had omitted when he related what had transpired at the book-store. His past work for the NSA was the only part of his past that he had never discussed with Linda. The only thing she did know was that sometime in the late 1950s or early 1960s he had done some work for them. He never explained his function with that supersecret agency, which was quite unusual for their rela-tionship. And Linda knew him too well to press him on this issue. She knew that if he wanted to discuss it with her, he would bring it up himself, in his own time.

"No, they definitely don't," he responded lightly. "However, if you want to put in an official proposal, I'll use my good offices to transmit it to the highest authority . . . to the head of the CIA himself."

He slid his palm along her flat stomach and cupped one of her breasts through her unbuttoned shirt. "Because I'll be damned if I let that dirty old man get anywhere near you."

"Is he really a dirty old man?" she whispered in a low seductive voice.

Sartain felt an uncontrollable urge sweeping through him. His hand left her breast, slid past the hardened nipple toward her neck, circling it behind, bringing her closer to him as he whispered in her ear, "Not half as dirty as this old man." And as she pretended to struggle away, he added, "What do they say about Geminis? That they are the greatest lovers in the world? Isn't it so?"

"No," she barely managed to utter before his hungry mouth closed on hers, "Libras are."

"You—" But her lips were already sealing his lips, her tongue searching his tongue, her thin long fingers caressing tenderly the back of his head through his soft hair. They rolled onto the thick grass, letting nature absorb and participate in their exploding fusion.

Later, when he lay on top of her, depleted, he could feel the sun's rays low against his bare back. He knew they would have to leave soon to catch the last ferry, but he refused to pull away, not yet. He looked down at her. Her eyes were closed, her long golden hair spread and mixed with the grass, a peaceful look on her radiant face. He touched her lips lightly, gently, drawing a lazy, content smile from her.

He felt lucky to be so happy, yet a certain fear gnawed at him. There, in her arms, totally possessing and being possessed by her, life was too sweet.

Sadness swept over him. This is too perfect, something kept telling him, it just cannot last. It was all so ephemeral, and he wanted it to last forever.

"I'm getting old," he complained as he rolled off to let her up.

"Not if you ask me, you're not," Linda grinned coyly, rising to gather her clothes, unaware of the turmoil within him.

Watching her dress, he felt guilty for not spending more time with her on the coast. "I'm going to try to cut out some of my obligations at Georgetown. I want to spend more time here, with you."

She looked at him as if to say she'd heard it before.

"No, truly," he protested, pulling on his pants. "I'm getting older, and I want to enjoy myself before I get too old and cranky, before you throw me away."

She glanced up from the blanket she was folding, struck by his show of vulnerability. "You are younger than anyone I know, Sam, including my fellow grad students, believe me."

He loved her for saying that, because he knew she meant it. "C'mon," he said, "if we don't hurry, we'll miss the boat and have to spend the night here."

She gave him a mischievous grin as she dropped the backpack she was holding and sat down beside it. "Is that a threat or an invitation, Professor?"

He laughed, pulling her to her feet. "I've got work to do, Linda. Much as I'd love not to do it."

Later, on the ferry to Tiburon, they drank hot chocolate from paper cups, watching the peninsula approaching them, black against the reddened sky. A few lingering sailboats lolled in the dusky breeze.

"Let's see if Steve and Luana will go sailing with us tomorrow when they come up from Berkeley," Linda suggested, knowing Sartain would like the idea of a day on the boat talking politics with his son and his girl friend.

"Sounds great. Whose boat?"

"Well, the Shermans said we could use theirs any time," Linda said.

"If the kids are up to it, it's fine with me."

"Good," Linda said. "I know Steve loves to sail, and so does Luana. Although it all depends on what kind of mood your son is in," she added. "After all, isn't he a Libra too?"

"Will you cut it out?" Sartain pleaded in mock exasperation, grabbing her by the neck and pulling her toward him as the horn sounded to announce the boat's approach to the dock.

CHAPTER FIVE

DARK heavy drapes, the only thing of substance in the sparsely furnished room, were tightly drawn, preventing the daylight from reaching in. Two cheap standing lamps cast light and shadow across the dimness, revealing a sagging, threadbare couch, behind which stood a drop-leaf table adorned with a dying potted plant and circled by assorted odd chairs. An old chest of drawers stood in the alcove next to a tier of bookshelves, empty save for a few legal texts. A mock-Persian rug covered only half of the dull parquet floor.

On the wall opposite the bookshelves, askew, hung a frameless oil landscape of a dreary winter day. Underneath it, on two adjacent straight chairs, sat two grim-looking men, their hulking bodies dwarfing the small seats to which they had been relegated.

The darker one sported a full beard that covered most of his face and set off his stony, dark gaze. The other one, sandy haired, was of softer countenance, but his yellow-green eyes were as steely as those of his bearded neighbor.

They sat rigid, arms folded, watching the elegantly dressed man who was pacing up and back across the room like an enraged panther.

At the table sat a blond woman, withdrawn in the face of the fury heaped on her by the raving Carlos. Her strikingly plain face was drawn into a mask of weariness.

Fusako was sitting on the sofa, straining to follow the exchange in German, a language which she did not speak but could somewhat understand. Her slanted eyes, behind the tinted glasses she wore, shifted back and forth between the fuming Jackal and the blonde. She ignored the two men who sat there, statuelike.

"Did you tell her it's absolutely vital to the cause? Did you remind her that we've just suffered a major defeat and that the whole movement is in mortal danger? Did you tell her it's of key importance to the revolution? Did you?"

Gertrude nodded, "Carlos, I'm sorry," she pleaded with a strong Bavarian accent. "I tried to persuade her, but you don't know Helga. She just wouldn't listen. She insisted that either Brigitte, Ilse, and Erika escape with her, or else she stays. They are very close, you know."

"No, I don't know!" he thundered. "All I know is that the goddamn bitch is willing to jeopardize my . . . our plan because she has suddenly discovered true love!"

The woman knew it was useless to respond. She eyed him warily as he stopped pacing and stood over her.

He was dressed in a three-piece suit, and his high-heeled patent shoes added a full two inches to his height, allowing him to tower over her. His gray-flecked hair, recently straightened, was neatly smoothed back with a touch of brilliantine. It glistened when it caught some light. His powder-blue shirt and the dotted tie perfectly complemented his well-tailored gray suit. His fingernails were immaculately manicured. He could easily have passed for a top executive in any of the prosperous industrial German firms which his fellow terrorists of the Baader-Meinhof and the June Second gangs were after.

Fusako watched; she couldn't help but muse that, in this latest costume, Carlos looked like the perfect candidate for a kidnapping. No one would have placed such a fine-looking gentleman in such shabby surroundings, except, paradoxically, as a hostage.

"I can't understand it. Why was Helga ready to go, alone, when Haddad demanded her release in exchange for the Entebbe hostages? She didn't insist then that the others leave with her." Carlos shook his head. "Explain that to me!" he snapped. *"Das ist doch zum verrückt werden!* It's crazy!"

"Well . . ." The woman hesitated under the Jackal's accusing glare. "She claims those were different circumstances then. She was in no position to make any demands. But now, I guess, she thinks that it's as easy to get four out as it is one."

"Easy, ah?" Carlos interjected acidly. He raised his voice again. "What am I? Some sort of a goddamn bank? Where does the bitch think I'm going to get the extra fifty thousand, the extra weapons. What about the risks involved? I just can't believe it. Are you Germans fighting a revolution or do you think this is some sort of a party?"

The German woman shrugged helplessly. "I don't know what to tell you." She sighed. "I tried my best. I even warned her there was a chance they may be transferred soon from Lehrter to the Stammheim maximum security prison." She saw the puzzled look on Carlos's face and explained. "Ever since Entebbe they have been pretty edgy at Lehrter. I was told the government is considering moving at least Helga out of there. I suppose it's because of the demand for her release . . . particularly when you asked for her and not for Baader or Ensslim. I don't exactly know what to make of it, but once Helga is at Stammheim, forget it, it's all over. You'll never get her out of there."

Carlos looked stunned. It took him a long second to absorb what the blonde had just told him. For the first time he turned to Fusako. "Did you understand what she said?" he asked in English. The Japanese nodded. "Stammheim," she muttered, thinking aloud. "Well, once Helga is there . . . Gertrude is right. Once she is there, forget it. We'll never get her out of there."

Carlos turned on the blonde again, still ignoring the two silent Germans. "When did you find this out?" he demanded, his voice betraying signs of deflation under the weight of this latest possible setback to his plans. "Why didn't you tell me this before? Do you realize what it all means?"

"Of course I do," the woman shrugged helplessly. "I tried to tell you . . . but . . . you kept interrupting me. I'm sorry. I can understand your being angry, but there wasn't much I could do. Helga is a very stubborn woman. As for the transfer, I heard the rumor only the other day, just before I saw Helga. I didn't say the transfer is definite, just that I heard they're considering it. But, at the same time, it would be logical for the prison to transfer them, at least Helga. It makes sense, doesn't it? Considering everything that has happened."

"Goddamn Haddad," Carlos swore to himself as he fell silent. If he had done what he was supposed to do in the first place, they wouldn't have to go through all this mess. And now that Ahmad was dead, it wouldn't be that easy to get the extra money. He cursed the dead Arab.

Carlos turned on the blonde again. "You mean to tell me that

Helga knows that she may be transferred to Stammheim, and she still refuses to break out alone?"

The woman nodded silently.

"*Verflückte Scheisse!*" Carlos shouted, startling even the stolid Germans.

"Carlos," Fusako interrupted him as she rose from the couch, "may I talk with you?" She walked over to him, her sleek black hair, rippling behind her, following in her wake. With her small well-proportioned figure and catlike gait, she looked different, softer and more sensual than the somber and angry pictures of her which appeared in the media. She took his arm and led him to the small foyer by the front door where they couldn't be seen by the others.

"Carlos," she said in a gentle voice, trying to calm him down, "Gertrude is right. I know Helga. I was with her in Southern Yemen. She won't budge . . . and I'm sure she won't leave Brigitte behind. Believe me, she'd rather rot in there than leave Brigitte. Forget about her and Ralf, that's all over. She is into Brigitte now."

"*Wunderbar!*" he muttered disgustedly.

"Well, you know the way she is. That's why we need her, don't we? Now listen to me. I've thought about it, and in the long run it may not be such a bad idea to spring all of them. After all, if you think about it, Helga was the surprise name on the Entebbe list . . . and a couple of weeks later she is the only one we try to get out. Well someone will surely be putting two and two together, and before we know it, our mission will be just that much more difficult. On the other hand," she continued, pleased that she was getting through to him, "if we get all four out, I doubt that anyone will suspect that something is up and that it has to do with Helga. Besides they'll be looking for four fugitives instead of one which will make it easier for Helga to cross to East Berlin. We can use the others as decoys, sending them in opposite directions. And let's not forget that if we get all four out, it will be more of a coup. It will be good for the morale . . ."

Carlos urbanely drew a gold pocket watch from his vest, clicked it open, checked the time, and slipped it back into place. "That's all very nice," said Carlos. "Not that I haven't thought about it, but the problem is that I don't have the extra money right now. And one thing I don't want to do is wait too long. You heard what Gertrude said, they may decide to move her to Stammheim any time now."

"Well, that's what I've been trying to tell you. If you've no objection in principle, I can come up with thirty thousand marks almost immediately. The question is, can you get the remaining twenty?"

He watched her as a proud smile crossed her lips. She looked very appealing when she smiled. He knew that she knew that he could come up with the money, that he always had that kind of "pocket money" around. "Okay," he agreed, "but let's get one thing clear. I don't want those two together after the breakout, not until the American thing is over."

Fusako's smile turned cruel. "Don't worry," she said, "I'll take care of it. I can promise you that." The perverse glee in her slanted eyes quickened his pulse. He felt his flesh twitch with excitement. He smiled back. She didn't have to tell him exactly what she had in mind; he knew he would be avenged. They were two of a kind, he and Fusako, a match made in hell's inferno.

"By the way, what about these two?" Carlos nodded in the direction of the room. "What do you think?"

"Don't worry," she said. "They're as professional as they come. They are no Arabs." She smiled, already cognizant of the Azzawi episode. She remembered how he had come to her afterward, surging with insatiable desire. "They are former Ministerium für Staatssicherheit, trained by Wolf himself. We won't have any problems with them."

"Are they familiar with all the details?"

"I briefed them today."

"Did you tell them to use spikes?"

"They were going to anyway . . ."

"*Gut*," Carlos said, nodding in satisfaction. "*Sehr gut.*" Employing East Germany's finest suited him. He knew that, for once, he could count on a professional performance. "It's about time," he sighed. "Now when can you get me the money?"

"By tonight, if you want."

"Perfect."

By the time the pair returned to the room, Carlos's mood had changed radically. While before he was fuming and dejected, now he was almost cheerful and confident. He even patted the relieved Gertrude on the shoulder, complimenting her on the job she was doing. He realized, he told her, it was no fault of hers that Helga was giving them such a hard time. He apologized for having turned on her.

Carlos assured Gertrude that he would come up with the extra money needed to bribe the guards, telling her that she should have it no later than the following morning. He added, however, that he was steadfast against any attempt to smuggle more weapons into the prison. It was much too risky, and if discovered, it could lead to the exposure of the whole plot. He saw no reason why Helga's gun should not be sufficient.

"And," Carlos added, his voice tense again with the importance of this last edict, "these three comrades of ours had better be told that everything must be done to get Helga out unharmed, even if they have to shield her from bullets with their own bodies. Helga must escape unharmed. Without her, alive and free, they are as good as dead. Tell them that."

CHAPTER SIX

"COME about, Sam!" Sherman shouted desperately, as his Cal-25 nearly slid into the side of the tanker under full steam. "You're gonna run us into them for sure! Release the jib!"

The transport was so close it looked like a mountain.

"Heads down!" Sartain yelled to the other five on board. They all complied, hearts pounding.

The boom swung, the halyards clanged loudly against the mast as the luffing sails sought for wind. The sloop lurched sideways, then settled into its new tack. They had escaped the near disaster.

"Damn it, Sam," Sherman said, trying to smile good-naturedly, "I wish you wouldn't take such chances with my boat."

"Oh, c'mon, Peter," Sartain grinned, totally unnerved, "I can't help it if you people panicked . . . I knew what I was doing all along."

"My ass," the ususally placid Sherman replied. "I suggest you hand me that tiller before you kill us all. I don't know about everyone else here, but my wife and I would like to see the sun come up tomorrow."

"Yea!" the others cheered loudly.

"Hear! hear!" even Steve, a daredevil in his own right, joined the protest against his father's risky sailing maneuvers.

"Okay, okay," Sartain conceded. "I know when I'm not appreciated. I can take a hint." And with that he handed the tiller to his neighbor and climbed forward to sunbathe at the bow.

"So tell me, Luana, I haven't had a chance to ask you before. How is school?" Linda was trying to start the conversation again, now that the boat was safely on course.

"School? Now?" Luana was baffled by the question.

"Uh-huh. How do you like your courses, your instructors?"

"Oh, I . . . I thought you knew. I'm not taking anything this summer."

"Oh! Of course," Linda said shaking her head. "How stupid of me to forget! I assume that just because I am a masochist, everybody else is too." She wrapped her arm affectionately around Luana's shoulders.

"Well," Luana said, obviously touched by the genuine display of affection, "I guess everyone else does, I mean . . . I don't mean . . . I don't mean being a masochist . . . I . . ."

Linda let out a laugh, relishing Luana's childlike simplicity.

"What I mean is, Mr. Sartain is teaching this summer, and Steve is taking French and rewriting his thesis, so I guess I am just about the only one who . . . who just goofs off."

"And if you ask me," Linda said fondly, "you're just about the only smart one in this family. We should have all taken the summer off."

Linda looked at Luana with a maternal gaze. The girl's flaxen hair whipped against her face in the stiff breeze. She would have made a perfect flower child back in the sixties, she thought. The girl was so loving, so fresh and vulnerable. Linda silently wondered how she and Steve were getting along.

Mrs. Sherman, sitting starboard directly across from Linda, huge dark glasses covering the top half of her sun-wrinkled face, spoke up. "Well, Linda, I hear you've got yourself a scholarship at Stanford." Bitsy Sherman had been a housewife and mother more than half her life, and years of cocktail party giving had honed her into an eager conversationalist. She managed to fit herself into any kind of group.

"How are you managing? I mean between your job with the magazine and Stanford?" Mrs. Sherman continued.

"Well, it hasn't been too difficult so far," Linda responded. "I'm preparing a series of articles for the fall issues called 'Women and Crime,' and as it turned out, I was able to use part of that material for a term paper in my sociology class. And . . . I guess I'm just lucky . . . the term paper was accepted as the basis for my master's thesis. In fact, my adviser suggested that I consider expanding it into a Ph.D. dissertation. So I'm really quite happy with the way things have turned out. It's definitely a fertile subject. The professor there steered me right this time," she nodded in Sartain's direction, winking, "for a change."

"That's really super," Luana uttered with unconcealed admiration. "I'm glad to hear you're not having as hard a time as Steve . . ." She broke off, glancing quickly in Steve's direction. She hoped it hadn't sounded deprecating. Steve, however, busy below getting another beer from the cooler, didn't seem to have heard.

"As a matter of fact," Linda continued, passing over Luana's remark, "the subject of women's criminality has become such a hot issue now, with the steep rise in women's crime in the seventies, that the genius over there," she raised her voice this time as she nodded again toward Sartain, "thinks it will make a good book—maybe even a nonfiction best seller if . . . we work on it together."

Sartain, lying on his back, eyes closed, didn't respond. He was enjoying the peaceful isolation of the bow, the gentle rocking of the boat, the icy spray which tingled his sun-soaked chest.

His mind wandered in and out of the conversation at hand, which he could barely hear from where he was. He caught, however, Luana's impulsive remark, as she was sitting nearest to him, and it started him thinking.

He reflected on the brief talk he had had that morning with Steve when they were left alone for a while at the house. Once again he became aware of the difficulties his son had with his master's thesis. Steve's thesis was about the students' rebellion in the sixties, and as it turned out, his first thesis supervisor thought he approached his subject on a much too subjective level, not at all as an "objective social scientist."

This conversation led Sartain to think about those days in the sixties. He wondered if his active involvement then did indeed influence Steve as much as his adviser had suggested. It must have. But did Steve really understand his father's position at the time? Did he really grasp why Sartain had involved himself in the protest movement in the first place? Why he had cut his ties with the Agency? In retrospect he wondered if anyone ever really understood his reasons in those days of turmoil.

That misinterpretation of his true stand bothered him at times. Later, however, that outright involvement reinforced and spread his reputation as a "liberal," and opened doors for him to different revolutionary circles throughout the world. That, in turn, proved tremendously helpful in his research on the subject of guerrilla and revolutionary warfare and later in his studies of terrorism.

Sartain's thoughts shifted to his meeting up with Atkins when his son's voice came through. "I read recently," Steve said, sipping his beer, "that as a result of all these new female criminals skulking the streets, many social scientists are having to recant their earlier theories about the passivity of women—which I, for one, never really bought in the first place. As one of these emerging 'superwomen,'" he smiled broadly revealing a set of perfect white teeth, "how do you feel about it?"

Mr. Sherman interrupted then, asking if Steve would take over at the tiller, so Linda didn't respond immediately to the question. She watched the athletically built Steve as he moved aft. In many ways he resembled his father, although he was a full two inches shorter. He had the professor's strong chin, but he also had inherited some of his mother's softer facial features. His hair was also lighter and less curly than the professor's. On the other hand Steve was an amazingly muscular man, exceedingly so for Linda's taste, who knew that he had been on the wrestling team as an undergraduate and still practiced daily judo and karate. His self-conscious masculinity was something that bothered Linda at times, but he was bright, highly inquisitive, and charming when he wanted to be, and that was primarily how she related to him. She didn't know exactly how to interpret his remark about her being a "superwoman," so she decided to let it go.

"Now, if you're talking about crime," Linda replied, realizing that both Steve and Luana were interested in what she had to say, and that even the Shermans were listening, "did you know that in Germany today girls under fourteen are committing as much assault and theft as their male counterparts. Amazing, isn't it? Only the other day I came across statistics that show that since 1971 something like three times as many girls have been sent to juvenile prisons as in former years . . ."

"Perhaps," Steve had to raise his voice for them to hear him, "the German female's attitude toward the use of force changed as a result of the bombs and bullets they were exposed to in World War II. Or . . . perhaps it's the fact that so many of them grew up without fathers, lost in the war. You think that had something to do with it? Have you looked into that at all?"

"Not really," Linda replied. "There is of course something to what you say, but you see, Steve, the phenomenon is not at all limited to Germany. In the United States, for example, where we have not experienced war at our doorsteps, the number of women jailed since nineteen seventy has risen three times faster than the number of men. It's really a universal circumstance. Take Great Britain, where the increase has been twofold within the last seven years, or Canada, where it doubled within the last sixteen, or even Japan, hitherto known for the passive and submissive role of its women, where it has risen twenty-two percent in the last five years."

Since Steve had a hard time hearing Linda from where he sat, he handed back the tiller to Mr. Sherman, who was more than happy to comply. It was obvious that statistics didn't interest him whatsoever. Sartain remained at the bow, half lost in thought, half listening, but the two other women seemed eager to hear more on the topic.

"But, you're right about one thing, Steve," Linda continued once he sat next to her again. "Nowhere has the increase in female crime been more startling than in the Federal Republic of Germany where—"

"She means West Germany," Sartain interrupted, moving down from the bow, stretching himself. "Here she is sounding like some pedantic Ph.D. before she even gets her master's."

"It takes one to know one," Linda retorted genially. And then she added with a victorious smile, "You can't take the competition, can you?"

The professor only laughed loudly in response, delighted at Linda's quick wit.

"But seriously," she continued, intent on pursuing the discussion, "in West Germany, if that makes everyone feel better"—she granted Sartain a sly smile—"one in three criminals today is a woman, when only a decade ago, it was one in ten."

"That's quite incredible!" Bitsy Sherman volunteered her opinion. "I just can't see it. I always thought the Germans were so orderly!"

"These unfortunately happen to be the facts," Linda answered, "and more horrifying than anything else is the fact that it is the increase in violent crimes which has been the most staggering. Up something like five, six hundred percent over the past few years. That's one of the reasons I'm going to make West Germany my most important case study."

"And that's why," Steve joked, "the next time I see a woman on the street, I'll cross as fast as I can to the other side, particularly if she has Teutonic features."

"Like father, like son," Linda commented, laughing with the others. "Two male chauvinist pigs!"

When the laughing stopped, silence fell over the boat. The bay had calmed, and in the late-afternoon quiescence most boats had begun their final tack toward harbor. Sherman glanced at the flat sails. "Well," he announced, "I think we'll head in now. Not much wind left today. Takes at least another half hour to make the marina. Heads down, I'm coming about."

They all ducked and for a time continued to be silent, listening to the boat sounds as it eased into its new tangent.

Luana, whose fascination with Linda was evident, spoke up. "Wasn't it a German woman who commanded the Entebbe hijacking?"

"Well, I don't really know if the woman you're referring to, Luana, was actually in charge, but she seemed to have definitely played a major role. I still haven't been able to identify her though. It was widely reported that she was Gabriele Kröcher-Tiedeman, who last year was exchanged for the kidnapped leader of Berlin's Christian Democratic Party—"

"Peter Lorenz," Steve helped even though it didn't seem she needed it.

"Yes, Peter Lorenz," Linda continued with the same pace. "She later reemerged to participate with Carlos in his raid on the OPEC headquarters in Vienna. But Sam strongly doubts that she was the German woman who took part in the hijacking."

"He does?" Steve interjected again. "Why?"

"Ask him," Linda said. "He's the expert. I guess he's privy to some confidential information we, the simple people, aren't." She looked impishly at Sartain. "Anyway—"

"Why, Dad?" Steve interrupted, pursuing the question. "I read the other day that the German woman who was killed at Entebbe was definitely identified as Gabriele Kröcher-Tiedeman."

Sartain, however, begged out. "This is Linda's subject. I'm on vacation today. Besides," he winked, "maybe I can pick up a few points for my next class."

"Bravo!" Mrs. Sherman applauded.

"Let's hear it for the women!" Luana chimed in.

As they neared land, Linda obliged her female audience, recounting some of the more fascinating stories involving women terrorists. She talked about the Palestinian hijacker Leila Khaled, about the Japanese Fusako Shigenobu, who sent her husband on a suicidal mission to Ben-Gurion Airport, and about Rose Dugdale, the young college professor who burglarized her own father's estate to aid the IRA.

Linda was at her best when it came to narrating personal stories. Her journalistic experience came clearly through, and she managed to get even Peter Sherman out of his dream world. He listened with interest to the stories about those curious women—the so-called weaker sex—who tote guns and toss bombs, the gun molls who refused to play second fiddle to their men. It was indeed a strange world out there, he thought to himself as he steered the boat toward Tiburon harbor.

But as the sun began to set, flecking the water with gold, the air was peaceful. With the coming nightfall everything around was calm and beautiful. The world of violence was so remote it might as well have been on another planet. Here all was serene. It all reminded Sherman of the bedtime fairy tales and monster stories his mother used to tell him, and his mind once again drifted off while the boat floated on through the dreamy, dusky landscape as if painted there by some French Impressionist.

CHAPTER SEVEN

I T was a moonless night, and the black Volkswagen van blended well into the darkness of the deserted street. The Ku-Damm may have still been aglow with glittering neons and the streaming lights of the late partygoers' traffic, but Lehrterstrasse was still, its darkness only here and there broken by a few patches of dim light cast down from the street-lamps.

Parked under a branchy oak, the two stone-faced men inside the van sat silently opposite each other. Their eyes had become accustomed to the near blackness in the rear of the van where they sat; they were able to make out each other's silhouettes. They had been there since nine o'clock, hardly exchanging a word, frequently consulting their phosphorescent watches. Earlier, headlights of passing cars had intermittently illuminated the van, but ever since midnight, when the guards' shift took place at Lehrter women's prison two hundred yards down the road, only one single car, a green Mercedes-Benz, passed by.

"It's five minutes to two," the blond one said, having consulted his watch again. "In five minutes they should start making their move." There was a note of anticipation in his voice.

"No," responded the bearded one. "In five minutes the hourly check will take place. They won't make their move until five or ten minutes later." He scratched his whiskers. "It will take them another ten to fifteen minutes to reach the outside wall, if they don't run into any problems."

"*Scheisse!*" the blond cursed. "I'm dying for a cigarette. I've got a pack of Americans too."

"You should have quit smoking a long time ago. In this business . . ."

"Don't worry, fuzz face, I'll live longer than you."

"I hope so," responded the bearded one as he pulled the .32 automatic from his holster. He checked it and loaded it quickly and expertly in the dark, not having to glance at it at all. Fusako was right, they were professionals. "I just hope you can hold your liquor," he added with a snide grin on his face which the blond couldn't really see but easily guessed at.

"I told you, don't worry about me," he said as he brought the whiskey bottle to his lips and took one more swig. Stinking of whiskey was the one part of the ploy that compensated for the boredom and discomfort of having to squat for hours, unable to smoke, in a tight tuxedo. "What I'm worried about is that he may not be here on time with the Mercedes."

"He will. He's probably already parked around the corner on Moabit Street. He can be counted on."

"You hope," said the blond as he downed another gulp.

"I'm sure!" the man with the beard snapped. "But I'm not so sure anymore about you. The whiskey is already making you talk too much. Just do us all a favor and don't get drunk."

"How do I smell?"

"You stink! I suggest you quit now and don't drink again until just before you reach the checkpoint. And leave some for Helga."

"*Jawohl!*"

The bearded one consulted his watch again. "I think I better move to the front and start watching," he said, slowly rising. Stooping forward, he positioned himself behind the driver's seat, where he could scan the high mossy brick walls of the prison.

Inside the aging turn-of-the-century prison the two guards had just completed their hourly routine check. They moved quietly, so as not to disturb the sleep of the women prisoners: those were the specific instructions of the warden. Having satisfied themselves that all was in order in the cellblock, they proceeded to the guards' lounge to have their coffee, read some old crime magazines, and gossip a little before their next hourly rounds.

Inside her cell terrorist Helga Denz lay in bed, fully clothed. She rolled from under the coarse blanket just as she heard the door click behind the two guards. Her thick blond hair was in curlers, and her face was all made up. Unlike some of the other German prisons, at Lehrter women prisoners were allowed to use cosmetics if they wished to do so. Most, understandably, never bothered.

Even with the curlers and ugly drab prison uniform Helga was definitely an attractive woman. Her strong features rather than detracting from her femininity only added an element of sexuality to her looks.

Helga coughed twice—the agreed upon signal. The jailbreak was under way. She was relieved to hear a responding cough from the adjacent cell, then another further down. It was the next (and last) one she worried about, since Erika was a chronic sleeper. Helga was afraid the girl would not be able to remain awake that late at night. At last a third cough came from even further down the row. So far so good, Helga thought as she began removing a loosened brick from the wall next to her.

It didn't take long to reach the gun, which she had assembled the night before from pieces smuggled in part by part. From the niche she also removed four keys and a pair of elongated pincers which she had designed especially for this moment. She walked over to the cell door which could be unlocked only from the outside.

Helga placed one of the keys between the tool's gripping jaws and stretched her right arm through the metal bars beside the steel door. Holding her breath, she extended as far as she could reach and within seconds managed to insert the key into the keyhole.

Taking a deep breath, she gingerly rotated the key. But to no avail. Something was wrong; the key wouldn't turn, no matter how much pressure she applied.

Helga rested a moment cursing softly. Renewing her efforts, she tried again. But the key wouldn't budge, and she began to fear it would bend. She felt hot and cold at the same time. The tension was creeping over her, even though she concentrated on keeping calm. Trying her best not to make any noise, every second turned into eternity. She began to perspire.

Trying not to think about the three women who were waiting for her, she decided to pull the key out and then reinsert it. She knew from the night before that it was much harder to wrench the key out than it was to get it in. She replaced it as smoothly as she could, with all the patience she could muster, yet the key still refused to give.

In their individual cells, Brigitte, Ilse, and Erika were wondering what had gone wrong. Why was it taking Helga so long? They were dressed in their prison garments, their bed sheets wrapped around their bodies. But unlike Helga they wore no makeup. All three were armed with metal pipes ripped from their toilets. They were getting anxious, unable to figure out what was going on. But they kept silent.

Helga rested again, exasperated. She couldn't quite figure out what had gone wrong. She had tried the key the night before, and it worked. What could have happened? She knew they didn't change the lock . . . Then it dawned on her: perhaps she was using the wrong key! But how? They were all marked. She decided to check anyway and reached for the three keys in her pocket. There among the three was the one she wanted. She caught herself from sighing audibly in relief. There wasn't time to ask herself how she could have possibly made such an error; there were only a few precious minutes left.

Within seconds the cell door was unlocked, and quickly wrapping her bed sheet around her, Helga proceeded as silently as she could to open the doors to her comrades' cells.

Swiftly, soundlessly, the foursome stole down the hall. Helga led the way, gun in hand, while the other three followed closely behind, holding their metal pipes upright, ready to swing them like makeshift riot clubs.

The two guards—both middle-aged and rather harmless looking, as were most of the male guards assigned to the women's prison—were stunned at the sight of the four armed Amazons bursting into the lounge. One of them let his coffee cup drop to the floor, splashing the hot liquid all over his and his partner's shoes and pants. The other, who had been preoccupied with a crossword puzzle, instinctively went for his revolver as he stood up. He realized that very instant that he had made a big mistake, but it was too late. Helga's gun whipped so hard across his face that it knocked him down unconscious, his nose a bloody mass.

Helga coldly aimed her gun at the other guard, who backed toward the wall, his arms above his head.

"You just keep quiet," she growled, "and you won't be harmed."

The terrified guard nodded; he would not give them a hard time. The look on his face conveyed clearly that all he wanted was not to be harmed. He avoided looking at his partner on the floor. "I have three children," he began to whimper.

"Shut up!" Helga snapped harshly. "I'm not interested in your family life. All I want from you are the keys to that corridor over there and to the library."

Still trembling, he pointed to the metal file cabinet where the keys were kept.

"Get them out for me!" Helga commanded. And as he unlocked the drawer and took out the keys to hand them over to her, she motioned to Ilse. The latter, without a trace of hesitation, and with unnecessary brutality, struck the poor man on the back of the head so hard with the pipe that they could clearly hear the sound of his skull cracking. Brigitte looked away to avoid watching the bloody scene, but the other two showed no emotion. Ilse smiled cruelly, content.

As the stricken man fell forward, his head hit the second guard's chest. The latter, who had lain motionless on the floor, twitched and began gurgling blood. As he moved his head, it became clear that he was regaining consciousness. Helga wanted to take no chances: he might be able to sound the alarm before they could get safely away from the prison. She once again motioned to Ilse, who was happy to comply. Her metal club swung once again, landing on his head. But when she sadistically prepared to hit the helpless man again, Brigitte, the youngest and most feminine of the foursome, could not endure any more. She turned to Helga with pleading eyes, "No!" she begged.

"That's enough!" Helga grabbed Ilse's arm. "Let him be. He's harmless. Come on, let's not waste time." And as they turned to flee the lounge, she briefly laid her hand on Brigitte's shoulder, gently squeezing with uncharacteristic tenderness.

Once inside the library the four women made use of the solid bookshelves to climb and reach one of the high windows which opened onto a narrow cement ledge. It was the top of the outside wall. From there it was a drop of over thirty feet to the street below, but the four sheets rolled and tied together gave them a makeshift rope twenty feet long, and the van was already parked underneath, against the wall.

Just as the fleeing terrorists began to slide down the makeshift rope, Helga first, the green Mercedes returned, this time with its headlights doused. It came to a full stop directly behind the van, and had there been any light, one could have readily noted that it carried diplomatic license plates.

The bearded East German was standing on the van's roof

ready to catch the women as they dropped the few extra feet from the end of the sheet-rope onto the top of the car. The blond, on the ground, grabbed Helga by the arm and quickly led her to the Mercedes, where she took the front seat. He replaced the man at the wheel, who in turn rushed to help at the van.

"Brigitte?" Helga demanded as the blond backed the car away from the van.

"Don't worry," he said, shifting gears to drive away. "They will all be okay. We've got to move separately and in different directions."

Helga didn't respond. She turned around to see her three friends entering the back of the van.

"Here," her escort said, handing her an evening dress. "Change quickly. We don't have much time. You were late, and the sooner we cross to the other side, the better." As Helga began to change clothes, he made a sudden turn and proceeded southeast in the direction of Tiergarten and Checkpoint Charlie.

He drove calmly, that late at night, making sure he checked all traffic signals so as not to call any unnecessary attention to the car.

The others who escaped in the van were speeding west into the heart of the Western Sector; the bearded one was spreading spikes on the road to delay any pursuers.

"Take a few sips," the blond offered Helga the whiskey bottle, "and make sure you kiss me and my collar."

Helga, putting the last touches on her dress and makeup, looked at him quizzically. "Your collar?"

"Yes, yes, the collar. I want it smudged with your lipstick."

"Oh, okay," she nodded. "How do I look?" She shook her long, curled hair from side to side, now loose from its curlers.

He turned to look at her. "Perfect," he said and smiled for the first time, which made him look so much more appealing. "You're very pretty, you know." He raised his right arm and wrapped it around her shoulders. Even through the tuxedo she could feel the steel muscles as he pressed her toward him. She buried her head in his neck, kissing him softly, as he continued to drive with one hand on the wheel. It was in this embrace that they approached the checkpoint into the Eastern Sector.

CHAPTER EIGHT

IT so happened that just about the time Helga Denz and her companion crossed safely into East Berlin, several thousand miles and six time zones away Professor Samuel Sartain was meeting Fred Atkins for dinner.

Sartain was both disappointed and puzzled by the sudden change in their plans for dining at the Atkinses' home. He had looked forward to seeing Beverly, whose company and cooking he had always enjoyed in the past. But as Fred explained on the telephone, something unexpected had come up, and the two of them would have to dine out, alone. He did not elaborate.

Both men arrived within seconds of each other, reminding Sartain of the obsession with punctuality that he and his former boss had always shared. It took Sartain a moment, as when he saw Fred at the bookstore, to adjust to Atkins's new appearance. As they were shown to their table, he wondered what on earth had motivated Atkins to grow a beard when he knew very well that it was the kind of conspicuous unorthodoxy frowned upon by the Agency.

They were seated at a secluded table in the farthest corner of the restaurant. Sartain wondered if Atkins had especially requested to be seated there when he made the reservation. They couldn't be overheard, tucked away like this. What did Fred have in mind? Or was he again reading too much into it?

"I've never eaten here before," Sartain said, surveying the place. It was an old-fashioned Italian restaurant, typically fitted out with red-checkered tablecloths, straw-wrapped Chianti bottles, and plastic grapes hanging from lattice arbors.

"Oh," Atkins smiled apologetically, "it's certainly not the most elegant place in town, but the food is delicious. And this corner is quiet. We won't be disturbed. I've conducted business from here more than once."

Business. Sartain's mind stuck on that word as the waiter brought his Campari and soda and Atkins's bourbon.

"Cheers," Sartain toasted, reserving comment on Atkins's last remark.

"To the renewal of old friendship!" Atkins replied, grinning cheerfully, although his eyes continued to examine the professor carefully.

Something was definitely in the wind. Sartain could feel it at the nape of his neck. He read it in the man's eyes. The old fox couldn't fool him with his casual manner, his expansive mood. He decided to play along: there was no need yet to broach the subject. He would let Fred call the shots for the time being. Besides he could be mistaken, but he didn't think he was.

Atkins placed his drink on the table and leaned back in his chair as if to get a better focus on Sartain through his heavy-rimmed glasses. "It's been a long time, Professor," he began.

Sartain nodded as their eyes locked. "Indeed it has."

Suddenly he was overcome by a determination to get right there and then to what had been eating at him for the last few days. "Fred," he began, "tell me one thing. Your being at the bookstore the other day . . . was that totally coincidental?"

Atkins answered slowly. He had expected the question to surface. "If you mean did I just happen to be there that day, the answer is no." He studied the sudden tightening of Sartain's face. "But, if you mean that, like most everyone else, I read about it somewhere and came to hear what you had to say and have a couple of your books autographed"—his face broke into a broad smile again—"then the answer is yes."

Sartain sensed that his old boss was telling the truth, and he felt slightly embarrassed by his paranoia. "I'm sorry, Fred," he said simply. "I guess the past still haunts me."

They were interrupted by the waiter, who showed up to take their order. After briefly consulting the menu, Atkins recommended the saltimbocca and requested it for himself too. They ordered another round of drinks.

As soon as the waiter left, Atkins asked, "What is all this about your spending so much time on the West Coast?"

Sartain examined his mentor and saw nothing but sincere interest. More at ease now he decided to be open with his old friend. He felt a strong desire to unload his feelings and thoughts to another man, and he once again felt very close to Fred. The years that had separated them suddenly melted away; the intimacy was restored. It seemed like only yesterday that he had sat with Atkins, announcing his irrevocable decision to sever all ties with the ultrasecret agency, opening himself to recrimination by his former employers. He had counted on the friendship and integrity of one man to protect him. This same man was sitting across from him now, eager to hear what he had to say.

"I spent my sabbatical three years ago at the Center for Advanced Behavioral Studies at Stanford," Sartain began. "It was then that I wrote my textbook on guerrilla warfare, and it was then that I met Linda." He glanced at Atkins. Fred's smile told him he had suspected there was a woman involved in the story. With somewhat less confidence he continued. "She was attending the grad school there, part time, and free-lancing for some West Coast based magazines. She'd just returned from a long stay in Europe. Anyway we met one evening in the library lounge. I can't tell you it was love at first sight. On the contrary." Sartain smiled as his mind slid back to the incident. "But within a few weeks, we were . . . inseparable . . . in a way I've never been before, at least not since Jane died."

Atkins's countenance changed when Sartain mentioned his wife's tragic death. He remembered all too well having to deliver the heartbreaking news to his friend. He remained silent, waiting for Sartain to continue.

"Well, to make a long story short, in one of our excursions to Tiburon, a place we were both taken by, and which I designated as the ideal place for retiring to write the Great American Novel, we ran into this empty house. It was pretty much in disrepair, having been left to the elements for some time. But it had obviously been a grand house at one time. We kidded around, fantasizing how we would fix it to our own taste if it was ours." Sartain paused as if waiting for a comment. When none came, he continued.

"I don't know what got into me the next day—it was only several weeks before I was scheduled to leave California and come back here to resume teaching at Georgetown—but I decided to check and discovered that the house was selling for much less than I expected. Considering the location and the view it had, it was an amazing find. It definitely needed a lot of work, that's why it was selling for such a low price, but Linda immediately begged to help me fix it. She had much experience in that sort of thing, she assured me, and she was good at it." He paused again, grinning in recollection. "She sure was," he said.

"Anyway," Sartain continued, "I just couldn't let such an excellent investment go by me. I did have some cash at the time. I sold some of my blue chips and became the new owner. That's how I ended up with the fellowship at Truman. And, incidentally, most of the novel was written on those long plane rides back and forth." He could tell that Atkins found his last remark amusing, so he added, "Linda, by the way, claims I owe the airlines a fat commission."

Atkins laughed.

"And also," Sartain continued, "since Steve goes to school now at Berkeley and Sally is married to one of Brown's people in Sacramento, well, it turned out just perfectly." Seeing the waiter approaching with the food, Sartain quickly concluded. "So basically that's where things are at with me."

Once served, Atkins was curious to find out how serious the relationship with Linda was. "What are your plans, Sam? Am I correct in assuming that she is much younger than you?" he ventured, not at all sure that he hadn't overstepped his renewed friendship.

Sartain, however, didn't mind the question. "Linda is about twenty years younger than I, an entire generation, but she is an extremely intelligent and mature young woman. She is definitely no kid, if that's what you mean.

"Now, as to your other question, I've given it much thought. I think I'm going to marry her. I've been procrastinating so far, not so much because of the difference in age," he hesitated, "but because I didn't really know if I wanted any more children at my age. And, yet, I didn't want to deprive her of having her own children. She said it's not that important to her, but I know differently. But now, not only do I not mind having more children, I look forward to raising kids with her. I know it seems odd, particularly since my grandchildren may be my own children's peers.

"But . . . I don't know quite how to explain it, I feel much younger since I moved to California. Linda has a lot to do with it. Since I met her, I make sure I take care of myself even more than I used to, I'm not embarrassed to admit it. I'm in top shape, never felt better. I jog every morning, I swim at every opportunity, and whenever I can, I play tennis or squash."

Sartain paused, fearful that Atkins would find his newfound life somewhat frivolous. At least outwardly, however, his old mentor appeared noncommittal. The professor continued. "Don't laugh, Fred, but she's even got me disco dancing every once in a while. What can I tell you? I feel rejuvenated, physically, emotionally, and even intellectually. I feel like I've gotten another shot at life, at least from a different angle."

Sartain was surprised at his own openness. It had been years since he had been able to reveal his inner feelings in such a way to another man. It was strange, he didn't feel the least awkward. Something within him told him he had done the right thing, although he couldn't really explain the feeling. Now, however, that he had said it all, he was eager to hear about Fred's life. Suddenly he was very curious and was hoping that his old boss would reciprocate with the same candor. "I've bored you longer than I intended, Fred. Now tell me about yourself," he said, refilling their wineglasses.

Atkins glanced at the man opposite him thoughtfully. Sartain could not have known that since he last saw him at the bookstore, Atkins had been appointed to head the newly formed Counterterrorism Coordinating Committee. Any information concerning the organization was considered top secret. The mere existence of such an international body, dedicated to the eradication of terrorism, was regarded as too sensitive a matter to divulge to the media and the public, at least for the time being.

Atkins decided to forgo any preliminaries. "Sam, what I want to talk to you about is confidential. Can I have your word that you won't discuss it with anyone?" His tone was more urgent than he had intended.

Sartain looked at him. Suddenly the veal in his mouth tasted like sawdust. So his initial reaction had been correct. Something was in the wind after all. He wanted to shake his head, to say he didn't really want to hear what Atkins wanted to talk about.

Instead he heard himself ask, "Are you sure you want me to hear what you have to say? I mean, you know where I stand now."

Atkins nodded. "It's nothing really that you should feel reluctant to know. Trust me."

"All right then, you've my word. But only as long as we understand that it's nothing that, if I keep it to myself, will compromise what I believe in."

Atkins reflected sadly on how tarnished the reputation of the Agency, whose main task was to protect the security of the United States, had become. "As you may or may not know," he began, "for the last eighteen months I've been the deputy director of coordination at Langley."

"I did hear at the time about your transfer to the 'company,'" Sartain responded. "But I didn't know about your present position. Three years ago, when I was in Paris, someone told me you were the chief of station there, and that was the last I heard. Was that true?"

"Yes, I was. It was my last tour of duty abroad. And as I recall, you were there twice during that time." Atkins said it matter-of-factly, not quite sure why he had to add it. Was it professional pride, demonstrating the Agency's efficiency? Or was it meant to show his continuous personal interest in his old friend?

"I see," Sartain commented simply, pondering why Atkins would suddenly choose to contact him now and to reveal confidential information to boot.

"Anyway what I am trying to tell you," Atkins was anxious to continue, "is that over the last weekend I've been appointed to head the newly formed Counterterrorism Coordinating Committee. Yes, I know it's a mouthful," he added smiling apologetically. "We've already decided to nickname it the Triple C."

Atkins's smile broadened at the sight of Sartain's puzzled expression. "It's not the Cabinet Committee to Combat Terrorism that you might be thinking of, Sam. This is an international body. As I'm sure you know, after the Munich Olympics, the chiefs of the different Western intelligence services have been conferring every six months over problems relating to international terrorism and hijacking. But the purpose of those meetings was limited to the exchange of information and the sharing of ideas, nothing more. Now, however, we're trying to achieve unified, coordinated action. Yes, it's a whole new ball game."

Sartain was enthusiastic. "A good move, Fred. I've come not to expect much from the United Nations. They're incapable of concurring on what terrorism is, let alone take some action against it. It's primarily a problem of the free world, and I'm glad to see that at long last the Western democracies are trying to do something about it, in concert."

Atkins nodded. "I was hoping you would be glad to hear the news," he said.

Assuming that his old friend told him about the Triple C because of his preoccupation with the subject of terrorism, Sartain thanked Atkins for letting him in on the confidential and dramatic news and added, "To be quite frank with you, Fred, and believe me, I'm saying this without a trace of impartiality, I don't think your superiors could have made a better choice. I honestly cannot think of a better man for this job. I wish you the best of luck. You've got your work cut out for you. I don't envy such a responsibility."

"The point is," Atkins responded quickly, but then hesitated. ". . . the point is, Sam, that I didn't call you here just to tell you about my new appointment . . . the point is . . . that I want you to work for us."

Stunned, the professor put his fork down. "I don't understand," he said slowly.

"I want you to work for the Triple C, Sam. I want to employ you, if possible, on a full-time basis—perhaps as my deputy, as second in command. We need someone like you, Sam. Someone who can see into the mind of the terrorist, to quote yourself; someone who can write future scenarios, not merely postmortem analyses. Yes, someone who can help us preempt terrorist attacks, not direct reaction to them. We need you, Sam. *I* need you."

A bitter smile crossed Sartain's lips. "Now let me digest this, Fred. Do you mean to tell me that you've cleared my name and—"

"No, not officially," Atkins interjected, knowing full well what Sartain meant. "I haven't yet, but I know it won't be a problem if you agree. I'm certain I can arrange it, I—"

"It doesn't really matter," Sartain interrupted this time, "because I won't do it anyway. I'm sorry, Fred. I'm highly flattered, you can be assured of that, but I just can't do it. I'm really sorry." He hoped the negative sounded as firm as he meant it to.

"But why, Sam?" The Triple C chief leaned across the table. "I mean, you believe in the whole thing; you just said so yourself. You know how important it is, and . . . and it's definitely an opportunity to implement what you've been preaching all along. So why not?"

"Because for one thing, I promised myself some time ago that I would never again work for any governmental agency, particularly not an intelligence agency. Not after what has happened, not again." He pushed himself away from the table as if to underscore his rejection of the offer.

"But—" Atkins tried to say something.

"Fred, I hate to refuse you." The professor leaned in again, intent on making himself clear. "I owe you a lot, but I just can't do it. As for the project itself, I think you overestimate my qualifications. I'm sure you can do well without me. I understand what you're trying to do, but I also know that nowadays there are men out there who can do a better job than I can. Men who are younger, have been more active than I have recently, and who are attuned to working within an organizational framework."

"No, Sam," Atkins interjected forcefully. "It's exactly for this very reason that I need someone like you, someone *without* the organizational mentality you're talking about. Someone who can think differently and independently. And please, Sam," he motioned with his hand, "let me finish. I can see your objection to working for the 'company,' for the NSA, but . . . but this is different, totally different. It's an international organ with a specific task, a mission which you admit you wholeheartedly believe in."

"This all may be true," Sartain responded, trying to keep his voice down. "But who is really behind it?"

"But things have changed, Sam. I don't have to tell you that. Things have changed radically since the days of Vietnam and Nixon. The 'company' has been purged, revamped; there is a new director; there are new, clear-cut policies. If anything, we may have become overly timid, hesitant to make decisions, fearful of taking action, particularly with the media breathing down our neck. Sam, you know all that . . . and, more important, you know the potential dangers of terrorism. You're at least as aware as I am of the threat to the same democratic institutions that you yourself have fought so bravely to protect, both within the ranks and outside, fighting the system itself."

It was the first time that Atkins let Sartain know, that he, for one, had interpreted the professor's active participation in the anti-Vietnam war protest movement as a courageous act in defense of the republic.

But he didn't give Sartain a chance to dwell on that revelation. He pushed on. "It's you, after all, who's been warning that everything until now has been child's play compared to what is in store. It's you who's been trying to sound the alarm, who's been concerned about the lack of cohesive response, who . . ." Atkins ran out of air. He stopped to let the professor respond.

"I'm going west, so to speak," Sartain said quietly, "and I'm about to begin a new life with someone I love very much. It's not as though I'm running away from my responsibilities. I'll just have to do my share through my writings. I'm not a man of action anymore, Fred. That period in my life is over. You know, very recently I promised myself that I would begin to say 'no' much more firmly. I'm deeply sorry," Sartain added with sadness in his voice, "that it's you I have to say it to."

Atkins looked at the professor thoughtfully, resigning himself to the fact that he might not get his man. "Sam, I'm sorry I leaned on you. I really didn't mean to. I guess I was just over-eager to have you on our team. But I do understand your reasons for turning me down." He eyed him carefully before he continued. "But I won't go away without something for having tried. What are the chances of your working for us on a part-time basis, informally, as a consultant or something, from the West Coast, if you wish? Can we work something out?"

Sartain sighed. "I was hoping you wouldn't ask me that. I really would like not to have to. You may not realize it, Fred, but I'm still tormented by my past association with the Agency, particularly, the Lebanese affair. Yes, I still feel guilt, and shame. I still feel like some undiscovered criminal." He raised his hand, and Atkins let him continue.

"I can understand why I did it at the time, and I can rationalize my silence," he smiled ruefully. "But I have no wish whatsoever to add to the burden. And frankly there are other reasons. I do not want to jeopardize my academic career and reputation, not to speak of compromising my research contacts in certain circles if word got out."

Sartain shook his head, fighting a battle inside. "I just can't do it, Fred. I just can't be associated anymore with any organization on an undercover basis, and that's obviously what it would be. Whatever I did for the airlines, perhaps was not publicized, but it was still in the open. It was a totally different thing, overt, and as such it was tolerated. But this would never be. I don't have to tell you that."

Sartain was deeply perplexed. He hated turning Atkins down. He was torn between wanting to help his friend and his conviction that he shouldn't get involved, that he deserved a new life, one free of the past. But it was not just a question of friendship and loyalty; there was more to his reluctance to totally turn the man down. He not only understood the reasoning behind the creation of the Triple C, he supported it without reservations. But still . . .

"Okay," Sartain finally said with a clear note of resignation in his sigh. "If you wish as a friend, and I mean just as a friend, to discuss in the future certain problems, to exchange insights—but again, I must emphasize on an informal and infrequent basis—then I guess it can be done. But *absolutely* no more."

Atkins nodded. "Agreed," he said. He leaned back and focused intently on Sartain again. The professor could not have guessed his next question.

"If you knew where Carlos was, would you tell me?"

A bemused smile crossed the professor's face. "You don't waste any time, do you, boss?"

Atkins only shrugged. He wanted to say something but then changed his mind.

"Even if I could tell you where Carlos was, what would you do? What would any government do? Correct me if I'm wrong, Fred, but I strongly suspect that even if some of the Western governments had a chance to lay their hands on Carlos, they would prefer not to. I believe most of them fear the consequences of his incarceration and trial more than what he might do if left alone. They would certainly deny it," Sartain added, not without contempt, "but you and I know that, unfortunately, this happens to be the case."

The Triple C chief could not disagree. Too often Western governments had been exceedingly eager to release captured terrorists for fear of retaliation by their angered comrades. He couldn't help but think about what the surviving DST agent said when he explained why the three of them had decided to act on their own when they went after Azzawi.

"Not anymore," Atkins stated with as much conviction as he could muster, knowing that he could only hope that would be the case. "This is one of the reasons the Triple C came into being. It is exactly that kind of malaise that we have to try and cure. By combined action we may be able to allay the fears of individual governments. But you still haven't answered my question: do you have any idea where Carlos may be at this point?"

"That wasn't exactly your question," Sartain needled his friend. "Where do you think he is?"

"We don't know. Our guess is that he's most probably hiding in one of his sanctuaries in Libya, Southern Yemen, or Iraq. Ever since Entebbe we've totally lost track of him. We do think, however, that he's planning something of unprecedented magnitude, a grand-scale retaliation, and that he may strike shortly, perhaps very soon. That's why I've asked your educated opinion."

"Well, I wouldn't be at all surprised if he were. You heard what I told that group at the bookstore. I, for one, am convinced that he's planning something with Wadi Haddad. But, at the same time, I'll be surprised if it takes place as soon as you suggest. I think it'll take him some time to plan the next one. He can't afford to fail again, not in any large-scale operation. His reputation as the invincible Jackal, as the world's terrorist extraordinaire, is on the line. And if I read him well, and I think I do, then success, not speed, is what counts the most with him at the moment."

Sartain paused for a second, reflecting on something, then continued. "Of course it's also a question of whether or not he gets his way. There have recently been some indications, as I'm sure some of your people may well be aware of, that there has been some tension between Carlos and Haddad. This, incidentally, in addition to the growing rift between both of them and the PFLP chief, Dr. Habash. So it's not at all that simple. The Arabs need a quick something, and they may act sooner but in a more limited manner."

Atkins listened attentively, not wanting to interrupt the professor's line of thought.

"But anyway," Sartain continued, "I don't really know where your man is right now. He could very well be in any of the places you mentioned. But I tend to doubt it. In fact I doubt it very much—particularly if our assumption about a grand action is correct. I just can't see him actively planning it from there. If anything, it would be from Algeria, which is more accessible to Europe and the rest of the West.

"Also, you have to keep in mind that Carlos has one major handicap which works in our favor: he himself may be an evil genius incarnate, but the people he has to work with—with the exception of very few like Fusako Shigenobu—are not the most capable in the world. Thank God! In other words he can't be too far from where he intends to act; he'll remember Entebbe just too well . . ."

Atkins nodded. "It makes sense," he said taking mental notes of what the professor had been telling him.

"But," the professor continued, "if it's Carlos you're after right now, Fred, don't ever expect him to be where you think he is. One lesson I've learned from studying the man is that he'll always emerge where you least expect him to. He's a master at that game. He'll always try to avoid being where he thinks you think he may be."

"So?" Atkins questioned when he realized that Sartain wasn't saying any more.

"So, I'm afraid that's as much as I can help you with. And now can we talk about something else? I've already overstepped the limits we agreed on."

Atkins nodded. He knew this was not the time to press the professor any further. "How about some zabaglione?" he asked. "I highly recommend it here."

"You know me too well," the professor nodded his agreement, smiling.

CHAPTER NINE

RIPLE fencing, the innermost one electrified, surrounded the hundreds of acres of woods, lawns, and flower gardens which constituted the well-groomed grounds of the Central Intelligence Agency headquarters. Of the structures in the vast complex none could be observed clearly from any public roads, and the entry lanes were identified by misleading signs. Guardhouses, armed patrols with trained dogs, and an elaborate underground grid of sensory wires insured against any trespassers.

The modern buildings studding the landscape were spare, but well appointed, and everywhere there was a feeling of lavish space, marble, glass, and sparkling metal. The compound was a far cry from the shabby, run-down wooden buildings alongside the reflecting pool between the Lincoln and Washington monuments which until 1962 used to house the CIA headquarters. Now the Agency was a few miles upstream and across the Potomac River in Langley, Virginia, its most visible landmark the seven-story main edifice which covered an area the equivalent of two city blocks.

In many ways the small building selected to serve as the Triple C headquarters was not much different from the others on the CIA campus, or the "Pickle Factory" as the Washington headquarters was still referred to by some of the old hands. Its most unique feature was its location; it was the most secluded and isolated structure in the compound. Even though it was only a few hundred yards from the central structure, it was separated from the rest of the buildings by a small grove of Virginia pines. But most important it had its own special side entrance which could be used to get in and out of the complex, independent of the main gate. It was originally built and designed to allow outsiders, or foreign nationals, to work closely with the Agency under conditions of strict security and confidentiality and yet to limit their access to the rest of the compound. Thus it was the perfect facility for the convening of the Triple C.

"Gentlemen, it is indeed a great honor to have you here," the director of the Central Intelligence Agency began his welcoming remarks.

Fred Atkins surveyed the impressive gathering. It was the first general meeting of the Triple C, and in a few brief moments the director, in addition to asking him to chair the meeting would formally announce Atkins's appointment as the first chief coordinator of the newly formed counterterrorist organization. Thus the most demanding and challenging job of his career would officially begin. As that moment approached, and as Atkins once again scanned the faces around him, some doubts began to creep in. He was awed by the caliber of the men present and apprehensive of his ability to successfully manage the immense task ahead.

Since this was the founding conference of the Triple C, in addition to the recently appointed permanent representatives, the actual heads of the intelligence establishments of each of the member countries were present as well. Some of the people in attendance were already legends in their own time within the international intelligence community. It was going to be anything but simple to handle them as a cohesive unit.

There was Daniel Owens, the lanky, moustachioed, old chief of MI6, the British secret service, puffing slowly on the Peterson briar eternally clamped between his teeth, a permanent scorn in his clear blue eyes. He fought "terrs" way back when the Union Jack was still flying over a large chunk of the globe, when Jewish terrorists in Palestine were Britain's main headache. Now, thirty years later having reached the top position in the British clandestine services, he also topped the IRA's death list. Atkins already knew he was going to prove difficult.

Next to the Briton was another legendary figure, General Pierre Laval, a short, bald man with thin silver glasses, the imperator of the French Deuxième Bureau. As unimpressive and unassuming as the frail man looked, Atkins well remembered he had been the only man de Gaulle counted on to successfully purge the SDECE and the DST of the infestation of KGB agents. It was due to his efforts that cooperation between the French intelligence service and the CIA continued after France pulled out of NATO. Atkins knew him personally from his tour of duty as chief of station in Paris and had great respect for the man.

A few seats over, General Ulrich von Hindenburg, the head of the BND, the West German intelligence service, was exchanging written notes with Colonel Kurt Demmer, commander of Border Guard Group Nine (GSG-9), the elite German antiterrorist unit. Demmer had taken part in the Entebbe raid as an observer, and Atkins hoped that the rugged *para*, who had already worked closely with the Israelis, would stay on as the permanent representative. But he knew that the German government wanted Demmer back home.

And so down and around the table were the heads of the intelligence services and the permanent representatives. No aides, no interpreters. They all spoke English. A most fascinating group of individuals to watch, these members of the second oldest profession. Each man looked and sounded so different, each man with his own peculiar mannerisms. And yet, Atkins mused, and yet as a group they betrayed a distinct commonality. Perhaps it was because they all wore the masks of highly accomplished poker players, each a master at the deadly game of intrigue, the game where the stakes piled higher with each technological advance, where human lives were often nothing more than small chips.

Sartain, collecting his lecture notes, was about to leave his book-crammed office at Georgetown when the phone rang. "I'm not here," he told Ethel, the secretary he shared with his younger colleague. She nodded and picked up the receiver.

His hand was already on the doorknob when she covered the mouthpiece and said it was Linda on the line, calling from San Francisco.

Sartain hesitated, a little surprised. "Can she call—" he didn't finish. Instead he consulted his watch. "Okay," he said, turning back toward his office, "I'll take it."

Before Linda could say anything, Sartain told her he was in a hurry. He had a class in exactly eleven minutes. "What's up?" he asked.

"I'm sorry to disturb you, Sam," her voice carried her excitement across the wires. "I'm going to Berlin tomorrow, and I thought you should be the first to know."

"You're going where?" the professor was puzzled, not quite sure he heard her right.

"Berlin, West Berlin, Germany."

"I don't understand," Sartain said, still mystified. "What for?"

"To cover the jailbreak . . . you know, of the four women terrorists . . . we talked about it. Anyway, Sam, listen. I managed to convince good old George that right now it's the perfect story to begin the series on 'Women and Crime.' Are you with me?"

"Yes, I am. Go on." He didn't bother to sit down.

"Anyway I told George and the other editors what you had said, that there is probably much more to it than meets the eye, that it can throw some light on the whole Entebbe thing."

"You did?"

"Yes. The others wouldn't go for it at first, but George that foxy old-timer, he can smell a good story. Especially with all the interest generated by Entebbe . . . the films and all. Well anyway, I know you're in a hurry, so to make a long story short, he agreed. They're going for it. All expenses paid. What d'you say?"

"That's great. Congratulations. How long are you planning to be gone?"

"I don't know exactly. A week or two. Anyway, listen, I almost forgot. I'm flying in to see you tomorrow. I'm booked on a flight to Berlin Thursday, from Kennedy . . . so I'll be leaving here tomorrow for Washington. We can spend the night together, and I'll go to New York the next morning. How about it?"

"Sounds good." He consulted his watch, realizing he would have to leave immediately if he was going to make it on time.

"Will you pick me up at the airport? I'll be coming on flight—"

"I will, but can we talk about it tonight? I've really got to go. I'm sorry."

"I understand. I'll call you tonight. Love you."

"Good-bye, love . . . and . . . congratulations again." He hung up and shook his head, smiling. He gathered his papers, his mind already concentrating on the lecture, constructing the opening sentences. He would have time later to assimilate what Linda had said. He consulted his watch. It was six minutes to ten; he had another five minutes, he quickened his pace hoping he would make it on time. He hated being late.

Atkins checked the clock on the wall opposite him. It was five minutes to ten. He had been speaking for over ten minutes now, the time he had alloted himself for opening remarks. He took great care during his brief exposition to play the middle ground. With all those powerhouses present this was not the time to be overly assertive. Yet, as he offered his interpretations of the main objectives of the Triple C, his innate forcefulness let the intelligence chiefs and their permanent representatives know that if anyone was going to call the shots in the new, loosely structured organization, it was going to be he and no one else.

He quickly stole a glance at the CIA director who seemed pleased with his tactful performance. It was time to call on Israel's Echad to make his presentation.

The head of the Mossad, Israel's renowned external intelligence agency, was a bearish man in his mid-fifties. He was of Russian-Jewish parentage from which he inherited his deep sea-blue eyes and sandy hair. His old crest had receded, extending even further his freckled broad brow. He had a large prominent nose and a strong jaw. Yet his most unique feature was his huge, hairy hands. With those bare peasant's hands, it was rumored, he had crushed to death two Nazi agents during World War II in Palestine, one in each hand. And yet when the man smiled, which was not often, the roughness evaporated and was replaced by an avuncular warmth. He offered a flicker of a smile when called upon by Atkins to make his presentation.

The Mossad, which in Hebrew means "the institute," was the shorter version of the organization's full title—the Central Institute for Intelligence and Special Assignments. In structure and goals it was comparable to the American CIA or the British MI6, but considering the Jewish state's special security problems, it carried much more authority, had a wider range of responsibilities, and enjoyed more freedom of action. The organization attracted world attention for the first time with Eichmann's capture in Argentina and the successful war of terror it conducted against Nazi rocket experts employed by Nasser's Egypt in the 1950s.

Atkins, like everyone else in the room, knew that Echad was not the rugged man's real name. "Echad" means "number one" in Hebrew. The head of the Mossad was never referred to by name. His true identity was considered a top state secret. And as Atkins ceded the floor to his nameless colleague, he could not help but reflect that the daring raid on Entebbe, which was successful primarily because of the superb intelligence work of the Mossad, had made this man "number one" the world over. Indeed it was in deference to that amazing operation that he called on Echad first.

Echad, however, had no intention of dwelling on Entebbe. For him, he told his audience in a deep, gravelly voice, that escapade was history. "The lessons drawn from it? Here," he said as he motioned to the Israeli permanent representative, Colonel Joseph Navon. Navon, who was sitting to his right, began distributing thin blue folders as Echad continued. "It's all in there," he said with unconcealed pride. "Concise, operational evaluations, prepared especially for you, gentlemen, by our top analysts. What I want to talk about today, however, is the aftermath of Entebbe and how we can best jointly prepare for it."

Atkins had no real feelings one way or another about Echad, but he took an immediate liking to the young, handsome Navon. While Echad obviously suffered from the characteristic Israeli arrogance, which Atkins considered to be the Israelis' Achilles' heel, the soft-spoken Navon was totally unassuming. If anything, he was shy. Yet the young reserved man was no newcomer to the game of espionage and counterterrorism.

Like each of the other Triple C permanent representatives Navon was also assigned a cover role at his embassy, his fictitious title a very innocuous one. Atkins, however, who over the past three days had been studying the bios of the different representatives, already knew that the young ex-commando officer had many achievements to his record, particularly in the field of external counterterrorism. For one, Navon had been the deputy commander of the "Wrath of God" (WOG), the much feared Mossad antiterrorist unit.

The Wrath of God, also nicknamed "Israel's long arm," was formed in response to the Munich Olympics' massacre of Israeli athletes in 1972. Its mission was to identify, search out, and liquidate Arab terrorist leaders operating in Europe, particularly those associated with the infamous Black September Palestinian terror group which took credit for the massacre.

The hit team managed within a relatively short time to trace down and eliminate twelve prominent terrorist figures. One of those eradicated by the young Israeli colonel was Mohammad Boudia. Boudia, an Algerian by birth, had been the commander

of the European cell of Habash's Popular Front for the Liberation of Palestine. A professional actor using the cover of a theatrical director in Paris, he was also a legendary womanizer.
Some of the women whom he had managed to sweep off their feet
he duped into going on suicidal missions for him. Boudia was the
man who originally recruited Carlos to the PFLP ranks and became his mentor and idol. After the death of his friend at the
hands of Navon, Carlos, who assumed command of the European
cell, named it Commando Boudia.

The Wrath of God was disbanded less than two years after its
formation as a result of mounting political pressure from Western European governments who resented the Israelis taking the
law into their own hands inside their countries' sovereign
boundaries. Consequently Lieutenant Colonel Navon was returned to Mossad headquarters in Tel Aviv to head its training
school. Two years later, anxious for action abroad, he was dis-
patched to Washington, D.C. as a full colonel and his country's
Triple C representative. Atkins was gratified to have him on his
team, hoping he would help mete out the same fate to Boudia's
successor as well.

"What we have witnessed," Echad rumbled on, referring to
the first major terrorist attack against Israel to follow Entebbe,
"is the initial attempt at retaliation by Haddad's people. It was
put together in a hurry, and as such, was relatively ill planned.
The four Palestinians, who carried Kuwaiti passports, were all
recent recruits with little training."

The incident Echad was describing took place at Istanbul's
Yesilkoy Airport, where a group of mostly Israeli passengers
were waiting at the transit lounge to board El Al flight 582 to
Tel Aviv. Twenty-six people were wounded when the terrorists
opened fire on the passengers with submachine guns and grenades. Four were killed: two Israelis, one Japanese, and one
American, a young staff aide to Republican senator Jacob Javits
from New York.

When Echad mentioned the foreign casualties, he eyed the
two Japanese intelligence men from underneath his bushy eyebrows. "My sympathies," he said curtly. He looked toward
Atkins and the director and nodded quietly, acknowledging their
loss.

It reminded Atkins of the briefing he read the other morning about the PFLP boastfully claiming that the murder of the "important American official" had been premeditated: "the first reprisal for the American collusion in the Israeli raid on Uganda." He had little doubt that it was nothing but ex post facto propaganda, that it was only a coincidence that an American happened to be at the Turkish airport at the time of the attack—and that he was killed. Yet he pondered the allegation. There had been too many reports circulating in the past few days about the American involvement in Entebbe. The most persistent pointed to the fact that it was American pressure that forced the Kenyan government to allow the Israeli planes to refuel at Nairobi on their way back from Entebbe, a crucial factor in the success of the final stage of the operation. Even though, as far as he knew, the stories were a total fabrication, it was their acceptance by the Palestinians which disturbed him. He couldn't forget Sartain's final words when they shook hands outside the Italian restaurant: "Incidentally, Fred, if I were you, I wouldn't at all discount this country as the most likely target for Carlos's next big move . . ."

Echad, in the meantime, went on to praise the Turkish airport security forces for preventing the terrorists from taking over the El Al plane. According to him this had been their original intention. "I want to thank my Turkish colleagues for responding with such alacrity to the request we made, after our raid on Entebbe, for increased security at Yesilkoy. It most definitely helped avert the hijacking and considerably reduced the number of casualties." He explained that when the would-be skyjackers saw the armed guards carefully searching the luggage of the transit passengers lining up for the El Al plane, they had no choice but to alter their original plans of reaching the liner itself. Thwarted, they opted to unleash their attack in the lounge. The swift and effective fusillade of the alert Turkish security agents prevented more serious bloodshed.

The Turkish delegate beamed as he responded to Echad's compliments. "We're happy to have managed to prevent the hijacking of the El Al plane. We're deeply sorry about the casualties, and I can assure all of you that after we complete the interrogation of the three surviving hijackers, they'll be brought to trial and will be punished severely."

They all must have reflected on the fact that Turkey was the only Triple C member that had capital punishment for crimes involving terrorism. At least some of them must have felt envious.

The French permanent representative, François Darlan, who until then was the commander of the Brigade Anti-Commando (BAC)—a small, elite police counterinsurgency unit with a tough reputation—interjected. "Can copies of the interrogation be made available to Paris?" he asked with a deep, nasal French accent.

"We shall of course be glad to provide you with any information which may be relevant," the Turk began to respond.

Atkins felt compelled to intervene at that point. Wasn't this after all why they had established the Triple C? "Copies of the minutes of the interrogation will first be sent here," he said authoritatively as he addressed the Frenchman, "to the Triple C headquarters . . . as will be the case with all other terrorist-related material from each of the member countries. Our task, among other things, is to see to it that all pertinent material will be made available for *everyone* to analyze."

Atkins's interruption was greeted with mixed reactions. While some nodded in approval, others granted him a curious and even a suspicious look. He couldn't quite interpret old Owens's gaze. If anything, the man seemed amused. Yet the point had to be made—no more optional bilateral agreements.

He was grateful that Echad didn't linger but pushed on with his remarks, his first sentence an indirect, but clear endorsement of Atkins's position. "I'm confident, gentlemen, that coordinating our activities through the Triple C will enable all of us to fight terrorism much more effectively. Now," he paused and looked at some papers in front of him, "I would like to address myself to a very sensitive issue related to the terrorist attack at Istanbul's airport. As much as I hate to do it"—he raised his eyes from the paper in front of him and looked in the direction of the two Italians—"I must point out that security at Fiumicino, Rome's airport, was lacking . . . to say the least."

Here we go, Atkins thought. Why couldn't the tough son of a bitch be a little more diplomatic? He could at least have omitted the editorial "to say the least." Didn't he know that the inclusion of Israel was still a matter of contention with some of them? Damn!

The Italian chief of intelligence, who practically jumped out of his seat to protest, wasn't able to say much because Echad raised his mammoth hand and cut in. "Please let me explain. *Prego*. I'm not trying to single out anyone for criticism. All I'm trying to do is to point out a recurring weak spot in our preventive airport security, and it is by no means something which is limited only to Fiumicino. The fact is, however, that the four terrorists who attacked the El Al passengers at Yesilkoy had passed unchecked through the Rome airport on their way from Libya to Istanbul. I've no doubt whatsoever that if they had selected Rome as their point of departure, and would have tried to board a plane there with their weapons, that they would have been spotted immediately by our friends." He gestured in the Italian's direction, who seemed appeased.

"The trouble is, however, that like Fiumicino most international airports still have lax, if any, search procedures at the transit lounges. They assume incorrectly, or take for granted, that the passengers have been thoroughly checked at their original port of departure. This, however, is not always the case. I can name at least half a dozen international airports where it doesn't happen." Echad glanced around the room. "None of them, of course, in the countries represented here. But that's not the point. The point is that we all have to increase the scrutiny of transit passengers at our international airports, particularly of those who had arrived from airports without strict security procedures. We've been doing it at Ben-Gurion airport for some time now, and we will be very happy to share our experience in this area with all of you. May I also underscore my point by adding that the written reports Colonel Navon had just passed around point to the fact that better security at the transit lounge in Athens's airport would have prevented the hijacking of the French airbus to Entebbe."

Atkins winced again at Echad's last remark. It was bad enough to criticize the Italians in such a forum, but to put down the Greeks just after having praised the Turks . . . he girded himself for the reaction.

To Atkins's surprise, however, the men in the room, including the Italians and the Greeks, were in total agreement that what Echad had said not only made sense but had to be corrected, and the sooner the better. He was relieved to see that national sensitivity and pride were put aside. He realized now that they were all professionals who came there to do a job, not to fish for compliments or play one-upmanship. The Israelis had pinpointed a major loophole in their countries' counterhijacking security. It was now up to the Triple C to recommend how they could jointly, and effectively, plug this loophole. It was a constructive beginning after all, Atkins mused. The task ahead didn't seem as unmanageable as before.

CHAPTER TEN

AS he navigated the red-carpeted concrete tunnel toward the TWA gate, Sartain felt overcome by eagerness. Lately he was finding it more and more difficult to tolerate Linda's absences. And now her work in Germany was separating them by an ocean and another continent. It made him anxious to think of her so far away, without him.

Linda had managed to reach him in time to warn him that she had missed her original flight because of a tie-up on the freeway. She had had no problems getting a seat on the next flight out but was forced to make a stop in Chicago, thus arriving at Washington's National Airport instead of Dulles. Sartain, always prompt, arrived at the nearer airport with time to kill.

In anticipation of Linda's arrival he had forced himself to labor the previous night and that morning on putting the finishing touches on his overdue article for the *Political Science Review*. It had been a difficult piece to write, but he was quite pleased with the results. The article discussed the danger, in an age when conventional wars are too destructive and too expensive to be practical, of transnational terrorism becoming the vehicle by which nations waged surrogate wars. The manuscript should have been completed weeks before, but commitments stemming from the success of *The Rescue* prevented him from meeting his deadline.

Now that he had sent it in, Sartain felt mentally unburdened, his thoughts free to wander at will. Yes, he chuckled inwardly, even the ability to roam a terminal at leisure, just watching the people, his mind disengaged, seemed a luxury to him. He chose an unoccupied chair in the midst of the foot traffic and, lighting his pipe, settled back to observe.

Airports always held a special fascination for Sartain. The continuous stream of people, different people, from all walks of life, flowing, surging in countercurrents. The hugs and kisses, the tears, the laughter and timid smiles, the hellos and good-byes, the constant unfolding of a plentitude of human drama. To him it was a true microcosm of twentieth-century life, as real as any.

He enjoyed this role of observer. He found himself following small groups of twos or threes as they greeted each other and strode off together. Occasionally he focused on one person: that man in the skinny tie and white socks—a conventioneer from Des Moines? The young woman with the small girl clinging to her skirt, eyes peering out the great broad window toward the runway, no doubt anticipating the arrival of her husband's plane.

And that dark, slender woman breezing past. Very chic, Sartain commented to himself. Exquisitely cut, elegant light suit, carriage like a gazelle, that fine combination of self-assurance and femininity. She must be European, a model or actress he mused, Italian most probably . . .

He felt like a voyeur. His work for military intelligence and later for the NSA had trained him to pay attention to the most obscure details. This, coupled with a fertile imagination . . . Sartain would be the first to admit that some of his fictionalized characters had found their way into his books through his observances in transcontinental lounges.

Sartain let the hubbub melt to a blur. What would all these ordinary, complacent people do if a few terrorists in the crowd suddenly opened on them with a burst of machine-gun fire . . . His mind began to write the bloody scenario. These perverse thoughts were interrupted by the announcement of the arrival of Linda's flight. "For another time," Sartain muttered as he cleaned his pipe into an ashtray and rose to find her in the crowd.

Tara Kafir was not Italian, and she was European only in that she was Hungarian by birth and had lived in Hungary with her parents for seven years before they all emigrated to Palestine, having survived the Holocaust with the help of some good-hearted Gentile friends.

When the professor noticed Tara at the airport, she had just arrived on a flight from New York where she had been residing for the past two and half years. Though still a ravishing dark beauty at thirty-eight, she was neither a professional model nor an actress, although she was often mistaken for one. She was known as the very capable U.S. representative of some of the top fashion houses in Israel. Due to her relentless efforts, and a superbly orchestrated public relations campaign which she conducted, two of the Israeli firms she represented—one which specialized in leather goods and one in fashionable swimsuits— became household names in the American vogue market.

Through her own flourishing import and export company, Kafir Inc., Tara also was the chief buyer for Shalom Inc., the largest department-store chain in Israel.

Her looks, her unbounded energy, and her remarkable success in business helped the Israeli widow of a noted American scientist to emerge within an astonishingly short time as a top socialite in New York, her new home base. She had come to Washington to attend, among other things, yet another evening with the crème de la crème of New York and Washington society.

Tara was applying the last touches of makeup when she heard the three knocks on the door. She was in the bathroom, which, in the best tradition of the elegant Madison Hotel, was conservatively appointed yet had all the modern amenities.

There were three more knocks when she quickly stood up and walked through her plush suite toward the door, her low-cut, formal gown swishing at her ankles. She checked through the peephole. A pleased smile crossed her face. She opened the door and let in a handsome young man in black tie.

The man entered the room hesitantly. It was obvious that he felt rather uncomfortable in his formal attire.

"You look absolutely wonderful," Tara said with an affectionate smile. "Please, Itzik, turn around," she switched to Hebrew, one of the six languages she spoke. "C'mon don't be shy, let's see."

As the young man awkwardly, and rather reluctantly, swiveled around, Tara assessed the tall, wiry youth. His dark hair and deep tan set off his ice blue eyes. "Great!" she exclaimed. "Believe me, you look good enough to model in one of my shows . . . Of course, you can't do it with that Beretta of yours . . . every bulge shows, you know." She winked and laughed heartily.

Itzik was clearly embarrassed.

"Okay, let's go," she said, trying to ease his discomfort. "I'm ready and we don't have much time. I've got to be back here"—she consulted her Tiffany watch—"in forty minutes at the most."

Arm in arm they strolled out of the room and rode the elevator down to the fourth floor.

Four floors below, Tara pointed to the two seventeenth-century clocks just outside the elevator. "These are very rare. They've a number of them here."

"Uh-huh," the young Israeli kibbutznick mumbled, disinterested, as he led the way.

Arm in arm still, they reached the end of the corridor and turned left, stopping at the third door to the right. A "do not disturb" sign hung on the knob. Itzik removed the sign, unlocked the door, and walked in first.

The room was dark, lighted only by the television set. Itzik scanned the room and switched on the light before he motioned Tara to enter. He walked to the door connecting to the other room. He knocked five times and waited motionless, glancing at Tara. They heard the door being unlocked from the inside, and then it opened.

"*Shalom*, Tara. Please come in," said Echad, the head of the Mossad, extending toward her his huge mitt, his face one big, welcoming smile.

"I doubt very much that they'll let you see her, let alone interview her," Sartain said. "It's too soon. They'll be working on her themselves for some time."

"If I can only gain access to the interrogation records," Linda said wishfully.

"How? I don't have these kind of contacts, not with the German police anyway."

They were drinking at Nathan's on the corner of M and Wisconsin, having changed their mind in the last moment about dining at the Rive Gauche, the more sumptuous French restaurant on the other side of the busy Georgetown intersection. They were having a before-dinner discussion about the arrest in Berlin the night before of Erika Küzler, one of the four escapees from the Lehrterstrasse prison, who was apprehended while strolling the Ku-Damm in midday.

"Speaking of contacts," Linda diverged, remembering something, "Steve came over last night. He was a real sweetheart. I had called him to let him know that I was leaving for Berlin, and he insisted on coming over and wanted to know if there was anything he could do to help."

"He's a good boy."

"Yes, he is. He said he would drop by the house every so often to make sure things are all right while we're gone. He even offered to water the plants and the garden. He insisted I take the name of a friend of his, a German student he met at Berkeley. Someone by the name of Horst Vogel."

The professor shook his head. He didn't know the man.

"He's a teaching assistant now at the Free University, a radical of sorts, and according to Steve he knows intimately some of the more revolutionary activists there, many of them ardent supporters of the Baader-Meinhof."

"I don't know how much use this man can be to you, but Steve is right about the Free University. Since it was opened—when the old Humboldt University ended up in the communist East Sector—the Free University, implying the old one was not, has been a noted hotbed for German revolutionaries and has often served as a recruitment pool for the Baader-Meinhof gang." Sartain stopped when he noticed a certain twinkle in Linda's eye.

"Rehashing a lecture again?" Linda asked grinning. "Sometimes you make me feel I should be paying you tuition."

He pretended to be hurt. He knew he had the tendency to forget himself and by force of habit to become overly didactic in ordinary, casual conversations.

Linda apologized. "Sorry I disrupted class."

"Then I'll continue with the lecture," Sartain droned soberly, squeezing her knee with a straight face. "Before I was so rudely interrupted, I was about to say that one of the men I noted for you to see in West Berlin is also teaching sociology at the Free University, Professor Kuno Grundman. He's been studying the German radical movement longer than anyone else and personally knows many of its leaders. I met him a few years back when I visited the Free University, and we still correspond."

Another man Sartain thought Linda should see was Klaus Rainer Röhl. The publisher of the leftist *Konkret* was Ulrike Meinhof's former husband.

Ulrike, who began her career as a journalist advocating paci-

fist causes, strongly opposing nuclear weaponry, became gradually more and more interested in the German radical movement
after she left her husband and twin daughters in 1967. Her involvement was sealed in a daring, bloody attack when she
managed to free a prominent anarchist by the name of Andreas
Baader. Andreas, a few years younger than Ulrike, became her
lover, and with him she went underground to form the Red
Army Faction—an anarchist, ultraviolent terrorist group spe-
cializing in bank robberies and which soon was nicknamed after
the pair. Even after the couple was captured, the Baader-
Meinhof gang continued with relentless frenzy to terrorize
Germany, and with Carlos's supervision, other Western nations
as well.

On May 9, 1976, the forty-two-year-old Ulrike, the "bandit
queen," as she was often referred to, took her own life in prison.
She used a makeshift rope of towels to hang herself from her cell
window. Carlos was in Athens putting the final touches to his
Entebbe operation when he heard of it. He had met Ulrike the
first time in 1970 when she and other German comrades were
training in guerrilla tactics at a PFLP camp in Jordan. He didn't
care much for Andreas Baader, thought him too "soft," his assertive machismo style notwithstanding, but he took an immediate
liking to Ulrike. He was shaken by the news of her death and
wanted to name his prospective operation after her. Haddad,
however, objected, refusing to dilute the necessary "Palestinian"
image of the drama.

"On second thought," Sartain backtracked, "I'm not so sure
you should see Röhl."

Linda was puzzled. "Why?"

"Well, I've just finished reading his novel, *Die Genossin*. It's a
fictionalized account of Ulrike's life. It rubbed me the wrong
way."

"How?"

"Well, it's misleading. He portrays Andreas Baader, for example, as a tool for the CIA . . . I mean . . ." Sartain shrugged
and shook his head in obvious disapproval. "He may just steer you
in the wrong direction. No, don't call him."

"I can handle him." Linda sounded disappointed, petulant.

"Most probably you can," he answered, reaching for her hand
and squeezing it. "But why don't you wait and see if I can make

it to Berlin first. Then between the two of us he won't have a chance." Sartain smiled affectionately.

"Do you really think you can make it?"

"Well, as I told you, I'll do my damnedest to finish everything here ahead of time so I can make it there on my way to Tel Aviv."

A few months earlier Sartain had received an invitation from Tel Aviv University to present a paper at a conference on TFB (terrorism, fanaticism, and blackmail). Sartain declined the invitation because, at the time, the long trip didn't appeal to him. He had preferred relaxing the rest of the summer in Tiburon with Linda. But when he found out about the change in her plans, he called his friend Professor Amir at the Shiloach Center to find out if the invitation was still standing. It was.

"I'll have the scampi marinara," Sartain said after Linda ordered.

"I'm sorry, sir," the waiter apologized, "but we don't have that today."

"How about the saltimbocca?" Linda suggested.

The professor shook his head. "It's good here, but I just had it the other day." Atkins's image reared its bearded head. He turned to the waiter, "I'll have the veal Florentina."

It may have been the reference to the Italian food which he had with Atkins the other day, it may have been something else which triggered it, but suddenly Sartain had the strong urge to tell her.

"Something I want to talk to you about," he eyed her seriously. "A few days ago I was asked to work for the government again. I mean working in the area of counterterrorism . . . a consultant sort of." He stopped, not sure exactly how to continue.

"Did you accept?"

"No."

He stopped again, staring intently at the salt shaker, then raising his gaze to meet her searching eyes. "You see it's for . . . well, it's for a clandestine organization." Again he paused. "Well, the whole thing is kind of confidential, I don't know why exactly . . . or I do . . . but after all even the Agency's employees are allowed to discuss some things with their spouses. Did you know that?"

Linda shook her head. She wanted to say that she, after all, was not his wife, but she held back. It wasn't the time to chance being misinterpreted. She sensed he was trying to tell her something important. Her silence was an invitation.

"They call it the Triple C," Sartain accepted, describing in rough detail the nature of the new organization, adding that it was his former boss at the NSA, Fred Atkins, a dear friend, who was selected by the CIA to run it. And then he told her how they had met.

Linda remained silent while he talked, pausing from time to time in search of the right words, making sure he wasn't overstepping boundaries. There were many things she wanted to ask, some things she didn't quite understand, but she dared not interrupt. She was both anxious and flattered; nervous about the confidential information, pleased that he at long last had come to trust her. She could sense that this was only the start, that there was more he needed to confide, tales of his covert work for the NSA which she knew had been tormenting him for so long. But for now she could accept this first trickle as a beginning.

"But I told him that I would never work again for a clandestine organization. I . . ." For the first time since he started to talk, his face lost its tenseness. "Well, I told him I can't, because of you."

Linda was shocked. "Me?"

Sartain nodded silently, but a slow smile was edging its way across his face. He looked around the room. Luckily, since the place was not busy that night, they had some privacy.

"It may not be the most appropriate place or time," Sartain reached for her hand, "but I want to tell you something which is even more important and of graver consequence than what I've just told you." He rolled his eyes dramatically. "Now, can you keep a secret?"

She nodded silently, baffled by the contradiction in the tone of his voice and the smile in his eyes.

"Well then," he took a big breath, "I've decided. No more delays. When you're back from Germany and you're finished with that series of yours . . . I want us to get married."

"Will you have the salad first, sir?" the waiter, tray poised above his head, broke in.

Sam and Linda burst into laughter.

"Shall we?" she said.
"Why not?"

That night their lovemaking carried more meaning and deep-rooted pleasure than even they had known existed. Afterward, peaceful, he told her at last what he had never told a soul. He told her the full story of what had happened in Lebanon.

CHAPTER ELEVEN

"WE must stop meeting like this," Echad said with a twinkle in his eye. "You know how much we pay for this suite?"

Tara nodded.

"A hundred and eighty-five dollars a night!" he continued. "That's almost half my monthly salary . . ."

Tara knew all too well that the man in the white shirt with the rolled-up sleeves was not exaggerating. Translated into Israeli pounds, that was indeed about half the basic pay of the chief of Israeli intelligence. She also knew, however, that in this regard he was not alone. A Cabinet minister in Israel was not making much more, nor for that matter was the prime minister himself. She felt guilty at times about her luxurious life-style. Yet her job demanded it. It was after all an integral part of her cover.

"You should have become a fashion entrepreneur, or a terrorist," she teased as she eased herself into the comfortable armchair at one corner of the room. "If it's a lucrative occupation you're after . . ."

"The so-called revolutionaries," he scoffed as he pulled a chair away from the desk and turned it to face her. He recalled a recent report revealing that many of the high-ranking officers of Al Fatah were averaging five thousand dollars a month. "It's a strange world," he sighed, "where 'freedom fighters' make more than the bureaucrats."

"Well, what do you expect?" Tara asked rhetorically. "It's a world run on oil, not milk and honey. And speaking of oil," she glanced at her watch and decided to get right to the point, "I still haven't been able to come up with any hard evidence to support your suspicions."

"Meaning?"

"Meaning, all we can prove is that Mahdi and Husseini did meet in Houston with some top oil executives. But we don't know what transpired, if money changed hands, or what they came for."

"In other words we've nothing." Echad didn't hide his disappointment.

"Not yet anyway." Tara wanted to say something more, but she changed her mind.

Echad rose from his chair and walked to the bed where he opened the attaché case which lay on top. He pulled out a large brown envelope and handed it to Tara. "It's the complete copy, word for word, of Abu Latif's interrogation," he said. "Everything is there, not just the allegations against the oil companies. Go over it very carefully. Perhaps you'll be able to get more out of it than we did. There may be something we've overlooked."

She opened the envelope and looked inside; there were at least fifty pages of transcript. "You never know," she said, tucking the envelope under her fur wrap.

"If we could establish that Arafat and his gang have been receiving funds from one single oil company, then we've got them all by the balls," Echad encouraged. "And I mean it, damn it, we'll go public. It's no longer merely discriminatory practices in employment or compliance with the economic boycott. This is the real thing, Tara; this is money which is financing the murder of women and children . . . some of them American."

Tara knew exactly what Echad hoped to uncover. She had been working on it for weeks now but to no avail. Penetrating the inner structure of the multinationals proved to be anything but easy.

A captured terrorist by the name of Salim Abu Latif had started to sing, charging under interrogation that some of the oil companies were paying the Palestinian terrorists large sums of money to keep them off their tail. And Tara, as the Mossad operative responsible for Israeli counterterrorism in the United States, was charged with the task of finding some hard evidence that would stand the sure, furious denials. She had no difficulty believing that Abu Latif's claims were true. Believing it and proving it, however, were two entirely different things.

"I'm sorry I haven't been able to deliver on this matter," Tara said, feeling he was unfair to expect so much so soon. "But the

surveillance we kept on those two did lead us to Abdul Muzrack."

Echad seemed somewhat surprised. The report he had seen
before he left Israel didn't specify exactly how Tara's network
found the Al Fatah recruiter in the United States.

"We got to him indirectly through Mahdi and Husseini," Tara
continued. "When they stopped in New York, on their way to
Houston, they contacted three people. We watched our new
birds and sure enough, two days later one of them showed us
right to Muzrack's doorstep. Yesterday I sent to the Kirya"—a
reference in the parlance of Israeli intelligence to the Mossad's
headquarters in that quarter of Tel Aviv—"microfilmed lists of
recent Al Fatah recruits and names of those he plans to hit on
soon. The beauty of it is he still thinks he's incognito."

This was a remarkable coup, Echad had to admit. For some
time the Mossad had suspected that the Palestinians were busy
establishing a network of activists in the U.S., one which would
consist primarily of Arab students and young Americans of Arab
descent. It was to be patterned after similar networks in Europe,
which had already proved to be of invaluable assistance to Palestinian operations there.

But Muzrack's uncloaking posed a dilemma to the Mossad.
Should they blow the whistle on this Muzrack? Or should they
just send him quietly to a better world? Among Israeli intelligence veterans, sending someone to "a better world," or "to a
world all full of bliss," were euphemisms for eliminating enemy
agents. In the same way sending a certain individual "on vacation" meant that person was to be merely incapacitated; the
extent of his injury depended on whether he was to be sent on a
"brief" or "long" vacation.

Echad posed the question to Tara: exposure or elimination.

"Neither," Tara said with decisiveness. "If we blow the whistle
on him, where does it get us? The man is attached to the U.N.
and carries a diplomatic passport. So the worst that could happen is that he would be asked to leave the country . . . and before
too long he'd be replaced by someone else, someone we don't
know, someone who would develop his own roster of recruits,
leaving us again very much in the dark."

She pushed the butt of her spent cigarette against the ashtray
before she continued, "And if we eliminate him quietly, what do

we gain? It's the same story. I think it's to our advantage to let him be. Let him continue his machinations, but with us always one step ahead of him. After all, in addition to knowing who their present operatives are, we know also who their future recruits are going to be. One day we may need all this information. We can always get rid of him if he stops being useful."

The Mossad's chief agreed. He had already learned to value Tara's clear, calculating mind. Tara had never failed him, yet he couldn't quite bring himself to stop relating to her as a woman. And now, even though it was certainly no fault of hers, he felt frustrated at the lack of valid incriminating evidence against the oil companies.

His intense hatred for the oil companies had begun way back, when he first found out that one of the largest U.S. oil companies maintained close relations with Nazi Germany in the thirties, especially with the firm of I. G. Farben. That industrial concern was deeply involved with the planning of concentration camps and the development of mass-extermination techniques, including the Zyklon-B gas which was used to exterminate Jews in the "communal showers" of Auschwitz, Dachau, Treblinka, and other death camps. Echad had lost most of his family to the showers of those camps.

He later became convinced that the corporate heirs of those wartime oil executives were now assisting Israel's enemies, who in his eyes were moral descendents of the Nazis. Yet he knew he needed more than just the confession of an Arab terrorist to establish this fact in the eyes of the world. He was determined to get the evidence he needed.

He rose and walked to the connecting door. "Would you like a drink? We've got a stocked bar here."

"No, thank you."

The burly man unlocked the door and asked Itzik, who was glued to a TV western in the other room, to fix him a screwdriver. "Be easy on the vodka, ah," the chief of intelligence cautioned his bodyguard.

Tara didn't suppress a smile as she reflected on the sissy drinking habits of her countrymen. After all, Israel had the only armed forces in the Western world whose soldiers would try to dispel routine barracks boredom with a fifth of something as potent as sweet wine or . . . banana liqueur.

"Incidentally," Echad said as he shut the door again and turned to face Tara, "I was asked the other day if we know of any link between some of the local underground and any of the Palestinian groups. Anything more than the last report you sent us? What about that San Francisco based group. What do you call it?"

"The New World Liberation Front?"

"Yes. You didn't mention it at all."

"Who asked you about them?"

"Fred Atkins. You know, the CIA man, the Triple C coordinator. He's concerned about the possibility of a major terrorist attack here, some sort of a combined effort, perhaps, between a local group and our 'cousins.' "

"Cousins" was a common Israeli reference to the Arabs—an allusion to the common descent of the two warring Semitic people from the patriarch Abraham.

"There is nothing of significance to add to my last report," Tara said. "As for the NWLF, I didn't mention it because, like everyone else, we hardly know anything about them. They really constitute an enigma to everyone concerned. Whether they are linked to the Weather Underground or the SLA remnants or are something else altogether, no one really knows. They do seem to be well organized and very selective in terms of their targets. They don't hit at random, they operate on a small scale, and at least so far have been avoiding unnecessary bloodshed. Their propaganda is sophisticated and hits home. In spite of numerous bombing attacks not one of their members has ever been captured. They have pretty much limited themselves to the West Coast, so I doubt that they have any ties with a transnational group. What did Atkins have to say about them?"

"Not much. They seem to be in the dark, too, when it comes to this group. The FBI apparently had been trying to penetrate for some time now, with no luck. They thought that perhaps we may have some leads. Frankly it would make my day to be able to tell them what's going on in their own backyard." He gave the beautiful woman sitting across from him a wink.

Itzik knocked on the door. The drink his boss had requested was ready. Locking the door again, the Mossad chief turned to Tara and toasted, "L'chaim!" He took one long sip and then winked at her. "Truly, between us, I much prefer pure orange juice, but as the French say, noblesse oblige."

He welcomed Tara's knowing smile, and as he sipped, he thought of their many years of close acquaintance. They met for the first time in 1956 when he was still an aspiring young colonel in Modi'in, Israel's military intelligence branch, and she, an eighteen-year-old conscript assigned to his unit. It was during the hectic days and sleepless nights of that year's Suez campaign, when the tenderfoot soldier girl displayed an incredible amount of resolve and veteran proficiency, that the relationship between the two had been launched. The thirty-five-year-old Echad was then still a happily married man with two children, and the relationship, despite a great attraction, was and remained over the years a platonic one.

It was Echad who prevailed on Tara, when her two-year conscription term came to an end, to apply for the officers' training course which required an additional year of service. Tara did and became a full lieutenant at the age of twenty-two and a captain three years later when Echad himself was promoted to brigadier and deputy commander of Modi'in. The two continued to maintain contact even after Tara, by then a major, left the army to marry the noted American scientist, Aaron Berman. Echad, by then Modi'in chief, was one of the four *chupah* bearers at Tara's wedding in Jerusalem.

After the violent death of her husband and child Tara joined the Mossad. She suspected that Echad, who had divorced his wife, was secretly in love with her. Tara's feelings, however, were confined to the kindest affection. To her the rugged, bearish man epitomized the strength and resilience of her country. He was simple in manner, yet brilliant; rough and tough, yet kind and generous at heart. She felt warmth toward Echad, who once again was her boss, but it stopped there.

Echad sat down now on top of the bed. He had piled the three pillows on top of each other, and reclining against them, drink in hand, he seemed unusually relaxed and comfortable. Tara sensed that he was ready for some social chitchat. She, however, preferred to let the conversation flow in another direction.

"Well," she said, "how was it? How did the first Triple C meeting go?"

Echad, who must have read her mind, gave her a foxy smile and shrugged. On the whole he was quite satisfied with the way it went. Particularly for a first meeting, he said, it was not too bad at all. He told her that he himself talked primarily about the recent attack at Yesilkoy Airport. As a result he felt that some kind of coordinated action would be taken, at long last, to beef up security at the transit areas of the member states' airports. He didn't believe, however, that his recommendation that most airports should have separate areas for departing and arriving passengers was taken very seriously. He shrugged again and then related how embarrassed the Germans were at having to explain the jailbreak of the four women terrorists only weeks after the successful raid on Entebbe. But as if to sound fair, he added that the Germans were at least heartened by the recent capture of one of the women, and that they felt that sooner or later the other three would be caught too.

When he questioned the Germans and the French, Echad said, about the bizarre shoot-out in Berlin, they had nothing to reveal. Apparently nothing of significance was found on the body of the Arab who killed the two DST agents.

Echad, resigned now to the fact that their conversation was to remain purely professional, briefed Tara about some of the new antiterrorist gadgets which were introduced at the conference. He, for one, was particularly interested in the British "numb grenades," which exploded without shrapnel and which he felt would have saved even more lives at Entebbe if the Israelis had them. He then told her that toward the end of the meeting the discussion centered on Carlos.

"It's obvious," he remarked, "that Atkins is preoccupied with the man. He is convinced that our friend Ilich is planning something big. And he was in total agreement with me that the Yesilkoy attack didn't have the Jackal's print on it."

"What do they plan to do about Carlos?"

"Well, Atkins really pushed for the first Triple C multinational task force to concentrate on the capture of the Jackal . . . or at least to preempt his plans. The good news is," Echad added with a broad grin, "that Navon was selected to head it."

"That is good news," Tara beamed. "I was concerned if some of them would cooperate with us and . . . and here they pick Yossi to head the first team."

"Atkins in particular seemed really to like him. Well, you know Yossi. Who doesn't like him?"

She smiled. "And what are your feelings about Atkins?"

"I like him," Echad said matter-of-factly. "As Yankee as they come but a real professional, and I like working with professionals." He winked.

"Well, I better get back upstairs," Tara said as she consulted her watch, "or *my* Yankee date will beat me to my room."

Echad nodded, smiling knowingly as he got up. "I understand, duty calls. Where to, my dear? And with whom; if I may so ask?"

"It's none of your business," Tara teased. "However, if you really want to know, I'm going with Charles Blair the third, president of Blair Enterprises, to a diplomatic party at the Venezuelan Embassy."

Echad, who was about to open the door for her, stopped and looked at her quizzically.

"Coincidence!" she said, realizing what went through his head, "just coincidence."

She knew as well as he that, before his cover was blown by Moukarbel in Paris, Carlos used to frequent the parties at the Venezuelan Embassy in London, enjoying his cover as a typical Latin playboy.

"Although," she added, "nothing would make me happier than to run into him there."

"I am sure he would say the very same thing if he knew who you were," Echad spoke softly as he unlocked the door, "my dear Mata Hari."

CHAPTER TWELVE

THE first time Carlos saw the red and white catamaran was two days earlier. Caught in his rented car in a rush-hour traffic jam on the Fourteenth Street bridge, he looked out at the Washington channel. It was his very first visit to the American Capital, and he did not then imagine that his options would be reduced to the use of a boat. But he did make a mental note of it. He didn't really like boats or anything associated with the sea. In fact he had a touch of thalassophobia.

As an eight-year-old boy in Venezuela, in a summer camp on a Maiquetía beach, he came very close to drowning in the surf. He still remembered the ground slipping from underneath his feet, the crushing waves covering him, the choking sensation, and the terrible fright that gripped him before his counselor grabbed him by the hair and lifted his head above water. It was early in life when he saw death eye to eye, Carlos was fond of telling his comrades in later years, his account of the story somewhat embellished, the paralyzing fear never mentioned.

Standing in line at Pier 4 about to purchase the fare for the boat ride to Mount Vernon, he was hoping that the large, lightweight catamaran would do. For the previous two days he had roamed the city searching for the right target. He had examined such possibilities as the Capitol, the Washington Monument, clearly seen now from where he was standing, the several museums along the National Mall, and other public buildings and facilities. He even bothered to take a good look at the White House. None of them, however, turned out to be suitable for his plans, not for the one before the big one. And the latter depended very much on the complete success of the former. Thus he couldn't afford to make a wrong move with this Washington diversion. One single error and the effort of a whole year could go down the drain.

He congratulated himself for coming to Washington in person. The risk involved was outweighed by the strong suspicion that the fools would have picked the wrong target. Once again he recalled Entebbe and shuddered at the thought. That's why he was hoping that the boat would prove to be the answer to his dilemma. Already he was pleased by the size of the line. The one-page brochure advertised the fact that each of the three Thomas Line's catamarans carried as many as three hundred ninety-four passengers. In fact it would be perfect. He estimated by the length of the line now that at least three hundred sightseers were about to take the four-hour cruise.

"Round trip?" the cashier at the booth asked.

"Yes, please, one round-trip ticket," Carlos said in a pleasant, only mildly accented voice. "Excuse me, madame, do you happen to have student fares?"

"No, I'm sorry," the thickset, middle-aged woman replied somewhat impatiently. "The reduced rates are for children only."

"I see," said Carlos, who was about to pull out his student ID card. The card would have testified to the fact that Rafael Rojas Restrepo from Colombia was a full-time student at the University of California at Berkeley. Indeed there was nothing in Carlos's appearance to contradict this new identity. Everything, from the beard to the worn-out gym shoes and the frayed denim shorts, supported that image.

Carlos closely watched the young blond couple ahead of him. They seemed to be Scandinavian students and were just proceeding through the metal gate. It was their backpacks that attracted his attention. Theirs were at least twice the size of his, and he was curious to find out if they would be searched. To his great relief they were not. And, indeed, a few people later he himself handed over his ticket and was motioned through the gate in the direction of the catamaran whose name appeared on the bow in large white letters. It was called *Fraternity*.

Carlos boarded the boat at the stern and proceeded directly to the main-deck cabin. The cabin's aluminum walls were not painted and felt cold. A stark atmosphere pervaded the huge room. But that was not what interested Carlos. He fast surveyed the place with a professional eye and quickly came to the conclusion that the main cabin was large enough, if necessary, to accommodate all the passengers, particularly if the boat was not full to capacity. It would be uncomfortably tight, but it could be done, and he was not concerned about the comfort of his hostages.

Carlos also noted with increased satisfaction that the eight windows on each side were hermetically sealed, and that the exits in the rear and in the middle, plus the staircase in the front leading to the deck above, could be guarded by as few as three people, if he didn't have more to spare. So far, so good, he sighed with satisfaction before he continued with his inspection.

He rested his backpack on one of the tables at the main cabin and pulled out a college notebook. He began to take down notes in Spanish: "The length of the main cabin is approximately 30 meters and its width almost 12. The men's room in the front right is about 4 by 2.5 meters. It has 2 seats and 2 urinals. No windows . . ." Carlos assumed that the ladies' room on the left was of similar size and was also without windows. He noted down for himself to check that last detail. He also added that the snack bar and the storage place for the life jackets were located between the rest rooms.

As Carlos climbed the stairs to the boat-deck cabin, he silently counted them. Again he meticulously noted the information down. He wasn't taking any chances. As far as he was concerned, the most minute detail could be of some significance. His former KGB instructors at Patrice Lumumba People's Friendship University, in Moscow, would have been proud of him, he mused. The fools! They would yet learn to value his true talents and respect his ingenuity. He could never forgive the humiliation they had caused him, and they would yet learn to regret his expulsion. No, he wasn't going to overlook a damn thing. It was the first and the last time he was going to be on that boat, and the four-hour trip would have to provide him with all the information he needed.

The indoor staircase to the upper cabin led him right to the front of the pilothouse's door. Carlos hesitated for only a few seconds when he realized where he was. He consulted his watch. The boat was not scheduled to leave for another twelve minutes. He made up his mind and went for the door's handle. He was ready with an excuse. The metal door opened with a squeak; he expected someone to confront him, but no one was there.

Four short steps led to the cockpit itself, but Carlos didn't climb them. From where he stood, with the door still held open, he just quickly glanced around, his pupils transmitting to the brain a barrage of information. His trained mind ingested all the details he could lay his eyes on, all in these brief, precious seconds. Digestion would come later.

He closed the door. It was not necessary to cause suspicion, he would gain entry before the cruise was over. His mind was already formulating a number of tentative plans. At this point it was sufficient to ascertain that the door to the bridge was kept unlocked prior to the boat's departure. In this day and age—Carlos shook his head—what a blessed laxity! He was beginning to feel the hunter's excitement but strongly resisted the temptation to immediately declare the catamaran to be the prey he was looking for.

The Jackal turned back and walked into the boat-deck cabin. It looked very much the same as the main cabin, only half its size. It also had two doors in the back and two more in the middle, opening to the weather decks which surrounded the boat. But there was no indoor connection to the hurricane deck above. He would have much preferred it if there was such an indoor staircase but concluded that it was no major obstacle.

As he crossed the boat-deck cabin, Carlos inspected the people who began to crowd it, attempting to determine their makeup. He detected quite a few foreign nationals and was particularly pleased by the large number of women and children. He recalled the white marble statue he had seen before on the waterfront, only a few yards from where he boarded the boat. It was a monument dedicated by the women of America to the brave men who perished on the *Titanic* to save the lives of the women and children.

Yes the time of the year was definitely perfect, Carlos thought as he patted the curly head of the cute tot who ran into him. The more, the better . . . children in particular held a special place in the heart of Americans. It would be like driving the blade in and then twisting and twisting . . . It was the only time that the constantly pleasant smile on the Jackal's face turned, for a split second, ugly.

Carlos climbed the companionway to the hurricane deck where three dozen passengers were sitting in the bright sun on cheap plastic chairs. The two Scandinavian-looking students were there, their backs leaning against the rail, their feet resting on the backpacks in front of them. They stared at him as he walked in their direction. The girl was pretty, and she acknowledged his smile with a slight nod. Her companion, however, ignored him and turned to engage his mate in a conversation in a language Carlos couldn't understand but guessed was Swedish.

Carlos was amused at the display of the male's possessiveness. His smile had been nonflirtatious. In fact he wasn't at all attracted to this blonde and it wasn't just because he was preoccupied with his work. Now the petite, dark girl he met the other night at one of Georgetown's hangouts, she did turn him on, and he enjoyed her until the wee hours of the morning. He had to, as she didn't give in until two or three in the morning. But when she did . . . He had almost been tempted to take her with him on the cruise but discarded the notion after a cold morning shower in her apartment. Now it took him a few seconds to remember her name, but he had written it and the telephone number down. She seemed to have fallen for him, and one never knew, she may become handy one day. Women had been of tremendous help to him in the past. Boudia used to say: a good woman is worth three men, and she's six times more fun.

As he examined the boat from where he stood, he realized that it would be impossible for anyone to leap from the top deck to the channel's waters. A person would have to be a super athlete to clear the two weather decks below. And as he turned to climb back down, catching again a hostile glance from the Swede, he mused that he would have liked to see the arrogant son of a bitch make a try for it.

Carlos was on the lowest weather deck next to the main cabin, and he figured that the unmarked door must be the one leading to the below-deck compartments, to the engine room itself. He looked around him. There was no one close to him, but a few people were looking down from the deck above him. There was no way that he would not be seen. So he decided that if he just behaved in the most casual manner, no one would suspect what he was up to. He would just be some overly curious tourist when he tried the door.

It opened without a hitch. Not hesitating, he proceeded down the metal staircase.

"Anybody here? Hello . . ." His voice echoed, but the only response was from the hushed ticking of some machines.

Should he continue to explore? He glanced at his watch. The boat would leave in four minutes. He found it very strange that no one was there yet. Someone would surely show up any moment. He climbed the steps with his back to the door, again his mind incessantly registering, memorizing every detail.

When the packed boat finally did take off with only a few minutes' delay, Carlos observed from a vantage point that there were two men in the pilothouse—the aging captain at the helm and another young man. The latter began to talk into the mike; he was the tour narrator. Carlos was impatient to find out the exact size of the crew. So far, besides the captain and the guide, he could identify only one other person as belonging to the ship's personnel, a young man in a blue shirt whom he had observed before helping untie the boat from the deck. It was difficult to tell who the others were, since only the captain wore any kind of uniform.

Failing to spot any other crew members and convinced that a boat of that size would need a crew of more than three, Carlos decided to approach the young man in the blue shirt.

"Sir," he addressed him quietly, feigning timidity, "can you tell me please how many people man this boat?"

The steward was used to all kinds of questions about the boat by inquisitive passengers. He had learned to answer them politely but coolly, making sure he wasn't sucked into any lengthy chatter. "Three. The captain and two deckhands."

"Only three?" Carlos was truly surprised. Indeed he didn't know much about boats.

At that point the guide's voice announced through the speakers that they were passing Fort McNair on the left and East Potomac Park on the right. He added some statistics about the park's golf course, but Carlos was only half listening.

"What about him?" Carlos asked, nodding in the direction of the bridge.

"What about who?"

"The man with the mike, the broadcaster." He didn't quite know the correct word in English.

"You mean the guide? Oh, that includes him. One of the two deckhands serves also as narrator."

"I see," Carlos said, not quite sure whether he should probe further.

"Why do you ask?" The steward suddenly sounded suspicious.

"Oh," Carlos shrugged, "I am a foreign student and I've got to do a paper for my English composition class, so I've decided to write one about this boat." It was the best story he could come up with at that moment. Apparently it sounded convincing.

"Where are you from?" the deckhand asked.

"I am from Colombia, from Bogotá. Have you heard of it?"

"No. I mean I've heard of Colombia, it's in South America somewhere, isn't it? But I've never heard of Bugo . . . Bugota, was it?"

"Bogotá. It's the capital," Carlos responded with all the shyness he could muster.

"I see," the young deckman said, turning away slightly, his span of attention having reached its limit. Carlos sensed it and quickly asked where he could get some food.

"I believe," the young man said, glad at the opportunity to disengage politely, "the galley is open. It's down the main-deck cabin. Take these stairs down," he pointed and with that walked away.

Two black girls staffed the snack bar, and Carlos ordered a hot dog and a cola. While he was waiting for the food, he calculated that if the boat was taken over soon after it left the dock, there should be enough food on board to last, if rationed carefully, for at least three days. That would be sufficient for his plans. Not having to rely on food from the outside would be a tremendous advantage. He assumed in addition that the boat was provided with adequate first-aid supplies and that, if they were lucky, there would be a physician or two among the hostages.

The *Fraternity* was circling Hains Point as it moved from the Washington Channel into the much wider Potomac River, which at that juncture was almost a mile wide. To the boat's left lay the facilities of the Naval Research Laboratory and to its right the land-filled Washington National Airport appeared. Planes were landing and taking off from the runways which ran parallel to the river, and there was no fence, no buildings, nothing between them and the water. Carlos, who stood on the upper weather deck, was snapping pictures with his Minolta faster than any Japanese tourist on board. He had already made up his mind that the catamaran was to be his target.

As the Jackal stood there watching the planes, recognizing the Pentagon in the far distance to the right, the whole operation started to take shape in his mind. He calculated the exact number of people he would need to take over the boat, the kind of weapons, explosives, and logistics required. There was only one more piece of information be needed to complete the jigsaw puzzle, and he was convinced that before he left the boat, he would have it.

Having almost given up earlier on the Washington scheme, Carlos found it difficult now to resist the excitement that was sweeping over him. In his mind he could already imagine the whole operation unfolding, stage by stage. God, he almost said out loud, there was absolutely no experience, not even fucking a new woman . . . there was absolutely nothing that could match the sensation that spread, prickling, through every pore of his skin. But the most exhilarating thing to him was that, in spite of all the excitement, his mind remained clear, cool, alert, attentive, still absorbing information, still not letting a thing escape him. He was in total control. Yes, he was in command. He was the one who was the real captain of the boat . . . the lives of all these people were in his hands. The adrenaline surged. He could see the faces of the terror-stricken passengers as they were taken hostage, imagine the new black and green flag of Terror International, recently designed by him, being raised to replace the Stars and Stripes. Oh he could already see it flapping in the wind . . . right there in the middle of the most powerful capital on earth, right at the center of capitalism and imperialism. He almost shivered with excitement thinking about it.

"Commando Boudia has taken over," he could hear the first announcement on the boat's intercom, repeated again and again in headlines and broadcasts throughout the world.

He was a toreador at the center of the arena with the throng cheering wildly: Carlos! Carlos! Carlos! Tears welled in his eyes. Yes, they would come by the thousands, the tens of thousands, to watch from the river's banks, terrified, fascinated, spellbound . . . and then he would hit them with the big one. He gripped tight the rail as he almost screamed for release, fighting the climax.

CHAPTER THIRTEEN

"PROFESSOR Grundman? Kuno Grundman?"

"*Ja. Das ist Professor Grundman. Wer ist das, bitte?*"

"Professor Grundman . . . er, do you speak English?"

"*Ja, ja, sicher.* I am sorry, yes, yes, sure."

"My name is Linda Wexler. I'm Professor Samuel Sartain's friend. He asked me to call you."

"Oh, *ja.* Professor Sartain. *Ja, er ist ein gut* . . . I'm sorry . . . yes, he is a good friend. Sure. Are you . . . here as a tourist?"

"No, not really. I'm a journalist. I'm here to do some research on the role of women in the terrorist movement over here, and Sam, Professor Sartain, assured me that, being an authority on the subject, you may be able to help me."

"Oh, *ja ja.* I remember now. You are a journalist, *ja?*"

"*Ja, ja.*" Linda chuckled to herself at being caught by the German inclination to resort to an abundance of "jas."

"*Nun,* how can I be of help to you, Fräulein Wexler?"

"Well, I would like to meet you, if it's at all possible, and discuss some things. Perhaps you could guide me. I think the best thing would be if we could meet and—"

"*Ja, ja,* absolutely. I would be delighted. Where are you staying, Fräulein?"

"Hotel Kempinski. It's on—"

"*Ja, ja.* I know it. You shouldn't have any difficulty getting here from there. Perhaps we can meet tomorrow at my office. Seven o'clock will be all right?"

"In the evening?"

"*Nein.* Seven in the morning. Unless it's too early for you?"

"Er . . . no, that will be all right." Linda was not a morning person, but if the man would see her, she was resigned to be there any time he wanted.

"*Gut.* I'll see you at seven. You know how to get to the university?"

"I don't think I'll have any problems. It's in Dahlem, isn't it?"

"*Ja, ja.* Just ask at the gate for the department of sociology. I am at room three-eleven. *Auf Wiedersehen!*"

"*Auf Wiedersehen, und danke!*" Linda responded using the little German she knew.

It was a clear, beautiful summer day, and Linda leaned back against her chair to take in the scenery out the window. The previous afternoon, when she landed at Tegel, a belt of smog had hung like a shroud over the vast city. Now a gentle wind helped dissipate the haze, and only a few white cumuli stood in the blue expanse like so many grazing sheep.

A few blocks away, dominating the skyline, in contrast with the blackened tower-ruin of the Kaiser Wilhelm church, Linda spotted the modern Europa-Centre. At night one could see its huge rotating Mercedes-Benz emblem glow bluish from miles away. To Linda it symbolized the power of German industry. It was hard to imagine a postwar Berlin when the whole downtown area was nothing but a pile of burnt-out rubble.

Incredible, Linda mused, the industriousness of these people. The question now was whether this booming democracy could survive the onslaught of a new kind of destruction. Terrorism. A new horror which stemmed, in large part, from the very phenomenon of the *Wirtschaftswunder*—the "economic miracle," the amazingly quick reconstruction after 1945. She recalled what I. F. Stone wrote about the Weathermen radicals in her own country: "The ultimate menace they fear is their own secret selves in their own parents."

As she looked out upon the myriad totems of power, she pondered what Sam had once told her. In West Germany, he had said, parents carried the burden of moral ambiguity inherent in the *Wirtschaftswunder*. There was something in the very robustness of the German economy which alienated the new German radicals and which they deemed to be profoundly obscene. Indeed, Sartain told Linda, it was the same kind of revulsion also reflected in many contemporary German films and in much of its modern literature. To some of these rebellious young Germans the sins of Auschwitz were never expiated. Instead they witnessed a guilty society rising sleek and fat from defeat. Thus these young men and women, who were raised to take the new German affluence for granted, and nearly all of them were products of middle- and upper-middle-class families, recoiled in revulsion from it and resorted to nihilist and anarchist violence.

Linda turned away from the window, unsettled by these notions, yet determined to pursue them. She consulted her address book again. She found the name she wanted but hesitated. She remembered Sartain's explicit cautionary words, but she justified to herself that all she really wanted to do was to make sure that Röhl would be in Berlin the following week when Sartain might be there.

Resolved, Linda reached for the telephone and dialed the radical magazine. Its publisher, however, was not there, but the secretary assured her he would call her back the next day. Linda decided not to use Sartain's name, explaining only that she was an American journalist who wanted to interview Ulrike's former husband.

As soon as Linda laid down the receiver, reflecting again on what made her disregard Sam's express warning, there was a knock on the door.

The blond blue-suited bellhop clicked his heels together as he handed Linda the bouquet of red roses. Yet even when he bowed in a theatrical display of respect, his hazel eyes continued to linger on Linda's California-tanned body which revealed itself in places through the sheer peignoir.

Surprised and delighted, Linda unwrapped the rustling, transparent paper. The note, welcoming her to Berlin, was signed by a Horst Vogel. It took her a brief second to recall that he was Steve's radical friend. "Sweet Steve . . . ," she said aloud. She was touched by this unexpected gesture, realizing that Steve must have called his friend in advance of her coming. She tried to remember, as she filled the vase with water, if she had ever told Steve that red roses were her favorite flowers. She set the arrangement on the dresser and stood back to admire the flowers. "Sweet Steve," she said again, "always full of surprises."

Horst Vogel was a tall, rail-thin man with shoulder-length sandy hair. Bushy eyebrows protruded over his narrow, ice-blue eyes which fought for dominance over his strong jutting chin. He seemed older, Linda thought, than twenty-seven. He resembled a cowboy star whose name she couldn't recall. He was not what one would call handsome, yet Linda could appreciate that his offbeat, rugged looks could appeal to many a woman. *"Prosit,"* he toasted as he eyed Linda with a mixture of curiosity and unabashed male appreciation.

The two were sitting under one of the bright orange umbrellas, a trademark of the Carrousel, the elegant outdoor café on the Kurfürstendamm. It was well after six, and the day crowd was being replaced by a more chic evening lot who, by and large, seemed to take their leisure more soberly. The neon lights were slowly winning a battle with the twilight, and the promenade was busy as ever with pedestrians and cars.

Horst was talking of his year spent at Berkeley and the mixed feelings he had about the place. He had expected the environment to be far more radically oriented and was disappointed with the students' growing apathy toward revolutionary causes. Linda reasoned that since the end of the war in Vietnam, and with the resolution of Watergate and Nixon's resignation, things had mellowed down considerably.

"Yes," Horst admitted ruefully. "Unfortunately the pendulum had swung back, not only in your country, but also here and in the rest of Western Europe. But not for too long, I can promise you that . . ." A faint smile crossed his thin lips. "To use an American expression, I can see the light at the end of the tunnel."

Linda didn't respond. She studied him with increased curiosity. He smiled and began relating the humorous circumstances that had brought him and Steve together.

It had to do with a traffic ticket, Horst confessed, which he would have gotten if it had not been for Steve. Riding a motorcycle, Horst was picked up at a Berkeley intersection for what the cop said was failure to come to a complete halt at a stop sign. Steve Sartain, then a total stranger, happened to be walking by at the time. Steve faked an epileptic attack which forced the policeman to let Horst go as he rushed to Steve's aid.

"He just didn't like ticket-giving cops . . . that's how he explained it later," Horst shrugged, grinning.

Linda burst into unrestrained glee as Vogel once again imitated Steve's heroic act.

"I love the way you laugh," Vogel said suddenly, slowly, "It's free and pure, and it rings like many little bells clinking together in the wind."

The tone of his voice caught Linda by total surprise. She

began to feel ill at ease. The flowers, the intimate statement didn't seem to match up with the man who sat across from her. Neither did, in fact, the worn-out jeans, the short-sleeve shirt and . . . the black woolen tie.

She didn't know whether to be amused or amazed by the young man's infatuation with her. Horst didn't try to hide the fact that he was taken by her, even though she had a few years on him. She decided to pretend she really hadn't noticed, to interpret his advances as gestures of friendliness. Steve must have forgotten to tell his friend the nature of the relationship between her and his father. Above all, this was a business appointment, and it was time to forgo the pleasantries and pursue the subject she came to explore.

She began to question him about the general political situation in Germany, leading him into a discussion of the Baader-Meinhof and their ilk. Eventually the conversation turned to the jailbreak.

"How was it possible for the four women to escape unnoticed? What kind of outside help did they have? Are they still in West Berlin or West Germany? And how could they hide effectively in a city like West Berlin?" Linda blushed at the onslaught of questions that erupted from her like a barrage of bullets.

Horst, however, calmly responded that he didn't really know much more than what was reported in the media. "I thought," he added, looking at her quizzically, "that your article was going to be about the subject of 'Women and Crime.' Why this interest in that particular jailbreak? After all there have been other escapes. Don't tell me you came all the way to Berlin just for that?"

"I want to begin my series with a dramatic illustration," Linda quickly explained. "What better vehicle than a story about these four women? Four women, whose freedom had been demanded by the Entebbe hijackers; four women, who made a mockery of the German authorities and their counterterrorism campaign."

"One woman," Horst corrected. "It was the freedom of only one woman the skyjackers demanded."

"I know, I know," Linda said somewhat impatiently. "But it makes no real difference. The point is—"

"Okay, okay." Horst raised his hand, smiling. "I got the message. It's not a bad idea. But tell me one thing, Ms. Wexler," his eyes forced themselves into hers, "why not get the material from the police?"

"This is the whole point. I don't want just the official version. That's not the way I work. I want to write a balanced story. I want to learn about these women from less biased sources. I want to find out about their personal lives, about their true motives. I—"

"All right, all right, I have it," Horst interrupted her again. He leaned back in his chair. His eyes narrowed even more as he studied her carefully before conceding that although he personally couldn't tell her much, he would be willing to introduce her to some friends at the Free University who, he was reasonably confident, could help her as long as she didn't use the information to hurt their movement.

"I'm not here to hurt anyone," she assured him. "All I want is to write a good, impartial story. Besides, who knows? It may turn out to be a golden opportunity for your friends to bring their cause to the attention of the American public. After all," she added, unable to stop what she knew would insult him, "isn't it true the media is the terrorists' best ally?"

"My friends are not terrorists!" the young German shot back, a flush of color in his face. "They are revolutionaries, real revolutionaries. Perhaps the only true revolutionaries left in Germany. They are idealists rebelling against the ultramaterialist society we've created, against the new kind of fascism which is masquerading as free enterprise, capitalism, and liberalism. Who are we really kidding?" he asked, full of contempt.

"But that's exactly why I came here," Linda appeased, "to find out the truth. And I assure you I came with an open mind."

"Okay, I'll help you," Horst said, mollified. He motioned to the waiter to refill his glass. "You want a good story, you'll have a good story." He leaned back, most of the tension drained from his face. "But let's talk about you, Linda. I am curious to know how you feel, as a Jewess, to be here in Germany?"

"How do you—"

"Steve told me . . . and the name . . ."

Linda felt awkward. Why would Steve mention that she was Jewish, particularly since she was Jewish only on her father's side. She took her time before responding. She was being tested. But why? She wanted very much to meet Horst's contacts, convinced that they would be invaluably helpful, but she was not sure of what he wanted to hear. She recalled stories of the viciously anti-Semitic, German woman terrorist who took part in the Entebbe hijacking. On the other hand . . . No, there was no point but to be as frank as possible. "Well, the truth is that the first time I was here, I really had mixed feelings—"

"You've been here before?" Horst sounded surprised.

"Yes," she answered. "I covered the Munich Olympics for a magazine back home. And to be honest, in the beginning it felt strange to be enjoying myself in a country which had perpetrated such horrible atrocities against my people . . . my people, at least on my father's side. And then, when the Israeli athletes were so brutally massacred, it was hard not to think that it was Germany again, that once more the Jews were being slaughtered on German soil."

Linda paused and searched Horst's face for reaction. There was none. He seemed to have accepted what she said without questioning it.

"But, quite frankly," she felt compelled to add, "in the days that followed, when I witnessed what appeared to be true shock on the part of most Germans to what had happened; when I continued to meet many Germans who were kind, warm, and friendly, I found it increasingly difficult to pass judgment on a whole people, to be faulted with the same kind of prejudice I had been condemning . . .

"After all," she added, smiling, "here I am, having a drink with you, and you're German . . . and I see you simply as a sincere, kind, and charming person."

"*Danke, danke,*" Horst said, not without a trace of condescension. "I really do appreciate your candor, your American openness." He hitched up his chair and leaned forward, his metallic eyes locking on hers. "Tell me then, Ms. Wexler, would you be able to go to bed with a sincere, kind, and charming German?"

"What?" she recoiled in her chair, taken aback by the straightforwardness of the question.

There was a long silence before she tried to soften her initial surprised, angry reaction with an explanation. "For that matter, Horst, I wouldn't sleep with an American, Englishman, or Bulgarian. You see, I happen to be a one-man woman, and I've already got my man . . . who happens to be Steve's father."

CHAPTER FOURTEEN

THE narrow, unpaved alley was dark, and Hans Huber, a Mossad agent whose true name was Saul Friedman, had to strain his eyes to avoid any missteps as he followed the man they called Fritz. The man ahead moved so fast, and with such confidence, that Saul surmised either he was very familiar with the place or had cat's eyes. He glanced back and satisfied himself that Kurt Barz, also a deep-cover agent whose real name was Itamar Shaked, was keeping pace right behind.

Fritz stopped suddenly, and Saul barely avoided running into him. He pointed at the back of a medium-size building which had one lit window on the second floor. "There," Fritz said in a hushed voice. "Follow me!"

They climbed over the low brick fence and approached the rear entrance. Fritz tried the handle. It was locked. He fished in his pocket and came up with the key. The door opened with only a slight, faint squeal. "Quiet," he whispered as they sneaked soundlessly into the dark stairway and up the steps.

Saul had been steeling himself for this moment, yet he still felt his heart pounding with almost uncontrollable excitement. At long last, after so much effort, he and Itamar were finally going to have a face-to-face confrontation with Fusako Shigenobu . . . God Almighty! If this meeting went well, then the road to Carlos, to the Jackal himself, would be open. Their eighteen-month-old scheme had worked after all, and now that it was so near, within grasp, he could hardly believe it. He and Itamar had been subjected to all kinds of incredible tests, had gone through hell on earth, and had overcome insurmountable obstacles in order to penetrate Carlos's inner circle. Could it? Could it be that their suicidal task was about to succeed after all?

When Yossi Navon had asked for volunteers, he said he needed kamikazes. He was more than just telling the truth. But even kamikazes needed a target to blow themselves against.

Saul suddenly felt Fritz's palm against his chest, and he froze on his heels, as did Itamar right behind him. They were now in the second-floor corridor and only dim light came through a glass-paned door only a few feet away from them. They could now hear muffled voices emanating from behind that door. Fritz had his forefinger on his lips to signal silence. He tiptoed in the direction of the lit room, motioning them to follow. They did.

When Fritz reached the glass door, he didn't stop but continued past it. Through the translucent glass, Saul could detect the blurred images of two people. He couldn't really tell what sex they were, although the hushed tones sounded like male voices.

What's going on? Saul wanted to ask but kept silent as they continued down the hall past the lit door. He didn't like the look of it; something just didn't seem right. What the hell was going on?

When the trio reached the end of the corridor, Fritz opened another door, and they entered a room where the only light came through the window which opened onto the street.

To Saul's and Itamar's surprise Fritz pulled two silencer-equipped revolvers from underneath his jacket and handed each of them one. "Just a side operation before we meet with Fusako," he explained in a low voice.

"But—" Saul tried to protest the sudden change of plans.

"It's something that just came up," the German didn't let him finish. "These are Fusako's specific orders. Have you ever heard of Michael Limon?"

Saul could feel anxiety seeping into his spine. "No," he whispered, trying to sound convincing. Itamar just shook his head, avoiding Saul's eyes lest he reveal his concern. Saul's grip on the gun tightened. Somehow the cold-metal feel was the only comforting thing he had at that moment.

"He is a top Mossad agent, one of the original members of the Wrath of God team. He usually goes by the cover name 'Mongoose.' He is meeting there, in the lit room we passed, with someone who has betrayed us. I want you to burst in and shoot them. Shoot to kill!"

Saul felt the blood curdling in his veins. Good God! He knew

Mike Limon personally. He was his instructor at BAHAD 18, the training facility for undercover agents. What are they to do? So this was the real test, the final acid test. Not only did he know Mike, he knew his wife Orna, and their two small children. Even if he didn't . . . to kill another Israeli agent . . . let alone one he personally knew. No! They couldn't. Not even if the opportunity to get to Carlos after all this time, and after all these efforts, could slip forever. No! Nothing could justify it.

Saul didn't know what his former instructor would do under the same circumstances; that sort of a scenario was never brought up during his training. He did know, however, that Itamar was watching for a signal from him. He held the equivalent rank of a major in the Mossad and was of a higher rank than Itamar. It was his responsibility to make the crucial decision.

God! Saul couldn't help but waver, to get all the way here. The test was deadly, decisively deadly. But why did they choose Limon? Could it be coincidence? Was their cover blown? Have they been playing with them all along, even while watching them both partake in those bombing attacks?

Incredible how much could go through a person's mind in just a few short seconds when a man has to make such a crucial decision.

Fritz, slimmer and much shorter than Saul, watched him carefully through his metal-rimmed glasses. He didn't move his wirethin lips but only gestured with his head as if to say: what the hell are you waiting for?

Saul didn't wait. There was just no way he was going to kill Limon. No way! With a heavy heart—or was it a sense of premonition?—he stuck his gun at the man's rib cage.

The German smiled.

Even in the very dim light Saul could detect the sardonic cruelty of that smile. He knew then that he had been had, that both he and Itamar were done with. Nevertheless he pulled the trigger.

The very moment Saul heard the empty "click," he felt the blade tearing into him from behind. Surprisingly there was no pain, only slight remorse mixed increasingly with mellower tranquility. He was a five-year-old child, his long blond curls flying in the wind as he kept running and running in slow motion toward his mother's open arms.

Saul's and Itamar's bodies hit the floor at the same time.

"*Schweines!* Jewish pigs!" the German hissed as the two Arabs wiped the blood off their Shabarrias' pointed blades.

It was a warm sunny day, and Linda, who was crossing the small Gieselbrechtstrasse circle, wore a short-sleeved white dress which nicely accentuated her tanned, slim arms. She moved lightly and gracefully, but if Gertrude and the bearded man who sat by the wheel could see her face, they would have been able to read the anxiety and concern registered on it.

Linda walked into the indoor part of the London Tavern, a bar-restaurant establishment on the Giezerbrecht and Sybel corner of the circle. Even through the glass windows that were shadowed somewhat by a wide red and blue canopy, the couple in the car could tell that she was looking for someone. She seemed to hesitate for a moment, and then they saw her approaching a lone man in a gray suit. It was only his back, however, that they could see.

The bearded man, one of the two East German agents who had helped the four female terrorists escape, and who was known to the rest of the group only by the name of Ulrich, touched Gertrude's arm. "Okay," he said, "why don't you just walk over there very casually and see if you can tell who the man is? At least let's find out what he looks like."

"You mean I should go inside?"

"No, first just walk close to the place and see if you can get a good look at him from outside."

Gertrude obeyed and got out of the silver Audi which they had parked opposite the restaurant, by the Kurbel movie theater. As instructed, she proceeded to stroll casually by the bar-restaurant.

Ulrich soon realized that Gertrude was unable to see the face of the man sitting with Linda. Either accidentally or intentionally the man in the gray suit was facing away from the window.

Gertrude hesitated and cast a questioning glance at her comrade in the car. Ulrich nodded.

The blond German grabbed the opportunity to follow a young couple into the restaurant as though she were part of their party. Once inside the place she crossed past the long mahogany bar and sought the ladies' room.

Noticing the sign on the far left, she strode right toward it. Only once did she cast a quick look behind her, in the direction of where the man with the gray suit was animatedly conversing with Linda. Even though she could only catch the man's profile for a split second, her heart skipped a beat. She didn't look back again until she reached the rest rooms.

Once inside the ladies' room Gertrude walked without hesitation into one of the stalls and, fully clothed, sat on the toilet to give some thought to what she had just seen. Or had she? Was it really Professor Günther? Could it really be he? It must have been . . . it would have been hard to mistake his prominent features . . . that nose, those huge ears, that lock of hair. No, it must be he and . . . if you give the woman credit, it also makes sense.

She got up and was careful to flush the water. True, no one was in the rest room, but as her instructor in Aden had told her, nothing like keeping good habits, even when they are deemed to be totally unnecessary. And as she walked out of the stall, she took the time again to touch up her makeup in front of the mirror and fix her hair before she left the room.

Now that Gertrude had a chance to have a better look at the man with the gray suit, she had no doubt he was indeed Professor Günther. She didn't linger but walked out and, a true professional, took the long way back to the car.

She could hardly contain herself when she told Ulrich, who all that time never took his eyes off Linda, that the man with the gray suit was Professor Günther.

"Who?"

"Günther, you know, the nuclear scientist . . ."

"Are you sure?"

"Go and see for yourself. But I tell you, it's him all right."

Ulrich wrung his hands. "I knew it, I knew the bitch was up to something," he muttered. His eyes narrowed ominously as he glanced in Linda's direction. "She is not going to get away with it," he said, touching instinctively the gun in his shoulder holster.

CHAPTER FIFTEEN

IT was already ten o'clock at night when Professor Sartain returned to his small house on Nineteenth Street. From his maid's note he learned that Linda had called around five P.M. and left the number of the Hotel Kempinski to call her back. Sartain looked at the electric clock on his desk and quickly calculated the time difference: it would be after three o'clock in the morning in Berlin. As much as he wanted to talk to Linda, it would have been unkind to wake her up at such an hour. No, he decided with some disappointment, he would call her in the morning. He would make it a point to get up earlier than usual.

Having given his mail only a cursory check, he walked over to the small kitchen to prepare himself a cup of hot chocolate, a favorite drink of his when he was tired and alone. Waiting for the water to boil, Sartain mulled over what he should do for the rest of the evening. He wouldn't have minded hitting the sack or at least lying down with a good novel. But there were many other things he should do, among them working on his own novel. He wondered whether he was too tired to go over Kesselman's Ph.D. dissertation; whether, being that sleepy, he would do it justice. He decided to give it a try.

The professor settled down in the soft leather chair in his study and began reading the four-hundred-eighty-page dissertation entitled: "The Role of the Armed Forces in the Process of National Integration in the New Developing States of Tropical Africa," flinching before the formidable title. He rubbed his eyes, took another sip of hot chocolate, and longed for the suspense novel at his bedside table. More than anything he wished Linda were there to knead his stiff, fatigued back.

He had had a long, arduous day, trying hard to finish as much business at the university as was humanly possible so that he could leave early and stop in Berlin prior to the Tel Aviv conference. Contrarily, now that the term was nearing its end, more and more people pressed to see him before he departed, knowing that he would be away for some time.

Sartain went through two hundred pages of dissertation, to the quiet music of Bach and Mozart, before his eyelids began to give, refusing to remain open. Concentration was slowly, steadily, waning. He lacked the energy even to refill his pipe with his favorite Erinmore mixture, continuing instead to puff on the bitter, smoked-out residue.

It was time to go to bed, or he would end up falling asleep right there, paying for it the next day with aching bones. He leafed through the remaining two hundred eighty pages and pushed against the chair's arms. He must be aging after all, he thought, he used to be able to take much more than that.

The following morning the professor, who habitually awakened on his own at exactly quarter to eight, twisted and wriggled in bed before mustering enough determination to roll off and lumber over to the other side of the room to turn off the buzzing alarm clock. It took another dose of resolve to fight the strong urge to crawl back under the tempting sheets.

The professor grabbed a long-handled, hard-bristled brush and forcefully began rubbing his body with it. Starting with his toes, he inched it up his torso, stroking the tough natural bristles rhythmically in the direction of the heart. It was something he learned from a Kurdish revolutionary he helped out a few years back. It never failed to wake him up, no matter how drowsy he felt, and it did wonders for the condition of his skin. In the beginning he found it difficult to tolerate the grazing of the coarse Siberian-boar bristles against the more tender areas of his body. But with time Sartain learned not only to brave the unpleasant scratching, but indeed to enjoy the rough sensation.

In a few minutes Sartain's body heated up. As a result of the constant, hard rubbing, his blood rushed from the capillaries to his veins and was being pumped forcefully into his heart. He turned on the cold water in the shower to a full blast and puffed and groaned under the impact of the icy water. But when he walked out of it, drying himself with a towel, he felt totally awake and rejuvenated. By the time he did his customary sixty morning push-ups, he was fully prepared to face the day ahead. A cup of coffee, milk but no sugar, and twenty minutes after he woke up, Sartain was ready to place his overseas call to Linda.

Linda walked out of her hotel room and was about to shut the door behind her when she heard the telephone ring. She quickly glanced at her wrist watch, it was five minutes to twelve. She hesitated for a second: should she or shouldn't she answer? She was on her way to meet some of Horst's radical friends for lunch at twelve thirty. She didn't want to be late.

It may be Sam, it occurred to her as she rushed back to pick up the receiver.

"Sam . . . Sam, it's so good to hear your voice. I was already out the door when the phone rang. I'm so glad I picked it up. I miss you, Sam, I miss you very much."

"I miss you too. How are you?" Sartain's voice was calm and confident. Linda almost wanted to lean against it for support.

"Oh, just fine. really enjoying it. I've been meeting a lot of people. Many good leads. In fact I—"

Linda paused as she heard Sartain starting to say something on the other end; the connection was not as good as before. "What Sam? I couldn't hear you."

"I said, I've got good news." Sartain's voice sounded stronger and clearer again. "It looks like I'll be able to come to Berlin and see you after all. It hasn't been easy, but I think I'll be able to pull it off."

"Oh please, Sam, you must . . . in fact, that's what I've been trying to tell you before, the reason I called you last night . . ." She tried to remain calm and not to sound alarmed. "Sam, listen. I don't want to pressure you, but you must come here, Sam, you must. You've been right all along and—"

There was a double click on the line as if someone had hung up.

"Sam, can you hear me? Sam, are you there?"

"Yes, Linda, I'm right here." His voice once again sounded fainter.

"Something is wrong with the connection, I can barely hear you."

"I can hear you. Do you want me to hang up and try again?"

"No, no," Linda responded quickly, "I can hear you better

now, just raise your voice a little. Besides I really don't have much time. I'm already late. Listen, I can't say much now, not on the phone, but I'm into something, and it's big. Much bigger and more horrifying than what you prepared me for."

Just then there was another click on the phone.

"Sam!"

"Yes!"

"Sam, I can't discuss it on the phone. I've got to rush. But please, please come, and as soon as you can. I'll call you when I get back. I love you! I'll talk to you—"

"Linda!"

"Yes?"

"Please be careful!"

"Don't worry."

"Linda, come hell or high water, I promise you I'll be there. I love you and I miss you very much."

"Sam . . ."

"Yes?"

"I'm crazy about you!"

She hung up.

Sitting in his new office at Triple C headquarters, Atkins sensed that something was wrong, very wrong. Colonel Navon had telephoned to ask to see him immediately. His voice held a tense note of urgency. Waiting for the colonel now, Atkins knew it would not be good news that Navon carried.

Considering his rank, Atkins's Triple C office was a very modest one, much smaller than the one he occupied on the seventh floor of the CIA central building. For the time being he left the bulk of nonactive dossiers at the old office. At these new headquarters extensive filing systems, and the latest in modern communications systems (a gift of the American government) would take up all the available work space not already designated for Jeremy, as the recently acquired, but not yet installed, ultrasophisticated IBM computer was already nicknamed.

Atkins spent the morning studying the daily reports collated, evaluated, and synthesized by the permanent representatives and their staff. Most of the raw information itself was supplied on a daily basis by the intelligence services of the fourteen member states.

One of the main thrusts of the new organization was to search out the whereabouts of Carlos, presently to no avail. The Jackal had disappeared as if swallowed up by the earth. When Navon entered his office, Atkins briefly entertained the hope that the Israeli in charge of Task Force Three had some new information about Carlos. After all, a few days earlier Navon had implied that the Mossad was up to something and that he was hoping for a major breakthrough. But now the look on the man's face told Atkins that whatever the young colonel had to say, it was anything but good news. He braced himself for the worst.

"We lost two of our best agents," Navon said gravely. "And I mean two of the best . . ." He looked beaten.

Atkins remained silent, nodding solemnly. He wondered what it all meant. The death of two Mossad agents was hardly the end of the world and didn't warrant an emergency meeting. He felt somewhat ashamed. Had he become inured to death?

"I knew one of them personally," Navon continued sadly. "Intimately, you may say," he sighed, clearing his throat. "But that's not the point. The point is that with them dead, we lost the best chance we ever had of getting Carlos . . ."

Atkins felt his back stiffen. He now realized what the man was trying to tell him. It was the end of the "breakthrough" Navon had talked about. "Damn! Damn!" he wanted to exclaim. But instead he only somberly said, "Go on, please."

"Eighteen months ago these two had successfully managed to infiltrate the June Second movement in Germany . . . or, so at least we were led to believe . . . they distinguished themselves in action, they rose fast in the movement." He paused and eyed Atkins carefully, assessing the impact of what he had just said.

Atkins's brow furrowed. The message was not lost on him. "Good God!" he thought, wondering which atrocities the undercover agents had been forced to perpetrate for the sake of their mission.

"Recently," Navon continued, "they were told they were being promoted, that they would join the ranks of the international network, that they would be working closely with the Rengo Sekigun."

The Israeli colonel didn't have to explicate. Atkins knew he meant Fusako Shigenobu's group, the United Red Army which, no longer able to operate effectively in Japan, had become the most dedicated core group of Terror International.

"In fact," Navon continued, "in the last communication we

had from them, they advised us that they were about to meet with Fusako. They were to work directly under her." He nodded sadly as he paused again. "It was a once-in-a-lifetime opportunity to penetrate Carlos's inner circle."

"Too bad," Atkins said, trying to hide his disappointment. "What actually happened?"

"We don't have all the details. About two hours ago I received a message from Mossad headquarters that their bodies were recovered—both were knifed in the back. Attached to the body of one of them was a handwritten note. It said: 'Good try.' It was signed by Carlos."

He paused again before he continued, letting the meaning sink in. "Their bodies arrived this morning at our embassy in Rome, in a sealed trunk. It was an air shipment from Libya."

"Good God!" Atkins said. He could vividly imagine the shocked faces of the people who opened the trunk.

"The worst thing is," Navon stared directly into Atkins's eyes, "that there was not a single sign of torture on their bodies." His voice sounded ominous.

Atkins was puzzled. Navon's last statement didn't make any sense.

Navon waited for Atkins to show that he understood, but the man looked genuinely baffled.

"I don't understand," Atkins said.

"It means they didn't need to interrogate them," the colonel explained. "It means they felt they knew all there was to know."

"I see," Atkins said soberly, grasping now the full implication of it.

"It shows the devil's son"—Navon resorted in his frustration to a Hebrew expression—"is ten steps ahead of us, not one."

They both were silent, two professionals, two highly capable and experienced men who recognized the genius of their adversary.

It was Atkins who broke the silence, asking what alternative plans the colonel intended to pursue now that the Mossad's attempted infiltration had failed so tragically.

Navon had a number of schemes in mind, but as he himself admitted, they were all at a preliminary stage, needed a great amount of further research, and involved elaborate and intricate planning. All of which meant time.

As he listened to Navon, it became frustratingly clear to the

Triple C chief that the Jackal was in no immediate danger, that he was winning the game. Now he could only hope that Sartain was right, that Carlos was indeed far from ready to make his next big move, that he also had to take his time.

Thinking of Sartain, Atkins wished the professor was there to aid them. Maybe then, he mused somewhat self-deprecatingly, instead of ten steps, to use the colonel's own words, the Jackal would be only one step ahead of them. He reminded himself to call Sartain. Perhaps they could meet and he could pick his brain some more. He could not have expected the circumstances which were to bring him and his old friend together again so soon.

CHAPTER SIXTEEN

ULRICH, the bearded one, paced back and forth in front of Linda, alternately whacking the leather crop against hip, thigh, and the palm of his hand. His stony, dark gaze revealed no emotion. Every so often he stopped, playing the frayed tip of the crop across his fingertips.

"Why were you trying to find Dr. Karl Baumann?" Ulrich's voice thundered at her again in a heavy German accent.

Linda didn't respond. She had already learned there was no point. She stared away at the frameless painting of a dreary winter landscape. She couldn't have known that only a few weeks earlier, the two archterrorists, Carlos and Fusako, had met in the very same room with her present tormentor and set in motion the events which in a bizarre, coincidental way led to her present predicament.

Her peripheral vision caught the motion of his hand before she felt the crop lash against her face, before she felt the scorching pain.

"Look at me, you bitch! When I talk to you, you look at me!" Ulrich hissed venomously.

Linda, reeling from the blow, complied. She turned her face up to him. There was no fear in it, only scorn. The look was not lost on the East German. It infuriated him.

He went at her again, this time smacking her face with the back of his hand. He hit her with such force that she felt as if her head had been torn away from the neck. She could taste blood in her mouth. Blood dripped slowly into the shreds of her white blouse, remnants of the fierce struggle she had put up against her three abductors.

The taste of blood made Linda thirstier. But she had given up begging for water. She could have all the water she wanted, they told her, if she answered their questions, if she told them what they wanted to hear.

"What did Professor Günther tell you? Why were you meeting with him? How long have you known him? Who led you to him?"

Linda stared at her bearded interrogator. The contempt was gone from her eyes. Now the only thing they registered was sadness. She opened her mouth to respond for nearly the hundredth time to the same questions but then changed her mind and clenched her jaws together in regained defiance. There was no use. They didn't believe anything she said anyway. They knew she was lying.

This time the crop found her left ear. Ever since regaining consciousness after her abduction, it was the piercing, intermittent pain in her ear that drained her the most. Triggered again by the new blow, the searing pain was beyond tolerance, forcing her to scream in agony.

An ugly, triumphant smile crossed the German's face as he glared at Gertrude who was busy writing at the small, drop-leaf table in the corner. She raised her head and smiled back at him. Only Walter, the soft-looking, youngest member of the trio, shuddered at the scream as he boiled water in the small kitchenette.

Linda quickly recovered and bit her lower lip against the pain. She was determined not to let the Germans relish her torment.

She was surprised at her own courage. If there was a bright side to all this, it was the pride she took in her own resources of endurance. She had read a lot about men and women, such as members of the resistance groups during the Nazi occupation of Europe, who never broke, even under the worst kind of torture. It had made her wonder how much physical punishment she would be able to take under similar circumstances. And now she was discovering her own true, inner strength when it was too late, when it was all over.

"What 'big thing' are you into, my dear?" The German kept at her, mocking. "What horrible things have you discovered?"

Linda's suspicion that her kidnappers had overheard her conversation with Sartain grew stronger now. She recalled the strange clicks, which she had attributed to the bad overseas connection. Indeed her telephone at the Hotel Kempinski must have been tapped. They, whoever they were, had proven dangerously skillful.

"Who are you working for? The Mossad? The CIA? Who? Who are your contacts? Why did you come to Berlin? Why?"

The questions, the accusations continued. And again, as she failed to respond, her inquisitor lashed at her, inflicting more pain. Yet, even in her condition, she perceived that there was no real method to his questioning. He seemed only to be deriving personal pleasure from hurting her physically, from abusing her verbally. Whether he managed to extract any information from her seemed entirely secondary.

Thus, in spite of the pain that diminished her thought processes, Linda sensed that this interrogation was only a preliminary tactic. Deep inside she knew that the worst was yet to come.

Her lack of fear, the calm acceptance of her fate, continued to surprise Linda. When she was captured, when she mistook their white Mercedes for a regular Berlin cab, she fought like a wildcat. The marks of fingernails on the faces of both men were heartening evidence of the fight she had put up. Later, however, when she regained consciousness in that miserable place, she realized there was no hope. Her captors did not bother to hide their faces or identities, which confirmed her worst suspicions. Unless some miracle took place, and she was not one to believe in miracles, she was doomed, and she knew it.

What troubled Linda the most was that she might die in vain. She desperately hoped that if she were to be killed, that somehow Sam would figure out what, and who, was behind it all. She prayed that the little she had told him on the phone would prove sufficient to lead him to her killers. She did not doubt for a minute that he would try to find them.

Oh, how she wished he had called a little earlier, even just five minutes earlier . . . perhaps she would have had time to give him some more information, a few more clues. On the other hand, she carried her thoughts, if she had told him everything she knew, and if their conversation was tapped, it would have put him in the same predicament she was in. She didn't want that. And besides, if she hadn't returned to the room to answer the phone, he wouldn't have known anything, he wouldn't have had a clue.

136
SABI H. SHABTAI

And she would not have gotten to talk to him, to hear his voice that one, blessed, last time.

Try to look at the bright side of things, she tried to comfort herself as a bitter smile crossed her bruised lips. The bright side indeed.

"You goddamn Jewish bitch!" Ulrich exploded shaking the crop at her face. "I'll teach you to smile, you slut! A journalist, ah? Women and Crime, ah? I'll teach you about women and punishment!" he laughed sadistically at his own cleverness.

His arm swung. The piercing pain shot from her ear through her brain. She felt that her head was about to explode. Her spine stiffened, every nerve and muscle tightened to its limit. She clenched her teeth and somehow managed not to scream. Gradually her body loosened, slowly growing numb, immune to any more pain.

"A very clever cover indeed," Ulrich sneered, "You dirty Jews are very clever, aren't you?"

Linda didn't respond, slipping gradually into semi-consciousness. Her unresponsiveness, however, pushed the East German into hysteria.

"You scum! You scum! You scum!" he shrieked, striking her alternately with his bare fists and his crop until her face was a bloody pulp and her chest and arms showed red and blue.

Linda's head dropped. She was close to passing out when Gertrude suddenly grabbed Ulrich's arm.

"Stop it, Ulrich. You'll kill her! Not now, please! We need her alive. Please, not yet!"

The East German, struggling to free his arm from Gertrude's hold, regained control of himself. He let her raise Linda's head and check her eyes to see that she was still alive. He turned away and walked to the sagging, threadbare sofa where he slumped down, scowling.

"Get me a cup of coffee!" he ordered the young German at the kitchenette.

Walter nodded silently. He had never liked Ulrich. He liked him now even less.

Linda's pain was superseded only by her thirst. *"Wasser, bitte,"* she begged, turning to Gertrude, using the little German she knew.

Gertrude looked at Ulrich.

"*Nein!*" he shook his head. "She should be grateful she is still alive. *Nein!*"

Linda wished she had lost all consciousness. To take her mind off the pain and thirst, she thought again of Sam.

If she had only five minutes with him, what would she tell him? There were so many things, there was so much, so much she wanted to say, so much she wanted to explain.

There was a knock at the door. For a brief second Linda saw a faint ray of hope. But she caught the smile on Ulrich's face. When the knocks repeated themselves in the same pattern, she realized with disappointment that someone had been expected.

Ulrich motioned to Walter, and the young man disappeared into the small foyer.

Linda heard the door being unbolted and opened. She could hear an exchange of male voices, of greetings in German.

A few seconds later, when she saw the man who followed Walter into the room, her heart almost stopped beating.

Oh, God! she thought. Now it all began to fall into place. Oh God! How could she have been so stupid, so blind? Now it all made sense . . . deadly, evil sense.

The tall, thin man who entered the room was none other than Horst Vogel.

Vogel granted Linda only a very brief glance, devoid of any recognition. He smiled at Ulrich who rose from the couch to greet him.

"I have it," he said in German and pulled out of his pocket what seemed to be a vial of serum. "This should make her talk."

Ulrich nodded. "It will." His voice was even, and once again his face had become expressionless.

As Horst pulled a syringe from another pocket and handed it and the vial to Gertrude, he turned and with a cruel smile winked at the crushed and bruised woman who only a few days before he had welcomed to Berlin with a bouquet of red roses.

Linda's heart sank as she was gripped by a final despair. She knew she had been bested. She would be forced to talk in spite of her resolve. "Oh, Sam," she cried silently, and the first tears rolled down her cheeks, turning crimson as they mixed with her own blood.

CHAPTER SEVENTEEN

SARTAIN'S movements were mechanical, robotlike. He removed the two guns from the leather case and began dismantling the smaller-caliber one first, the .22 Walther. It was the shorter PPk model, preferable to him for certain purposes to the PP. He considered the German Walther the best semiautomatic in the world.

With a proficiency he never lost the professor pulled the trigger guard downward, pushing it sideways with his right index finger and allowing it to rest on the underside of the frame. Continuing to hold the trigger guard in that position, he pulled the slide all the way back and then lifted it off to allow it to glide forward. Now that the pistol had been taken down to its three main components, he began cleaning it, alternating between the cleaning rod and the gun cloth. His face was a total blank, and even though he stared at the gun in his hands, he never really saw it.

When he hadn't heard from her, Sartain felt in his bones that something was wrong. He had tried to call her twice that evening, but she didn't answer. And when there was no response to the messages he left, and when he discovered that she never returned to her room that night, he knew something was very wrong. He had braced himself for the worst.

Ever since that beautiful day at Angel Island that faint sense of dread had never left him. Now she was dead, and in the most perverse manner possible his instincts had been vindicated. How he had known, as they made love among the eucalypti, that the serenity of the moment would not be his to hold, he could not say. But he had known it. The only thing he had never suspected was that it would be Linda who would have to pay . . . The hand gripping the barrel quivered slightly.

If only it had been his life they took. The pain was unbearable. He would not think. He would concentrate on what he was doing, on what he planned to do. But her image came alive in his mind, and against his will his memory forced him to see scenes of them, together, forced him to know what he refused to know: that he would never see her again, that she was gone forever . . . that she was now an immobile, lifeless corpse, his Linda. No, there was no other way but to shut his mind to it.

And to hate. To hate with all his soul, and to contemplate the revenge he was going to extract from those who were responsible. Those who had taken the life of what to him was the incarnation of everything good, pure, and beautiful on this earth.

He reassembled the Walther, loaded both magazines with seven rounds each, and laid the gun aside by its shoulder holster.

He pulled the Colt Python from the case and weighed and fondled it mindlessly in his hands. It was a .357 magnum, a high-caliber revolver he had been partial to and had trusted for many years. It had seen much action in his hands and had never failed him. He rotated the drum with an expert, familiar touch and began taking it apart.

If only he could cry . . . but he couldn't. He didn't know how anymore. And even if he could, he wasn't sure he wanted to. It might soften him, it might impede him. No, he preferred it this way, with every emotion a creek flowing into one big river of hate. Every other feeling would be kept numb. He would stay away from sorrow, from grief, from self-pity. He had kept himself apart from everyone, refused to talk about Linda's death, refused to mourn. At the university none knew about his personal tragedy. In the last few days he held himself together, completing his business as usual. Perhaps he was a tad more reserved, taciturn; but no one noticed.

Satisfied that the magnum also was in perfect working order and thoroughly cleaned, he began to reassemble it. Revenge, he thought, came first. Nothing else mattered. Tomorrow was death to Linda's killers. The day after tomorrow didn't exist.

He collected the guns, the silencers, the holster, and the ammunition and walked to the bedroom. Deep inside him there was still something of the old Sartain, something which questioned his motives, something which he refused to acknowledge. He had convinced himself that Linda would want him to avenge her, and the conviction inured him against any self-doubt. It gave him strength he hadn't realized in years. In the past forty-eight hours he had not shut his eyes, nor had he eaten as much as a piece of bread. And yet his hands were steady, and he felt no fatigue, as if he had acquired superhuman powers.

He had awakened that sorrowful day at 5 A.M., trembling all over, covered with cold sweat, his heart palpitating. Later the coroner's examination determined Linda's time of death at around midnight Berlin time. He knew she was thinking of him when she died, when they killed her, when they killed him.

He neatly packed the weapons and the other accessories into the specially designed compartment in the false-bottomed suitcase. He hadn't used the case for this purpose in many years, centuries, it seemed.

Carefully locking the compartment, he proceeded mindlessly to pack his clothes. As much as he kept fighting it, the image of her being tortured, battered, and molested flashed vividly on his mind screen, as if piercing his brain with a long sharp needle. He shut his eyes hard against the pain, forcing the picture blank.

Only once had he let go. It was right after he was notified by telephone. Sitting at the kitchen table, staring nowhere, both fists raised in anguish, the first reality of her death shot searingly into his mind, and his fists came down crushing with such ferocity that the wooden table caved in on his knees, its shattered pieces grazing his legs. But the physical pain was a welcomed relief from the mental torment. That had been two days ago, yet it seemed like time had stopped and he was stuck in an eternity of hell.

Ready to fasten the large Samsonite suitcase, he glimpsed Linda's picture which stood atop one of the bookshelves. He had taken the snapshot in their backyard at Tiburon only a few months before. He had caught her unawares leaning over a rosebush about to smell the blossom which she held in her long, delicate fingers.

He took the picture from the shelf and touched it longingly. How he wished he could crawl back through the lens into that gone-forever day. Linda! Linda! he cried out without words. Linda!

"Good evening, sir. Where to?" the cabbie greeted the professor respectfully.

"Dulles Airport." Sartain's reply was curt.

The driver nodded and noted the time and destination in his book. As he pulled out of the driveway, he studied his wide-shouldered passenger in the rear-view mirror. He could tell by the grim expression on the man's face that he was not in a conversational mood. He decided to forgo the customary chitchat on the weather and instead concentrate on driving.

As they headed for Key Bridge and the Washington Memorial Parkway, neither the cabdriver nor the professor were aware of the black Chevrolet which had been following them from the very moment they pulled away from Sartain's building.

"Whatcha carrying there?" the blond ticket agent at the Pan American counter winked. So far she had been unsuccessful at eliciting a smile from the professor, whom she found exceptionally handsome despite the stern expression on his face. He was definitely her type, she mused. She had a thing for mature, sophisticated-looking men.

Sartain, in a sporty camel suit with an open-neck brown shirt which perfectly suited his complexion, granted her a quizzical look. "I'm sorry, I didn't hear what you said."

"I said you're a few pounds overweight. I mean . . . your luggage." She blushed coquettishly as she pointed at the large gray Samsonite on the scales. "But it's okay, I'll let it go. It's only a few pounds," she winked again. She was a pretty young woman, and she knew it.

"Thank you," Sartain answered brusquely, without a trace of the acknowledgment she seemed to have expected.

Snubbed and all business now, the agent tagged his suitcase and returned his passport and ticket without looking up. She handed him the boarding card which told him his flight to Frankfurt would be leaving from gate five. "Your flight is on time," she said, "so you should easily make your connecting flight to Berlin tomorrow morning. I sent your baggage through to Berlin, and you'll have fifty-five minutes between arrival and departure in Frankfurt. Have a good flight, Professor Sartain." She tried one last dazzling smile.

Sartain nodded absentmindedly, grabbed his briefcase and headed toward the escalator. As the twice-rebuffed blonde followed him with her large green eyes, she shook her head. Pity such an attractive man never smiled. She shrugged and turned to attend the next passenger in line, a tall young man with a big friendly grin.

Having passed through the metal detectors at the screening gate, Sartain proceeded to the boarding area. He took a seat, lighted his pipe, and waited for the call to board the modern mobile lounge which would take him to the DC-10.

Even the airport hubbub could not stir Sartain from his thoughts. His mind was in Berlin, planning, calculating his next move. His brain was functioning normally, rationally, ordered to be undisturbed by the pain in his soul.

He hadn't yet figured out the exact motives behind Linda's murder, but he could begin to guess. Whoever did it would pay, he swore to himself. He kept repeating it in the back of his mind, as if he was also making a silent promise to Linda.

The danger, the risks involved, were of absolutely no consequence to him. Without Linda life had become totally meaningless. He knew he might get himself killed. But it didn't matter as long as he could take some of them with him.

It was different now than it had been in Saipan when his closest buddy, Dave, was cut down by Japanese fire. It had been a total blind fury which swept over him when he grabbed the flamethrower from the corporal and stormed forward alone against the blazing machine-gun nests. Then it was a temporary insanity, and years after he still had difficulty reconciling himself to the act which had earned him a Silver Star.

Linda had once suggested that perhaps what overtook him in Saipan was not so much an uncontrolled thirst for revenge as it was a release, after endless months of combat, of long, bottled-in fear. But if there was fear then, there was none now.

"Pan American flight sixty-nine is ready for boarding at gate number five," the disembodied voice poured through the lounge.

Sartain rose slowly, gathering the briefcase from the floor beside him. Proceeding toward the gate, his way was suddenly blocked by two stout-looking fellows, taller even than he was.

"Professor Sartain?" the one in the blue blazer inquired.

The professor nodded cautiously.

The man reached inside his blazer.

Sartain's eyes hardened as he followed the sudden move. He quickly stepped back; his grip tightened around the briefcase handle as the heavy valise became a weapon about to let loose.

Instead of a gun, however, the man pulled out a badge. "Airport security," he uttered officially as he showed it to Sartain. "Please come with us."

The professor was led to a sizable, modern, windowless office, lit by harsh fluorescent lights. The nameplate on the imposing bare desk identified it as the bastion of one Paul H. Williamson, DIRECTOR OF AIRPORT SECURITY. The name was unfamiliar.

Sartain sat on the vinyl chair whose thin armrests were made of cold stainless metal and stared blankly at the heavy armchair behind the desk. He awaited the appearance of Mr. Williamson.

Fifteen minutes passed, and the director still failed to show up. Growing irritable, Sartain rose from the chair and walked to the door. As soon as he opened it, he was confronted by the two officers in mufti.

"How long do I have to wait here? Where in blazes is that director of yours? Why the hell are you holding me anyway?" Sartain demanded. "My flight is leaving in twelve minutes, and I sure as hell don't want to miss it."

The guard assured him he would make his flight, saying that its departure had been delayed at least forty minutes. The director would be there soon.

"Am I being detained? If I am—"

"No, sir, you're certainly not," the officer in the dark blue blazer hastened to assure him. "But please, sir, try to understand. We're only doing what we're told, we're only doing our job."

Sartain studied the young man in front of him and then without saying another word closed the door and returned to his chair.

Moments later he heard the door being reopened. He didn't bother to turn around to face the person who walked in. But when the man lay a friendly hand on his shoulder, Sartain looked up, startled. Gazing down at him was the face of the Triple C chief.

CHAPTER EIGHTEEN

THEY had already passed the Army and Navy Country Club on the Shirley Memorial Highway when Colonel Joseph Navon finally brought himself to tell his wife what had been occupying his thoughts all evening. The two of them had just finished a delightful dinner, Middle Eastern style, at the home of another Israeli couple in Georgetown. Now they were heading southwest toward their home in the suburb of Monticello Park in Alexandria. It was the house which had been on his mind.

They had inherited it from the former cultural attaché at the Israeli Embassy who had been abruptly ordered home before the end of his term just when Colonel Navon and his family arrived at the capital looking for a place to live.

It was definitely a *metzia*, a real find. A well-furnished house in a good neighborhood for very little money. It belonged to a family that had moved to Israel a couple of years back but had decided to hold on to their Washington property as a rent house. The Israeli cultural attaché had been a close friend, and when he was forced suddenly to leave, they were only too happy to arrange through him for another Israeli official to have the place.

Thus, for what they would have had to pay for a much smaller place in town, the Navons had a real house with ample yard in a peaceful, verdant suburb where the kids could spend much time outdoors. It was not a very large house by any means, nor was it very new, but it did have three large bedrooms and a small swimming pool. It was the pool which made the real difference for the children, who for the second time in their lives had been uprooted from their home in Zahala, a charming, treed community north of Tel Aviv where they had romped with other children of the Israeli defense establishment.

"Sarah," the young colonel began in Hebrew, "I've some bad

news." He kept his eyes on the road, where the traffic was heavy for so late in the evening. He could feel her turn to watch his face in the lights of the oncoming cars; her large almond eyes studying his facial expression.

The two of them had been together ever since Joseph could remember, from the first time when he gave her a ride home on his bicycle as they were returning from an afternoon at the Youth Movement's "hut." He was fourteen then, and she was a year younger. He could still recall that wonderful sensation he felt with her scented hair brushing his face as she rode sideways on the top brace of his bicycle, leaning lightly against his arm. It was a feeling he would never forget as long as he lived.

Sarah used to wear her thick wavy hair very long then. She had lots of freckles and the cutest pointed nose he had ever seen, "a real *shikse* nose," as her elders used to affectionately tease her. Everyone loved her then. Twenty years later she still had the cutest nose, and in the summer her freckles came alive. Her hair was cut fashionably short now, at Sassoon's. Everyone still loved and respected Sarah, but no one more than her husband.

Those who knew the young colonel well dubbed him the Rock of Gibraltar, referring to his strength and reliability. But the soft-spoken man knew that much of his resilience drew itself from Sarah and the durability of their relationship.

"It's not that bad," Navon was quick to reassure her as he took his hand off the wheel and softly caressed her knee. "I'm not going away again, nothing like that . . ." He knew how much she hated his long periods of absence. When he was in charge of some of the Wrath of God actions in Europe, he had had to disappear for as long as six months at a time, without being able to let her know where he was. She always accepted it, but he knew how difficult it was for her and the children.

Navon once, inadvertently, came across a hidden bundle of letters; there must have been at least a hundred of them there. They were letters written by her and addressed to him; letters which had never been sent. They were full of love, longing, and loneliness. He never revealed that he had read the letters; he knew she wouldn't want him to know how much she suffered when he was away. He knew she was afraid it would weaken him if he were conscious of her pining. Yet he planned to tell her one day. Perhaps when he retired. Then he would tell her and thank her. For now he could generalize by airing his opinion that it was the wives and sweethearts back home who were the true stalwarts of Israel's struggle for survival.

". . . It's just that we'll have to move into the city and very soon." He let it all out in one breath. "My request for special permission to remain in the house has been irrevocably denied," he explained. "They want us to move in no more than a month."

She was silent for a moment, then spoke. "That's a shame," she said. "The children love it so much there." There was a note of sadness, of disappointment, in her voice, but she quickly composed herself. She knew it was hard enough for him without adding her own feelings of loss. "Where will we have to move?" she asked much more matter-of-factly.

"Well, like the rest of them, we'll have to move into a security building."

Sarah knew that by the "rest of them" her husband meant the other high-ranking Embassy officials, and that by a "security building" he meant any of the city's high-rises which had a doorman and twenty-four-hour security. She was familiar with the strict regulations; the flat could not be located, for example, on the first two floors of the building nor on the top one—a precautionary measure aimed at making access to the apartment from either the ground level, or the roof as difficult as possible.

"I'm going to look at a couple of buildings on Wisconsin Avenue tomorrow. Would you like to join me?"

"Of course I would," she said as she squeezed the hand on her knee encouragingly. She was thinking at the same time how she would break the news to the children. They had made friends already with some of the neighbors' kids, and she knew all too well that they would find it very difficult to adapt to confined apartment life. She almost sighed but held it back. She could easily imagine how much Yossi hated having to tell her, and she was not going to make it even more difficult for him.

Ten minutes later, when they reached their home, Navon pulled into the gravel driveway to let his wife out at the front door before he drove the extra fifty feet to the garage.

"Would you put on some water for me," Navon said as Sarah stepped out of the car. "I would love to have a good cup of coffee. I really have to do some reading tonight before I hit the sack."

"Of course," she said affectionately, making sure there was not a shade of sadness in her eyes. "How about a Turkish coffee?"

"No thanks," he shook his head. "Too strong."

"All right. Now don't take too long, ah . . ." She winked at him, smiling, and shut the door.

Navon stopped the station wagon in front of the garage and got out. As he bent down to grasp the handle of the aluminum garage door, about to pull it up, he heard a soft male voice calling him by his Hebrew name "Yossi!"

Puzzled, Navon stood up, turning toward the voice. Blinded somewhat by his car's headlights, he shaded his eyes with his hand. "*Me ze?* Who is that?" he asked both in Hebrew and English.

The soft, teasing voice which came from behind the dark bushes answered in a slightly Latin-accented English: "It's me, Yossi. I hear you've been looking for me. Well, I've been looking for you too. Remember Boudia?"

The very instant he heard the name of Carlos's Algerian mentor, Colonel Navon, the product of the finest commando training in the world, reacted reflexively, without the slightest hesitation.

He dived sideways to the ground, out of the car's light beam. Even before he hit the ground, his hand had reached for the Beretta which he always carried tucked behind in his belt.

But it was too late, even for him; he was a sitting duck. Two quick, muffled shots barely disturbed the quiet suburban night. Neither of them came from Navon's only half-drawn gun.

"Sa-rah!" the dying Israeli war hero screamed, shattering the heavy silence. "Sa-rah!"

As she came out of the house, running frantically toward the garage, her desperate cry "Yossi!" was almost drowned in the noise of a car roaring away.

"I should have known you had something to do with this," the professor responded to Atkins's greeting without a tinge of warmth or humor in his voice.

Atkins shrugged apologetically in the face of his friend's indignation. He had expected it. "Well," the Triple C chief said, retaining his amicable posture, "I see you're off to Berlin. May I ask for what reason?"

"Pal," Sartain said, obviously hostile, "I'm sorry I have to be blunt, but it's none of your goddamn business." He glanced at his watch and rose from the chair, heading for the door.

"One moment, Sam!" Atkins blocked the door, trying to remain pleasant under the difficult circumstances. "Gerry!" he called.

The door opened immediately, and the young man in the blue blazer walked in. He shot a quick glance at the professor who had stopped, annoyance registered all over his face.

"Gerry, will you please bring in the suitcase."

Gerry nodded and disappeared behind the door.

The professor stared down angrily at the much shorter, bearded man who had beads of perspiration beginning to form on his forehead.

Atkins refused to be intimidated. "What are you planning to do in Berlin, Sam?" He wiped his sweaty brow with the back of his hand.

Sartain was about to say something, but then reconsidered. Granting his old boss a contemptuous glare, he turned and went back to his chair. He sat, jaw clenched, and resumed his silence.

"Sam," Atkins said softly, trying to mollify him, "I'm your friend, Sam. I'm only trying to help." He sat also and pulled the chair up facing his friend, who did not respond.

There was a knock on the door. "Sir?"

"Okay, Gerry. You can come in."

The tall young man entered, carrying Sartain's gray Samsonite. Atkins motioned in the direction of the large desk, and the young man placed the heavy suitcase on top of it. He exchanged a quick look with his boss and left the room.

Atkins walked behind the desk and without saying a word opened the suitcase. He reached under the garments for the hidden mechanism and quickly unlocked the false-bottomed compartment, revealing the two wrapped pistols and the other accessories.

"You forget, Sam, we were the ones who gave you this case."

The professor remained silent, sitting straight in the chair, his unflinching gaze fixed on an invisible spot on the wall opposite.

Failing to draw a reaction, the Triple C chief decided to change his approach.

"Listen, Sam, I know how you feel. I know. Believe me, Sam, it grieves me to no end. I know how much you loved her. I'm sorry, truly sorry." He studied the professor's face for some sign of acknowledgment. There was none.

"I also read the German police report," he continued and then paused briefly to let what he had to say sink in. "I can assure you that I for one do not accept its conclusion. I do not accept," he hesitated slightly, "that it was a rape-homicide perpetrated by some deranged psychopath."

Sartain remained mute, but his expression did change. Facial muscles twitched involuntarily. He closed his eyes and bit his lips together, betraying the inner torment.

Atkins resumed his monologue. "Correct me if I'm wrong, Sam, but I presume that you suspect Linda's murder to be the work of German terrorists. More specifically the Baader-Meinhof gang. I think you suspect that Linda had uncovered something in her journalistic research. Most probably certain information which imperiled the . . . the bastards and . . . and they decided to do away with her, disguising it as a common crime of assault by some sex maniac." He shrugged sadly. "Well, am I right?"

Atkins waited for Sartain to answer. The silence was heavy. And then the professor's jaws unclenched. His lips finally moved. "It was no ordinary sex crime." His voice was tight, barely audible.

"Then, am I wrong to deduce," said the Triple C chief encouraged by the response, however terse, "that the reason you're going to Berlin, toting guns like some wild cowboy, is to avenge the death of your fiancée?"

Realizing, by the expression on the professor's face, that he might have pushed a bit too far, Atkins immediately apologized for sounding sarcastic. "I'm sorry. I just couldn't help it, Sam. Your behavior is so confounded irrational that . . ."

"Fred," Sartain didn't let him finish. There was a new, strange expression in his face as he enunciated each word in a steely voice. "Not you, nor the Agency, nor anyone else can stop me. Put it straight into your head. They killed the one woman I loved, and I'm going to get whoever did it, if it's the last thing I do. You can delay me, but you can't stop me."

Atkins shook his head incredulously. "Are you going to do it alone?"

"Alone," said the professor, determined, "and don't be smug with me, Fred. Save it for someone else, for one of your boys." He motioned contemptuously with his head in the direction of the door. "You know me better than that."

"True," said Atkins, "I do know you better than that. That's why I can't comprehend . . . I just can't believe that you, of all people, would go off half-cocked like this, knowing the kind of people you are up against." He shook his head again.

Sartain kept silent, uncompromising. He checked his watch impatiently as if everything Atkins had said was merely boring small talk.

"The way I see it," Atkins went on, unwilling to give up just yet, "is that you're—I don't know exactly how to put it—that you're so obsessed with your personal grief that you must be entertaining some sort of a death wish . . . which, believe me, Linda's killers will be more than happy to fulfill.

"This obsession of yours, my dear friend, is blinding you to the facts. It makes you even more vulnerable than any simple Joe Blow out there. Sam, you've been under constant surveillance ever since yesterday, and you didn't know it. You didn't even notice that you were being followed by my 'boys' from the moment you left your house this evening. Now, tell me, what kind of a chance do you think you really have all alone in Berlin?"

"I know exactly what I'm doing," Sartain retorted stubbornly, yet with slightly less conviction. Could he have been that unaware?

"You do, ah?" Atkins challenged him. "Do you know, for example, that more likely than not the man responsible for Linda's murder is Ilich Ramirez Sanchez?"

Atkins had touched a raw nerve.

"Carlos?" the professor gasped. He was suddenly fully alert, his gaze sharp and penetrating.

"Yes, Sam. The Jackal himself."

The professor didn't say anything, but his eyes implored Atkins to continue.

"The Germans," Atkins said, "managed to extract out of the recaptured Erika Küzler—she was one of the four women—"

"I know," the professor nodded.

". . . that Fusako Shigenobu was in Berlin at the time of her capture. In fact Erika admitted that it was Fusako who had sent her on the errand that led to her arrest. Anyway we also have reason to suspect now that Carlos was in Berlin after the Entebbe raid." Atkins paused briefly before he continued. "A gun used recently by a PFLP man in Berlin to kill two French DST agents who tailed him was found to be the same one that Carlos used to shoot that Jewish British tycoon . . . I forget his name."

"Sieff, Joseph Edward Sieff the president of Marks and Spencer."

"Right. That was almost three years back," Atkins said, thinking at the same time, that if the professor's personal tragedy affected his actions, at least it didn't seem to cloud his phenomenal memory. "Anyway I strongly suspect that Linda was on to something, something big, and that's why they did away with her."

"Carlos!" the professor demanded impatiently. "Carlos? You said the Jackal was behind it. So far you haven't told me anything to substantiate it. How do you know Carlos was responsible?"

"I didn't say I know for sure, Sam," Atkins answered defensively. "I said 'more likely than not.' We have good reason to believe—"

"What good reason? What evidence? The fact that some Arab used a gun which supposedly belonged to Carlos?" Sartain was becoming angry and scornful again.

The Triple C chief chose his words carefully. "Linda, we've just now discovered, may have tried to leave us a message."

"A message?" Sartain couldn't contain himself. "I wasn't told anything about a message! What are you trying to say?" He rose from his chair and stepped toward Atkins. "What have you been hiding from me?"

"Sit down, please," Atkins begged as he himself sank back into the heavy desk chair. "We haven't been hiding anything. Please sit down and listen."

The professor reluctantly retreated.

"When I first learned of Linda's murder, because of her connection to you and the subject of her assignment, I asked the Verfassungsschutz to look into the case." Atkins took for granted that the professor was familiar with the federal Office for the Protection of the Constitution, the West German equivalent of the FBI. "A closer examination by them revealed some things which went undetected in the first autopsy. Besides discovering that Linda had been drugged with a truth serum some fourteen hours before her death, scratches on the small of her back, initially attributed to the sexual assault, along with the many other bruises, formed what looked like four awkwardly etched letters.

The professor's back stiffened. "What four letters?"

"C, A, R, L."

"C, A, R, L? Carl?"

"Yes, Carl. Or at least that was the name we thought the crude letters indicated. There were two possibilities: either the deranged killer left his incised mark on his victim's body"—Atkins wished he didn't have to go into specifics as he sadly watched the torment on the professor's face—"or Linda managed somehow, with hands still tied behind her back, to scratch her assailant's name into her own flesh. After all Carl is a common German name."

"Not with a C," the professor stated soberly.

"I know," Atkins said, "the German representative pointed that out to me, and indeed a closer inspection of Linda's fingernails revealed traces of her own skin and blood underneath their tips. It led the Germans to conclude that, being an American, she just didn't know how to spell her assailant's name the German way. But I had my own doubts by then. And sure enough, further examination revealed that the scratches attributed to Linda's nails consisted of the name Carl plus a sort of apostrophe at the end. Only that I strongly suspect," his eyes locked into the professor's, "that it was no apostrophe, but the beginning of another letter, the letter O. My guess is that Linda was interrupted when she was desperately trying to tell us it was Carlos."

"Carlos," Sartain whispered, his brow creased in deep, painful thought. There was a long silence before the professor muttered half audibly, as though speaking to himself. "She was trying to tell me . . . it had to do with Carlos . . . poor Linda." He shook his head with half-closed eyes as if vividly imagining what she had to go through, her suffering; his fists tightened until the knuckles almost burst through the taut, stretched skin.

"That's what I've been trying to tell you, Sam," Atkins finally endeavored to resume his argument. "Alone, you just don't stand a chance. Not against him and his international gang. It would be pure suicide. If you really want to avenge Linda's death, then do it with us.

"Come aboard, Sam. We need you and you need us. That man is up to something new, something horrible which, as you yourself said, may take place here. Together we may be able to stop him. How about it?"

Just then, the white telephone on the director's desk rang. Atkins, disturbed by the inopportune interruption, let it ring for a few seconds before reaching for it.

The Triple C chief's expression changed drastically as he listened to the voice on the other end, and when he put down the receiver, he looked unusually stern.

"It may be already beginning," he said in a grim voice. "The Israeli representative to the Triple C, Colonel Joseph Navon, was just shot to death in front of his house in Monticello Park. The assassins got away." Atkins's gaze under the puckered, bushy eyebrows was piercing. "Well, Sam?"

The professor stared back at him and then at the suitcase and the guns on the desk. He kept silent, but the struggle within him was apparent.

Atkins moved from behind the desk and strode toward the door. "I'm sorry, Sam," he said, not bothering to conceal his growing ire, "but I no longer have the time, nor the patience, to mollycoddle you. You want to go to Berlin, you can go. Nobody is going to stop you. As far as I am concerned, you can bloody well go to hell too."

He opened the door and was about to slam it shut behind him when the professor moved toward it.

"Wait, Fred!" he called after his disgruntled friend. "Wait!"

Atkins turned.

"We'll both wind up in hell sooner or later," Sartain acceded. "We might as well go there together."

PART 2

CHAPTER NINETEEN

I T had been exactly six weeks since the fleeing Helga Denz had crossed the border to East Berlin, and now she was heading south on another continent, down Interstate 55. The drive through the remarkably flat Illinois countryside was exceedingly monotonous. The freeway stretched on for miles and miles, with gas stations and McDonald's proving to be welcomed points of interest along the road. Here and there some scattered farmhouses rendered the landscape a little more appealing. But, by and large, even they were daubed in drab grayish tints.

Helga was not disappointed. She had already been told that the trip south would be anything but exciting. Yet she found it hard to remain alert, to take in details as she probably should have. The monotony of the drive made it too difficult; her mind kept wandering off to the preceding days. They had been eventful, she reflected, particularly on the day she snuck across the Canadian border into Vermont.

She had first landed in Montreal with her newly forged passport. She liked Montreal. Beside being remarkably beautiful, it was a large, vibrant city, as cosmopolitan as any. It was an ideal place to melt into the multinational crowd, to become inconspicuous. It was the sort of place where one's accent or foreign habits attracted little attention. There she still felt very safe. Even Chicago failed to give her that sense of security: it was much too American. She recalled what one of her fellow teachers at the kindergarten had said upon returning from a summer vacation in the States. "Chicago," she had stated, "is the largest American city. New York and Los Angeles are international cities, but they're not really American . . ."

Helga had never been to New York or Los Angeles, but from what she had gathered, that remark must have been true. At least the three major cities she passed through on that long Greyhound ride from Vermont to Chicago—Buffalo, Cleveland, and Detroit—were all very American in character, and very much the smaller replicas of Chicago. Next time, Helga promised herself, she would try to go to New York and Los Angeles. She would have particularly liked to see Disneyland. Ever since childhood she had craved to go there; it held a special fascination for her. In the meantime, and for a long time, she would just have to be satisfied with life in Morris, Illinois. From what she already knew about the place, it was no Disneyland. She knew that for some time she would probably long for those few days she spent in Chicago; that even Cleveland, Ohio, would seem like a dream city.

The green freeway sign told Helga in bold white letters that she was approaching the Illinois 30 exit. She reached for the Standard Oil map and placed it against the steering wheel. She consulted it briefly, only slightly easing her foot off the gas pedal, and estimated that she had another twenty to twenty-five minutes before she would have to change to Interstate 80.

Her thoughts now drifted to Karl. It had been more than eight years since she last saw him. What was he like now? Had he aged much? "Now let's see," she muttered to herself as she tried to remember. He must be forty-six by now . . . yes she recalled, he was thirteen years older than she. Would he fall for her again? Did he know about her recent past? He must. Her capture the year before was not much publicized, not abroad anyway, but her recent escape was. Unless he read just local papers . . . her name would not have appeared there.

Helga shook her head. No, she couldn't count on it. He must know. And if he didn't, it wouldn't take long before he did. Would he turn her in? A bitter smile crossed her lips. This, after all, was the sixty-four-thousand-dollar question. He did have a wife now and two kids.

It was indeed a great risk Carlos had asked her to take, Helga thought. Yet the whole plan, the biggest and most daring ever, now depended on her. She had been catapulted from the rank and file of the Red Army Faction, and being merely Ralf's girl friend, to the innermost circle of Carlos's Terror International.

She had been told by the Jackal that outside himself and Fusako no one else knew as much about the operation as she did, not even Wadi Haddad.

To be entrusted with such an enormous responsibility was naturally a bit unsettling, yet Helga savored it, the great risks involved notwithstanding. Besides, it was better than being cooped up in the Lehrterstrasse prison. She knew all too well that if it had not been for her indispensability to the operation, and all due to a bizarre coincidence, Carlos would not have considered breaking her out.

She was no fool. No one would have gone to such trouble and expense just for her, while far more important comrades were still languishing behind bars. Worse comes to worse, she comforted herself, she would be back where she was before, in jail. And before they parted, both Carlos and Fusako had assured her that if that came to pass, she would be at the top of the list of those whose freedom they would demand in any future hostage-taking operation. Any way she looked at it, she couldn't really complain; even Morris would be better than the Berlin prison. If only she could have Brigitte with her.

The highway sign indicated fifteen miles to Interstate 80. Well it wouldn't be long now before she would be in Karl's town. As her thoughts began drifting back to him, she felt a warm, tingling sensation in her genitals. It felt odd, almost foreign. She had been without a man for a long time, ever since her imprisonment. The first few weeks had been the most difficult, forcing her to heavy masturbation. But then slowly and gradually she took sex and men completely out of her mind, concentrating her attention and affection on Brigitte instead. Subconsciously she must have always had latent lesbian tendencies which until prison had found their expression every so often in strange, freakish heterosexual relationships.

When Helga escaped from the Lehrterstrasse prison, her mind was on anything but sex with men. If she missed anything at all, it was Brigitte. Moreover Fusako explicitly warned her to stay away, until the whole thing was over, from either men or women. Now, however, when she thought about the nearing encounter with Karl, she was suddenly overtaken by a sudden upsurge of passion. More than lustful, she felt thrilled, agitated. All in a way which she never felt about Brigitte. The young, delicate prisonmate unearthed in her totally different emotions. They were feelings of unbounded tenderness, of warmth and protectiveness which she had never really experienced before. Karl, on the other hand, triggered feverish sensations which bordered on violence. With him she used to feel constantly on the verge of exploding into tiny little pieces, as if her whole existence was about to end any moment.

Helga knew that it was not really Karl himself, but the nature of their relationship which turned her on. She realized that if she was to remain in control, that if she was again to be so totally irresistible to him, she must never show that she too enjoyed the relationship. She must show no pleasure, not until the very moment of climax, always to be followed by remorse, by disdain.

When she thought about it, Karl's sexual hang-ups seemed to have little to do with the classic sadist-masochist relationship. She was neither psychologist nor psychiatrist, but she intuitively gathered that what Karl Baumann craved for was of a far more complicated nature, a sort of masochist-masochist relationship, singularly built on the twisted excitement of suffering both physical pain and mental anguish. As much as he enjoyed his own physical abuse, he savored what he viewed as her own mental distress in being forced to partake in it.

The flashing blue light of the highway patrol snapped her from her thoughts. Helga's initial reaction was to press hard on the gas pedal, but the cool professional in her took over. The squad car may not be after her, and if it is, it may only be for a simple moving violation. No, she should be careful not to jump the gun. Her papers were all in order, prepared by Klaus von Brückner himself, the top East German expert on forgery. There was no reason for undue alarm, not yet anyway.

She checked the speedometer and slightly reduced her speed. She had been cruising well within the fifty-five-mile speed limit. She had been sticking to the right lane all along, and she didn't recall passing anyone for some time.

The careening police car closed in, and now she could already see in the side-view mirror the officer's moustached face. He wore dark glasses, and she couldn't really tell if he was focusing on her or not. His face, as much as she could tell, seemed very official and expressionless.

Within seconds his white and blue car zoomed by her at top speed, overtaking a few more cars ahead of her as well, disappearing fast into the horizon. Her chest heaved a sigh of relief, the grip on the 9-mm Smith and Wesson beside her eased. It was Carlos who had insisted that she use an American-made gun.

CHAPTER TWENTY

IF any of the permanent representatives attending the general meeting of the Triple C harbored any private thoughts regarding the murder of Colonel Joseph Navon, they kept them to themselves. Yet none of them could seriously accept the theory advanced by the FBI that the colonel was merely a victim of just another too frequent D.C. attempted armed robbery. They knew better. For them all it served as a tangible danger signal, an ominous precedent. One of their most distinguished and competent members had been liquidated within miles of their headquarters, and the killers had managed to escape without a trace. The ramifications were rendered even more sinister considering that the Israeli colonel had been selected only the month prior to head TF-3, the unit assigned to track down Carlos and his close lieutenants.

"I spoke with Echad recently," Fred Atkins looked around the room at the gloomy faces of the representatives. "He promised me that the Mossad will replace Colonel Navon with an equally qualified member of their intelligence community. The Israelis do not even suggest that it was a security breach on our part that led to the colonel's death. If anything, they seem to be blaming themselves for the lack of adequate protective measures. Echad, however, no longer considers diplomatic cover to be sufficiently secure, and the Mossad's new representative, whoever he may be, will likely have a far more intricate cover.

"Without causing any undue alarm," Atkins continued as he surveyed the select group in front of him," may I suggest, gentlemen, that the cover problem should be considered by the rest of you . . . of course, in consultation with your respective governments as the agreement stipulates. I say this particularly in view of the recent increase in the number of attacks on our own chiefs of station, all of whom were also operating under the guise of an embassy assignment. Just this morning I received a report that ballistics tests demonstrated conclusively that the forty-five-caliber pistol used to gun down a police official in Athens the other day was the very same weapon employed in the assassination of the CIA chief of station there. As most of you know, Dick Welch, very much like Navon, was shot outside his suburban home upon returning from a Christmas party at the Embassy."

"Any leads in this case, Mr. Atkins?" The Italian representative was the first to interject a question into the chief's somber monologue.

Atkins shook his head. "Not really. The group claiming responsibility for both killings, 'the Revolutionary Organization of November Seventeenth,' or something like that, is little known to us. We don't know its size, whether it is an indigenous group or an offshoot of some sort. Anyway I've already asked General Diamandopulos," he looked briefly in the direction of the robust Greek representative, "to prepare a written report on the case with as many details as possible on the new organization. I trust you'll have it on your desks by the end of the week."

Having finished with the unpleasant business, Atkins quickly surveyed the room and pushed on with the next subject on the agenda.

"I'm gratified, as the chief coordinator," he began and cleared his throat, "to recommend a new, extremely qualified man to head the Task Force Three in place of the late Colonel Navon." Atkins paused, collecting his thoughts. "This man has worked with me in the past, and I would like to think of him as an old friend, although I can assure you that our personal association has not in any way prejudiced my decision to recommend him to you. There is not the slightest doubt in my mind that he is the best man for the job."

At that point Atkins turned toward Sartain, who was sitting to his left, and officially introduced him to the assembly. It was clear from the low murmur of approval which spread through the room that the professor was hardly unknown to the membership. Sartain, thumbing through some papers in front of him, acknowledged the reaction with a dry smile devoid of either modesty or satisfaction.

"I've asked the professor," Atkins announced, his tone officially dramatic, "to prepare and present to us this morning a comprehensive analysis of the man who is by far our most dangerous adversary . . . namely . . . Ilich Ramirez Sanchez . . . alias Carlos Martinez . . . alias the Jackal. This first report which is based on Dr. Sartain's personal research over the last few years, and the files made available to him after he joined our ranks, should assist you, gentlemen, in making your decision on my proposal to nominate him . . . as the new head of Task Force Three.

"I would like to point out . . . that a copy of the professor's personal file—which includes a biographical history, a collection of his writings, military and NSA records, and other pertinent information—is in the large yellow envelope in front of each one of you.

"Incidentally," Atkins continued in the same slow, dramatic manner, "you'll find that the file also includes an unusual item. It is a personal letter from Dr. Sartain regarding the recent murder of Linda Wexler in Berlin. As you may know, the late Ms. Wexler, who we strongly suspect was assassinated either by Carlos himself or his henchmen, was a close friend of Professor Sartain." Atkins stole a quick, uneasy glance at the man to his left. "She was in fact his fiancée. The letter was written in response to those of you who had legitimately questioned whether the professor's willingness to undertake the specific task of hunting the Jackal is fueled by personal vendetta. May I add that I, for one, am fully satisfied with the content of the letter and have no qualms whatsoever about the professor's motives."

God will forgive my little white lies, Atkins thought as he turned toward the professor.

Sartain glanced one last time at the papers in front of him and commenced his presentation in a deep, resonant voice, forgoing any preliminary remarks. Once he began speaking, he relied solely on his memory, never once having to consult his extensive notes. As in his classes he talked directly to his audience, his piercing gaze occasionally zeroing in on one person as if to drill home the point.

Atkins could easily tell that Sartain's listeners were taken by the clarity and the authoritative manner in which the rugged-looking professor presented his arguments, as well as his command of the subject and his amazing ability to recall even the most minute details. The Triple C chief was pleased that he had decided to let the professor sell himself. His earlier apprehension that Linda's death would affect Sartain's usual performance was unfounded. As for the permanent representatives, if any had been smug enough to consider himself thoroughly familiar with the background and nature of the "most wanted man in the world," he soon learned how much he didn't know.

Sartain's account began with Ilich Ramirez Sanchez's family roots. His forebears, according to the professor, came from the rainy, mountainous town of San Cristóbal, three thousand feet up in the mists of the Venezuelan Andes. It was from this area, the professor pointed out, that a succession of tough, ambitious men, such as General Marcos Perez Jimenez and President Carlos Andreas Perez, had descended to impose their will on the much mellower people of the plains.

Both Carlos's father and mother were from San Cristóbal. The father, Dr. José Altagracia Ramirez, was born on a ranch just outside the town. At one time he had thoughts of dedicating his life to the church but changed his mind and moved to Bogotá, the capital of neighboring Colombia, to study law. It was there that he met Gustavo Macheado, an exiled leader of the outlawed Venezuelan Communist Party. And it was Macheado, who later returned to Venezuela to head the legalized Party, that turned the young law student into a Marxist.

Sartain took time to analyze the paradoxical man who was Carlos's father. Though a devoted Marxist, Ramirez never took the further step to become card-carrying member of the Party. He was a lawyer, whose Marxist antiexploitation beliefs did not prevent him from wheeling and dealing in real-estate holdings and becoming a millionaire. He was a patriotic Venezuelan who named his three sons after Lenin: Ilich, who was born in Caracas in 1949, Lenin, who was born two years later, and Vladimir, who was born in 1958.

"If the father was a Marxist," Sartain let a drop of sarcasm tinge his voice, "then his sons' early upbringing hardly reflected it. For a number of years, starting in nineteen fifty-eight, the three children, accompanied by their mother, traveled around the Caribbean, spending months at a time in Mexico, Jamaica, Brazil, Florida, and Colombia. The trips were generously financed by Dr. Ramirez, and the children were provided at all times with the best private tutors money could buy. The father would occasionally fly in for a visit but never stayed for too long as the Ramirezes had marital problems.

"It was during that extended Caribbean tour," the professor pointed out, "that Carlos had the opportunity not only to become fluent in English at an early age but also to develop cosmopolitan attitudes and habits. In spite of Dr. Ramirez's convictions, however, the family didn't travel to Cuba. It is another discrepancy in the father's behavior which is well worth noting. In later years Dr. Ramirez always stood steadfastly behind his son's revolutionary actions. Unlike the cases of many other disgruntled young radicals, whose rebellion against society was as much a rebellion against their parents, one could be tempted to conclude that this was not so in the case of our Ilich.

"The father, for example, when explaining his political philosophy recently, charged that the Communist parties, almost without exception, have become too conservative for his taste and that his sympathies have been with the extreme left ever since Khrushchev started leaning toward coexistence with the West. It was Ramirez's opinion that a change from capitalism to socialism was possible only through armed struggle, and he claimed that philosophically and politically he was in total agreement with his son . . . even though, to quote him, 'we may diverge a little on strategic matters.'

"So, on the surface," the professor continued, "the Marxist father turned radical even before his son did, and instead of the more usual intergenerational conflict we are asked to witness a convergence of revolutionary views between father and son. Yet the divergence, the discrepancy, is still in my opinion very much there. The father had always been a talker from the very moment he turned Marxist but would never really practice what he preached. He was a man who, literally, never put his money where his mouth was. He was a man of words, while his son became a man dedicated to action.

"My feelings are that if we are to understand our man, we can not disregard what is to me the son's revolt against his father's inertia, against what he might have interpreted as hypocrisy. After all, a disenchantment within middle- and upper-middle-class families is not unfamiliar. Only in this case Ilich carried it to the extreme, stripping his revolutionary activity of all its doctrinal and ideological trappings, resorting to action for the sake of action, turning to the old anarchist device of Propaganda by Deed."

The professor reached for his pipe, filled it, and lit up with a disposable lighter which Atkins handed him. As he drew on it slowly, smoke billowing with each puff, his countenance was one of typical academic pensiveness. His audience waited silently for him to continue.

Atkins remarked to himself that if there was a change in Sartain's manner, it was that the man hardly smiled anymore, and when he did, it was forced. Definitely not the old warm, disarming smile, one which used to balance so well his intellectual earnestness. Atkins's thoughts carried him back to the professor's presentation at the bookstore. Was it really only a few weeks ago? It seemed like years.

Sartain removed the pipe from his mouth and holding it absentmindedly in both hands went on to explain why he considered it so important to understand the inner motives of the man they were after, to comprehend what really made him tick.

"We're all quite aware of what the man is capable of in the professional, technical sense of the word," Sartain said. "The question remains, however, what is he capable of mentally? How far will he be willing to go? In other words are we dealing here with a true revolutionary, a man dedicated to some tangible political cause—no matter how much we don't agree with it—or with a man whose own personal problems and complexes only find their expression in extreme political violence? Are we dealing here with a twisted individual who has made terrorism his profession, his permanent vocation? Indeed much in the same way that the late Mayor Daley of Chicago when asked in court what his profession was, retorted matter-of-factly, 'Mayor of Chicago' . . ."

Some of the people in the room grinned at the allusion, but the professor kept his somber semblance, puffing on his pipe before continuing. "Pinpointing the inner motives of the man, comprehending his frame of mind, stepping into his emotional shoes, I believe would greatly help us determine whether the most able terrorist today is capable also of taking that extra step on the road to holocaust, by testing a more unconventional terrorism, be it nuclear, chemical, bacteriological, or whatever.

"It is my belief that a true revolutionary, someone who really believes in the cause of the people he is fighting for, would balk at resorting to such an irrevocable act. The question then remains: what kind of a person is the Jackal?"

For the following two hours Sartain spoke with hardly a pause about the man he suspected to be responsible for the death of the woman he loved. He dug into the childhood of the plump, curly headed boy who never distinguished himself in competitive sports and whose nickname was "El Gordo"—"the fat one." He related the boy's experiences when at the age of fourteen, after years of private tutoring and schooling, he was sent to a public school. It was the Collegio Fermin Toro, Caracas's biggest state school where for the very first time Carlos took part in violent political action, when he enthusiastically joined stone-throwing street demonstrations against the Betancourt regime and in support of the once again banned Communist Party. He dwelled on the fact that Ilich, who as a child couldn't stand the sight of blood, yet to make up for his physical appearance was fond of telling friends that "bullets are the only thing that really make sense." Often, however, the bold talk by the then chubby boy only elicited ridicule from his stronger, more athletic peers.

Sartain told the Triple C members how, in the summer of 1966, when the Ramirezes finally concluded that they could not make a life together, the mother and the three children left for England. They resided in London in some of the more posh neighborhoods and continued to be supported by the wealthy Dr. Ramirez. It was after one year of living in England that Ilich and his younger brother Lenin, encouraged by their father who came to visit, applied and were admitted to the Patrice Lumumba People's Friendship University in Moscow, a place often suspected of serving as a KGB recruitment pool and training center for young revolutionaries from Third World countries.

Enrolling at the Patrice Lumumba University was a major turning point in the life of young Ilich, Sartain suggested. He refuted, however, the assumption prevalent among some of the Western intelligence services that the young Ramirez was recruited during that time by the KGB and became a Russian agent with the specific task of infiltrating the ranks of the Palestinian terrorists. He pooh-poohed as much too simplistic the common premise that Carlos's expulsion from the university for "disreputable morals" and "provocative activities" was merely an attempt by the KGB to whitewash their newly recruited agent.

His research, Sartain claimed, demonstrated that Carlos's incessant pursuit of girls and bourgeois pleasures—facilitated by the generous checks with which Dr. Ramirez augmented his regular scholarship—and his constant disregard for his Russian instructors and the political indoctrination courses, was genuine and very much consistent with his maverick personality. Besides, Sartain added, the PFLP had also been aware of these allegations and ran a thorough check on him.

Sartain raised some eyebrows by proclaiming his conviction that if anything, the humiliating expulsion had turned Carlos into as much of an anti-Russian and anticommunist as he was anti-capitalist. As a matter of fact, his later spectacular terrorist actions were as much aimed at impressing his former mentors as they were designed to shock the Western world.

Atkins thanked his good fortune that no new Israeli representative was yet there to attend the meeting. He knew all too well the consistent charge by the Mossad, often for quite obvious reasons, that Carlos's Terror International was not only funded secretly by the KGB but also operated by them, and that the Jackal was an undercover Soviet agent maintaining contact with his true masters at Moscow's Dzerzhinsky Square through the Cuba Dirección General de Inteligencia (DGI). He knew that had there been an Israeli representative at the meeting, he would, regardless of his own personal convictions, challenge the professor in much stronger terms than those of the Turkish representative, who was the first to question the professor's statement.

Sartain, however, stuck to his theory and went as far as to state that at times he wished Carlos was indeed a Russian agent. If that were the case, he claimed, everyone need not fear that he would resort to unconventional terror tactics, whose unpredictable consequences could hardly be beneficial to the Russians.

Sartain proferred his own interpretation of how the young Venezuelan student became an international terrorist. According to the professor rather than being recruited by the Russians, Carlos offered his services to the Palestinians on his own initiative. Apparently at the Patrice Lumumba University Ilich had befriended a number of Palestinian students with whom he was fascinated, and who, very much like him, loathed the university's tedious, stuffy, and thoroughly boring political indoctrination. He was turned on by their stories of the real guerrilla war that was going on across the Jordan River and along the Lebanese border. He felt very much attracted to these volatile, macho men who like him believed that "bullets were the only thing that made sense."

Sartain named names, dates, locations, and incidents, presenting much solid evidence to support his argument. Many of the representatives took notes; some, who still had doubts, would study them carefully later to look for holes in the professor's theories.

Sartain proceeded to examine Carlos's diverse exploits, from the moment he turned urban guerrilla under the command of Mohammad Boudia to his emergence as the master terrorist and the linchpin of Terror International. He analyzed the massacres at Ben-Gurion Airport and the Munich Olympics, the sabotage of the Trieste oil refineries, the murder of the French DST agents, the assault on the French Embassy in Holland, the rocket attack at Orly Airport, the kidnapping of the OPEC ministers in Vienna, the recent Entebbe hijacking, and a number of other incidents, which hitherto had not been attributed to the Jackal and whose mention triggered surprised reactions. But again the professor substantiated his claims with evidence which they all were hard put to challenge. Indeed it was the first real chance for each of them to fully comprehend the magnitude of the evil genius of the world's foremost terrorist.

With measured, habitual movements the professor emptied his pipe into the large glass ashtray in front of him. He instinctively reached for the tobacco pouch but then, realizing that the pipe's bowl was still on the warm side, changed his mind and didn't refill it. Instead he crossed his fingers and rested both hands on the table as his penetrating gaze traveled the room, making brief contact with each one of his listeners.

"Yes, I definitely believe, having studied the man for some time now, that he is capable of taking that extra step. Frankly I doubt that even Wadi Haddad would be willing to resort to anything which goes beyond hijacking, sabotage, assassination, and other ordinary acts of terrorism. With all his fanaticism even Haddad is well aware of what the repercussions of such a move could be to the cause of the Palestinians. But Haddad, I hear, has cancer."

There was a ripple of shock in the room at that piece of news. Where did this imposing man get his information? Incredible . . . Haddad has cancer . . . now that's something . . . one should inform headquarters immediately. Only Atkins seemed unimpressed, a sly, content grin flickering at the sides of his mouth.

". . . his position has been weakened," the professor continued, totally oblivious to the reaction his remarks had generated, "since his debacle at Entebbe. The question now is: how much does Haddad control Carlos, Terror International's real keystone, and for how long?

"It is for this reason, among others, that Carlos may decide, if he hasn't done so already, to move to more neutral ground. I am quite convinced, in fact, that in the future he will choose to operate from a place which is more accessible to Europe than Iraq and Southern Yemen. If my assumption is correct, then there are only two other reasonably safe alternatives for him: Libya, where he has been residing off and on for some time now, but which can also prove to be very limiting under the constant scrutiny of the unpredictable Khadaffi; and Algeria, which is more moderate and somewhat less sympathetic to the terrorist cause than the other three states but which, on the other hand, provides much better accessibility to the rest of the world. Furthermore its larger size, greater sophistication, and higher degree of pluralism will afford the Jackal far more maneuverability.

"As I've already told the chief," Sartain asserted confidently, turning toward Atkins, "I'm willing to stick my neck out . . . and gamble on Algeria as Carlos's next base of operation."

Having ventured his opinion in such a nonacademic fashion, the professor admitted that accurately guessing the Jackal's next base of operations amounted to no more than placing the very first piece in an intricate jigsaw puzzle. Carlos, no doubt, was up to something big, the magnitude of which was not in any way constricted by any moral bounds. But what? how? where? and when? These were the crucial questions: the answers were probably known to no one but the terrorist's closest lieutenants.

"Unfortunately," Sartain said, consulting his watch as he reached the final remarks of his presentation, "the modern, democratic, open societies we live in are highly vulnerable to terrorists of Carlos's ilk. Static security in itself is not the answer;

there is just no way in the world that we can protect all the potential targets without becoming some sort of an Orwellian police state."

As if to make his point all the more tangible, Sartain enumerated several of what he claimed were practically thousands of exposed and pregnable sensitive targets. Targets, which if hit by the terrorists, would result in damage of catastrophic proportions. He chilled their marrow when he illustrated how all alone he could, if he were determined to do it, wipe out half of Boston with one well-aimed, single shell from a high-powered bazooka. They all knew how vulnerable they were, but until now they either refused to admit it even to themselves or it had never been articulated to them in such ominous, concrete terms.

"And yet, if for the sake of protecting ourselves effectively against such monstrous acts," the professor continued in the same vein, "we are forced to give up our freedoms, our civil liberties, then where are we? Won't we be playing right into the terrorists' hands? Forcing them perhaps to lose the battle, but letting them win the war itself.

"Well," Sartain acknowledged, drawing back from the large mahogany table, his gaze encompassing the whole conference room, "we all know very well what the problems and pitfalls are. It is for this reason, after all, that you all have assembled here, representing the ever-dwindling number of truly free nations. My recommendation is very simple, and hardly very original: if we can not afford to wait anymore for terrorists such as Carlos to strike first, triggering reactions which at least are bound to undermine our democratic institutions and affect our way of life, then we have no other choice but to go after them. In practical terms it means that we have to make every effort to infiltrate their tightly closed organizations; we must preempt their plans before they have a chance to act, before it is too late.

"I am well aware that this is easier said than done," Sartain said, carefully examining the disappointed expressions on at least some of his listeners' faces, bitterly remarking to himself that they couldn't have expected him to offer some magic solution, to pull some tricks out of his academic bag. "But we must do it despite the fact that most of the terrorist groups today are quite alert to this kind of modus operandi. Many of them indeed have been extremely wary in recent years of recruiting any new members, which makes our task all the more difficult. But having studied the problem for years now, always with an eye to the future, I don't see that in the long run we have any alternative. In the final analysis I am convinced that this is the only really effective way to combat organized terrorism in the nuclear age, the only hope we have to win over a group such as Carlos's Terror International. It's as simple as that."

Later, when Sartain left the room and the hand ballot was taken, it turned out that the membership of the Triple C selected him almost unanimously to head the TF-3.

The only two representatives who abstained were the Turkish and the Japanese. The former because he personally still suspected that the Jackal was a Russian agent. The latter because the professor in a recent interview refused to condemn violent demonstrations by farmers and students against the newly built Tokyo Airport.

Atkins, however, couldn't have been more satisfied with the results.

CHAPTER TWENTY-ONE

THE Air France jumbo jet began its descent toward Ben-Gurion International, the passengers' faces glued to the portholes to glimpse the approaching shoreline of the Holy Land. Miep Steen felt her heartbeat quicken. Tension crept up her legs. She sought Pieter's hand for encouragement, only to find it moist with perspiration. He granted her an awkward, strained smile, far from reassuring, and returned to a professional journal of apiculture, as if it would afford him the ultimate cachet, that he was indeed who he claimed to be.

Miep studied her boyfriend, realizing that he was at least as nervous as she. After all, this was his very first mission. Thus the hand that had sought comfort found itself the comforter.

Tel Aviv's first rows of white buldings appeared below, shimmering bright against the deep blue September sea. It was the eve of the Jewish New Year, and many of the passengers were Jews traveling to Israel for the High Holidays. Such was the elderly couple from Kansas City sitting directly behind the two Dutch terrorists.

Miep, overhearing the old couple's exclamations of elation at seeing the land of their forefathers for the very first time, felt anger swell in her. What right do these Jews have? she thought. What right to come here like that while hundreds of thousands of displaced Palestinians, the legitimate owners of the land, are wasting away in the squalid refugee camps?

The powerful Rolls-Royce engines shook the wide-bodied aircraft as it suddenly lost altitude over the narrow coastal plain. From above, the verdant orange groves seemed helplessly squeezed by the sprawl of urban growth. Few aboard gave thought to the fact that if the 747 continued eastward for a few minutes longer, it would have crossed the pre-1967 boundary with the Hashemite Kingdom of Jordan. Indeed, from a bird's-eye view, the Jewish state seemed incredibly small and vulnerable, like its own helpless groves.

But as the man-size tires touched with surprising softness the cement runway, Miep's thoughts were not of Israel's geopolitical security problems. She was intently studying every detail on the airfield that she could spy.

As the plane taxied on the runway, Miep saw the main terminal. Considering the airport's world-wide fame, the building was anything but impressive. For one thing it lacked jetways, a common feature at any modern airport. It was a rather old, ugly structure, under continual renovation. Considering the millions already spent, the time wasted, the inconveniences caused, and the resultant aesthetic monstrosity, it would have been much better had the thing been torn down altogether and rebuilt from scratch.

Yet, ironically, the airport's continuous renovation held one security advantage: the ongoing modifications rendered almost useless any long-range planning of a terrorist attack on Ben-Gurion. As Miep had been briefed prior to leaving Amsterdam, it was difficult to know from one month to another the exact layout of the terminal. That was part of the reason for her being there.

Ever since the Israeli raid on Entebbe, security at Ben-Gurion had been beefed up to an unprecedented level in anticipation of a retaliation. One evidence of the increased wariness was the machine-gun-mounted jeep and the command car which shadowed the Air France jetliner from the moment it left the main runway. Both vehicles were manned by fierce-looking soldiers in battle fatigues. Their green berets testified that they were members of the renowned Border Guard which consisted largely of recruits from Israel's non-Arab minorities—the tough, martial Druze and the Circassians.

Miep took note that the 747 parked some distance from the main terminal and a few hundred yards away from any other jetliner.

The jumbo jet's heavy door swung open, and a tall, dark, sharp-featured officer walked in. He was followed by two soldiers carrying Uzi submachine guns in ready position. If Miep had not been forewarned about the tough security measures, she would have been petrified.

The lieutenant collected the entry forms which the passengers had completed during flight and skimmed through them quickly.

"How many are getting off here?" he asked in accented English.

"Eighty-four," the purser responded coolly.

"How many are going on to Teheran and New Delhi?"

"Sixty-seven."

"Any Israelis in first class?"

The purser shook his head, as if to say, "hardly." A faint grin crossed the lips of the two French flight attendants. It did not escape the young lieutenant, who, while thanking the purser politely, glared at him with undisguised contempt and stepped into the forward coach cabin.

"*Yesh po Israelim?*" he asked in Hebrew, raising his voice. "Are there any Israelis here?"

About a dozen hands went up.

He walked over to a young couple sitting with a six-year-old child at the center section, two rows ahead and to the left of Miep and Pieter.

The officer smiled at the curly headed boy who displayed fascination with the high-caliber revolver on his belt and asked the parents in Hebrew: "Have you noticed anything suspicious?"

The Israeli couple exchanged a hesitant look.

The non-Hebrew-speaking passengers seemed puzzled, nervous, unable to tell it was only a routine security procedure. The two grim-looking soldiers who held tight to their Uzis, their dark eyes ominously scrutinizing the passengers, added to the tension.

"Have you detected anyone acting strangely during the flight?" the officer elaborated.

"No," the man responded in Hebrew for both of them, "nothing that attracted our attention."

"How was the security check at de Gaulle?"

"Okay," the husband said tersely.

"*Kacha, kacha,*" his wife disagreed.

The officer stared at her quizzically. "What do you mean 'so-so'?"

"Well . . . in my opinion they really only checked the hand luggage closely."

The army man nodded his understanding. "*Toda raba,*" he thanked them and moved up the aisle passing Miep and Pieter, whose hearts skipped as he did.

Continuing to address other Israeli passengers, the officer received pretty much the same answers. Satisfied that no questionable characters had been spotted on the flight by his security-conscious countrymen and that the security procedures at the French airport, if not meticulously thorough, were at least satisfactory, the young lieutenant permitted the disembarkment of the Israel-bound passengers.

Miep kissed Pieter good-bye. He would continue on to Teheran and New Delhi. She deplaned with the other passengers and boarded a bus which went under Border Guard escort to the main terminal building.

A few short lines formed at the passport control area, and Miep found herself standing in front of the elderly couple from Kansas City. Both were exhilarated at having set foot on the Jewish homeland soil.

"Your husband?" the American woman questioned, noticing Miep was alone. "Where is your husband?"

"He's not my husband," Miep forced a smile, annoyed at the diversion of her attention from the study of the terminal layout. "He's my boyfriend. He had to fly on to New Delhi on business. I'll join him there later."

"What kind of business?" the nosy woman wouldn't let her disengage. "What kind of business is he in?"

"He's in honey."

"Honey?"

"Uh-huh."

"Well, that's sweet . . . Isn't it, Harold?" She turned to her husband, proud of her little pun.

Harold nodded his agreement disinterestedly.

The sober-faced passport officer examined Miep's papers and asked to see her plane ticket. As she complied, his eyes inspected her coldly.

What he saw was a petite baby-faced brunette, bangs almost covering her eyes, clad in a fashionable denim dress under a light, well-cut gray coat.

"What's the purpose of your stay here?" he asked while studying her ticket.

"Tourism. I wish to visit the holy places of Christianity," she said with rehearsed confidence.

"How long are you planning to stay? It shows here," he

pointed to the Air France ticket, "that New Delhi is your final destination."

She nodded. "I guess for about two days."

"Are you traveling alone?"

"Well . . . well here, yes. You see my fiancé continued on to New Delhi. He's on a business trip, and I'll join him later."

"I see," he said and proceeded to stamp her passport. He was about to hand it to her, when he suddenly asked: "What does he do?"

"Who?" The question had startled her.

"Your fiancé, of course."

"Oh . . . he's . . . an apiculturist."

"He's what?"

"He's an api-cul-tur-ist." She pronounced each vowel separately.

"What's that?"

"He's in honey."

"Oh," the man said, smiling for the very first time. He handed her the passport and ticket. "This is the land of milk and honey, you know. He should have stopped here too."

"Next time," she said and smiled politely, catching herself before she added: "He's planning on it."

The officer followed her with his eyes as she walked away from his window. His foot silently pressed a concealed button.

As Miep approached the baggage carousel assigned to her flight, a small girl in a scout uniform stopped her and handed her a flower.

"*Shana Tova!*" the child greeted her with a big, warm smile and then added in English, "Happy New Year!"

"Happy New Year to you too," the Dutch terrorist responded with genuine affection and paused briefly to watch the girl as she proceeded to greet the other passengers.

Miep waited patiently by the long conveyer for her suitcase, taking the time to absorb every detail, particularly any relating to the security setup in the large hall where four years earlier Japanese terrorists, also arriving on an Air France flight, had massacred twenty-eight people. She counted half a dozen armed soldiers and a small number of police. To her far right she saw a large heavy glass partition, probably bullet proof, behind which a waving crowd waited, many trying to catch a glimpse of their arriving friends and relatives.

A few minutes later Miep spotted her blue suitcase moving toward her slowly on the carousel. Just as she grabbed it and placed it beside her on the floor, she felt a hand on her shoulder.

Startled, she turned around to face a stocky young woman in police uniform who was standing next to a tall young man in civilian clothes.

"Are you Miep Steen?"

She nodded.

"Will you please come with us?" the policewoman said as the man leaned over to pick up the suitcase. Miep noticed the gun he was wearing under his jacket.

She paled, but quickly resumed control. Smiling, she asked: "Do I look like a smuggler?"

"It's only a routine check, Miss Steen. Not to worry," the policewoman explained.

Miep was led to a windowless room where the policewoman asked her politely to undress. She then proceeded to methodically inspect every item of her clothing, including her shoes. Finding nothing suspicious she asked the naked Dutch woman to turn around and lean against the low table with her legs apart.

"What for?" Miep protested, sensing what was coming.

"Not to worry," the henna-haired cop assured as she placed a thin, transparent glove on her right hand. "It will only take a minute. It's only routine."

"But—"

The policewoman shook her head to cut off useless argument.

Miep decided she would be better off cooperating. Clenching her teeth, she turned around. She squirmed with discomfort, humiliation, and anger as she felt the strong index finger groping her private parts. She longed for the revenge to come.

In the next room, ascertaining first that the blue suitcase was not in anyway booby-trapped, the tall Mossad agent was busy going through it and Miep's handbag. But he too failed to uncover anything inculpatory. There were no weapons, explosives, or suspicious papers. Nothing. Only fashionable clothing, cosmetics, and an expensive Minolta.

Four hours later Miep still found herself insisting that she was nothing but an innocent tourist. What did they want from her? And where in God's name did they ever get the notion that she was a terrorist? She said she regretted now that she hadn't flown on to New Delhi, that she had ever gotten the urge to visit

Jerusalem and Nazareth. She never in her wildest dreams thought that someone whose sole purpose was to visit the Holy Land, the places sacred to Christianity, would be subjected to such brutal treatment—particularly someone from Holland, whose people had consistently been Israel's staunchest supporters in Europe.

Miep's Mossad interrogators were unable to get anything out of her. Confident in the fact that there was absolutely nothing incriminating in her possession, she would admit to nothing, putting up a tough front.

As the Sabbath settled in, a bearish man with sandy hair walked into the room. His deep sea-blue eyes smiled at Miep as he extended his huge hand in greeting. As she took it and repeated his *"shalom,"* his eyes suddenly turned into icicles. His grip tightened.

A terrified scream ricocheted from one wall to another in the windowless room. He was hurting her beyond reason. And he wouldn't let go.

CHAPTER TWENTY-TWO

"**D**O you recall," Atkins asked, loosening his tie as he squirmed on the uncomfortable metal chair by Sartain's desk, "the incident three months ago when a German by the name of Bernard Hausman was blown to pieces at the Tel Aviv airport when he opened his briefcase for inspections?"

"You mean the one who carried a Dutch passport?"

"That's the one."

"A rather bizarre case," the professor shook his head. "It seemed he didn't know his case had been booby-trapped by whoever sent him. Why do you ask?"

"Well, it was Hausman's use of a passport belonging to a Dutch student by the name of Hugo Miller which led to the collaborative investigation by the Israelis and the Dutch into the various radical groups which have mushroomed in the Netherlands recently. As a result of this confidential cooperation, fortified more recently by the establishment of the Triple C," Atkins added not without a note of satisfaction, "the security people at Ben-Gurion managed to identify this Miep Steen and preempt the skyjack."

"I see," Sartain said, noting something on a small yellow pad among the many files on his desk. He had been busy studying them when Atkins dropped by the "cage," as Fred had named the professor's Triple C office. No larger than ten by six the small, narrow room was originally destined to serve as a storage area. But because all the available office space at the crammed headquarters had already been allocated to the permanent representatives and since Navon's empty office was to be taken by his Israeli replacement, it was the only way to satisfy Sartain's wish to have his own place at Langley.

At least the "cage" was on the second floor, had a small window overlooking a large pine, and afforded the professor some privacy, whereas the rest of the staff, other than the national representatives, had to be content with partitioned cubicles. Sartain's confined quarters didn't seem, however, to bother him. He was much too preoccupied with his work, and with his mourning of Linda's death, to pay any attention to any details of comfort.

Atkins came by to inform Sartain of what the Israelis considered a major coup—the thwarting of an elaborate skyjacking scheme. He had just conversed with Echad over the phone and learned that Miep Steen, a twenty-three-year-old social worker from the town of Berde in the Netherlands and her thirty-one-year-old boyfriend, a Dutch radical by the name of Pieter Hals, had been sent by the PFLP to inspect the security procedures at the airports of Tel Aviv, Teheran, and New Delhi. The information was needed for a group of six terrorists of different nationalities who were preparing to board an Air France flight in New Delhi. A flight whose destination was Paris but whose schedule called for two stops—Teheran and Tel Aviv.

According to Echad it was a well-planned operation, and again, like the one at Istanbul's Yesilkoy, in direct retaliation for the Israeli raid on Entebbe. Indeed its purpose was to demand the release of the very same jailed terrorists whose freedom had been sought by the Entebbe hijackers. With the one exception of the already freed Helga Denz.

Miep's interrogation revealed that the hijackers had planned to take over flight 193 at seven thirty A.M., right after it was to receive landing clearance from Ben-Gurion's control tower. The intention was to prevent the captain from warning the tower that the plane had been hijacked, precluding thus either midair interception by the Israeli air force or the blocking of the airport's runways—as was the case a few weeks earlier when other Palestinian terrorists, who had commandeered a KLM DC-9 over the Mediterranean, were prevented by Israeli Phantom jets from flying toward Tel Aviv.

Once the Air France plane was on the ground, the PFLP terrorists would have threatened to blow it up with the passengers unless their imprisoned comrades were released and turned over to them. The intention was to negotiate while the jet was parked at the Israeli terminal. Having it on the ground, in Israel, the terrorists figured, would have afforded them not only better control over the release of their comrades but also better leverage and bargaining position.

What led to Miep's detainment at Ben-Gurion was the collaborative investigation of a radical cell in her hometown Berde. It had identified her as an active member of the Marxist Educational Collective and placed her name on the list of suspected terrorists. Thus as innocent as the Dutch girl looked, and even though absolutely nothing incriminating was found on her or in her luggage, Echad was called in to personally take over her interrogation.

"Miep told him everything she knew," Atkins said matter-of-factly. "And Pieter, who masqueraded as a businessman dealing in honey, of all things, was picked up a few hours ago in New Delhi. The Mossad tends to believe that this time it was Carlos himself who was behind this elaborate plan.

"What do you think?" Atkins asked. "Do you believe it was the Jackal?"

Sartain pondered the question. "I don't know," he said finally with unmistakable skepticism. "I don't have all the information, so it's hard to tell. I've never heard of this Miep Steen, and I don't know too much about Berde's Marxist Educational Collective, except that it's an offshoot of the Amsterdam-based De Rode Jungd, or The Red Youth. Nevertheless I tend to doubt that it was Carlos's work, even though, I have to admit, at first glance it does seem a well-planned scheme. Could have been a smoke screen, but it seems far too elaborate for that."

Sartain paused, thoughtful, before he continued. "There are two main things here that make me doubtful: the scale of the operation—it's smaller than what I would have expected—and secondly the idea that Carlos, who has to be looking for a major success, would resort to using inexperienced amateurs such as Miep Steen or this Pieter Hals.

"No." Sartain shook his head. "The more I think about it, the more I tend to doubt it. No. I suspect it was Wadi Haddad again. And the unfortunate thing is that, if I'm right, it will only strengthen Carlos's position against the ailing doctor. I don't like it. If I had to choose between two evils, I'd rather see Haddad or one of his Palestinian henchmen in control than Carlos. When will we get all the details?"

"I assume the whole story will be fleshed out at the Tuesday meeting when Navon's replacement will be here."

"Who is he?" Sartain asked with only mild interest.

"I don't exactly know yet," Atkins hedged. He eyed Sartain with a sly smile, adding, "but I believe it will be a 'she,' not a 'he' . . ."

"A woman?" the professor sat up, failing to hide his surprise.

"Why not?" countered the Triple C chief, amused at his friend's reaction. "Women have always been an important part of their armed forces. A woman, after all, ran their country for years . . . and it seems she did a pretty damn good job at that. How did David Ben-Gurion put it when he was their first premier? 'Golda is the only man in my Cabinet.' There you have it," Atkins chuckled. "Besides there seems to be an increasing number of women in the various terrorist organizations. Maybe what we need is a feminine touch."

Suddenly Sartain's expression changed; Atkins's words had sparked a painful memory. His mind slid back to the day they were sailing in San Francisco Bay. Linda's soft, confident voice rang in his ears again, talking about the role of women in crime and terrorism. Oh, how he longed to really hear her voice again, to see her, to touch her again. How much he missed her, needed her . . . those long sleepless nights.

"Sam, are you with me?" Atkins's voice snapped the dazed professor back to reality.

"Yes, yes," he cleared his throat, the pain of remembrance still registered on his face.

Atkins pretended to ignore Sartain's momentary lapse and continued, "As I was saying, it may be a blessing in disguise."

"I beg your pardon?" Sartain said, still fighting the ghostly images. He had lost track of what Atkins had said.

"It's a blessing in disguise," Atkins said patiently again, "because Echad really hassled me for not replacing Colonel Navon with another Israeli as the head of Task Force Three. Not that I hadn't expected it. But now they'll have to realize that a woman would never be accepted by the other members as the head of the task force."

Atkins eyed the professor cautiously. "But whoever the new Israeli representative is," he added, "he or she will be in the task force. That much I had to concede to Echad. Is that all right with you?"

The professor shrugged. Still recovering from the sharp pain, he muttered somewhat melancholically, "It doesn't matter to me, Fred." Noting, however, Atkins's concerned look, he quickly added jokingly, "As long as it is not Golda Meir . . . I know the grand old lady, and she would take over in no time at all."

Atkins forced a laugh. He and Bev were concerned about the way the professor bottled in all his feelings in the aftermath of Linda's death; the way he hid behind an almost impenetrable mask, burying himself in his work, avoiding any personal contact which did not pertain to it.

Fred and his wife were the only two people Sam saw socially. And it took considerable arm twisting to convince the reclusive professor to come to dinner the two times he had. At supper the conversation centered almost exclusively on politics and the state of the economy. Sartain showed no inclination to talk about his tragedy nor anything else that related to his personal life. Linda's name was never mentioned.

Atkins could only imagine his friend's inner torment behind that stony façade. A few times he caught it in Sartain's gaze, in the involuntary twitch of certain facial muscles or in a momentary lapse such as he had just witnessed. He wanted to approach Sartain and coax him to vent his anguish, to share it. But Bev continuously cautioned him to let the man be. He must resolve it for himself, she counseled. Some men are like that. With a heavy heart Atkins complied.

Fred was at least grateful to have managed to persuade his friend to join the Triple C ranks. Though his motives were not totally unselfish, he was pleased to see the professor channeling his burning desire for revenge in constructive work. Indeed it seemed as if all his energy had synthesized into a relentless pursuit of that elusive trail which would lead them to Carlos. It became quite obvious that Linda's death affected neither Sartain's work-load capacity nor his acumen. Moreover Sartain was willing now to use the cover of writing a book on the Jackal to approach his old contacts among the Third World revolutionary circles. Circles to which traditional types like Atkins had only limited access or none at all.

While Atkins had assumed personal responsibility for the hard-nosed professor with known liberal views, Sartain's work for the Triple C was kept a secret known only to the CIA chief and a few of his top aides. In fact the very existence of the multinational

organization devoted to counterterrorism was still guarded as
highly confidential. Here and there a few vague references to it
managed to reach the international media, but nothing indicated
the true composition of the organization and the location of its
headquarters.

As for Sartain, he had decided after lengthy deliberation to
teach the fall semester at Georgetown. The academic cover
couldn't be more perfect. On campus only Mondays, Wednes-
days, and Fridays he could spend two full weekdays at the
Triple C headquarters.

To get there, Sartain used a blue 1975 Vega provided him by
the Triple C. He would switch to the Chevy from his own BMW
at a public garage in town and drive to Langley wearing impenetrable sunglasses and a tweed hat. A simple decoy, but one
which so far kept him unrecognized. He would ordinarily take
the George Washington Parkway, as if going to Dulles Airport.
But instead of exiting at the Bureau of Public Roads' sign which
marked the way to CIA headquarters, he would change to highway 123 which would take him to 193. He would stay on this
highway for less than a mile before cutting right into Turkey
Run Road. This country lane placed him at the undistinguished
back entrance to the CIA complex, where the Triple C building
stood apart.

Atkins rose and stretched his limbs and back. "Damned luxurious furniture we got you, Sam," he joked. He glanced over the
files piled high on Sartain's desk, recognizing some as part of the
FBI material the professor had requested earlier in the week.
Sartain was hoping to find something in them that would be
useful in his strategy to infiltrate Carlos's inner circle.

If indeed Carlos was planning to make his next big move in
the U.S., and if he was to operate out of Algeria, then, Sartain
figured, there was a good chance that Carlos might himself approach any of the credible American radicals who had sought
refuge in Algeria. The trick was to get to those people before
Carlos did.

"Any progress with the FBI stuff?" Atkins asked, halfway out
the door, not expecting a positive response

"Yes," Sartain nodded. Atkins stopped. "As a matter of fact I
was planning to have you see one film in particular this afternoon. It's part of the Bureau's debriefing of Tyrone Jackson. It

may give us the key we've been looking for. I was going over the transcripts before you dropped in, but I'd like you to watch the real thing."

Sartain reached for the metal cabinet squeezed into one corner of the small room and pulled out a reel of film. "Do you have about forty-five minutes, Fred?"

Atkins consulted his watch, debating.

"I believe it's important, Fred. Very important." The professor's natural impatience seemed to have quadrupled since Linda's death.

"All right," Atkins granted. "Can I use your phone? I'll have to postpone an appointment."

In the small screening room located in the basement right next to the lab which was still being assembled, Sartain mounted the reel on the 16-mm projector. *How many times has he done it this week?* Atkins wondered as he watched the professor expertly thread the film.

"This is reel number four," Sartain commented, adjusting the focus when the celluloid caught. Distorted figures appeared in rapid succession on the screen. "Part of a series of twelve films taken by hidden camera during Tyrone Jackson's FBI interrogation after he returned to the States last year."

As Sartain talked, the blurred images of a middle-aged black man appeared on the screen. Sartain teased the focusing knob, and the picture went sharp. The man sat in a bright, bare room facing the camera. He was addressing two men, one white and one black, dressed in suits and facing away from the camera.

Atkins had little difficulty recognizing Jackson's face from the heavy media exposure the revolutionary had endured in the past decade. He looked fatigued, older than his age. No longer was he menacing, this once fiery black man, who with his extremist followers managed to terrorize several police forces in the States. His close-cropped, kinky hair was flecked now with gray, as was his trim moustache. His expression was almost benevolent.

The beginning of reel four carried the continuation of a lengthy tirade by the former fugitive about his disillusionment with radical socialism, communism, and the Third World.

Atkins cast a quizzical look in Sartain's direction.

"Wait," the professor said calmly. "This is coming to an end."

As if on cue the white G-man on screen, tired of the endless jeremiad, halted the harangue and asked Jackson point-blank about his contacts with some of the terrorist groups.

Now the man was wary. It was all in the past, he claimed. Beads of perspiration formed on his brown forehead. He had begun to withdraw from that element some time ago. In fact they themselves kept him at arm's length, so he knew no more than the average person on the street about any of the terrorist groups' current activities.

The FBI interrogators let it ride. They continued with more specific questions about other American radicals who found refuge in Algeria, running down a prepared list of names. It was when they mentioned the third name on their list that the professor tapped Atkins lightly on the shoulder, telling him to pay close attention.

"What can you tell us about Jim Anders?" the black federal agent asked in a controlled monotone.

Jackson raised his eyebrows, hesitating. "Well, brother, not much, really." He knit his brows, concentrating. One could see his show of willingness. He wanted to look cooperative.

"All I know is that Jim was a Weatherman . . . perhaps still is. I don't know. I think you guys were after him for bombing the State Department or something, and when you were about to nab him, he hijacked a plane to Algeria." Jackson paused, his white teeth gleaming, but Atkins couldn't tell if he was grinning or seeking approbation.

"I also heard," Jackson continued, "that you did get his girl friend during the skyjack. Still serving time in some clink over here, right? Anyway last time I saw Jim he was teaching in some school in the Kasbah, an Arab school." He shook his head. "I guess that's about it," he added, shrugging.

Atkins suspected that the man he observed was walking a tightrope between old loyalties to fellow fugitives and his own self-preservation. The Triple C chief leaned toward the screen, watching the dilemma pass behind the black man's amiable façade as his questioners pressed for more on Jim Anders.

Jackson came forth. Jim Anders, it seemed, had enjoyed the confidence of many expatriate revolutionaries based in Algeria. He was well liked and traveled freely in their circles—quite unusual for a white American.

"Has he been involved in terrorist activity? Any links to the Palestinians, the PFLP, for example? Has he worked for them?" The two federal agents kept at him.

"I don't know. Perhaps. I'm sure he knows some of the Palestinian terrorists, but working for them?" He shook his head doubtfully. "Who knows, man? Everything's possible. I only met the dude a few times."

"What did you talk about? You must have talked, didn't you? After all, you were Americans," said the white agent, not without a tinge of sarcasm.

"I don't remember, man, give me a break," Jackson sighed, exasperated. He rubbed his eyes with the back of his forefingers as if the lights were suddenly too intense. "Whatever we bullshitted about just wasn't that memorable. I mean, we didn't exactly talk terrorism all the time. All we talked about . . ."

He suddenly stopped, squinting his eyes and contracting his brow as if suddenly reminded of something.

". . . Well, I do remember one night, I guess it was about a year ago. I gave the guy a ride home from some party thrown by a Cuban couple in Hamma. He was way down, you know, moody, very nostalgic. He told me that sometimes he really missed the U.S." He tugged on his earlobe, recollecting.

"Go on."

"Well he wasn't too coherent most of the time, but I remember him saying like that the war in Vietnam being over and all, and Nixon's resignation and . . . other stuff had made him rethink a lot of things. He said he was confused, like he'd lost some of his revolutionary zest. Something about really wishing he could be back with his girl friend, living somewhere quietly, in some small town in . . . Montana. Yeah, Montana. Where he was from originally. Yeah, all peaceful and quiet in Montana, away from politics, revolution, and all that."

"How did you react to it?"

"Man, I played cool. How did I know he wasn't setting me up?" he shrugged. "Anyway I wasn't about to advertise my own change of heart. So I just kept real quiet."

"Is that all he said?"

"Well . . . no," the black man answered, now varying his narrative. "He said that he had no choice but to fight on until the system changed, because that was the only way he'd ever be able to get home free . . . He said he'd never hack it living behind bars." Jackson stopped, cleared his throat, and added, "It was sad, man, very sad, because I knew exactly how he felt."

"What did he mean by fighting on?"

Jackson shrugged again. "I don't know, man. I don't know if he meant it literally or what. I didn't ask."

"Did you see him again after that?"

"Yes, I did. Once."

"Did he say anything more?"

"No. Not a word. Matter of fact I wondered if he even remembered what he'd told me. I mean the man was pretty stoned the night he talked to me."

Sartain turned off the projector and switched on some lights.

"That's our man!" he announced as he began rewinding the film. For the first time in weeks, Atkins noted, the professor was truly elated.

"You mean Jim Anders?"

"Yes. I mean Jim Anders." Sartain nodded, a victorious grin creeping over his usually stern visage.

"I see. Well . . . that's very interesting," the Triple C chief said tentatively. He didn't want to seem dense. "I'm still somewhat in the dark though, Sam. Who exactly is this Jim Anders anyway? You must know more about him than what I've just heard. Let me in on the rest."

Sartain glanced at the clock. "Do you have another fifteen minutes?"

Atkins conceded that he did. Sartain picked up a chair and swiveled it around to sit straddle-legged. He began relating the story of Jim Anders and his girl friend Amy Lahr.

Both were members of the Weathermen underground. On May 2, 1970—the very same day that Sartain himself was among those leading a peaceful protest march in Washington against the invasion of Cambodia—the pair attempted to place a pipe bomb, concealed inside a Samsonite briefcase, at one of the State Department hallways.

Intercepted by a guard on their way out of the building, Jim, then a twenty-four-year-old ex-marine, pulled his handgun and shot the man in the chest.

Thinking they had killed the guard and fearing identification by other witnesses, the young couple panicked and headed for

National Airport. Still armed, as passenger screening devices were introduced only two years later, they boarded the first flight they could get on, and commandeered the plane the moment it took off.

Forced to stop at Boston's Logan Field for refueling, the two were persuaded to free the passengers in exchange for the gas and one hundred thousand dollars. But once the women and children were evacuated, FBI agents who, disguised as mechanics, had been hiding under the jetliner since its refueling, rushed the plane. They attempted to overpower Jim while Amy had been lured to the tarmac to collect the ransom money. Though shot in the left arm, Jim managed to resume control of the situation by shooting one of the agents and disarming the other.

Fearing a further double cross, Jim ordered the pilot to take off immediately. As they set a course for Algeria, Jim's message was relayed to the control tower: "I'll come back to get you, Amy," he choked, "if it's the last thing I ever do . . . ."

"He didn't obviously?"

"No, he didn't," Sartain said. "But if he could have figured a way to do it, I'm convinced he would have."

"The FBI man? And the other guy he shot?"

"Totally recovered, both of them. But here's a real irony, Fred." Sartain paused, as if to assess his chief's readiness to hear what he was about to say. "Amy Lahr was a student of mine at Georgetown at the time. She was a poli-sci major, an A student, brilliant girl. I was aware, of course, of her radical opinions. She took a couple of my classes and wrote a few papers for me. In fact one of them dealt with the FLN and Algeria's violent struggle for independence. Yet I had no idea that she put her views into practice. Never occurred to me she might be an active member of the Weathermen."

The professor paused reminiscing. "I liked Amy," he recalled. "She was an excellent student. We had a good rapport. As a matter of fact, even though I was infuriated by what the Weathermen tried to do, which could have jeopardized the whole positive impact of the peace march, I agreed to testify at her trial . . . for the defense . . . as a character witness."

"I see," Atkins said tonelessly. "I didn't know about that."

The professor smiled. "I guess, Fred, there are a few things you don't know about me after all. Anyway, Amy, who is twenty-seven now, is serving a fifteen-year sentence at Terminal Island."

"Near Los Angeles?"

Sartain nodded. "Anyway the point I'm trying to make is . . . for the last few days I've been studying every minute detail about Jim Anders that the staff was able to dig up. I feel by now that I know the man better than he knows himself. And . . . I believe that he can be turned around."

Atkins looked puzzled.

"I believe he can become our key to the penetration of Terror International. I think he can be persuaded to work for us. You couldn't find anyone with better 'credentials.' "

Atkins was beginning to get the gist of Sartain's thinking.

"All I need," Sartain said as lightly as he could, "is to be able to offer him and his girl friend a full pardon in return for their service."

"What?" Atkins jumped as if a thousand volts shot through his body. "You must be out of your mind! Bombing the State Department, seriously wounding a guard, hijacking a plane, shooting federal agents? That guy deserves *at least* life imprisonment, and you . . ." He shook his head in amazement. "Come on, Sam. I can't do it. It's impossible. Find another way!" He turned to leave.

"Wait a minute, Fred!" Sartain snapped, grabbing him hard by the arm. "Just a goddamn minute! You asked me, you practically begged me to join this outfit to find a way, *any* way, to get to the Jackal. And now that I've got a sound, near-perfect plan to penetrate Carlos's organization with a genuine revolutionary, you tell me to forget it?"

Atkins stared at the strong fingers gripping his arm.

"Sorry," Sartain apologized as he quickly retreated. "But don't you see, Fred, this may be our only chance. Sure, it's no easy decision. But look at the choices. If you pardon an exiled skyjacker for a crime committed six years ago, you may get the only opportunity we have to crush Carlos and prevent what might be a major catastrophe, the loss of thousands of lives . . . What will it be?"

It was a tense silence that followed. The Triple C chief grappled with his thoughts.

"How do you know the man will accept the offer?" he asked finally.

"I don't. But if he doesn't, so what? We'll only be where we are now: nowhere."

"How are you going to approach him?"

"I have a scheme," the professor said cautiously. "First, we'll have to arrange for his girl friend to escape from prison."

"You're mad, Sam! Totally mad!" Atkins gasped, covering his ears with his hands as if refusing to hear anymore. "You are determined to get me into trouble, into deep, deep trouble. For Christ's sake, Sam, don't you know what the hell is going on in this country now? Don't you know they are raking agencies like ours over the coals for anything that begins to smack of 'dirty tricks.' A splendid way to establish the reputation of the Triple C!"

"Okay, okay," the professor raised his hands. "I know the risks. You know the risks. Now you think it over, my friend. But if your answer is still negative, you can count on my immediate resignation. I'll go it alone if I have to."

"You're serious, aren't you?" Atkins stared as if at a man gone crazy.

"I'm sorry, Fred," the professor responded very calmly. "I like you. I respect you. But you've still got only until tomorrow night to say yes, or . . . or you can have your 'Golda Meir' as the head of the task force."

Fully aware of the dilemma he had placed his old friend in, Sartain quietly collected the reel and left the room, leaving the perplexed Triple C chief to mutter in exasperation: "Professors!"

CHAPTER TWENTY-THREE

THE sales meeting at Macy's had gone extraordinarily well, so Tara felt little contrition for being late to her next appointment. Compulsive as she was about punctuality, there was nothing much to be done. The cabdriver weaved his yellow Checker expertly through Manhattan's congested late-afternoon traffic.

Yes, Tara reflected, the meeting had definitely been more productive than she had expected. In her slim crocodile attaché she carried a signed order for two hundred women's suede coats and three hundred jackets of the next season's collection. Furthermore they promised her an answer on the men's line by no later than Wednesday afternoon; she expected it to be positive. She smiled to herself, knowing that she had charmed the new buyer off his feet. He couldn't take his eyes off her. And he was no slouch himself—a twin for Mastroianni.

It was Trento he'd said he was originally from, and again she wondered why that name rang a familiar bell in her head. He himself said it was a nondescript town in northern Italy, certainly not one for the tour guides. He was surprised she had even heard of it.

Anyway, if the order did come through, it would be a hundred full-length leather coats plus two hundred jackets. She calculated it quickly in her mind: close to eighty-two thousand dollars. Not bad for one afternoon's work.

Yet, as the taxi maneuvered through traffic, reflections on the successful sale were overrun by thoughts of Echad's latest communiqué regarding her new assignment.

She had been on the Navon case from the very night he had been gunned down in front of his house. And yet, lamentably, she had come up with nothing, absolutely nothing! She could not blame the local police nor the FBI. It certainly was not due to any lack of effort, or competence, that no clues were found. As for the ballistics tests, they revealed nothing more significant than the fact that Joseph Navon had been hit by two identical slugs fired at close range from a new 9-mm Smith and Wesson— a gun seldom used by either Middle Eastern or European terrorists.

As soon as Tara had learned of Navon's murder, she issued instructions that all the key Al Fatah people residing in the U.S. be put under the tightest surveillance. But even her determined operatives failed to come up with anything substantial to point to who was behind the elimination of the Israeli colonel. A few of her own people began to question whether it was not just another ordinary crime.

Someone suggested kidnapping Abdul Muzrack to let the Mossad's interrogation team have a go at him.

Tara's objection, however, was adamant. Even though she was still convinced that Navon's killing was not an ordinary crime, she began to doubt that the Al Fatah had been the perpetrator. It was not yet worth it to her to expose her hard-won confidential identification of Yasir Arafat's top dog in the U.S. just to find out he had nothing to do with this particular operation.

Tara concluded that if Navon's murder was the work of Palestinian terrorists, it had to be the doing of the PFLP. But if the Popular Front for the Liberation of Palestine had an American-·based network, Tara and the Mossad knew nothing about it. One thought haunted her: if it was the PFLP that executed Navon, why weren't they claiming credit for it? After all, for the sake of propaganda and to boost their followers' morale, they frequently took credit for imaginary exploits. Why now would they fail to publicly credit themselves with such a sinister, successful action against their archenemy, the Israeli Mossad?

Her reverie was shattered when the taxi swerved sharply to avoid near collision with a green van cutting heedlessly in front of them. As the young bushy-haired cabbie swung in and out and back into his original lane, narrowly missing another car, he unleashed a flood of profanities in a mixture of Hebrew and Arabic. He could not be aware that his classy female passenger was well versed in both.

Tara, amused, shifted her attention to the driver's ID by the meter. MOSHE MIZRAHI it announced in bold black letters underneath a photograph which bore only slight resemblance to the cabbie. It was as common an Israeli name as they came. Now that the cab has resumed its slow, steady crawl with the rest of the traffic, she caught him observing her in the rear-view mirror.

"Dis crazy drivers," he shook his head as he addressed her in heavily accented English. "I don't understand who geeve dem a driving license."

Tara displayed disinterest as she feigned a search for something in her attaché case. She had nothing to gain by a conversation, and she certainly did not wish to identify herself as a compatriot. Too often a New York cabdriver turned out to be a fellow countryman. She had heard from the Israeli consul general that perhaps as many as twenty percent of the Big Apple's taxi drivers were *"yordim"*—as those who left Israel to settle in other countries were pejoratively labeled.

From pride ingrained in her since childhood, Tara couldn't help feeling personally humiliated by the phenomenon. That an Israeli would leave his country after all the toil, the sacrifices, the bloodshed, to come to New York to drive a taxi, she could not understand. It was as if by emigrating, these Israelis, many of them Sabras, native Israeli born, put a major dent in the raison d'être of the creation of the Jewish state. They betrayed and undermined the tenets of the Zionist movement, turned their back on a two-thousand-year-old dream. Thus she couldn't help but resent and despise the *yordim*, which in Hebrew meant, literally, those who "descend," as opposed to the *olim*, those who immigrate to the land of their ancestors, those who "ascend."

There was an opening suddenly in dense traffic when they reached Forty-eighth and Third, and the rebuffed cabbie slammed his foot on the gas without warning, jerking Tara against the back of the seat.

She could only see the back of his head, but somehow she sensed a smirk on the cabbie's face at having thrown his beautiful, haughty fare off-balance.

"Ben znunim!" she thought to herself in Hebrew, but caught herself before the epithet escaped her lips. Indeed she wished she could say it to him, just to see his expression at her calling him a son of a bitch in his own language. That would have startled him all right, she chuckled to herself.

Carlos. The thought came, tormenting. Could it have been the Jackal after all who killed Navon? Absolutely no helpful clues existed as to who the assassins were. She knew Carlos liked to operate alone at times, to pull the trigger himself; there had been enough precedents. But would he have come all the way to the States, to Washington, D.C., for the sole purpose of eliminating one person?

True, it was Navon who had been responsible for the liquidation of Carlos's idol, Mohammad Boudia. It was also Navon who had sent Saul and Itamar after the Jackal, and it was he who was selected to head the Triple C task force whose primary assignment was to nail the Venezuelan terrorist.

Yet, despite all these personal motives, it didn't quite fit. And besides, Tara argued to herself, all the Western intelligence services concurred in the opinion that Carlos was still hiding somewhere in the Middle East. No, he wouldn't come here just to get Navon. Unless . . .

"You said Bloomingdells? Dint you, lady?" the cabdriver interrupted her thoughts again as they neared Fifty-ninth and Third.

"I'm sorry, I didn't hear what you said?"

"Bloomingdells? You going to Bloomingdells?" he asked again impatiently.

"Yes. Please."

Anyway, Tara resumed her thoughts, now she would have the opportunity to check some of these outside theories. No more would she be confined just to one area, just to the United States. This was what she had secretly wanted ever since that horrible, bloody day at Ben-Gurion Airport, the day that changed her life.

The cab came to a screeching halt in front of the store's entrance. The driver turned around and leered. He was rather handsome, in a rugged kind of a way, with pronounced musculature. Tara wondered briefly what he had done in Zahal. Was he a tank commander? an infantry soldier? a paratrooper?

"Two dollars fifty."

What the hell are they all doing here, chasing the golden calf? Tara thought bitterly as she handed him three dollar bills.

"Keep the change," she said as she stepped out of the Checker. She could feel his dark, impudent eyes on her back as she strode toward the building.

A person has the right to choose where he wants to live and what he wants to do with his life, she reminded herself. Yet . . . No! She needed to clear her head of all such troubling thoughts. She had to focus on her imminent confrontation with the stern Ms. Sheldon, who was anything but an easily charmed, and charming, Italian.

Then, as she was about to enter the elevator, it struck her: the University of Trento—but of course, the place where the Red Brigades terrorist organization originated. She recalled now the files she had seen at Mossad headquarters. Handsome devils they all were. Very much like the Macy's buyer. And most of them didn't look like they had a mean bone in them, like they could hurt a fly.

During the ceremony at the cemetery chapel, Sartain felt numb; his suffering had already reached rock bottom. But later, as the casket was lowered into the gaping pit, when the subdued sobbing of Luana's mother and sister turned to a wailing, he was once again overcome by anguish. With this fresh pain his torment assumed a cumulative measure. He couldn't bear looking at the all-too-remindful sight of the coffin disappearing into that sinister black pit. He shifted his eyes, resting them on his son's tense, tearless face. He knew how Steve must feel.

Two days earlier when Sartain heard from Steve about Luana's murder, his decision to fly to California for the funeral was instantaneous. Both he and Linda had been very fond of Luana, that "pure, innocent flower of a child" as the Episcopalian minister so fittingly eulogized her. Sartain remembered how protective Linda had felt toward Luana, whose childlike purity deeply touched her. He wanted to be by his son; he felt he might be needed.

The coroner had confirmed that Luana died by strangulation. Her assailant, it was also established, tried first to rape her as evidenced by her torn clothes, but he never consummated his intent. He had either been interrupted or frightened by someone or something, and proceeded to kill her instead. It was possible, the police theorized, that he choked Luana to death in order to keep her from screaming.

The police also assumed that since most of the articles of value in the small house had vanished, the attacker might have originally intended only to burglarize the place. Apparently he had entered the one-story Berkeley home by forcing open the back door.

Time of death was placed at some time between seven and nine o'clock in the evening, when Steve was at the library a mile away. The burglar must have worn gloves, as not a single fingerprint aside from those of Steve and Luana was discovered in the house. The police had no suspects.

Luana's violent death so soon after Linda's had a traumatic effect on the professor, not only because it forced him to relive both Linda's and his wife's deaths. It also conjured some very disturbing, self-searching questions. It made him feel as if he were somehow personally responsible for the deaths of these three women. As if he were being made to pay for his violent past, for the lives he took . . . for Lebanon.

Moreover, ever since Sartain learned of the circumstances of Luana's death, he couldn't keep from questioning the plausibility of coincidence. The similarity in the way both women found their end kept haunting him. As irrational as it seemed, something within him insisted that there was a connection, that it was not all a coincidence. But how? And why Luana? Had he become so obsessed with conspiracy? With terrorism? With Carlos? Had Linda's death unsettled him that much? And if indeed they were after him, why strike at the people close to him? They killed Navon, not his wife.

These and other questions continued to trouble the professor as he drove his grieving son from Mountain View cemetery on the East Bay to his Tiburon home. He refused to let Steve remain at the house in Berkeley, the site of Luana's murder. So he talked him into staying with him in Tiburon, at least until he had to go back to Washington. Sartain candidly admitted to his son that he found it unbearable to be alone in a place whose every room conjured memories of Linda. Steve conceded without further argument.

"I can't stay here for too long, son," Sartain finally broke the silence as he slowed to approach the Bay Bridge toll gate. He was thinking about his telephone conversation with Atkins earlier that morning. Atkins had informed him that after a long deliberation he was willing to go along with his plan but wanted him back at the Capital as soon as possible.

"I don't expect you to, Dad," Steve murmured solemnly. "I'm grateful you came at all. I know how busy you are."

"I only wish I could do more," Sartain replied as he handed seventy-five cents to the black toll taker who greeted him toothlessly but cheerfully. He forced an acknowledging smile.

"What are your plans, son?" Sartain asked as he resumed speed over the bridge. "Are you planning to return to school right away?"

"I don't know. I haven't really thought about it yet. Except that I'm going to move out of the house. That's definite." Steve stared out at the unfolding panorama of Marin County to his right, seeing but not seeing it. "I think I would like to take off for a while. I don't feel like going back to school this quarter. I don't think I could."

"I understand, son. Believe me, I do."

"I may just travel. Go east, or maybe to Europe . . . or even to the Orient . . . I don't really know." He sounded lost, hurting. "Or maybe I should just keep busy, drown myself in work . . . like you. I don't know."

He absentmindedly toyed with the glove-compartment lock, punching it in and out. "I already miss her, Dad. I didn't realize how much a part of my life she had become. And I feel really bad for not treating her better. How could anyone do . . ." He couldn't finish his sentence; the pain on his face said it all.

"I've been thinking," Sartain began, clearing his throat. "Perhaps you should come with me to Washington."

There was no response, as if Steve hadn't heard him. But Sartain knew he had.

"I've wanted to talk to you about it," he continued. "I would like you to come live with me, at least for a while. I think it would help both of us." Why was it so difficult for him to say it? They used to be so close, so intimate, especially after Steve's mother's death. But ever since Steve went to college, things had changed. An intangible gulf had gradually developed. Not knowing how to deal with it, Sartain found it easier to ignore, telling himself it was only a natural, temporary, part of the process of growing up.

"Because *The Rescue* has become a success, I've managed to finagle a generous advance for my next book," he continued. "It will deal primarily with Carlos, and I could use you as a research assistant. I could easily pay you eight hundred a month . . . with free room and board. What d'you say?"

"It's very magnaminous of you, Dad . . . and kind. But do you really need me?"

"I certainly do. With my teaching and—" He paused, catching himself. ". . . and with the other consulting jobs I have I'll need an assistant anyway. Since I'll have to pay someone, it might as well be you."

Sartain knew his son's pride, the obsession for independence. From his very first year in college, Steve was reluctant to receive an allowance from his father, resorting instead to a tuition scholarship and part-time jobs around campus to support him.

"Besides," Sartain added as they left the Bay Bridge and circled the modern Embarcadero center heading toward the Golden Gate, "research for this book will require traveling to the Middle East, Europe, and perhaps South America. I don't see any reason why you couldn't accompany me there. In fact I would like you to."

Steve's eyes lighted up, the gloom temporarily disappeared from his face. The prospect of working and traveling with his father seemed to have excited him. If he didn't fully show it, it was perhaps because it wouldn't have been appropriate at this time.

"When would you want me, Dad?" he asked, controlling his enthusiasm.

"As soon as possible, son. If you want, you can fly back with me. The sooner the better."

"I don't know about leaving so soon, Dad. I'll have to notify the administration, store my stuff, and a few other things. But I guess I can get there in a week."

"That'll be perfect," Sartain said. "It will give me a chance to get your room ready and . . . You don't mind staying with me, do you?"

"No, Dad, not at all," Steve said gently. "That's what appeals to me most about the whole thing."

"Thanks, son. I'm glad." Sartain's voice revealed how deeply touched he was.

By the time they had crossed the fog-shrouded Golden Gate Bridge, they both felt heartened by their newfound closeness. Yet Sartain couldn't but muse how sad it was that it had required the tragic, violent deaths of the women they loved to restore their own past intimacy.

CHAPTER TWENTY-FOUR

D R. Karl Baumann examined Helga with curiosity and apprehension.

She looked quite different, he thought, older than he had expected. In a way he was relieved not to like her new, close-cropped hairstyle which only accentuated her lined features.

Helga seemed calmer, less spirited, no longer the vivacious, sprightly young woman he used to know. The tomboy in her which had aroused him so much in the past, he reflected with cool perception, had turned into a mature, masculine quality.

And yet, in spite of it all, she was still very much the same Helga he had craved all these years in recurring dreams, in many a lustful, sleepless night. She was still the woman who triggered in him the deepest primordial passions.

As much as Karl tried now to fight and resist them, he found himself unable to prevent the same old powerful and twisted desires from overtaking him, engulfing any prudent reason.

The previous day when the surprising, unsettling call had come at the plant, Karl agreed only after much indecision to meet Helga. He was determined, however, to let her know in no uncertain terms that it was for the last time, that he had no wish of ever laying eyes on her again.

He planned to say that she had caused him enough anguish, enough suffering to last a lifetime. He was going to tell her that he had totally changed since she left him, that his whole life had undergone a radical transformation since then. He had a wife and two children he very much cared for. He had a highly responsible job, a new citizenship, a comfortable existence. And now that he had managed to overcome the shock and misery of her forsaking him in such an abrupt and cruel manner, he would be damned if he would let her disturb his life again.

No! Karl kept telling himself all day after she called. He would refuse to have anything to do with her. She had been out of his life for eight years, and that was the way he wanted to keep it.

True, when she had disappeared, leaving only a brief, impersonal note behind, he was ready to kill himself. He would have done anything to get her back. But things had changed, he reassured himself when he left the plant to meet her for lunch. No longer was he a slave to his sordid fascination with her. She must leave him alone! She must go away! That's what he was going to tell her, unequivocally. He was his own man now.

But, when he sat facing her at the busy coffee shop on Division Street, Morris's main thoroughfare, he could not bring himself to do it. He realized he should have never agreed to come. She spoke but a few words, and the old feelings began to wash over him with such striking vividness that it seemed as if they had parted only the day before and not eight years ago.

An alarm sounded in Karl's head. He was slipping fast, but there was nothing he could do. Suddenly all that he could think about was that he wanted very much to be alone with her in some remote, secluded place.

In a strange way the fact that Helga had changed, the fact that she had aged and that there were things in her appearance not to his liking, made him want her even more. He had to fight the temptation to lean over, run his fingers through her short, sandy hair, and pull her head hard toward him so that he could tongue each age line on her face, so that . . .

"How did you find me?" he managed to ask in German, choking back the emotions. "However did you find me?"

She smiled, that same teasing smile. "I found you," she replied in German, her voice like velvet. "I found you, and that's all that counts. Didn't you know I was bound to find you one day?" She asked it as if it had been he who had suddenly vanished, leaving no trace.

Karl kept silent, searching her face. Was she mocking him? The hazel eyes stared directly at him. They seemed clear, truthful, and inviting. If there was ridicule in them, he couldn't detect it. He was overwhelmed with contradictory feelings.

"Deep inside me," she continued, whispering low, "I always knew we would be together again one day."

She mustn't say that! It isn't fair, it isn't fair at all!

His heart was beating wildly, but he managed to sound calm. "I have a wife and two children, Helga."

"I know," she nodded. "It makes no difference. All I want is to be near you. I don't want to own you. Believe me, Karl, I have no intention of disturbing your life. I don't want to stand between you and your family. I wouldn't think of doing it. I won't hurt your career. All I want, Karl, is to be with you . . . occasionally . . . like we used to be. I'm not asking very much."

He felt hot. He was perspiring heavily. Failing to find a handkerchief in his pocket, he used a paper napkin to dab his forehead.

"Why don't you take off your jacket?" Helga suggested sympathetically. "It's very warm in here."

Baumann removed his coat and hung it on the back of his chair. "Indian summer," he said apologetically as he loosened his tie and pushed his glasses tighter against his face.

"So I've heard." She smiled affectionately. "Do you feel better now?"

"*Ja. Ja.* Much better." He smiled meekly.

Suddenly he felt Helga's sharp fingernails dig hard into the hairy flesh of his lower arm. Stunned, he looked down at her hand and then up at her grinning face. But he didn't pull back, nor did he utter a single word. He quickly glanced around the coffee shop; no one took notice of the little drama unfolding at the corner table.

Still silent, Helga continued her grip on his flesh until she drew blood.

Karl's breath became heavy, but he felt euphoric, alive in a way he had not been in years. He welcomed the sweet pain and felt let down when Helga withdrew her fingers as suddenly as she had unleashed them.

He closed his eyes, his arm inert, resting on the Formica table.

When he raised his eyelids again, Helga was watching him indifferently.

"What have you been up to?" Karl ventured finally. He preferred, for now, to ignore her perverse overture. "You didn't marry, did you?"

He was relieved to hear that she hadn't. Not that it would have made much difference, but he already had begun to feel pangs of irrational jealousy.

By the manner in which Karl asked the question, Helga deduced that he didn't know about her underground activities and more importantly about her imprisonment and the recent escape. It was all for the best, she thought; it made her job much easier. There was less explaining to do. And by the time he did find out, it would be too late for him. She would have complete control of the situation.

"Have you been teaching?"

She nodded. "Off and on. I've done a lot of traveling. But yes, I did teach in Hamburg for a while and then in Stuttgart."

"Well, have you been happy? I mean . . ."

A bitter smile formed at the corners of her mouth. "Not with any man . . . Not like . . ." She didn't finish but instead touched with the tip of her forefinger the small drop of blood which had formed at the end of the scratch on his arm. She brought the finger slowly, dramatically, to her mouth and sucked and licked it clean.

He took a deep breath as she repeated the performance. His arm was leaden. He felt hypnotized. He began to envisage them together. Images of him crawling on the floor licking and sucking her toes one by one, the saliva dripping out of his mouth while she lashed his bare bottom with a black leather whip raced through his mind. His penis stood throbbing, pushing hard against his trousers. He held back a groan, imagining her sharp teeth biting hard at the back of his neck, at his shoulders . . . harder . . . deeper.

"Helga!" he uttered, jerking his head, somehow getting himself together. "I . . . I've got to leave. We can't be seen. I mean, we shouldn't be seen too often and for too long in public." He removed his glasses and wiped his sweaty face with the napkin again. "It's quite a small town, Morris, you know. Only ten thousand people."

"I gather then that you'll see me again," she said as she removed the finger from her mouth, eyeing him carefully.

He nodded.

"There will be no problems," Helga said quickly. "I'll be moving at the end of the month from the Park Motel to a small house on

Jackson Street. You won't have to worry about being seen with me there. In fact you won't have to see me that often. I'll be content if you see me once or twice a week. And when you can't, you can't."

Though grateful for her consideration, he felt disappointed. He wanted her to crave him, to be totally obsessed with him. But here was that same old indifference, that familiar distance.

"Incidentally," she winked at him, bending close to whisper, "when I stopped in Chicago on my way here, I visited some of the sex shops on State Street, and I've got some special things"— she wetted her lips with her tongue—"I think you'll really like them. I bought them just for you."

Karl was about to explode. All those years of suppressing his true sexual desires, burying them deep, ignoring them. He wanted to say: Let's go right now to your motel, I can't hold it anymore!

Helga looked at her watch coolly. "It's time to say good-bye, Karl. Incidentally," she added, "I won't call you. You can call whenever you wish."

"Do you need anything, Helga? Money? Anything?" He was stalling, not wanting to leave.

She smiled thinly and shook her head. "Nothing. Thank you. I've already got a job as a saleswoman at the Kroger department store. You know I can look after myself."

Once again he felt disappointed, rebuffed. He wished she had asked for something, anything.

As he put on his coat ready to leave, she touched his arm. "Karl," she whispered, "my name now is Helga Lang."

"Lang?" he said puzzled.

"Uh-huh. It's so that I can work. My green card goes by that name."

"I see." He nodded his understanding.

"*Auf Wiedersehen* then," she said affectionately.

"*Auf Wiedersehen*," he responded and headed toward the cashier to pay the bill.

Helga followed him with her eyes. He looked the image of an aging, middle-class American in his colorful double-knit suit. He had definitely aged these past eight years, she thought. He was bald at the crown now, and his once dark, thick hair had turned thin and silvery gray. He had a slight forward bent when he walked, and with those severe rimless glasses, he looked even older.

No, she concluded, he was anything but the object of a woman's sexual fantasy. But she had never really thought of him as handsome, or particularly masculine. That wasn't his appeal.

She stood up, and without glancing at him again, walked toward the rest rooms. It had almost been too easy, she remarked to herself. Carlos was right after all. People never really do change.

CHAPTER TWENTY-FIVE

ARTAIN was intrigued. He was convinced he had previously met the woman facing him across the conference table. But where? When? He had been searching his mind in vain. How could he have forgotten such a remarkably attractive woman? The sculptured features, the patrician nose, the stunning almond-shaped eyes, the glistening black hair, that slender figure. And yet the name Tara Kafir rang no bell. Neither did that captivating, slightly accented voice.

What troubled the professor even more was that he had the feeling that he had seen this new colleague of his not too long ago. But where? Damn it! Unless . . . unless it was her look-alike that he had seen on some TV commercial or magazine cover. No. He was certain he had seen her in person. Sooner or later it would come to him.

One thing for sure. The usually cool, suave François Darlan was strutting his stuff for her. They're amazing, these Frenchmen, Sartain reflected amused. Ordinarily they're cold as fish, preoccupied with their own selfish egos. But show them a beautiful female, and they would outdo any orangutan in heat.

"I'm telling you, ze man was as much of a technician for la Television Algerie . . . as I am!" The former commander of the Brigade Anti-Commando protested in his resonant voice, pounding his fist emphatically against his chest. "I rechecked weez le Deuxième Bureau, and zey are all convinced, weezout exception, zat eet was Carlos!"

The demonstrative Frenchman referred to reports which claimed that the Jackal had been in Yugoslavia the week before. Allegedly Carlos had been observed by both French and German intelligence agents as he boarded a plane for that neutral communist country.

Carlos was apparently traveling under disguise. He was

spotted, claimed the French and the Germans, because he was accompanied by the German terrorist, Hans-Joachim Klein. (Klein came to fame when he was seriously wounded and captured in the January raid on the OPEC headquarters in Vienna. On Carlos's insistence he was removed from the hospital's intensive care unit and brought to the plane which flew the raiders and their hostages to Algeria.) Sartain could still remember Carlos's unequivocal response to the protesting Austrian doctors: "I don't care if he dies on the flight; I'm not leaving him behind. We came together, and we will leave together."

According to the French and German agents there were three other unidentified men traveling with Carlos and Klein who appeared to be Carlos's bodyguards.

Both Paris and Bonn alerted the Yugoslavs, who claimed that they immediately placed the man alleged to be Carlos under tight surveillance. The French and the Austrians then officially requested that the suspect be arrested for possible extradition. The State Department, prodded by the Triple C chief, began exerting pressure on Belgrade to honor the request.

Four days later, however, to the dismay of the Americans and their allies (although not at all to Sartain's surprise), the Yugoslavs put the man alleged to be Carlos and the others on a jet for Baghdad, where they disappeared.

The Yugoslavs shrugged off Western protests, explaining that the whole episode was a case of mistaken identity. The suspect had been merely "an Algerian television technician."

The Yugoslavian government had good reason—or, more aptly, as Sartain suspected, a reasonable excuse—not to cooperate on this matter with the United States. Only a few days earlier, on September 10, Croatian terrorists had hijacked a New York to Chicago jetliner. The skyjackers had demanded that, in return for freeing the hostages, an eight-page communiqué pressing Croatian demands for independence from Yugoslavia must be printed on the front page of five major American newspapers. To show that they meant business, the hijackers' comrades gave the New York police directions to a bomb planted in a coin locker at Grand Central Station. The bomb, contained in a pressure cooker, exploded when the disposal squad tried to disarm it, killing one policeman and injuring three others.

At that point any earlier objections to dealing with the Croatian terrorists, or, as Atkins angrily protested, "conceding to the hijacking of the freedom of the press," were overruled. And in what both he and Sartain considered an extremely dangerous precedent, all of the terrorists' demands were met, including the air drop over London, Paris, New York, Chicago, and Montreal, of thousands of leaflets carrying the message of the self-styled "Fighters for Free Croatia."

Afterward, to the embarrassment of the American capitulators, the five hijackers were discovered to be unarmed. The "bombs," which they claimed they had smuggled aboard the plane in saucepans wrapped as gifts, proved to be fake.

The French had refused to negotiate with the hijackers when they landed at Charles de Gaulle Airport, and their Triple C representative, Darlan, now blamed the American submissive position for the Yugoslav noncooperation in the Carlos case. Indeed, as each of the TF-3 members around the table knew, the Yugoslavs, while praising the unyielding stand of the French, minced no words in assailing the United States' handling of the Croatian affair.

Yet, while Sartain did not state his skepticism outright, he doubted that the Yugoslavs had let Carlos go, if indeed it was Carlos, because of the U.S. handling of the Croatian hijacking. He still held the belief that even if some government had the chance to lay its hands on Carlos, it would prefer not to. Most of them feared the consequences of the Venezuelan terrorist's incarceration and trial more than what he might do if left alone. The Jackal had to be eliminated, killed, not captured alive.

"Zey didn't even demand zat ze men pull zeir hands out of zeir bulging pockets and prove zat zey had real guns," Darlan continued his protestation. "When zey knew zey had passed srough ze metal detectors at La Guardia in order to board ze plane! . . ."

"I agree." Tara Kafir spoke up, echoing the Frenchman's strong words. "What is the point of having all these devices if anyone can go through them and then simply pretend to be armed and in possession of explosives!"

"*Mais c'est vrai!* What is ze point?" The dark, hairy Frenchman seconded her, puffing victoriously.

"What I find particularly objectionable," Tara continued, barely acknowledging Darlan's support, "is the captain's outrageous behavior."

Tara pulled a sheet of paper from the blue folder in front of her. "With your permission, Professor," she turned to Sartain, "may I quote the captain's voluntary statement just before they all deplaned?"

As he nodded in response, Sartain searched in Tara's dark eyes for some sign of recognition, a signal that she had met him before. There was none.

"This is the captain." Tara began reading from the paper in her hands. " 'We've all been through an incredible experience. But it is over for us. No one is hurt. However, it is not over for our hijackers. Their ordeal is just beginning. They have a cause. They are brave, committed people. Idealistic, dedicated people. Like the people . . .' " Tara looked up and surveyed the room pointedly, her eyes lingering on Sartain, challenging.

" 'Like the people,' " Tara continued to read with unmistakable sarcasm, " 'who helped to shape our country. They are trying to do the same thing for theirs. I think we should all give them a hand.' "

Sartain exchanged a quick look with Atkins, who had been sitting in on this special meeting of the TF-3. The captain's statement was indeed distasteful, and they both knew that it had been pathetically followed by many of the American passengers' enthusiastic applause.

Again Sartain had been anything but surprised by the reaction of the TWA captain and the passengers. Only six months earlier he had published a lengthy article in *Commentary* analyzing such behavior. He termed it the "Hostage Syndrome." To him, while disturbing, it was an understandable phenomenon that some kidnap victims, rather than being outraged by their predicament, emerge from the shattering experience burbling warm praise for their captors, who turned out to be great folks just because they didn't kill their hostages.

Sartain wanted to remind Tara that Americans had no monopoly on such regrettable behavior. He kept silent, however, remembering Atkins's reference to the Israelis' resentment at not having one of their own replacing Navon as the head of the task force.

"Let's not forget that our brave captain gave the female hijacker a big hug in front of the press cameras," Tara hammered on. "Can anyone really blame the Yugoslavs for being so annoyed? And I don't have to tell you that we in Israel harbor no great love for Tito's government . . ."

Sartain could no longer contain himself. PR be damned. "I don't believe there is really any point crying over spilled milk," he said, forcing a pleasant look. "For whatever reasons, the Yugoslavs let Carlos go, if indeed it was Carlos. What's done is done. The question is: where do we go from here?"

Before anyone had a chance to respond, the professor quickly informed his multinational group which, beside the U.S., Israel, and France, consisted also of the representatives of Britain, Germany, and Japan, that he had a plan. A complicated one at that, but one which he believed had a fair chance of leading either to Carlos's capture or at least to the frustration of his future schemes.

Sartain explained that what he proposed involved some quasi-legal maneuverings and had taken some time and a great deal of persuasion to obtain approval from Washington. Nodding in Atkins's direction, he added that it was only due to the Triple C chief's relentless efforts that a green light was, albeit reluctantly, granted.

Atkins, who had remained conspicuously silent throughout the discussion, motioned for him to continue.

"In essence what we're talking about," the professor began, "is the same old formula which I'd suggested a few weeks ago at the general meeting. That is, an attempt to penetrate the inner circle of Carlos's Terror International. I've come to the conclusion that the best way of achieving such an objective is to use genuine American revolutionaries who have been living in Algeria. I'm saying Algeria because recent intelligence reports tend to confirm my earlier suspicions that it is there that Carlos is establishing his new headquarters. It is from there that he will probably plan his next move."

Sartain paused briefly to light his new briar and let what he had just said sink in.

"Professor Sartain," Tara seized the moment, accentuating his academic title in a way he didn't appreciate. "You are aware of course of our past attempts to infiltrate Carlos's group. Attempts which so far have been totally unsuccessful. The last one, an effort of eighteen months, ended in the death of two of our most capable operatives. Why, may I ask, do you think you'll do better? Especially since you are suggesting the use of American agents.

"Correct me if I am wrong, Professor," she added without attempting to mask her skepticism, "but I believe there are no Americans in Terror International, let alone in Carlos's inner circle . . ."

Suddenly, out of the blue, it hit Sartain where he had seen her. A sly smile of recognition involuntarily crossed his lips.

Tara ignored Sartain's queer reaction, challenging him on another issue. "You've also chosen, Professor, to brush aside the Yugoslavian incident when it could be of great significance in terms of what Carlos was doing there in the first place and why he went to Iraq. As a matter of fact, if I read you correctly, you've insinuated that, in spite of the French and German reports, you doubt it was Carlos at all. Why, may I ask?"

"Were you at National Airport about a month ago?" Sartain replied in non sequitur.

Tara's fierce expression was instantly reduced to one of total bafflement.

"I believe you were escorted by a short, stocky, middle-aged woman. You were wearing a light beige suit." Sartain addressed her in an uncharacteristically informal manner. "It was you, wasn't it?" He watched her confoundedness increase.

Tara glanced uncertainly at Atkins, who only shrugged noncommittally. "I don't . . . I don't understand what you're talking about," she muttered, her voice devoid of its earlier assertiveness. But then, regaining her self-possession, the Mossad's top female agent said harshly: "I don't see what that has to do with—"

"Oh," Sartain interrupted, retaining the friendly grin, "it really doesn't matter. It's just that you look so familiar, I've been searching my memory for where we'd met. And then, all of a sudden, it just hit me."

By now it was obvious that Tara's bewilderment had changed into annoyance. But before she had a chance to respond, Sartain quickly added: "But that's really not the point. The point is that, quite frankly, and with all due respect to our French and German colleagues, I'm still not totally convinced that it was Carlos who was on that Belgrade-bound flight.

"I keep questioning why, if Carlos traveled under disguise,

Klein did not? And why did he choose to travel with the one member of his inner circle who is perhaps the best known to us? The more I wonder about it, the more I become convinced that Carlos wanted us to think it was he who boarded that plane to Yugoslavia.

"But even if it was Carlos, and it could have been, I find it very difficult to accept that it was he who left for Iraq with Joachim Klein. Having spent years carefully studying the man's modus operandi, I'm convinced that it was a diversionary act. For whatever reasons, Carlos wanted us to believe that he left for Iraq with Klein."

Sartain paused, gesturing at the Triple C chief. "When I first learned of Carlos's alleged departure for Iraq, I told Mr. Atkins that if my assumption that Klein was nothing more than a clever decoy in this case is correct, then it would be easy to uncover his trail in Iraq . . ."

The professor rested his pipe in the glass ashtray and pulled a yellow sheet from his blue folder.

"This is an MI6 report which Jim handed me just before the meeting." Sartain motioned in the direction of the tall, moustachioed Briton who nodded in confirmation. "It states that on two separate occasions our Herr Klein has been spotted in Baghdad . . . rather conspicuously I might add."

Surveying the room, Sartain stated in a calm, assured voice, "I leave it up to each one of you to draw your own conclusions. In my opinion Carlos either never left Algeria or is already back there plotting his next move."

Once again locking his gaze on Tara, Sartain addressed himself to her other question. "I've also studied very carefully the Mossad reports, and in my judgment you failed to provide your two agents with sufficiently adequate cover-identity to infiltrate Carlos's organization. That is why your operation failed."

Sartain enunciated each word, both surprised and amused at the way he relished putting the attractive woman down. Not that he really disliked her, but after all, he justified, it was she who so arrogantly challenged and provoked him. He was only reciprocating in kind. Linda, he mused, chuckling, would have most probably labeled him a "male chauvinist pig," accusing him of trying to assert his masculine dominance.

If Sartain analyzed his last thoughts, he would have realized that it was the very first time since Linda's death that he was able to think of her without the accompanying pain. And if he could have been frank with himself, he would have to admit that he would never play a cat-and-mouse game with a woman unless he was intrigued, even fascinated by her.

"You used professional operatives," the professor continued, oblivious to his feelings, "and no matter how convincing they are, no matter how elaborate a background cover you provide them with, there is always a chance that a careful probe into their past could find some discrepancies and place them under suspicion. I understand where the Mossad in its anxiousness to get to Carlos would resort to such an alternative. But in the Jackal's case this is tantamount to a kamikaze action."

Sartain was pulling no punches, and he could tell by the sudden pallor of Tara's face that what he had said hit home.

She remained mute. Nervously she pulled from her purse a box of Sherman's cigarettelos. As she placed the brown cigarillo between her lips, now tightly drawn, Darlan hastened to light it for her.

Tara, who seldom smoked, nodded her thanks, inhaled once, and glared at Sartain coldly. But her feelings were mixed.

As much as she resented what the strong-minded professor with the incredibly powerful presence had to say, he did, unfortunately, make sound sense. She found it difficult to disagree with him. But there was more to it than that. Only she didn't know what or, perhaps, preferred not to.

"My plan, on the other hand, is to infiltrate Carlos's network with someone who is already a true, bona fide revolutionary," Sartain explained. "I intend to use agents whose credentials as genuine terrorists are beyond question and could withstand the most careful scrutiny."

He paused before he continued and stared pointedly at Tara. "That's where the crucial difference lies. And that's why I believe we have a reasonable chance of succeeding where others have failed."

Tara remained silent.

"Of course," Sartain added facetiously, "there is an even more effective way: that is, if we could talk one of Carlos's close lieutenants into double-crossing him and becoming an informer for us. But, as much as I know about this lot, you haven't got a prayer there. I can guarantee that even if somehow you did manage to approach any of Carlos's people, they would each turn you down with a bullet in your head."

Tara still showed no outward sign of approval, or disapproval. But as she listened to Sartain outlining his scheme, she was taken by strange, conflicting emotions. She told herself she didn't like the American who had replaced Navon, yet she had to admit that she found him intriguing. She felt a curiosity and awe that she hadn't experienced in a very long time. She wouldn't think of admitting that there was more to it, that from the very first moment she laid eyes on him, she had been attracted to the rugged professor. It was much more comfortable merely to resent him.

CHAPTER TWENTY-SIX

ARLOS'S arms jerked up as if to protect himself; his torso twitched once, twice. He sat up panting, gasping for air.

It took a full second before his sleep-filled eyes discerned the nude woman lying next to him, the tousled sheet wrapped around her narrow waist. A smile of relief came to his lips.

Fusako, whose face was concealed by her long black hair, breathed rhythmically, her slumber undisturbed by Carlos's abrupt awakening.

In the filmy dawn light that seeped through the ancient wooden shutters, Fusako looked incredibly young. Although thirty, two years older than Carlos, the Japanese terrorist had the figure of a fourteen-year-old girl. Her breasts were small and firm with tiny dark nipples, and her skin was ivory smooth. Like most Oriental women her body was practically hairless. A black, silky wisp barely hid her womanhood, which never failed to feel virgin tight.

Carlos had just endured a horrifying dream. He was somewhere in Japan's snowy mountains, subjected to a cruel, relentless *sokatsu* by Fusako. Little by little she forced him to admit that he was not a true revolutionary, all in front of the inner group of Terror International. Their hostile, hateful faces, particularly that of Abu Sherif, were still fresh in his mind.

Fusako was forcing him to confess that he rejected the basic tenets of collective action, that he was guilty of self-centered egotism, of looking after his own aggrandizement rather than that of the revolution.

And then, as he was forced to strip naked, Fusako, with bulging, horrid eyes, grabbed a *sai*, that ominous Okinawan trident, and was about to drive its sharp blades through his bare chest when he awakened covered with cold sweat.

Carlos shook his head, wiping some of the perspiration away with the back of his hand. In the distance he could hear the muezzin summoning the Kasbah's faithful to early morning prayer at the Sidi-Abderahmane Mosque. He knew exactly what had precipitated the bizarre dream. The night before, after they made love for the first time in weeks, he had finally gotten Fusako to tell him the story of the Snow Murders which had happened before they met.

Shortly before Fusako and her followers left for Lebanon in late 1971 in search of an international revolutionary base for the United Red Army, thirty URA members fled to Mount Haruna. Following the example of Mao's Long March, they had fled to the mountains not only to escape from a police crackdown in Tokyo but, more importantly, to plot the armed overthrow of the Japanese government.

Like Fusako, who studied at Tokyo's Meiji University, the group was made up mostly of students or college dropouts from middle- or upper-middle-class backgrounds. Isolated in the mountains as they were, and frustrated by their inability to plan and pursue a scheme of political action, they soon lost all sense of reality and turned the urge for violence in on themselves.

Tsuneo Mori, the group leader, launched a series of mock trials, bringing into play a Japanese-Buddhist process of logic called *sokatsu*—a questionable exercise which seeks to collate isolated facts into one concept. He used it as an excuse to cruelly persecute those who opposed him and his views. Once the process of *sokatsu* began, only death awaited the accused.

The procedure for the death sentence varied little. The victims were stripped naked, gagged, beaten, tortured, stabbed, strangled, and then tied outdoors in subfreezing temperatures and abandoned. After two days and nights of pleading for mercy, the victims' suffering came to an end.

One woman, eight months pregnant, was whipped with metal wire. Then, when pressing her abdomen failed to abort the child, she was tied to a tree and left to freeze to death.

Another woman was left bound and gagged under the floor of the hut for three days before dying where she could hear the others above cooking food and gossiping. A young man bled to death after biting off his tongue. One male member of the group was tortured and beaten after which his two younger brothers were ordered by Tsuneo to jointly plunge a knife into his heart. When they balked on their first effort, Tsuneo commanded them to do it again. In all, fourteen members died in the carnage within a few weeks.

With a sigh of relief Carlos rolled out of the wide bed onto the tiled floor. The coiled-spring mattress squeaked, and Fusako turned in her sleep, moaning softly. Carlos, tiptoeing barefoot around the bed toward the bathroom, paused to observe her.

She purred again and grabbed for the pillow, holding it tight between her arms, bending her knees to expose her small rounded buttocks. She seemed so sweetly innocent, so harmless, like a kitten. And yet . . . as Carlos recalled the previous night's lovemaking, the games she knew so expertly how to play!

He chuckled inwardly at the way she had been portrayed in the international media: "Pretty, but generally a rather sexless woman whose one great love is the Red Army," one magazine article described her. Others alleged that Fusako was a cold-hearted lesbian, dwelling on the fact that her marriage to Tsuyoshi Okudira was never consummated, that she had consented to be his wife for the sole purpose of using his name to get to Lebanon on her "honeymoon." They accused her of consciously and deliberately sending him to his death when she assigned him to the May 1972, suicidal mission at Lod (Ben-Gurion) Airport.

"Cold, frigid, passionless." Carlos smiled. If only they knew. If only they knew, for example, that when she worked part-time in a Ginza bar to raise money for the fledgling URA, when she proclaimed, "I saw every drink a customer bought as yet another rice ball for the Red Army," that there was more to it, that she indeed enjoyed prostituting her body. She had confided to him that as much as she hated the "capitalist pigs" who mauled and degraded her, she derived immense pleasure from the sexual act itself. Her salacious stories of her many exploits turned them both on, leading usually to explosions of passion he rarely experienced with any other woman.

In many ways, Carlos thought, as he quietly unlocked the door to the toilet, he was in love with Fusako. And he knew that, in her own way, she loved him too.

Two hours later Carlos, clad in a North African burnous over his normal clothing, and Fusako, in a white haik and a yashmak with only her dark eyes showing, walked the Kasbah's age-old labyrinth of dark alleys and narrow, winding passageways.

The Kasbah remained the last ancient Muslim remnant in the city of Algiers, which in Arabic derived its name from Al-Jazá'ir, "the islands." The reference was to the several small islands that formerly existed in the bay, all but one of which had been since connected to the shore or obliterated by the harbor works and jetties. Many of Algiers' old buildings had given way under French colonial rule and heavy European settlement to modern apartment houses and office complexes built in the white southern-European style. The trend continued after independence in 1962, and only the Kasbah remained intact with its maze of ancient, sometimes centuries-old structures crawling one on top of the other.

It was in the Kasbah that Carlos, primarily for reasons of security, had chosen, upon his return from Yugoslavia, to establish his new headquarters. He had politely rejected Boumedienne's offer of a large, secluded villa by the Sidi-Ferruch's beach outside Algiers.

In the Kasbah any Western-looking person, any stranger, any unusual, suspicious movement, could be quickly spotted by a network of lookouts and informers. And ever since the Jackal had learned of the Mossad's provisional plans to use its Shayetet 13, the noted Underwater Demolition Commando Team, to raid his beach house in Libya, he decided to stay away from such isolated, easily identifiable targets, no matter how fortified they were. Deep in the marrow of the Algerian Kasbah he felt safe, protected even from the agents of the host government. No matter how friendly the government was at present, a sudden about-face was not uncommon in Arab politics. The unpredictable consequences of the Jackal's next big move could make the working relationships even more tenuous.

As Carlos and Fusako approached a three-story house a few blocks from the Cemetery of the Princesses, their entrance was blocked by two burly Arabs in dark, flowing robes.

"Where are you going?" they asked ominously, hands gripping the pointed Shabarrias through the djelabahs' folds.

"To the well," Carlos responded soberly. His Arabic was distinctively Palestinian.

"What for?"

"To drink."

"To drink what?"

"Blood," Carlos answered, a flicker of a contented smile under his new moustache.

"Your numbers?"

"One-oh-one."

"One-oh-two," Fusako spoke for the first time.

The Arabs bowed and motioned them in. On the second floor were another two giant sentries armed this time with Kalashnikov AKN-47 rifles, whose folding stock allowed them to be easily tucked away under overgarments.

The exchange of watchwords repeated itself, only that this time instead of going to the well to drink blood, the passwords indicated a trip to the cowshed to milk oil. Their code numbers, however, remained the same.

The Jackal and the Red Army Queen climbed one more flight of aged limestone stairs where they met yet another sentry who showed them into a medium-sized room with a high, arched whitewashed ceiling.

In a semicircle, on chairs, ottomans, rugs, and an old divan sat ten of the innermost group of Terror International. Those among them whose identity had been known crowned the most-wanted lists of several countries.

Ulrich, Gertrude, Horst, and Fritz—the Kraut Squad, as Carlos was fond of referring to them—sat grouped together on the left side of the room. On the extreme right was Manuel Lattore, a Uruguayan Tupamaro and Carlos's oldest Latin American accomplice, who had looked amazingly like the Jackal prior to the latter's plastic surgery. To his right, sitting on a Persian rug, was Professor Tukahashi Takemoto, a former professor of eighteenth-century French literature at Rikkyo University and Fusako's most trusted confidant who had been in charge of the URA's European network since 1973.

Next to the Japanese professor sat the scar-faced, brutish-looking Mustafa Saka, Carlos's link to the Turkish Peoples Liberation Army, who with two fingers had gouged out the eyes of the Israeli consul general in Istanbul before shooting him to death. Behind him, on the divan, sat Ahmad Hashem and Halil Said, two Arab hit men who had been in the group ever since their recruitment by Carlos's predecessor, Mohammad Boudia. To their long list of victims they had recently added the names of Saul and Itamar. Like the German Fritz, who partook in the slaying of the two undercover Mossad agents, their identities were unknown to any of the Western intelligence services, a big plus in any future operation.

At the center of the room, by the two empty chairs reserved for Carlos and Fusako, sat a tall, handsome, moustachioed Arab. He wore a stylish three-piece suit in light beige tones. Wrapped around his head, and held in place by a black opal, was a traditional white kaffiyeh which accentuated his sharp, sculptured features and his dark, fierce eyes.

The man's renowned *nom de guerre* was Abu Sherif, and at the age of thirty-six he was one of the most admired figures of the Palestinian terrorist movement. Although a relative newcomer to the PFLP ranks, he was a veteran guerrilla who until two years before had been the Black September deputy chief of operations. A serious falling out between the ambitious Abu Sherif and Yasir Arafat in the spring of 1974, however, led the former to defect later that year from the Al Fatah ranks and join Dr. Wadi Haddad in Iraq. Within a very short time the charismatic man managed to gain the dentist terrorist's confidence and emerge as his unofficial right-hand man.

It was Abu Sherif who had been the subject of the coded message delivered by Ahmad Azzawi to Carlos on that unfortunate July day in Berlin. No wonder that poor Azzawi feared the subsequent fury of the Jackal. He knew that while Wadi Haddad had sent the money and the green light for the German operation he unexpectedly demanded that his new confidant, Abu Sherif, play a more prominent role in any of Carlos's future operations, "to enhance the shattered Palestinian cause."

Carlos had met the former Black Septemberist several times within the previous two years, and although he had nothing but respect for the Arab's operational skills, each time he had to deal with Abu Sherif, he liked him less. There was little question that the feeling was mutual, stemming from an intense, though concealed, personal rivalry between the two equally ruthless terrorists.

Both, however, were clever enough not to display these feelings openly, viewing each other as too dangerously powerful in his individual sphere to seek an open confrontation. Neither thought the time was ripe for a showdown. So they both waited for the opportune moment to come.

Carlos was well aware that Abu Sherif had grown increasingly resentful of the operational leeway which the Jackal enjoyed outside the Middle East. He realized that the Palestinian was particularly envious of his personal hold over the transnational network which came to be known as Terror International after Carlos's expansion of the original Commando Boudia. It enjoyed far more autonomy vis-à-vis the PFLP than the Black September ever enjoyed within the Al Fatah organization, mostly due to the independent links which Carlos had cunningly cultivated with other terrorist organizations throughout the world.

At the same time it had become all too obvious to Carlos, particularly after his recent visit to Haddad in a remote Yugoslavian hospital, where the Palestinian leader went for radiotherapy for his cancer, that Abu Sherif was already on the move to succeed the PFLP chief. Haddad, as Carlos learned from the Yugoslavian doctor, had only one or two more years to live.

Carlos had little doubt that if Abu Sherif did manage to succeed Wadi Haddad, his own privileged position within the PFLP would be quickly terminated. And, unless he subjugated himself to the new chief, his life would be in danger. The Palestinian was just too personally ambitious, too power hungry himself to let Carlos continue to enjoy his reputation as the world's Number One Terrorist.

The previous night, when Carlos had related to Fusako the details of his Yugoslavian trip, of how he fooled everyone into believing that he had continued on to Iraq, he confided to her that Haddad's days were numbered.

Aware of the rivalry between the two, she asked what he was planning to do about Abu Sherif.

Carlos merely shrugged in response, commenting that, for the time being he would go along with Haddad's request. In fact, the Jackal elaborated, he planned to put the Palestinian in charge of "Operation Fraternity," the Washington operation.

"But why?" Fusako protested. "You planned it all, why let him rip—"

"It's all right," he touched his fingers to her lips, smiling. "Don't worry. The Jackal has his own way of—shall we call it?—'constructive elimination.'"

Now, however, at the inner circle's meeting, Carlos greeted

him with such warmth that Abu Sherif was hard put not to respond in kind. They hugged and kissed each other in the best Arab tradition, and Abu Sherif was careful to compliment Carlos on his latest disguise.

"You look more of an Arab than I do," the Palestinian gushed.

"Thank you, my friend, my brother. Coming from your lips, I consider it the highest compliment."

Having greeted everyone else in the room, the Venezuelan took his seat and opened the meeting by reporting on his mission to the American Capital. Feigning self-reproach, he admitted from the outset that ambushing Colonel Joseph Navon was most probably foolhardy on his part, but that it was something that he had to do.

Carlos was confident that those present not only agreed with him, but that avenging Boudia's death the way he did served only to further enhance their veneration of their revengeful leader. Even Abu Sherif seemed awed by the daring act, wishing at the same time that his rival comrade would indulge in even riskier personal exploits. After all, no one's luck lasts forever.

In a relaxed manner—and in English, the only language common to all present—Carlos related his difficulty in finding a suitable Washington target. He then told of his trip aboard the *Fraternity* to Mount Vernon. What he had thought was a long shot, Carlos explained, turned out to be an ideal target.

He described the large catamaran at length, having memorized the most minute detail from the college notebook the day before. He savored impressing his listeners by being able to recall even the number of steps between decks.

"We'll need two commandos for the pilothouse," Carlos outlined, "preferably with some navigational experience, two for the middle cabin, and two for the engine room. And for the initial stage two people for the hurricane deck and another two to cover the weather decks. All in all the operation can be carried out successfully by no more than a dozen guerrillas with four of them, after the outside decks are cleared, becoming reserves. In other words, while eight are on watch, four can either sleep or rest alternately. That is, of course, if we're forced to use only twelve persons." Carlos surveyed the room. "Not bad at all, I dare say, for a boat of such size and such a darling, precious cargo," he remarked smilingly in his best British accent.

225
FIVE MINUTES TO MIDNIGHT

Most people in the room nodded their agreement. Not all of them understood, or even liked the Jackal, but when it came to planning and executing an operation, there was no one they would trust more. Carlos was unquestionably Number One.

"But most important," and now Carlos addressed himself directly to Abu Sherif who had already been told that he was going to lead the raid, "unlike most naval hijacks the getaway here will be exceptionally safe and simple. You see, all three catamarans used by the Thomas Line draw seven feet. Now, I've found out—" He paused as he pulled from underneath his long robe a nautical chart of the Potomac River. "—that the water at several places along the land-filled National Airport is up to ten feet deep," he explained, pointing to the chart.

"This means," Carlos continued to address Abu Sherif, "that when you demand that the DC-10 be brought to the runway, it will be only ten meters from the water. You can dock, disembark, and walk the short, open distance to the plane with as many hostages as you choose and with absolutely, and I repeat, absolutely, no danger of being ambushed.

"This is not a suicidal mission, Ibrahim," Carlos called the Palestinian by his true first name. "You know I believe neither in fedayeen nor kamikaze," he prevaricated. "We want you and the rest back here, victorious, and more importantly, alive. This is why I searched painstakingly for such a suitable target."

The Palestinian, who was studying the chart spread on his knees, nodded silently, unsure of what to say.

"Now our intention, as I've already discussed with Haddad," the Venezuelan addressed himself to everyone in the room, "is to have at least a few Americans in the raiding party. It will help us not only in terms of manpower, local logistics, and intelligence gathering, but more important in lending the operation a true revolutionary character. We don't want them to palm it off as just a terrorist assault by foreign elements. Without going into unnecessary detail at this point, I do want to assure you that contacts have already been made with the most reliable, combat-seasoned, truly revolutionary group in the United States.

"Colonel Navon notwithstanding," Carlos winked triumphantly, "I promise you I didn't waste any time."

The group's response to the Jackal's plan was positive, even enthusiastic. After some discussion, during which Abu Sherif exhibited considerable aptitude for questioning the most minuscule, seemingly obscure, yet relevant, details, Carlos called the meeting to an end. He and Fusako left the room first, while the others, as a safety precaution, followed them in short, but irregular intervals.

Carlos and Fusako, however, didn't leave the building. Instead they entered a room on the first floor where they quickly changed their garments, Fusako into a dark peasant dress still concealing her face and Carlos into European clothing with his head, however, wrapped in a checkered kaffiyeh and his eyes covered by large, dark sunglasses. Moments later they observed through the window the first of their comrades to enter the street. It was Abu Sherif. The two exchanged a meaningful glance but did not move from their hiding place.

Fifteen minutes and four persons later Halil Said appeared on the stone pavement below the couple's window. He seemed somewhat nervous, his movements furtive, as he walked quickly down the narrow street, occasionally looking suspiciously over his shoulder.

But as vigilant as Halil was in skulking through the Kasbah's maze of winding, twisting arteries, which became more and more crowded as he neared the Grand Mosque, he missed the newly disguised pair of master terrorists close on his tail.

Soon Halil reached a small square adjacent to the mosque which at this noon hour was bustling with people and activity. A number of shabby, timeworn shops ringed the old stone plaza, but most of the business transactions took place at the pushcarts, where street merchants hawked noisily, peddling anything from contraband Gilette blades to an endless variety of local confectionery.

Halil stopped in front of a coffee shop with a worn-out sign that read Marhaba but which bore no resemblance whatsoever to the posh restaurant of the same name on rue Hamani. He carefully scanned the place. Most of the customers were busy either playing or observing Shesh Besh, the local backgammon game. Some sucked on their nargileh, the favorite Arab water pipe, while running through their fingers the beads of their musbahaha, the Muslim rosary.

Apparently failing to find whomever he was looking for, Halil took a seat by an overturned barrel that served as a table. Facing the busy circle, he studied the people through impenetrable sun-glasses. He failed, however, to detect the Venezuelan and the Japanese who were observing him from the dark entrance of one of the adjacent buildings.

"I knew it!" Carlos hissed suddenly, pointing in the direction of a tall Arab approaching the coffee shop from the other side of the plaza.

"Who is he?"

"Abu Dervish. He was Yasir Arafat's man in Morocco and is now the Al Fatah representative here."

Fusako stared at him quizzically. "Abu Sherif?"

"No." Carlos shook his head as he unbuttoned the right cuff of his shirt-sleeve. "I don't think he has anything to do with it. He is not a traitor. But this dirty Arab, this son of a bitch Halil, I've been suspecting of passing information to Al Fatah ever since Entebbe." He cursed crudely in Spanish. "Now you know why I was so careful not to mention anything at the meeting about the Morris plan."

She nodded, comprehending.

As Carlos removed the adhesive tape from his forearm, letting the sharp part of the metal blade slide into his right palm, they both saw that Halil had spotted Abu Dervish. He stood up, and having left some money on the table for the coffee he didn't finish, he walked toward the Al Fatah man.

"Okay," Carlos said. "I must move before he makes contact, before he has a chance to utter a word. Cover me."

As Halil left the coffee shop and walked toward Abu Dervish, Carlos moved quickly in their direction. He made certain he kept behind Halil, careful, at the same time, not to attract Abu Dervish's attention.

Once more he felt elated, flushed. His body was light, almost weightless, nothing but superbly synchronized muscles in action. He imagined himself a panther closing on his quarry. His nostrils flared, his grip on the ten-inch knife tightened. Almost all of the dagger was a thin, sharp blade, which, pressed against the under-side of his lower arm, felt part of him, an extension of the stalker.

He was never more himself than at such moments. Yet people wondered why he, the mastermind, the superb planner and or-ganizer, would condescend to doing the killings himself. They could not comprehend the joy such acts brought him.

The mediocre fools! He relished the irony. What do they know?

The distance between him and Halil had been reduced now to fifteen feet when the Arab suddenly turned his head.

Behind two pairs of sunglasses, one's eyes widened in terror, in recognition of the end; the other's narrowed in intense excitement, in anticipation of the kill.

Without the slightest hesitation, in tune with his walking movement, the Jackal's arm shot up and forward in such a quick motion that only a camera's lens could have captured it.

For one-hundredth of a second the steel blade glittered in the sun as it soundlessly sliced the air, then pierced the Arab's chest.

Before his victim, clutching the short shaft of the weapon implanted in his chest, hit the pavement, before anyone, including the Al Fatah man, realized that anything had happened, Carlos had swiveled and quickly, but casually, strolled away.

As he left the square, turning into a quieter street which led up toward the old fortress, he was joined by Fusako, whose hand still tightly gripped the Skorpion machine pistol under the folds of her peasant dress.

"Do you want me to make sure he's dead?" she whispered as she strode alongside him.

Carlos shook his head. "He's dead, all right," he said with a tone of finality.

"How can you be sure?" she persisted. "You went at him from fifteen feet. What if he's only seriously wounded? What if he talks? Can we risk it?" She was breathless as she strained to keep in pace with him.

Carlos slowed down and turned to face her. "I said," he snapped angrily, "he's dead!"

CHAPTER TWENTY-SEVEN

"**P**ROFESSOR Sartain?" The surprise registered on Amy Lahr's face as she was brought into the windowless room assigned by the warden. "Professor Sartain! What on earth are you doing here?" Though amazed, she clearly seemed pleased to see him.

Sartain was heartened by Amy's initial, amicable greeting. After all, he hadn't seen her since her trial six years back, and she had never since communicated with him, even though her attorney had assured him that she was deeply grateful for his favorable testimony. Driving down from Los Angeles to the Terminal Island penitentiary, he had tried to envision what her first reaction to his surprise visit would be.

"Well, I am here to see you," he smiled at her, extending his hand. She returned the smile and took his hand in hers.

They examined each other silently in the dim light of the solitary, caged bulb in the ceiling.

"I . . . I can't imagine why you've come to see me," she said, "but I'm sure glad to see you, Professor." Her prison-dulled eyes sparkled with pleasure.

"Please call me Sam, Amy. We're no longer at the university."

"Unfortunately," she said softly, her eyes momentarily regaining their shut-in glaze. "But I don't think I could just call you Sam. Apparently, Dr. Sartain, I am not as much of a radical as that," she winked.

If anything, Sartain thought, the six years behind bars seemed to have mellowed her once rather abrasive personality. He had always liked her, despite her rough edges, but he felt affection for her even more now.

"Well," he cleared his throat, not quite certain how to begin. "I . . . I have a few things I would like to discuss with you, Amy."

His expression changed. It was time to do business. He pointed to one of the two wooden chairs to his right. "Let's sit over there, and then we can talk."

The professor and his former pupil sat down facing each other.

"I've always thought of you, Amy, as a very bright, mature student. So I'd rather get straight to the point. You see, Amy, it's . . . it's about Jim that I came to talk to you."

"Jim?" she gasped, a terrible fear in her eyes. "Has something happened to him? Is he all right?"

"No, no, nothing of the sort," Sartain was quick to calm her, his hunch—that her all-consuming love for Jim Anders had not dwindled at all over the years—vindicated. "Nothing has happened to him. For all I know, he's fine. As a matter of fact it may turn out that I'm a bearer of good news for you two."

She sighed in relief, but the thought of harm having come to Jim made her anxious. She got up and paced the room. She tried to smile. "You sure scared the living hell out of me there, Doc. How many times have I dreaded the—" She shook her head and left the sentence incomplete. "Do you have a cigarette on you by any chance?" she asked.

"No. Sorry, Amy, I don't smoke. Only a pipe."

She shrugged.

"Do you want me to get you one. I can knock on the door and ask the guard."

"No, don't bother, it doesn't really matter. I'm not really a smoker myself. It's just that . . . Anyway," she smiled again, collecting herself, "you said something about good news. What good news? I could sure use some."

The professor examined her carefully. "In a sense," he said, "it all depends on you. In fact, on both of you."

Amy ceased pacing. She looked puzzled. "I don't get it," she said. "You speak in riddles. It can't be anything to do with a parole, can it? I won't be eligible for at least another four years." She stared at him, questioning.

Sartain shook his head. "No, it's not," he said. "But it does have something to do with getting you out of here, free. And . . ." he paused more dramatically than he intended, "with a possible pardon for Jim."

For a long while she was speechless, bewildered. Then she responded, unsmiling. "It's a very cruel joke you're playing on me, Doc, if what you say is not true."

"If you sit down," he said, reaching for her hand, "I'll explain everything to you."

Twenty minutes later, when Sartain finished explaining what he had in mind, Amy seemed dazed, overwhelmed, but to his relief, neither totally shocked nor put off.

"You do realize what you're asking me to do, don't you, Professor? And I'm not merely talking about the danger, the risks involved."

Sartain nodded solemnly. "I do. Very much so. But Amy, again, I'm not asking you to betray the movement nor your convictions. These people are not revolutionaries, they are terrorists, and you know there is a difference. They are not fighting for a better world, they are nihilists and anarchists of the worst kind. Most of them are nothing more than self-indulgent killers or fanatics insane with hatred who will stop at absolutely nothing. They are not committed to a people's cause, to the masses, to the working class. They have no regard for these. They consider themselves above everyone else; they are an elitist, fascist group hiding under the mantle of radical socialism."

Sartain paused. Staring directly into her eyes, he prodded, "Now deep inside you, Amy, you know all of this to be true. You know I'm right."

What Sartain didn't tell her, however, was that for a number of weeks now he had been carefully studying her intercepted correspondence with Jim. He was well aware of the gradual disillusionment of her fugitive boyfriend with the radical-socialist regime in Algeria. As a teacher in a crowded, understaffed and underbudgeted school, Jim had grown to resent the flow of most of the oil and gas revenues toward the military establishment and the purchase of unnecessary armaments from the Soviet block. This, while illiteracy was still as high as it had been under French colonialism, with almost fifty percent of the population still without any formal education.

Sartain couldn't tell Amy about the self-doubt he read between the lines of their letters. Doubt which they both were loath to articulate explicitly, lest their own personal sacrifices seem totally futile. He could only infer that underneath their continuous lip service to the cause, to their commitment, lingered some very grave questions with regard to the doctrines which they once had so readily espoused.

"I don't know," Amy said, confused. "I know that Haddad,

Carlos, Fusako, and the others are not exactly what they claim to be. Their actions, as their life-style, are at times anything but revolutionary. I'm not naïve, Doc, not anymore. But still, how do I know that what you are telling me is true? How do I know that Carlos is really planning the sort of craziness you claim he is? How do I know?"

"You don't," the professor responded quickly and sharply, expecting the question. "You don't. But this is why it's an open-end arrangement. We'll let you go, but then it's up to you to find out what Carlos and his gang are planning. Once you're out of this country, we can't force you to continue to cooperate with us. In fact, even if you and Jim are willing, there is no guarantee that you will be able to penetrate Terror International. But you two have a better chance than anyone else, providing you follow my instructions."

Seeking her eyes, Sartain continued. "You'll have to find out for yourself, Amy. But if you want to come back here with Jim, you can live a normal life again in the place you two were born and belong. This country has undergone tremendous changes since Vietnam, but it still needs people like you to carry on with the job of making it an even better place. If you want to be pardoned and cleared, if you want to stop being fugitives for the rest of your lives, then I'm offering you the best chance you'll ever have."

Amy rose and began pacing the room again. The professor remained silent, following his former student with his eyes, knowing full well what was going through her mind. He had done his best to convince her. It was all up to her now.

Sitting and watching her, Sartain realized he had forgotten how pretty she was. In fact she looked slimmer now, even in the baggy prison uniform, and it suited her. She also wore her wavy auburn hair shorter and tidier, revealing her fine features and those beautiful hazel eyes that radiated intelligence. Indeed, the professor mused, with her full, firm bosom she looked seductive enough to entice a male guard to break the rules.

Amy suddenly stopped pacing and turned toward him. "Do you need an answer right away?"

"No, not right away," he responded carefully. "But I would like you to make a decision soon. Let's say within a week at the latest. Don't forget that your escape has to go like clockwork and must appear genuine. Planning the details will take time. And we would like to have you in Algeria as soon as possible."

"I understand. But I still have to sort it out in my mind." She smiled bitterly. "The jailbreak better look believable, very believable, or my life ain't going to be worth a dime."

Sartain nodded. "We know that."

"Is the plan foolproof?"

"It is."

"What is it then?"

"Well," he cleared his throat, "it's rather simple. All I'll give you now is a rough sketch. A guard, who has been recently hired here and assigned to your bloc, is one of our undercover agents. He's going to make indirect, but noticeable advances toward you, to which you'll be coyly responsive. Now, on a prearranged night, you'll supposedly lure him into your cell and knock him unconscious with . . . let's say . . . the leg of your chair or your bed. You'll then remove the keys from him. Do you know corridor B?"

"You mean the one to the right of my cell?"

"Exactly. You'll follow it to the brown metal door on the northern, outside wall. It's not marked, but you'll have no problem telling which one it is, and you'll have the key to it. This door will lead you outside the building, directly opposite the Coast Guard base. Do you get it?"

She nodded silently.

"Okay. Now about ten yards to your left, right next to the service entrance gate, the two tall fences merge into one as they connect to the building itself. Almost at the end of this one fence, there is a small door. It's an emergency hatch in case of fire or earthquake. You will have also gotten the key to this door from the guard. Once you unlock it, you're home free."

"Not quite," Amy responded. "What about the watchtower with the searchlight just inside the service entrance? And what about the patrol car that cruises the road regularly?"

A wry smile flickered around Sartain's mouth. "I see you're quite familiar with the security arrangements here. Have you—"

"It crossed my mind," Amy replied before he finished his question. "But I soon realized there was no way I could pull it off." She shrugged. "Not without inside help."

"I see," Sartain said. "Anyway, don't worry about the searchlight or the patrol car. You'll be briefed in time about both. But what do you think of the plan in general? Does it help you to make up your mind?"

Amy hesitated. As she sat down again, she asked, "Can I have his gun?"

A momentary silence hung in the air between them as the professor carefully weighed the unanticipated request.

"Yes, I guess you can," he finally conceded, a tinge of uncertainty in his voice. "I guess it will only make the whole thing that much more convincing."

"You realize, Professor, that you're really putting yourself on the line here. If I use that gun . . ." She paused and studied his face directly. "If that gun goes off, you're through, finished."

A knowing smile crossed the professor's face. "We'll all be, sooner or later, if we don't incapacitate Terror International. I think it's well worth the risk."

She didn't comment.

"Well?"

"I still need to think about it," she said.

Sartain shrugged in understanding, resigned to the fact that he was not going to have her immediate consent. But there was something in his former pupil's clear, intelligent eyes which reminded him of Linda, and also of another woman whom he had only recently met. It was perhaps from it that he derived the confidence that in the end Amy would come through.

On the very same day that Professor Sartain visited Amy at the federal correctional institute on the tip of Terminal Island, Helga Denz, alias Helga Lang, moved from the Park Motel to a small furnished house on Morris's Jackson Street. It was an old, undistinguished brick building which was sheltered from the street and the neighboring houses by a cluster of evergreens and a tall wooden fence.

That evening, right after his day shift at the Dresden nuclear plant, the eager Dr. Karl Baumann came to see Helga at her new residence. It had been almost a month since Helga had first phoned to let him know that she was in town. During that time, despite much beseeching on his part, she had consented to meet him only once, and again only for a brief luncheon.

Having shown him the house, Helga led Karl back to the living room where they sat to face the fireplace on an old, Early American couch.

Placing his beer on the wooden coffee table in front of him, Karl turned toward Helga. He studied her profile as she watched the flames licking the logs like lizards' tongues. Touching her hair gently, he sighed. "I can't tell you how much I've missed you, Helga," he confessed. "All I've been able to think about these last few weeks is you. Only you. It's been very hard on me, not being able to see you more often. At times . . ." He paused, trying in vain to hold back. "At times I've considered forsaking everything and taking you off to some remote place . . ."

Helga slapped him with the back of her hand with such ferocity that his glasses flew off his nose.

"Aiee!" the scientist moaned in pain, groping for his glasses with one hand and soothing his hot cheek with the other.

"I don't want to hear you say that ever again!" Helga scolded ominously. "Never again!"

"Okay, okay," he coughed.

That's all she needed, Helga thought, for him to contemplate quitting his job at the nuclear facility. She was pleased, on the other hand, by his obsession with her. It would become very useful later.

"You have an important, prestigious job at the plant," she said, her tone mellowed. "I've told you before that the last thing I want is to interfere with your career or your family life. Is that clear?"

Karl nodded silently, reaching for his beer glass.

But before his grip closed on it, Helga grabbed him by his thinning hair and pulled his head to her. "Do you understand?"

"I understand. I do, I do."

"*Gut*," she let go of his hair. "But I still have to punish you for what you've said." She touched softly his reddened cheek with her cool hand, smiling suggestively.

The aging nuclear scientist nodded enthusiastically. "*Ja, ja. Bitte.* I do deserve punishment. I did misbehave."

"Well then, fetch me that whip over there." She pointed to the other side of the room.

Karl adjusted his glasses. "Where? Where?" he asked anxiously. "I can't see it."

She pointed to the mahogany dresser in the alcove. "There, inside the top drawer."

He scurried to the dresser and retrieved the black leather whip she had picked up in Chicago.

"Now undress," she ordered as she dimmed the standing lamp by the sofa and fed the fireplace more wood.

With trembling hands Karl undid his tie and began to unbutton his shirt. He never took his eyes off her. His heart pounded wildly, fearing, yet yearning for the approaching pain. His organ, which ordinarily required a great amount of fondling by his wife to achieve a semblance of an erection, was already bulging hard against his briefs.

Helga turned up the radio. "*Schnell! Schnell!*" she barked as she cracked the whip against the floor. "Quick, what are you waiting for, you lazy bum? You scum of the earth! You filthy Nazi!"

He quickly took off his shoes and unzipped his pants. He was about to remove his underwear, when she suddenly shrieked, "*Nein!*"

He froze. Stunned, puzzled.

"No," she repeated. "And leave the socks on too."

He stared at her as a child denied his candy. "Why, Helga? Why?"

"I told you, I don't want to leave any marks. You're married now, you know."

He nodded. The disappointment registered all over his face.

She approached him, stopping before him with her legs apart. In her high-heeled boots she was an inch or two taller than he. Pushing down on his shoulder with the butt of the whip, she forced him to his knees.

"Take off my boots," she said.

He did, very slowly.

"Now suck my toes!" she commanded.

He shook his head. "*Nein,*" he said, "I won't."

It was hard to believe, she thought, that more than eight years had passed. Everything came so second nature. She cracked the whip against the floor by him. "You'll do as I say," she growled. "Bend your stinking head down and lick my toes!"

A thin, defiant smile crossed Karl's lips as he shook his head stubbornly.

Pressing his neck down with her right foot, she flogged him on his back, buttock, and the bottom of his feet. She hit him quite forcefully, yet made sure she didn't touch any exposed flesh.

Karl groaned in delight. "Harder, harder. Please harder," he pleaded.

"Shut up!" she screamed annoyed as she removed her foot and went for his hair again. "I told you I don't want to leave any marks."

"Please!" he was desperate. He longed to strip his underpants and free his throbbing organ.

"No," she said and walked away. She too would have enjoyed the sight of blood, but it was not wise.

He sat on the floor, winded, deflated. How could she leave him like this? The hell with his wife.

Suddenly he brightened. "Helga?"

"No more, Karl."

"I know. I just wanted to tell you some good news."

She turned and looked down at him, curious.

"Betty will be going away soon with the kids. She's spending Christmas with her family in Savannah. That's in Georgia. We talked it over the other night, and she will be leaving early, about three weeks from now. She doesn't like the weather here this time of the year anyway. But I'll be staying behind because of work. I'll join them later, just for the holiday itself."

Helga reflected silently on the news. "I understand she is rich," she answered.

Karl smiled. "Oh, yes, quite. The old man is very wealthy. In fact they have a huge ranch out there."

"Any brothers?"

He shook his head. "No, just another sister."

"I would like to see what your wife looks like. Do you carry any pictures of her on you?"

"No, but I can bring some next time, if you want."

She nodded. "Bring some of the children too."

CHAPTER TWENTY-EIGHT

ATKINS thumbed one last time through the newspaper clippings of Amy Lahr's escape from Terminal Island. "Well," he remarked as he closed the folder and placed it on top of his desk, "so far, so good, Sam. The L.A. *Times* seems to be the only one to bother printing her picture, and then only on page six. That discovery of those huge arms caches in San Bernardino County got all the front-page play. Good timing."

Sartain, who had brought the clippings to Fred's office, nodded. "I was worried about too much media coverage, with pictures of her all over the place. All we need is for someone to recognize her and turn her in before she has a chance to cross the border. You can stage such a jailbreak only once, not twice."

"How long is she going to remain in the States?" Atkins asked. "Do you know where she is planning to cross the border?"

The professor shook his head. "I don't, and I only assume that she'll sneak across on land. She didn't really know herself. It depends on what her contacts in the underground think is safest."

The Triple C chief had seconded Sartain's decision to let Amy rely on her own connections within the underground for passage out of the country. Though riskier, and more time consuming, the more she relied on her radical comrades, the more credible her escape would become. If Carlos were to fall for it, the ruse would have to be perfect.

"How is the guard doing?"

"Oh, he's all right," Sartain responded. "She hit him a bit harder than we expected, but it's only a mild concussion. He's been hospitalized, but he'll be out for reassignment soon."

"I hope so," Atkins said as he handed over the folder. "What do we do now?"

"On this?" Sartain asked as he took the file. "Nothing. We wait."

"Just wait?"

"Yep. Just wait. Until we hear from her."

"I see . . . But what happens, Sam, if Carlos decides to make his move sooner than you expect him to?"

The professor took his time to respond. Leisurely he loaded his pipe. "Is it all right with you, Fred, if I smoke?"

Atkins nodded, amused. "I always liked your tobacco's aroma. You should know that by now. But you still haven't answered the question."

The professor struck a match, sucked, and watched the smoke waft toward the ceiling. "I didn't say we sit here and watch the grass grow. We need to pursue all other possible avenues to cover ourselves. But I'm still convinced that Jim and Amy are our best bet. In their case there isn't much we can do for the time being but sit and wait." He puffed again on his pipe, adding, "And if my hunch is right, we have time . . . probably until summer."

"Summer?" Atkins had clearly not expected so long a wait. "Why summer?"

The professor shrugged, regretting he had said anything. "Don't worry, it's only a hunch." He hurried to change the subject. "Incidentally, about Christmas dinner, will you tell Bev that I'd be honored to attend. Steve won't be able to though. He'll be in Vermont, skiing with some friends of his. In fact he'll be leaving already tomorrow to spend a few days in New York."

Atkins nodded his understanding. "Well, at least you can come, Sam. It will be a real pleasure having you with us. By the way, how's Steve doing? Is he still working with you on the book?"

"Yes, he's doing very well. He's been really a tremendous help to me. In fact," Sartain smiled proudly, "he's becoming more of an expert on Carlos and Terror International than I am."

"Perhaps we should replace you with him," Atkins teased. "Seriously though, does he know?"

"Does he know what?"

"Does he know about your work here?"

The professor hesitated, studying his pipe, which had gone out. "Yes, Fred, he does. I had to tell him. There was no other way. He's much too smart not to have guessed that there was more to it than just writing a book about Carlos." He paused to relight his pipe, reflecting momentarily on the long conversation he had had with Steve after his son had moved in. "I told him about my work here. He knows what we are trying to do, though, only in general terms. But, Fred, I do have total confidence in him. He wouldn't talk, not even inadvertently. He's one of the most tight-lipped people I've ever known."

"All right," Atkins granted, "as long as he doesn't talk. It's your personal safety which is first and foremost on the line here, and I'm sure he can see that."

The professor nodded. "He certainly does. I told you he has become as much of an authority on the subject of Carlos as I am."

Atkins regarded him speculatively, weighing the thought. "Sam, how much does Steve know about your work for NSA and one-oh-one?"

Sartain's expression tautened. "All he knows is that because of my army Intelligence background I did some work for the NSA back in the early fifties, and that that's how I met you. He knows absolutely nothing about one-oh-one, and I hope it remains that way, forever." His voice turned hard, quiet. "I'm not particularly proud of it, you know."

Atkins shrugged. "It was a different time, Sam. There is nothing to be ashamed of."

"I prefer to forget it," Sartain muttered bitterly.

Atkins shook his head. "You amaze me sometimes, Sam. Here you are, planning—" There was something in Sartain's hard stare which made him stop in mid-sentence.

Granted, Atkins mused, the 101 was probably the best intelligence unit ever put together; surely the most secret. He was proud to head it at the time. But Sam was right; it was quasi-legal at best, never really authorized by President Truman's 1952 directive which established its supersecret parent organization, the NSA.

Atkins changed the subject. "I was talking to Tara this morning, after the meeting. She told me the Mossad is convinced that Carlos's new base of operations is Algeria, and that you were also correct in your analysis that he never went to Iraq from Yugoslavia."

"Well, I'm glad they finally see things my way," Sartain remarked indifferently, collecting his papers, ready to leave.

"She asked some personal questions about you."

The professor shot him a glance, but quickly looked aside, feigning disinterest.

"In fact she admitted to me that in the beginning they were not quite sure about you," Atkins continued. "Your past stance on the Palestinian issue, your articles about the need for some sort of a Palestinian entity if there was ever to be peace there, did not exactly endear you to the Israelis, you know."

Sartain did not respond. There was something in his friend's tone which told him Fred was getting at something.

"I assured her, as I once did Echad, that even though you may be sympathetic to the idea of some form of Palestinian autonomy, you are anything but pro-PLO. I reminded her that your political views are shared by many Israelis, including your friend, Professor Amir, who is one of their top experts on terrorism."

Sartain shook his head. "I didn't know I was in need of an advocate. Anyway what did she say to that?"

Atkins smiled puckishly. "Oh, she understood perfectly. She's quite a remarkable woman, you know."

"I know."

"Do you really?"

"What do you mean by that?" Sartain defended, realizing only too late that he had swallowed the bait.

"I mean, how much do you really know about her? There is a human side to her, like—"

Sartain stood up, he had heard enough. "Fred," he interjected, "I know as much about her as I need to know. I'm not quite sure what you're driving at, but I have no interest in her personal life. None whatsoever. I have to leave now, I'll see you later. Goodbye."

As the inwardly agitated professor was about to open the door, Atkins called, "Sam . . ."

Sartain turned around, "Yes?"

"Sam, Tara is going to be staying in town for a few days, personal business. I wanted you to know that she'll be staying at the Madison Hotel under the name of Ruth Gordon."

Sartain studied his friend's foxy expression. "I fail to understand why you're telling me that. I don't think she needs a tour guide. I'm sure she is not lacking escorts." The sarcastic reference to Tara's active social life was blatantly clear.

"Well, I just thought, in case some emergency came up, that you might want to know where you could reach her. She'll be there through the twenty-second," Atkins said nonchalantly.

"Good-bye," Sartain snapped with finality and almost slammed the door behind him.

Left alone, the Triple C chief shook his head, smiling to himself. He pressed the intercom button on his desk. "Get me Mr. Colton, please," he asked. Minutes later he was talking to the CIA director.

Jim ran his fingers slowly, lightly, over Amy's face and down her taut, naked body toward the soft lips of her sex. He bent over and circled her hardened nipples with his tongue.

Amy moaned softly, her eyes closed, a contented smile on her face, "I thought you were tired," she whispered.

"I am," he smiled, only too aware that they had made love three times already that night. "You, my dear, are just irresistible."

"I'm glad," she said.

Jim moved his tongue up the side of her long neck until he found her ear. Biting gently on its lobe, he murmured, "I've kept all your letters, you know. All five hundred of them."

"All of them?"

"All of them."

"Why?"

"Oh," he drew back, laughing softly, "I intend to publish them one day."

"No way," she shook her head lazily on the pillow. "Leave that to Anita."

"Anita?"

"Anita Hoffman. I thought you knew she published her correspondence with Abbie in *Esquire*."

"In *Esquire*?" he shook his head, incredulous. "You must be kidding. When?"

Amy laughed. "Last spring, under the title, 'Love letters from the Underground.'"

"Was it good?" Jim sounded curious.

"Sad." She paused. "I cried for them when I read it, and for us. Must have been a mental block that I didn't mention it to you. They couldn't hack it, you see, went their own way."

"That much I knew," Jim said soberly. "I did hear that Abbie married another woman, became a bigamist." In the candle's faint light he saw Amy's smile turn sad. He sought her hand and squeezed it.

"It sure didn't take him long," she said with a tinge of bitterness. "Only a year. I'll never forget that line in his first letter to her: 'I think we are one of the greatest love stories of this or any other time.' "

Amy raised herself on her elbows and sat up against the wooden headboard. She stared at Jim's face, trying to take in each detail: the curly blond hair, the light blue eyes, the cleft chin which added strength to his otherwise soft features. She adored his body, which had the build of a swimmer—muscular, yet slim and light.

"Talking about the greatest love story . . ." Amy whispered, teasing the fine, golden curls on his chest. She completed her sentence with a smile.

They gazed into each other's eyes lovingly.

She took his hand and brought it to her lips. "Thank you," she said and kissed it.

"Don't," he whispered back, his fingers touching her mouth softly to silence her. "Don't thank me. It's I who am grateful to you. If I didn't crack up, if I didn't go mad, it's only thanks to you. It's because of the hope that one day we would be together again." He played his fingers through her hair. "In fact even now it seems like a fantasy, a dream I've dreamed so many times," he sighed. "I can't tell you how many times . . . Lying here, in my place, in each other's arms and . . ." he reflected, ". . . and there was always the candle, like the last time we made love in D.C. Remember?"

She nodded.

"And any moment now," Jim continued in the same low voice, "I expect to suddenly wake up and find that once again this is merely a dream, and that you're gone, that you're still locked in at Terminal Island." He took her in his arms, embracing her tightly, almost desperately.

"I know what you mean," Amy whispered, "a dream . . . a

fantasy." Tears welled in her eyes, tears of both joy and sorrow—joy for being reunited at long last, and sorrow for all the lost time, for all the misery they both had to endure.

"I love you," she said, "I love you, Jim. I love you so much it scares me, and yet . . . and yet, it makes me fear nothing, nothing at all."

"I'll never let you go, never, never ever again," he breathed in her ear and then showered her face with quick, light kisses. Their arched bodies responded to each other like dancers moving to the same undulating rhythms. His hands pushed her soft buttocks against his groin, and he felt she was ready and eager for him. He slid into her with such force and intensity, as if trying to consume the agony of the six-year separation through the blaze of their melting bodies. And when they came, they both cried out in protest, yet in triumphant declaration to the world, that they were one.

Later when they lay resting on their backs, sharing a cigarette, she was the first to break the silence. "We've got to do it, Jim. We've got to do it," she repeated, touching the subject which had been paramount in both their minds ever since she told him of Sartain's terms shortly after her arrival in Algiers.

"We must find out what it's all about," Amy continued. "I mean, if it is nonconventional, as Dr. Sartain claims, if it is nuclear or biological or anything like that, then it's insane, crazy. It negates everything we believe in. Regardless of the risk, Jim, we can't just let it happen."

Jim snuffed out the cigarette in the small metal ashtray he was holding for both of them. "I don't disagree, Amy; it's just . . . I mean, what can we do? I don't even know if we can join Carlos's group. And even if we do, there is still no guarantee that we can find out anything."

"I know there is no guarantee," Amy turned to face him, "but the least we can do is try. All we've got to do, the professor said, is find out where and when they're planning to strike. He doesn't expect us to uncover all the details. Just get him some information to go on. They will do the rest. Jim, we've got to at least try."

He shook his head. "I don't know, baby. I really don't know. It's just not that simple."

Amy was not about to give up. "Look at me, Jim," she appealed. He turned to face her. "Jim, I want to have a child. I want more than one child. I want to raise a family with you. Do you understand what I'm saying?" Her gaze was as intense as he had ever seen it. "It's what I've been dreaming all these last years. Do you understand, Jim? We've fought for something, haven't we? Well, I want our kids to have a future . . . I don't want them to be the children of fugitives, gypsies. I don't want to have to constantly hide. I want to raise them at home." Unintentionally she broke down, her tears falling softly on her breasts.

Jim had never seen her really cry before. "Please don't," he touched her moist cheeks.

"I'm sorry," she said, regaining control. "It's not fair. I shouldn't be asking so much of you. I'm being selfish. I'm sorry." She wiped the last of her tears. "I love you, Jim, and I'll go anywhere with you. It's you I want, not the children. I don't know what came over me."

He pulled her chin up to his face. "We'll give it a try," he said. "I don't want our children to grow up in a world full of crazy maniacs tossing nuclear bombs around. I didn't want to tell you before, but I have been approached several times about becoming more involved . . . I refused each time. I guess I was afraid I might get killed before I had a chance to see you again."

She kissed him. "I would have killed myself if anything had happened to you," she said. "Hoping to see you again was the only thing that kept me going."

He reached for the wine bottle on the table beside him, and emptied the last of it into their glasses. Handing her one, he toasted: "To Montana!"

"To Montana!" she repeated. "And to our children."

CHAPTER TWENTY-NINE

OUTSIDE, the colorful Christmas lights flickered against the soft white snow. Sartain sighed and glanced at the antique wooden clock in his study. The wrought silver hands showed half past eleven. He picked up the book and peered at it again, but the words failed to conjugate, the sentences conveyed no meaning. Earlier he had found it difficult to write or read any of the professional literature stacked up on his desk. Even Uris's novel about Ireland, which he liked, failed to hold his attention.

Yet it was not fatigue that disrupted his concentration. On the contrary he felt restless, agitated, and more than anything, painfully lonesome. Worse, he couldn't keep Tara out of his mind. The more he fought it back, the more her image crept into his thoughts.

He had thought about her before, at night when he was alone. And when he did, it was not without some guilt for betraying the memory of the woman he loved.

Once, the night Steve left for his ski trip, Sartain had experienced a vivid dream. He and Linda were skiing at Heavenly Valley when they stopped to rest atop one of the slopes. It was a bright, crisp day, and the view of the deep blue lake below was breathtaking.

Overwhelmed, Sartain took Linda into his arms and held her tightly, burying his face in the softness of her fragrant hair. Suddenly he was seized by a strange sensation that it was another woman he was embracing, that the hair had changed texture and color. He pulled back, startled to discover it was Tara he was holding. He awoke disturbed, consumed by guilt.

Since Linda's death, Sartain had not been with a woman. There were plenty of women more than willing to comfort his loneliness, but they held no interest for him. His mind was else-where, his heart still devoted to the memory of Linda. His one desire, the desire for revenge.

Sartain's acute melancholic restlessness now had less to do with Steve's departure, or the advent of the memory-filled Christmas holidays, than with the fact that it was the twenty-first of the month. Tomorrow Tara would leave Washington. Curiously he was gripped by a sudden, inexplicable longing for her presence. He yearned to be with her, talk to her, unload his deepest feelings on her. It was as if she alone in the world could comprehend the despair within him, as if she alone could help smooth the stinging pain in his heart.

The past few days Atkins's words kept buzzing in Sartain's head: "She is a remarkable woman, you know . . . asked some personal questions about you . . . how much do you really know her? . . . a human side to her . . . she will be staying through the twenty-second . . ."

Sartain glanced again at the old wooden clock. She wouldn't be in her room anyway, he tried to dissuade himself from any impulsive move. She's most probably partying with her society friends. Only the other day he had happened to see her name mentioned again in the gossip columns of the *Post*. Even if she was not out, she was most probably in bed by now.

His hand reached for the brown telephone by his armchair, and, as if he were a remote-control robot, he watched his fingers dial information.

"Number for the Madison Hotel, please," he heard himself ask the operator. "Eight, six, two, sixteen hundred? Thank you."

He hung up. Last chance to reconsider. He picked up the receiver and dialed the number.

"Mrs. . . . Ruth Gordon, please."

"Who is calling please?" the hotel operator queried.

"I'm sorry?" Sartain was surprised. All he had planned to do was check if she was there, to see . . .

"Sir, who may I say is calling Mrs. Gordon? We're requested to inform our guests at this late hour who is trying to reach them," the operator explained politely but firmly.

"Tell her it's, er . . . Dr. Sartain."

"Just a moment please, Doctor," she disappeared off the line.

He felt a strong urge to hang up. But it was too late; he had already given his name. What had he done? What in hell's name was he going to say to her? That he wanted to wake her up and wish her a Merry Christmas . . . or a happy Chanukah?

"Hello?"

She said only one word, yet he recognized the unmistakable voice. Thank God she didn't sound sleepy or disturbed.

Oh no! What if she had someone in her room? He felt like a fool.

"Hello? Dr. Sartain?" Her voice had more of an accent to it on the phone, but it sounded friendly.

"Mrs. Gordon . . . I'm sorry, I . . . mean Ms. Kafir?"

"Yes. What is it, Dr. Sartain? Is anything wrong?"

"No, not really. I just . . ." He paused. Christ Almighty, what was he going to say now? He wracked his mind. "I just . . . felt like talking to you," he managed to get out. He had never felt more embarrassed in his life.

"I see." She didn't sound surprised. "You do sound disturbed. Are you sure there is nothing wrong?"

"No, there is nothing," he responded quickly. "It's just that . . ." He paused awkwardly again. He would have given anything to be able to terminate the conversation with some dignity.

"Do you want to talk on the phone or would you prefer that we meet somewhere?" she helped. "As you may know, I am scheduled to leave for New York tomorrow morning and then to Israel for a couple of weeks. We may not have another opportunity for a while."

Sartain could hardly believe how casual and calm she sounded about the whole thing. He was grateful.

"Well, if you don't mind, I would rather speak with you in person. I mean, yes, I would like us to meet . . . tonight."

There was a long, unnerving silence at the other end. Sartain stared at the clock, as if only now realizing that it was almost midnight. He began to feel like a complete idiot. What in God's name could he say that would extricate him from this ridiculously embarrassing situation?

"Unless . . . ," he began hesitantly.

"It's okay," Tara's voice came reassuringly through the line. "I just got back to my room, and I'm still dressed. Where shall we meet? Would you like to come over here?"

He hesitated.

"There is a nice quaint bar downstairs, an English pub," she continued over his awkward silence. "It's quiet and I think they're open until two A.M. How fast can you get here?"

Sartain looked out the window. It had stopped snowing. Rubbing his fingers over his beard, he concluded he was in need of a quick shave. "Give me thirty minutes," he replied, regaining some of his usual confident tone.

Little more than a half hour later the professor and Tara were shyly toasting each other in the dimly lit pub.

Tara pulled a Sherman cigarillo from an expensive case, an admirer's gift, and offered one to Sartain. He shook his head but took her lighter and lit hers. He had forgotten his pipe in his haste to leave. She drew on the brown cylinder slowly, studying him, and waiting for him to open the conversation, her countenance was a mask, yet her dark, dazzling eyes seemed anything but cold in the amber candlelight.

"It's sort of difficult to explain," Sartain ventured, clearing his throat, "but I am not here really to talk shop."

"I didn't think you were," Tara said with an encouraging smile.

"Frankly," Sartain said, "there wasn't anything specific I came to talk to you about. It's just that . . ." He was still groping for words.

"It's just that you wanted to talk," Tara helped.

Sartain nodded. "You see," he tried again, "it's difficult, because I haven't really been with a woman . . . I haven't really spoken to anyone intimately since . . ." He paused before he let it out, ". . . since the death of someone I loved very much."

"I know," Tara said quietly.

He looked at her quizzically.

"I know about the murder of Linda Wexler," she explained.

Tara's utterance of the name startled Sartain. Somehow, coming from her lips, it sounded strange, improper. He felt the pangs of guilt again.

"I'm sorry," Tara said, noting the sudden change on his face, sensing she must have said something inappropriate.

"There is nothing for you to be sorry about."

"But why me? Why talk to me?"

The professor shook his head and shrugged. "I don't really know."

"Is it because I had a similar experience? Is that it?"

"I don't quite follow you," he said, genuinely nonplussed.

A slight bitter smile crossed Tara's lips. "It seems I know more about you than you know about me, Professor."

He could not tell her that he did not know much about her because he had been doing his damned best to block her out of his mind. "Your husband?" he asked.

Tara nodded. "And my child."

Sartain studied her face for a long silent moment. God! She is so exquisitely beautiful, he couldn't help but think. The strength that emanates from her. He had always been fascinated by strong women. If they intimidated other men, they enchanted him. He had never been really attracted to weak women, no matter how pretty or charming they were. He could like them, feel protective toward them, but he could never really respect them, let alone love them. His women had to be his equal, like Linda, like his late wife.

"I would like to know," Sartain said finally. "That is, if you don't mind telling me."

Tara reached for her glass and sipped slowly on the Remy Martin. She did not want to talk about her own personal tragedy. She would have preferred not even to think about it. Yet already the painful picture began forming in her mind, and something within prodded her to tell him, to relive those tragic moments for him.

She began slowly, as if the pain of the memory halted her speech. "It was May thirtieth, nineteen seventy-two. I drove to Lod Airport to meet my husband. I remember it was an exceptionally lovely day, with temperatures in the low seventies. Spring was just giving way to summer and it was not yet oppressively hot.

"Daniel, he was four, was strapped in his car seat next to me. I remember the windows were down and the air felt good." Even now, four years after, Tara could still vividly feel the wind play through her hair, its refreshing stroke against her flushed face. She could still recall the spring fragrances and the elation sweeping over her in anticipation of seeing Aaron after two long weeks of separation.

"My husband, Aaron Bergman, was returning from a biochemistry conference in Belgium. The conference itself lasted only one week, but he took some extra time to visit some colleagues who were doing cancer research in Paris and Rome. He was a brilliant scientist, my husband, American born, though he took Israeli citizenship when we married. He was almost twenty years older than I, eighteen years to be exact, and had devoted many years to the study of preventive medicine. In Israel he worked at the Weizmann Institute on a generous Ford Foundation grant. He worked hard, was very highly thought of, and many people believed he was going to win one day the Nobel prize in physiology." She stopped, lost in memory. Sartain politely waited for her to recover.

"I arrived at the airport early," she continued after a time. "The traffic had been lighter than I expected. In one of these coincidences which prove to be fateful, I ran into the officer in charge of security that evening, Shaike Gurevitz, an old friend from my days in Modi'in, military intelligence.

"Shaike, in the best Israeli tradition, wanted to show his clout, 'protectzia' we commonly call it in Israel. He insisted on arranging for me and my son to meet Aaron at the luggage area. At first he wanted to show he could get me out to the plane itself, but I thought enough was enough." She paused again, reflecting on the consequences of her choice that day.

"Only after Shaike made certain that I had a place to sit while I waited—the chair of a security guard in a corner—did he finally leave me alone. The young Yemenite guard took immediately to Daniel and began playing with him and entertaining him. I remember thinking how lucky I was to have such a beautiful, intelligent, and good-natured child. He was . . ." She didn't continue, refusing to get emotionally carried away.

"It was not long before the plane landed," she resumed her description of the events. "Aaron was one of the first to disembark from the Air France flight, which had come from Paris with a stop in Rome, and one of the first to go through passport controls and appear at the baggage area.

"He looked so tall and distinguished to me, and as he spotted us, I remember feeling so proud. Daniel saw him and began calling, 'Abba, Abba. Daddy, I'm over here!' He came over and lifted Daniel up and kissed us each several times. It's strange, but when I talk about it, I see it all as though it happened in slow motion. The details are what kill me, the bloody details. Remembering . . ."

Sartain leaned over. "You don't have to finish," he said softly, sympathetically.

"He kissed us," Tara continued abruptly, stubbornly struggling to overcome her grief and regain her composure, "and said how much he had missed us. 'Wait and see what I brought Danny,' he winked and kissed Daniel again. 'And what I brought you from good old Paris,' he whispered in my ear and smiled mysteriously.

"We hugged, again and he walked toward the carousel to get his luggage. I took Daniel to wait with me at customs.

"But my son wanted to go to his father, fearful he was leaving us again in spite of my explanations. Somehow he managed to pull away from my grip. 'Abba! Abba! Daddy! Daddy!' he yelled as he dashed toward Aaron before I could stop him.

"My husband turned around, and seeing Daniel running toward him, he grinned and bent down to receive him.

"It was then that I glimpsed the three Japanese men by the carousel. Later I learned that they had been on Aaron's flight. Their luggage, too, had just arrived, and I saw them open their cases and pull out submachine guns and some grenades. Before I could react, before anyone could react, they stood back to back, legs apart, forming a circle, and began firing from the hip into the crowd.

"I saw one of them aim his gun at Aaron and Daniel. The world went into an unreal slow motion. It was a dream, it was not true, it was not happening, I told myself. Paralyzed, helpless, I watched my husband gathering Daniel into his arms just as the bullets struck them both. They collapsed together, blood spurting . . ." Her voice went dead, and the hand holding the cigarette trembled.

"Then reality hit me. I screamed and ran hysterically toward them. Grenades were exploding now all over the place blowing dozens of people apart.

"I never reached my husband and son. They died instantly in each other's arms. I was knocked to the ground from behind by the Yemenite guard who for a long time after I hated for saving my life."

"The Lod massacre," Sartain muttered somberly. "I had no idea. I'm sorry."

Sartain remembered the much publicized outrage well. Two

of the Japanese were killed, the third, Kojo Okamoto, was captured. One of the two dead terrorists, the leader, Tsuyoshi Okudira, was the husband of Fusako Shigenobu. Okudira had inadvertently swung his gun too far, killing one of his comrades in the baggage area. The two remaining Japanese then raced out of the building to the tarmac, firing into passengers just stepping off an arriving El Al airliner. Running out of ammunition, Fusako's husband pulled the pin from his last grenade and, in what amounted to a modern-day hara-kiri, clutched it to his belly, the explosion decapitating him. Later Okamoto was taken.

Besides the two terrorists twenty-eight people were killed in the massacre, and dozens more were seriously wounded. Most of the victims were Puerto Rican tourists on a pilgrimage to the Holy Land. They understood little, if anything, of the Arab-Israeli conflict, let alone the role of Japanese kamikazes in it. They were victims of the PFLP philosophy that, in the eyes of a committed terrorist, "no one is innocent."

After the customary seven-day mourning period, Tara, a former military intelligence major, went to see Echad. She wanted to join the Mossad, she told him.

Echad, concerned about Tara's emotional state in the aftermath of her husband's and son's death, adamantly refused at first, resorting to Mossad regulations. As he pointed out, the Israeli Institute for Intelligence and Special Assignments, unlike most other intelligence services, almost never took in volunteers. This policy considerably reduced the risk of infiltration by double agents and helped prevent the enrollment of adventure seekers and those motivated by personal reasons—undesirable elements who could act impulsively and foolhardily and thus jeopardize at times an entire operation, endangering the lives of other operatives.

Tara, guessing Echad's reasons for turning her down and remembering his great disappointment when she had left Modi'in, confronted him point blank. She was not acting impulsively under emotional stress, she claimed. Nor was she seeking personal revenge, she argued forcefully, hoping she sounded convincing enough. She had left her intelligence work in order to marry and have children. Having lost her husband and son, what was she to do, sit home and mourn? She had no real interest in the world of fashion into which she had ventured only to occupy her time. So what was she to do? After all, hadn't it been Echad himself who openly admitted that her resignation was a great loss to the Israeli intelligence community? Hadn't he meant what he said?

Softened by Tara's arguments, the Mossad chief decided to put her to a test. It was to be grim, cruel, but it would prove beyond any shadow of doubt whether she was in control of her emotions and could be fully trusted.

Enrolled like all Mossad recruits for a six-month probationary period, one of Tara's first assignments was to interrogate Kojo Okamoto. The surviving Japanese terrorist had so far refused to divulge any information about the operation he took part in or the people who sent him. He had been told Tara had lost her family in the airport attack. Since all else had failed, it was explained to Tara, perhaps this knowledge would make him talk.

Echad secretly doubted that the Japanese would respond to Tara any differently, but that had not really been his reason for assigning Tara to this particular task. What Tara was not told was that the bullets in the Beretta she was given for protection were blanks and that the interrogation was to be secretly monitored by Echad and his aides.

Left alone with the man she had seen kill her husband and son, Tara never betrayed her true feelings, despite the fact that the Japanese showed no remorse whatsoever.

If anything he was particularly abusive toward her, as if indeed hoping that she would use her gun on him. Tara didn't know that some days before, he had been bluffed by Echad into divulging a bit of information in exchange for a loaded pistol with which to commit seppuku.

When the interrogation was over, only Tara's bleeding left palm, where her nails had left their mark, told what she must have gone through.

Tara was finishing her story now. The worst of it was over. She became more relaxed and sipped on her drink.

"The proceeds from Aaron's two hundred and fifty thousand dollar life-insurance policy plus a sizable settlement with Air France enabled me to establish a successful import and export business in New York. We had lived there in nineteen seventy and nineteen seventy-one, when Aaron was doing research at Columbia, so I was quite comfortable there."

Sartain couldn't help but add, "And that, of course, served as a perfect cover for the Mossad's top agent in charge of counter-terrorism here. That much I do know."

Tara shrugged. "Can I please have another drink?" she asked, lifting her empty glass.

"Certainly," Sartain motioned to the waiter and ordered two more cognacs.

"Do you know who Hector Hipodikon is?" Tara asked suddenly when the waiter left their table.

"Hector Hipodikon?" Sartain's forehead wrinkled in concentration. "Wasn't that a name on one of the false passports they found last year in the suitcase Carlos had left at his girl friend's apartment in London?"

"Yes. One of the things we discovered later, much later, in continuing to interrogate Okamoto, was that the single contact he and his two comrades had in Rome was Hector Hipodikon—the man who delivered the weapons and gave the final briefing."

The professor nodded grimly. "I knew Carlos was involved in the Lod massacre," he said, "but I didn't know in what exact role and to what extent. It all falls into place now."

The waiter returned with their drinks.

"Tell me then," Sartain asked when they were left alone, "is it personal revenge after all? Is that why you do it? Is that what you're after?"

Tara reached for her drink and sipped on it slowly. Sartain once again couldn't but admire her fine-boned face, like a carved mask, which even at close to forty needed hardly any makeup.

"What about you?" Tara responded with a question. "Are you in it only because of Linda?"

Sartain studied her for a long, silent moment. "No," he said. "Not only because of Linda. I am convinced, now more than ever, that we have only five minutes to midnight."

"Five minutes to midnight?" Tara asked puzzled, glancing at her watch.

"No, no," Sartain smiled for the very first time that evening. "I don't mean . . . Have you ever heard of the *Bulletin of the Atomic Scientists*?"

Tara, still perplexed, shook her head. "I don't believe so."

"It's a monthly out of Chicago," Sartain explained. "On its cover it displays a clock whose hands monitor man's race with nuclear doomsday. With the advent of détente the hands were moved slightly back from five minutes to midnight, where they had been during the height of the Cold War. Recently, though, with the sharp acceleration of international terrorism, and the threat of its going nuclear, the Doomsday Clock was set up again at five minutes to midnight."

The look on Tara's face said that she understood him completely. He was beginning to experience the unique closeness which he had shared previously with only one woman. All during the conversation with Tara he felt as if a wall of ice within him, which had shut him away from the rest of the world, was beginning to thaw. He began to feel touched, calm, even happy again. And yet, underneath it all, there was a sharp sense of guilt for being able to experience such feelings so soon, only months after Linda's death. As he looked into Tara's dark, compelling eyes, he felt that she empathized even with this unspoken guilt. In the very same way he understood the powerful mixture of emotions that he provoked in her.

When the pub closed and Sartain walked Tara to the elevator, they shook hands, silently, warmly. Like two partners who had just signed a lifelong contract against all odds. They knew that for a long time to come, perhaps forever, there was not to be any physical closeness between them. There was to be only the deepest intimacy between two powerful, lonely people whom fate had set on the same perilous course.

CHAPTER THIRTY

DESPITE the gloomy weather—it had been raining incessantly in Algiers for this last week in December—Carlos was in a buoyant mood. He had the irrepressible feeling that 1977 would be his year, the year of the Jackal.

"Let's give the professor a few more minutes to arrive, and then we shall begin," he advised patiently, surveying those assembled in the high-ceilinged room.

As if cued by his words, there was the agreed-upon knock at the heavy wooden door. The Jackal motioned to Manuel Lattore, his long-time Uruguayan comrade, who rose to let in the diminutive professor. The two Arab guards outside, following strict instructions, remained a good ten yards away from the door.

With Takemoto's arrival Carlos now had in this Kasbah gathering all the members of the inner circle who would be trusted with the outline of his big plan, the Morris plan. Besides himself, Lattore, and the Japanese professor of French literature, present also were Fusako and the Kraut Squad—Horst Vogel, Gertrude, Fritz, and Ulrich. Most were already vaguely familiar with some aspects of the ultimate scheme, but none of them, not even Fusako, knew all the pieces of the incredible jigsaw puzzle. The full kaleidoscopic configuration of that masterpiece of terror was still captive in the Jackal's genius, devilish mind.

Carlos stood and walked to the bare whitewashed wall behind him. From his breast pocket he pulled a folded paper. Spreading it open, he attached it to the wall with thumbtacks. It was a detailed 1:300:000 map of the state of Illinois. Standing in front of it, using his pen as pointer, he was about to begin the revelation of the Morris plan when he suddenly experienced a quick, uneasy paramnesia.

It was a throwback to the days when he taught Spanish part-time at Langham Secretarial College in London. He preferred not to remember those autumn days of 1970, when he was stalled in London waiting to be contacted by the PFLP. He was fresh from training in Jordan, where he had gone following the humiliating expulsion from Patrice Lumumba.

He had hoped that Langham College, attended primarily by middle-class young ladies, would provide a happy hunting ground for his overactive libido. But he soon experienced the intense xenophobia which young English women from such background commonly felt toward "dagos," particularly when they were overweight, flashy, self-appointed lady-killers. His students, without exception, rejected the coarse overtures of the wide-hipped, round-faced, thick-lipped Venezuelan. How different it would be today, the slimmed, muscular, post-plastic-surgery terrorist chuckled to himself, were those English rosebuds to know him as the legendary Jackal.

Recovered, Carlos pointed to the upper half of the map, where the Illinois and the Kankakee rivers met to form the Des Plaines River, and where Interstate 55 ran into Interstate 80.

"This is Morris, Illinois," he stated, touching the tiny black dot with his pen. "And here," he pointed to another dot, a few miles west along the Illinois River, "is Seneca." He moved the pen back to the right and slightly down the map. "And here, a few miles south, next to the Kankakee River, is Braidwood."

The Venezuelan terrorist circled the three towns on the map. "And here, within a radius of less than twenty miles, is the world's biggest center of nuclear plants, located"—he traced with his pen the Des Plaines River northeast to Lake Michigan—"only fifty miles from Chicago—America's second largest city, with a metropolitan population of close to eight million." Carlos paused, surveying the room with a portentous grin. "*And here,* my friends, is where we are going to make our most extraordinary strike."

Carlos was gratified that his statement drew some surprised gasps. From such a group of hard-bitten urban guerrillas, the career professionals of the terrorist movement, he could not have expected much more. He could only imagine what the reaction would have been, had there been some Arabs among them. He was exceedingly proud of this core group of his.

"My plan is to take over," Carlos continued, "in one coordinated attack, this atomic complex. That is, the three-unit Dresden nuclear plant near Morris, the two-unit La Salle plant adjacent to Seneca, and the two-unit Braidwood plant. Altogether we're talking about seven atomic reactors which, in monetary terms alone, are worth . . . ," he paused dramatically, ". . . over five *billion* dollars."

There were no gasps this time, only an awed silence. Even Fusako, who had known a bit more of the plan than the rest of them, had thought Carlos's scheme was limited to the Dresden plant alone. The prospect of taking over the entire nuclear complex, the largest in the world, was mind boggling.

"Why the whole complex?" Carlos asked rhetorically. "Simple. It increases our chances of success. This way, if we fail to capture one of the reactors, we will still have a chance to take over the others. In fact, even if we fail at two of the plants, controlling the third will be more than sufficient for our purposes. Furthermore once the alarms go off, there will not be enough police reinforcements in the area to cover all the installations under attack. Believe me, they won't know what hit them. And, if we do manage to take over the entire complex, well . . ." He smiled broadly, "we can ask for the world."

"What are we going to ask for?" the Japanese professor queried.

"Not much. Very little indeed." Carlos welcomed the question with glee. "Nothing impossible, nothing unreasonable."

His demands were definitely provocative, definitely humiliating, unprecedented, Carlos thought to himself, but, at the same time, he was careful not to make them too irrational, too unacceptable. He wanted to win this round decisively, and to win it big, bigger than ever. But he did not want to become a martyr.

As he pulled a small piece of paper from his pocket, he explained, "Now things may change by the time we carry out the operation, which, appropriately, is going to take place on July Fourth, but—"

"July Fourth?" both Ulrich and Gertrude interrupted.

"I'll explain later," Carlos raised his hand, dismissing their puzzlement with only slight impatience. "But first let me tell you about our demands as they stand now."

Knowing his tendency to roam from the point at times, Carlos consulted the scribbled paper in his hand. "First of all," he began, "we shall ask that all the imprisoned freedom fighters whose release we failed to secure during the Entebbe hijacking, plus a few others, will be freed. This operation, after all, is to a large extent meant to be in retaliation for Entebbe.

"Secondly we shall ask for a small amount of money. Let's say, ninety-nine million dollars."

"Ninety-nine? Why ninety-nine? Why not a hundred?" Manuel couldn't contain his puzzlement.

"We don't want to be greedy, do we?" Carlos winked. "However, if you insist, we can make it ninety-nine point nine million."

He was in an exceptionally exuberant mood. He had been waiting for a long time to unfold his big plan, and now he was making the most of it. "We shall, of course, demand that half the money be in European currencies and in gold. With their steep inflation, and the big negative gap in their balance of trade," he winked again, "the dollar *ain't* what it used to be."

With the exception of Fritz, who never smiled, they all grinned.

"Thirdly," Carlos continued, "we, as a true revolutionary movement, supporting all oppressed people, shall demand that the President of the United States publicly declare his support for the establishment of a Palestinian state, Puerto Rican independence, and the right of the American Indians to full compensation for the land taken away from them.

"Fourthly," Carlos glanced at the piece of paper, "as a symbolic act we will demand the lowering of the flag in all federal buildings in the U.S. in memory of our revolutionary brothers who perished at Entebbe.

"And finally, to add insult to injury," he smoothed his trimmed moustache, grinning, "we shall demand that Israel be forced, in addition to freeing our comrades, to reimburse our friend President Idi Amin for the damage done at Entebbe." Carlos had no great love for the uncouth African buffoon, but he would have loved to see the faces of the Israelis when coerced by the American government to comply with this humiliating demand.

"Now, after all these demands are met," he continued, pleased with his performance so far, "we shall ask for Hercules C-one thirty transport planes to fly us, and some of our hostages, from the nuclear plants to a destination of our choice."

"Hercules C-one thirty?" Fusako, who questioned the use of propeller planes, asked. "Isn't that carrying the symbolic identification with Entebbe a bit too far?"

"No." Carlos smiled cunningly. "Some of us will not wind up at any airport. I told you at the time, when it comes to this operation, I trust no one. Some of us will parachute at different points along the way, and I certainly am not going to jump out of any jetliner."

"So that's how . . ." Fusako gasped at his craftiness.

Carlos smiled and nodded. "Exactly. All of us here will not be going to any airport, be it in Libya, Algeria, Iraq, or anywhere. We'll bail out of the planes beforehand. Let the Americans think, if they want, that we're asking for the Hercules because those were the planes the Israelis used in their raid on Entebbe."

As Fusako shook her head admiringly at the ingenious plan, Gertrude raised her hand somewhat timidly.

"What is it, Gertrude?" Carlos asked.

"I don't know how to parachute," she confessed, reluctant to admit she suffered from acrophobia.

"Don't worry," Carlos assured her sympathetically. "You are not the only one. When the time comes, you all will know how to parachute. It's being taken care of."

The Jackal began to explain why he chose July 4 as the target date. There was the psychological angle, he said. It was, after all, the anniversary of the Israeli raid on Entebbe. But there are other, more practical reasons. They would not be able to initiate the diversionary attack on the Washington boat—an integral part of the whole operation—until the summer tourist season anyway. The extra time could well be used for planning, preparation work, and training. Furthermore he had already discovered that on that major American holiday, security at the plants tended to be exceptionally lax. "So, since we have to wait until summer anyway," Carlos concluded, "I couldn't think of a more perfectly appropriate day."

The group collectively nodded in agreement.

"There is one more thing. The winds during that time of year tend to blow northeast, in the direction of the lake and downtown Chicago. This is an added advantage, because the potential damage in terms of the spread of radioactivity depends very much on the force and direction of the wind."

This last statement was followed by a heavy silence. It was as if for the very first time they all began to grasp the full implication of their leader's scheme. The vision of a deadly poisonous radioactive cloud permeating the atmosphere couldn't but send a chill through the marrow of even these cold-blooded terrorists.

It was again the German woman who broke the silence. "What are we going to do if our demands are not met?"

"We'll threaten to kill the hostages and damage the plants," Carlos responded matter-of-factly. "And if that doesn't work, to blow up the reactors."

"Blow up the reactors?" This time it was Manuel Lattore. "You mean . . ." He traced in the air with his hands a large mushroom. "You mean like an atom bomb? Like Hiroshima?"

Carlos broke into laughter. "Not exactly, Manuel. A commercial nuclear plant is not exactly a nuclear bomb. The concentration of fissile fuel in it is far too low to trigger an atomic explosion. To create a nuclear weapon, one needs a high concentration of fissile material, usually in the form of either pure plutonium or uranium which has been enriched to about ninety percent in the isotope uranium-two thirty-five."

Carlos was proud to demonstrate some of the extensive knowledge he had secretly acquired on the subject of nuclear technology. He was well aware that he was talking above their heads, but the sooner they were exposed to the subject, the better. Between now and July 4, he told himself, they would have to learn far more about it.

"To put it very simply," Carlos expounded, "in a nuclear weapon the object is to initiate a chain reaction that will bring a large number of nuclei to fission in a very short period of time. Now this sort of reaction can be obtained only if a certain minimal amount of nuclear material, or what they call 'critical mass,' is present. With less than this quantity, an explosion will never occur."

Lattore, like most of the others in the room, seemed baffled. "Then where is—"

"Where is our nuclear leverage?" Carlos saw the question coming.

The Uruguayan terrorist nodded silently.

A patient, paternalistic smile formed around the corners of the Jackal's mouth. The truth was that he himself had been as ignorant of all this until only eighteen months before, when he began studying the subject intensively under the guidance of one of the top experts in the field, Professor Günther.

"Well, we may not be able to trigger an atomic explosion à la Hiroshima," Carlos conceded. "But if we know what we're doing, we can still cause a . . . shall we call it a 'nuclear accident'? One whose consequences can prove to be almost as lethal."

Detecting the questioning look in his comrades' eyes, Carlos continued, "Very briefly, and very much on the surface, since all of you are not yet ready to digest many of the intricate technical details involved, we can threaten to cause a 'core meltdown.' We can quite easily do it by disrupting the reactor's cooling system. All it really takes is knowing exactly where to place the charges. The reactor's core, deprived of its essential coolant, would immediately begin to overheat, and with the control rods withdrawn and a shutdown aborted—and for that incidentally we'll need inside help, and we'll have it—it would melt the fuel pins.

"If, at the same time, we break through the protective shieldings with the explosives," he continued, sitting down again, "and breach the containment dome, radioactive aerosols, and other fissile products, will escape into the atmosphere in quantities that, with the right wind, will be enough to poison the entire population of Chicago. If we blow up all the reactors, we can transform that whole area into a virtual wasteland." He paused before he asked with a teasing grin, "Now is that a sufficient enough leverage for you?"

There was only total silence in the room.

Reading what was clearly on his comrades' minds, Carlos added with the same teasing smile, "I definitely hope, or shall we say, I'm counting on the fact that we'll not have to resort to such calamitous action. Obviously we too won't have the slightest chance of surviving it. That's why we must make certain that our threat to go all the way will never be questioned, that our resolution to die for the cause will not for a moment be doubted. This, I promise you, and I prefer not to go into details at this point, will be unequivocally demonstrated through the Washington diversionary attack on June twenty-seventh—the anniversary of the Entebbe skyjacking."

Fritz, the taciturn one, asked in a heavily accented voice, "The inside help, can you elaborate?"

"Helga is taking care of it," Carlos responded equally tersely. "When the time comes, I'll brief you."

Fritz nodded obediently, but the Japanese professor wanted to know where Carlos was planning to get the kind of manpower and local logistics required for an operation of such magnitude.

Once again Carlos welcomed the question. It offered him the opportunity to bring up that highly sensitive issue which had been in the back of his mind throughout the session. He lit a Gauloise and proceeded to tell his followers how, when he had casually raised the subject of an attack on a nuclear installation the previous year—just to test the water—he was told by Haddad and the rest of the PFLP leadership to forget it. There was too much danger, he was told, that such an act might eradicate any sympathy whatsoever for the Palestinian cause, and not only in the Western world. "As if sympathy ever got anything for anyone," Carlos commented contemptuously.

"I've become increasingly convinced, ever since the OPEC and the Entebbe operations," he continued, "that, very much like our Fatah friends, the Popular Front is becoming more and more exclusively concerned with the Palestinian cause. I am beginning to believe that the commitment of our Arab brethren to a world revolution is nothing more than lip service. Between you and me, I fear that if they get their lousy Palestine tomorrow, we would never again hear the faintest battle cry, or battle squeak, coming from their direction."

Carlos allowed himself such cutting remarks against the PFLP because he knew that none of those present harbored much love for their Semitic allies. Particularly not after the shocking betrayal of Halil Said, a long-time member of the inner circle. Thus, just as they had not questioned initially the absence of any Arabs at this important meeting, they were hardly surprised now at Carlos's bitter criticism of their financial sponsors. They listened expressionlessly as the Venezuelan revealed that the PFLP was under the erroneous impression that the attack on the Washington boat, to which Haddad had given his approval, was the main operation Carlos was busily planning.

Carlos went on to explain that while Palestinian guerrillas would take part in an assault on the boat led by Abu Sherif he wanted none to participate in the Morris operation. That naturally aggravated further the problem of having sufficient manpower for the large-scale operation. Moreover problems of logistics in the U.S. were far more difficult and complex than, for example, in Western Europe. It became clear to him early in the game, Carlos explained, that in order to successfully carry out the operation, they had to obtain the cooperation of a local radical group.

As it turned out, Carlos said, a major schism which had developed recently within the ranks of the Weather Underground offered him that opportunity. He briefly explained that the radical movement, struggling to maintain momentum in the post-Vietnam era, when even the militance of the black movement seemed to have died out, had split apart over a desire on the part of some of its fugitive leaders to come out into the open, to "surface." Apparently four of the five-person WUO leadership were strongly in favor of giving themselves up, part of a scheme to abandon violence for the time being so they could concentrate on open political work. The fifth, and most militant leader, however, a young woman whose underground code name was Rage, fiercely rejected the plan. She denounced it as a counterrevolutionary move, an act of cowardly betrayal, and was determined to fight it to the end, even at the risk of splitting the movement.

"This brave woman," Carlos said, "needs a major action, preferably in alliance with other world revolutionary forces, to reassert her dominance within the movement, to rekindle the revolutionary spirit in her country, to revitalize the people's struggle against the establishment."

The Jackal was well versed in all of the radical, leftist rhetoric. He seldom used it, however, and then, only for effect and only in moderation. He considered himself a true professional not a rabble-rouser.

"Rage believes," Carlos continued, "that the Morris plan suits her purposes perfectly. She is willing to go all the way; she feels she has nothing to lose. She can guarantee us at least a dozen die-hard revolutionaries who will balk at nothing. Of course, to be on the safe side, they will not be told about the true nature of the operation until the very last moment. She will also take care of most of the local logistics involved, help us prepare the arms caches, and provide us with safe houses. She—"

There was a slight noise outside the door which only a few of them noticed. As the sentence froze on his lips, the Jackal motioned with his eyebrow and a slight twist of his head to Manuel Lattore. The Uruguayan did not hesitate. While the rest remained silent, each going for his own weapon. Lattore quickly made it to the door and swiftly opened it, his Soviet Marakov ready to shoot.

There was no one there, however. Only the sound of a distant muezzin call could be heard. As Manuel peeked around the doorframe, a bemused smile crossed his face. He reshut the door and faced the room.

"What was it?" Carlos asked, now relaxed, his automatic already back in its shoulder holster. He could see from Manuel's familiar grin that it had been a false alarm.

"Nothing," the Uruguayan replied. "The guards were kneeling in their noon prayer. Must have been that faint noise you heard."

"Both at the same time?" Carlos asked.

Lattore nodded.

"The goddamn fools," Carlos shook his head, twisting his nose in disgust.

"At least their behinds were facing the door," Manuel joked.

"Well next time put a bullet right through them," Carlos quipped, causing everyone but Fritz to smile.

"As I was saying," Carlos continued, not allowing the brief incident to disrupt his line of thought. "Rage has little doubt that the operation can succeed. She is totally convinced, as I am, that the Americans will bow to our demands. She agrees that they would not risk a nuclear catastrophe. In fact she is quite confident that the whole thing will turn her into the new heroine of the antinuclear movement there. Come to think of it, we may add to our demands a promise by the American government of a total review of their nuclear program . . ."

He stopped to consider that last thought. "Yes," he finally said, "I don't see why not. As Horst here"—he turned to face the young German—"who made the initial contact with her, can tell you, the antinuclear issue has the potential to replace Vietnam as the cause célèbre of the new antiestablishment forces."

Vogel, who was sitting between Fusako and Gertrude, nodded silently. It had been his analysis after his return from his stay in the States which led Carlos in the first place to seek the cooperation of the Weather Underground dissidents.

"Thanks to Horst's help," Carlos felt like being exceptionally lavish in his praise, "we've also managed to recruit a number of exiled American revolutionaries here. I believe they'll prove quite useful to us in this operation." He didn't elaborate, and no one bothered to ask for details. There were far more important questions in their minds.

"What do you think the PFLP reaction will be, once it's all over?" Ulrich asked, expressing a concern shared by many of them. "And what about the Arab governments who have been supporting us all along?"

Carlos laughed. "We'll present them with a *fait accompli*, with a gift they cannot refuse. To begin with, *money*, lots of money, more money than the PFLP has ever seen. We will share it with them fifty, fifty. To show our generosity," Carlos winked wickedly, "we'll take the smaller fifty million. You and I know they won't turn us down, not those greedy bastards. They may publicly disassociate themselves from us, even denounce us, but they are clever enough to know that in the long run this whole thing will serve to enhance their own prestige and power.

"As for the Arab countries, once they see the strain our act will put on the relations between Israel and the United States— because as we know, Israel will at first refuse to comply with our demands, endangering the lives of millions of Americans—they also will come around. Perhaps, again, not publicly, but when did they ever do it in the open anyway?"

Carlos stood up, a familiar surge of excitement beginning to overtake him. "And as for the Russians," he scoffed, "you can rest assured that they are not going to shed tears over what may amount to a virtual death blow to their main rival's commercial nuclear program. Incidentally," he smiled wickedly, "there is one more thing which is destined to work for us. Neither the Americans, nor anyone else, will ever know for certain whether we have managed to spirit off from the plants some radioactive material. Not much, just enough to give us that extra leverage against those who might seek to confront us in the future."

Carlos was perspiring heavily now, in spite of the cold day. He reached for his pocket and pulled out a handkerchief with which he hastily wiped his face. "It will establish us as a superpower on our own," he continued excitedly. "We'll go down in history as those who dared to change the course of events in this century. If we are successful, and we will be, next year may be remembered as the most important year of the century. The year that small, multinational groups of determined individuals like us began to successfully challenge the mightiest nations on earth. It will herald the collapse of nation-states, of nationalism, of capitalism. It will lead to an unprecedented global upheaval, to a true world revolution. And we, us, you and me, will be the ones who triggered it, who were responsible for it all. We will make history, my friends, I can guarantee you that. We'll be remembered for generations to come, like Karl Marx, like Hitler, like Mao . . ."

The Jackal fought the tears which welled in his eyes. He wanted to embrace, to kiss each one of them, so overwhelmed was he with emotion. Almost choking, he concluded, "And so, my friends, I wish you all a Happy New Year. A Happy Nuclear Year."

PART 3

CHAPTER THIRTY-ONE

ARTAIN was lost in concentration when the telephone in his Triple C office buzzed. Slowly he pulled himself away from the uncharacteristically sentimental letter he was writing to answer.

"Dr. Sartain?" It was the unmistakable, nasal voice of Lucy, one of the three Triple C telephone operators.

"Yes."

"Dr. Sartain"—Lucy was always extra careful to respectfully emphasize his academic title—"you have a call on the outside line, the D.C. number."

"The D.C. number" was an ordinary Washington, D.C. number afforded primarily to agents and informers not permanently employed by the Triple C. It was their direct line of communication with the Langley headquarters. If one called that number, a female voice would always respond politely: "Department of Meteorological Instruments. May I help you?"

Those who accidentally called the number—and it happened more often than one would expect—would ordinarily either hang up immediately or apologize for dialing the wrong number. Those who called it intentionally, however, would say: "I would like to inquire if you still carry in your stock item number twenty-seven?" Or perhaps they would ask for item number twenty-three or thirty-one or seventeen. All depending on whom they wished to talk to. Sartain's assigned number was forty-nine.

"Who did he . . . or she, say it was?"

"Jody."

"Jody. You sure it was Jody?" Sartain's heart skipped a beat. Jody was the code name of Jim Anders.

"Yes, Dr. Sartain. I'm certain."

"Did he indicate where he was calling from?"

"No, sir. But it's definitely long distance. Would you like me to activate the recorder?"

"Yes, Lucy. Thank you."

"I'll put him on right now then, sir."

"Thank you." A couple of seconds later Sartain heard the click on the line which indicated that he was connected.

"Is that you, Jody?" he asked.

"Yes, it is. Is that you, Mr. Samuels?"

"Yes, Jody, it's me. It's good to hear your voice again. Where are you calling from?"

"I'm calling from Toronto, from a telephone booth."

"Good. What are you doing in Toronto?"

"Just visiting. I'm on my way to Chicago."

"Chicago?"

"Uh-huh. That's where I've been asked to go."

"I see." Sartain was quickly digesting the information. "When will you be there?"

"I intend to cross either tomorrow or the day after."

"Papers?"

"Everything is okay. I even look different, if you know what I mean. Nothing major though."

"I understand. It sounds okay. What about your sister? Is she with you?"

"No. I left her back home. She may join me later."

"Any news from Dad?" It had been predetermined that "Dad" would be the code name for Carlos.

"Sorry. Nothing so far. All I know is that I'll be going to Chicago. I may find something once I'm there. I'll call again from there. Anyway I better hang up now."

"Jody!"

"Yes?"

"Good luck. And remember, our deal is still as good as ever. You've nothing to worry about that."

"Thank you, sir. I'm counting on it. Good-bye." The line went dead.

Sartain pressed the intercom button. "Lucy," he said when she responded, "did you get it on tape?"

"Yes, Dr. Sartain. When do you need it?"

"Immediately. But can you first find out if Mr. Atkins can see me right away. Tell Kitty it's urgent, very urgent. I'll pick up the cassette on the way to his office. Okay?"

"Yes, sir."

Sartain sighed as he glanced at the paperweight calendar on his desk. It showed Wednesday, June 4. It had been six months, a full half year, since Amy's staged jailbreak. During all that time they had heard from her and Jim only twice. The first time, in the middle of January, in the form of a postcard which the professor received at his home address. The card depicted the Pecherie, Algiers' picturesque fishing port, and said little:

> Enjoying our visit immensely.
> Spent 3 days in Algiers. Plan to spend 2 more in Oran and one day in Constantine.
>
> Love,
> Jody and Ivy

As brief as the message was, it was the first encouraging sign. It meant that Amy had arrived safely in Algiers and that Jim was willing to go along with the professor's plan. It also meant that the agreed upon meeting between them and Sartain would take place in Algiers on March 21 at the designated place. Confirmation of the card's receipt was published a week later in *Le Monde* in the form of an innocuous ad that ran for two weeks.

On March 17, the first day of Easter recess at Georgetown University, the professor, accompanied by his son, left Washington, D.C. for Paris on what was supposedly a ten-day research trip to North Africa. On March 22 they were contacted by Amy at the Aurassi Hotel on Algiers' Avenue Frantz Fanon.

That same evening the Sartains dined at the Bacour on rue Ali Boumendjel, a few tables away from Jim and Amy. Without acknowledging the other two Americans, Jim rose and strode past their table toward the men's room. A minute later he was joined there by the professor. It was a very brief exchange, lasting barely three minutes.

The professor did learn, however, that Jim and Amy had been recruited by Terror International for a possible operation in the States, and that they were being trained in the use of weapons and guerrilla tactics. But other than the fact that their training was geared partially toward the hijacking of a boat, they were told nothing and managed to learn nothing about the intended operation.

In response to Sartain's question, Jim added that the training, though methodical and extensive, had been drawn out. There didn't seem to be any sense of urgency, which only served to reinforce the professor's conviction, when he later evaluated the information, that Carlos was not planning to strike before late spring at the earliest.

The men's-room meeting was the very last time the professor had seen or heard from the couple. The information about the boat intrigued him. Still strongly suspecting that Carlos was contemplating a nonconventional attack, he recommended to Atkins that all LNG transport tankers that entered U.S. territorial waters be carefully scrutinized and placed under tight security, especially those which came from Algeria.

The Triple C recommendation was still being considered and debated by the National Security Council when Jim placed his call from Canada. In the meantime, in order not to seem totally inert and irresolute, the NSC informed the U.S. Coast Guard of the possible danger and instructed it to keep an eye on all such tankers.

Both the professor and Atkins were becoming resentfully accustomed to the new administration's lack of real concern for, or understanding of, the increasing danger of terrorism. At times it seemed as if the new policy makers in Washington were wavering between lip service to preparedness to total capitulation. In one particular incident the President himself set what he admitted was a "dangerous precedent" by bowing to the demands of a sole gunman, calling the man personally in Ohio to hear his grievances in return for the release of a hostage.

The "doves" were riding high again in Washington, and the fact that it was the badly tarnished CIA that provided the main link with the Triple C only further served to undermine their trust in the multinational counterterrorist organization. The Hanafi Black Muslim seizure of the Capital's B'nai B'rith headquarters and National Islamic Center pointed to both the lack of sufficient intelligence on such groups and the absence of a force adequately trained to cope with such emergencies. But even the portentous death of some six hundred air passengers on a runway in the Canary Islands as an indirect result of a terrorist bomb failed to convince the new administration of the impending danger. The "ins" did not share Atkins's and Sartain's fears that in the future, within the context of a nonconventional terrorist threat, even six hundred casualties could become a small number indeed.

There were also grave problems within the Triple C itself. The Abu Daoud affair had highlighted the chronic problem of not being able to achieve full cooperation among the member states, each country having its own national priorities. This time it had been the French government, who for its own political and economic reasons acceded to the demands of the Arabs. Acting against the expressed wishes of other Triple C members and their own counterintelligence service, the Quai d'Orsay arranged the release of Abu Daoud—a high-ranking Palestinian terrorist sought by both Israel and Germany for planning the 1972 Munich Olympics massacre. He had been deliberately and precipitously arrested a few days earlier by DST agents, who were still eager to avenge the killings of their comrades by the Jackal.

The humiliated François Darlan resigned from the Triple C and the DST in protest of his government's cowardice to be replaced a month later by a permanent representative more in tune with his country's need of Arab oil.

The Israelis, reeling in anger over the action, became less and less forthcoming in supplying intelligence information—still the best in the Western world on terrorist matters—to the Triple C. Echad, in fact, did not hesitate to justify his country's stance by implying that the Mossad could no longer be certain that its confidential reports would not find their way into the hands of unfriendly elements.

Tara, who had successfully discouraged Echad's early impulse to withdraw from the multinational organization, told Sartain that the Mossad chief was finally persuaded to give it another try only because of his respect for the Triple C chief. She warned Sartain, however, that the capture of Carlos remained the acid test. If the TF-3 proved successful, then the Triple C would regain its earlier stature; otherwise the Mossad would cooperate only minimally or withdraw altogether.

During those turbulent early months of the Triple C organization the relationship between the professor and Tara had bloomed into a unique romantic friendship—one which defied definition. There had grown between them a special independent closeness found only between two strong, powerful, yet vulnerable and lonely people. Forced by fate into solitude, they suddenly discovered in each other a magnetic attraction and a singular professional bond. Yet that strong attraction, physical as well as mental, had not developed into a sexual relationship.

There were several reasons for their avoidance of physical intimacy. In the early stages of their infrequent meetings Sartain sensed a distinct wrongness to the prospect. Too soon after Linda's death it would have constituted a betrayal of her memory. He did not deceive himself; he knew that physical intimacy with Tara would only transform their feelings for each other into a complete love relationship for which he was not ready.

At first Sartain had justified their nascent amity as the simple need for companionship, nothing more than pure friendship between two people who understood each other, who were involved in the same deadly, ugly business and who could talk about it freely, without the danger of a security breach.

Yet Sartain, who still denied himself sex with any woman, found that he wanted Tara more and more. He solemnly promised himself that he would not initiate anything until Linda's death had been avenged. Too, he feared that any forward move could ruin what they already had. He would not take that risk.

Tara had her own reservations about a full-fledged love affair with the Gentile professor who headed the TF-3. So she contented herself with their platonic intimacy.

When Jim Anders called, the professor had been in the midst of writing Tara a letter, one which he knew he would not send. Tara had been in Israel for the previous two weeks on personal business and her quarterly Mossad briefing. Sartain was surprised how much more difficult it had been for him to endure her absence this time. If in the past there had been doubt in his mind, in his heart it now vanished. As he wrote in his letter, he recognized now that he was much more in love with her than he had ever been willing to admit to himself. She was no longer just filling a need for a meaningful companionship. She was no more a substitute, a replacement for Linda. He would always love Linda, would never cease to cherish her memory. But he now also recognized that he loved the Israeli woman no less.

The fact that it was Linda's death which had indirectly led him to Tara disturbed Sartain and unavoidably filled him with guilt. She was dead, and here he was emotionally involved again.

Yet it had not prevented him from falling in love with Tara. It was as if the inner conflict only added to the intensity of his emotions. The sexual abstinence only served to deepen the hunger in his soul.

He was very much hoping, Sartain wrote in the letter, that Tara would finish her business in Israel and be back in time for his birthday, a little over a week away. She was the only one, he conceded, he really cared to be with on that day.

Steve, who was still working closely with his father on the Carlos book, traveling with him to Europe and North Africa back in March, had moved out of his father's house shortly after their return. He had recovered from Luana's death, had a new girl friend, and both he and the professor agreed that he needed his own place and privacy. He rented a small apartment on Nineteenth Street, not far from his father's and within walking distance of Georgetown University, where his girl friend attended classes and where he used the library for a good deal of his research.

Since the day of Luana's funeral, when Steve had revealed his vulnerability, his inner feelings, and fears, he was never again as open with his father. He continued to remain considerate, respectful, and even amiable, but the same old aloofness, that reserved distance surfaced again. The professor and his son conversed much about politics, terrorism, and, of course, the book, but they no longer discussed their innermost feelings.

The telephone's buzz once again disrupted Sartain's thoughts. It was Kitty, Atkins's secretary, calling to inform him that her boss was ready to see him.

As he hung up, Sartain stared at the letter to Tara for a second, undecided about what to do with it. Should he tear it up now, or wait until he returned to his desk and could reread it once more? Finally he folded it neatly and tucked it away in the inside pocket of his suede jacket. He then headed for the first floor to pick up the cassette from Lucy.

"What do you make of it then?" the Triple C chief asked when Sartain turned off the tape recorder.

"Well, I'm encouraged," the professor said as he sat down again across from Atkins. "I would have been happier if he could have told us more. But as we expected, Carlos is not forthcoming with information. I think though that sooner or later Jim will find out something about the Jackal's plan, enough to go on and hopefully, preempt it."

"Why Chicago?" Atkins asked. "Why do you think he was sent to Chicago? Does that tell you anything?"

Sartain shrugged. "I don't know, Fred. It may or may not be his final destination. But, at this point, until we hear from Anders again, we should do absolutely nothing."

"Why? I don't quite follow you."

"If it is indeed to be Chicago, and we start beefing up security there all of a sudden, without knowing what we are up against, all we may accomplish is to alarm and forewarn Carlos that we have inside information. It could jeopardize our whole plan. I'm afraid we'll just have to wait patiently until we hear from Jim again."

Sartain reached inside his jacket for his tobacco pouch to fill his pipe. Inadvertently, he touched the unfinished letter. He could use the communication with Jim Anders to bring her back early. Would it be too presumptuous? Too selfish?

"What if we don't have enough time?" Atkins interrupted his reverie. "What if Carlos decides to strike soon, a few days from now? What if Jim Anders finds out about it only just before zero hour? Don't you think we should have at least a few operatives there, ready for any eventuality?"

"You could," Sartain conceded. "But only in a very low profile. Under no circumstances, though, should we contact the Bureau or the local police. No telling where Carlos might have informers. In any case I very much doubt that he'll strike so soon."

Sartain paused to light his pipe. "Perhaps we should recapitulate what we have learned from Jim's call. Shall we?"

Atkins nodded.

The professor consulted the note pad in his hand. "Jim is in Toronto. He's planning to cross the border sometime within the next forty-eight hours. How? We don't know. All we know is that he's been provided with forged papers and that he has a new appearance, 'nothing major though'—that is, he has not undergone plastic surgery. It could be a moustache, a beard, different haircut and coloring . . . any, or all of these, and more."

"Do you think that will be sufficient?"

Sartain shrugged, "I don't know," he said very calmly. "I assume Carlos knows what he's doing."

A bitter smile crossed Atkins's face. Sartain never really failed to amaze him. How could the son of a bitch remain so cool?

"We also know," Sartain continued matter-of-factly, "that Amy is not with Jim. But most important, according to him, she is still in Algeria, and since she went through the same training, and since he expects her to join them later, it means that the operation is not imminent.

"And again, if my hunch is right, and if I read Carlos's flair for the dramatic correctly, and if we take into account the reports from our other sources that the PFLP in no way has given up on its desire for a major retaliation for the Entebbe debacle, then it will take place on either June twenty-seventh—the first anniversary of the hijacking itself—or even more probably on July Fourth, which is both the anniversary of the Israeli raid and our Independence Day. Don't forget how that raid was interpreted here at the time: 'the best possible present Israel could have given us for our bicentennial celebration.' I have a strong feeling Carlos would love to give us another 'present' on that day, one which we shall not forget."

Sartain paused and then added slowly, thoughtfully, "Yes, Fred, the more I think about it, the more my nose tells me it will be July Fourth."

"How can you be so goddamn certain?" Atkins asked slightly irritated at the professor's conjectural forecast.

"I didn't say I was certain," Sartain responded patiently. "You can call it an educated guess, a common-sense hunch, reading into the mind of the terrorist . . . whatever."

He suddenly leaned forward and stared straight into Atkins's eyes. "If you were Carlos, Fred, what would you do? What day within the next few months would you choose?"

Atkins sat back, slightly jarred by the unexpected question. He took a moment to think. Then a cunning smile crossed the lips above the beard. "July fifth!" he uttered triumphantly. "I would pick July fifth."

Sartain shook his head and smiled wryly. "Very clever, Fred. Very clever, and cautious indeed. But you see, my dear Fred, you are *not* the Jackal . . ."

CHAPTER THIRTY-TWO

FOR the two days following Jim Anders's call, both Atkins and the professor waited anxiously for him to contact them from Chicago. Sartain was the less apprehensive of the two, confident more than ever that his intricate, long-nurtured scheme was at last going to bear fruit. Convinced that Carlos was planning to strike either on June 27 or July 4, he regarded Jim's early arrival on the scene as a promising omen. He was certain that such a long preparatory stay in the States would afford Jim the opportunity to come upon some indication as to what Carlos had planned. For once, the professor felt, they had a chance to be one step ahead of the Jackal.

On the third morning, after a late night at Triple C headquarters, Sartain arose earlier than usual, resorting to his brush, push-up, and cold-shower routine to fully awaken him. While shaving, he contemplated the day ahead. He had to spend a couple of hours at his university office to finish up some last remaining business. If he got there by seven thirty, he figured, he could be out of there, on his way to Langley, by no later than nine thirty. He was grateful the school's summer vacation had started the week before. Now he would be able to devote all of his time and energy to Triple C business. Indeed Carlos could not have been more accommodating, he mused sarcastically, waiting for summer vacation before hatching his sinister plan.

Sartain was definitely cheered that morning. He had a strong premonition that he would hear from Jim Anders that day, and, if he were really lucky, perhaps also from Tara. He was not unaware of Atkins's own initiative in contacting Mossad headquarters in Tel Aviv, requesting the immediate return of its

Triple C representative to Washington, due to the recent important developments in the Carlos case.

"Son of a bitch!" Sartain cursed suddenly. He leaned toward the mirror to examine the cut on the underside of his nose. Sure enough, it was deep and began to bleed profusely. He cursed again.

He plucked a speck of toilet paper and stuck it against the cut to stop the flow of blood. He should be a bit more careful shaving, he admonished himself, somewhat more amused at himself now. He shouldn't let his mind wander off like that too often, or one day he would find himself without a nostril. What the hell was he standing in front of a mirror for, if he didn't bother looking at it?

The imperious whistle of the kettle sent him to the kitchen where he hastily poured himself a cup of instant coffee. Since Steve had moved out, Sartain had reverted to instant coffee, no longer bothering to take time to brew coffee just for himself. Into the toaster he dropped a piece of rye bread, which, with margarine and a few slices of his favorite Monterey cheese, would constitute breakfast, to be consumed while he read the morning paper.

As he opened the door and bent down to pick up his delivered copy of the *Washington Post*, Sartain's heart stopped.

It was difficult to recognize Jim Anders behind the glasses, the beard, and the darkened hair, yet the bold front-page letters above the photo announced unmistakably:

FUGITIVE SKYJACKER CAUGHT CROSSING BORDER INTO U.S.

Sartain was still standing in his doorway, gulping down the details of Jim's capture by the FBI at Niagara Falls, when the telephone rang. It was Atkins.

"Did you see the paper?" the Triple C chief asked.

"I'm just looking at it," the professor muttered grimly.

"What do you think?"

"What do I think?" What could I think? Sartain silently considered the question. Could it really be that all the painstaking efforts, all the calculation was in vain? . . . that everything had collapsed, irrevocably undermined by some goddamn G-men who had nothing else to do but botch up crucial operations?

How did these incompetent bastards get to him anyway? They couldn't find Tania for a whole year and a half, and here they pick up Jim before he had a chance to set foot . . .

"Sam?"

"I'll see you in your office within an hour. We'll discuss it then," Sartain replied coldly. He placed the telephone back into its cradle.

An hour later, when he walked into Atkins's office, his first question was: "How did it happen, Fred? How did they manage to nail him? That was a pretty damn good disguise he had. Were his papers sloppy?"

"No. They were perfect. It was a tip."

"A tip?" Sartain looked shocked. "From whom?"

"An anonymous caller," Atkins shrugged. "Male, with a French-Canadian accent."

"French-Canadian?"

Atkins nodded.

"*Merde!*" the professor uttered, his countenance revealing the disgust, the disappointment he couldn't help but feel. "*Merde!*"

"You can say that again," Atkins commented. "I wonder who the hell your boy contacted when he was in Canada, and why they would choose to turn him in like that. Must have made some fast enemies"

Sartain shook his head. "I don't understand it either, Fred. Have you been in touch with the Bureau? Has he spilled anything about our agreement?" His voice held concern.

"Luckily, no. Nothing so far. He wouldn't talk to anyone but asked to see an attorney. I'm not worried about the FBI. George is already in charge of the case. But I don't want your Anders to shoot his mouth off to some damn lawyer. That's all we need."

"Don't worry about that," Sartain calmed. "He won't say a word. He'll wait until I contact him. Those were my specific instructions to him. Besides, he is not stupid. Amy is still in Algeria, and he knows what they will do to her if the truth ever came out. Believe me, he'd kill himself before endangering her in any way."

Somewhat relieved, Atkins offered, "Well, I can arrange for you to meet him, even today if you want to. The question is: where do we go from here? Is he of no use to us anymore now that he has been recognized and apprehended?"

Sartain remained silent for a moment, reflecting on the question, though he knew what the answer must be. "I'm afraid, Fred, that's exactly it. If it hadn't hit the papers, maybe then we would have been able somehow to hush up the whole thing and use him again. Although, quite frankly, I don't like that tip business. It doesn't fit. But we could have given it a try. Now, however," he shrugged in frustration, "it's much too late for that."

"What about . . ." Atkins hesitated. "What about staging a jailbreak for him?"

A bitter smile crossed the professor's lips. "No use, Fred. Carlos isn't going to fall for that one twice. He's no fool. All we'd achieve is to put Amy in jeopardy. And aside from assuring her personal safety, she is now the only chance we probably have."

"Yes. I can see that. Well I guess the main question remaining is, What will Carlos do? Will he give up on his plan altogether because of Anders's capture or will he go ahead with it?"

Sartain stood up and began to pace in front of Atkins's desk. He absentmindedly toyed with the unlit pipe in his hands. Finally, as though talking to himself, he said, "On the way here I tried to place myself in Carlos's shoes. I tried to see how I would react to Jim's arrest if I were planning a major attack in the near future."

Atkins followed him with his eyes, keeping silent.

Forehead wrinkled in deep concentration, Sartain continued. "To begin with, I tried to figure out how much Jim really knows about Carlos's plan and how much damage that knowledge could do. Now, if what Jim told me is true, and I have no reason to doubt it, then he really doesn't know much. In fact, he knows very little. The media have already reported that Anders's explanation for returning to the U.S. was that he missed his country. No one knows that Amy has been with him in Algeria all this time, so the media are further speculating that he really attempted to sneak back here in order to be with her. No one seems to even suspect that Jim is still involved with any terrorist group, let alone Terror International. Looking at it then from Carlos's point of view, there would be no reason for Jim to reveal his true purpose in returning. There is absolutely nothing for him to gain by doing so. If anything, it would only aggravate his own situation. Moreover Carlos knows that Jim is fully aware that if he did open his mouth, he would seal Amy's fate. So why would he?"

Sartain stopped pacing and stood facing Atkins, staring through him. Fred wanted to say something, but the professor waved his hand, indicating he didn't want to be interrupted yet.

"Furthermore let's say the FBI does manage somehow to extract the truth from Anders. What will they really find out?" Sartain asked rhetorically, pacing again. "Only that Terror International, or the PFLP, is contemplating an attack here, in the U.S. But where exactly, what, when, and how? Jim knows practically nothing. At least not enough for Carlos to give up on his operation. Particularly when he can safely assume that Jim won't dare to reveal even the little he does know."

Once again Sartain stopped pacing to stare at Atkins. "No," he shook his head with conviction. "Carlos will not quit now. Would you?"

Atkins nodded slowly, a mocking look wrinkling up the corners of his eyes. "But, of course . . . I'm not the Jackal. Am I?"

Any other time Sartain would have most probably found his friend's retort amusing. Now he dismissed it, continuing his line of thought. "It makes no difference. We just can't take the chance one way or another. Unless we see convincing evidence to the contrary, we must proceed on the assumption that Carlos's plans haven't changed."

Back in his crammed office, preparing for a special meeting of the TF-3 later that morning, Sartain reexamined the possible consequences of Jim's unexpected detention. He still hoped, as he had told Atkins, that Amy's position within the terrorist group would not be drastically affected by the capture of her boyfriend, that she would still somehow be exposed to some meaningful information and be able to communciate it to them in time. Yet he knew he couldn't count on it. In truth he was even less hopeful than he had led Atkins to believe.

He had relied too heavily on his infiltration scheme, Sartain reproached himself. He should have pursued other avenues more diligently, researched other alternatives more vigorously, not allowed himself to put all the eggs in one basket. Somewhere out there, there were bound to be clues as to what Carlos was planning. Even Linda, during her assignment in Berlin, had apparently come across such information. She must have. What shred of incriminating evidence did she stumble on that had exacted its price in her torture and death? "You've been right all along," she said to him in that last telephone conversation. "It's even bigger and more horrifying than what you predicted . . ."

Sartain sighed. What had he been right about? What had he predicted? He had pondered these questions a thousand and one times and couldn't come up with anything specific. True, he had told her he expected Carlos to retaliate for Entebbe, or at least to use the debacle as an excuse. He had also expressed his fears that terrorism would turn to nonconventional methods, that it would go nuclear. But what specific thing had she found? What else was she trying to tell him when she etched Carlos's name into her own flesh? Would her death be in vain after all?

We may have to start from scratch again, Sartain concluded in frustration. But where to start? And is there enough time? He rubbed his eyes with his palms to clear his muddled head.

If Linda had found those leads in Berlin, then that was where he must take up the thread. She went to Berlin to investigate the escape of the four Baader-Meinhof women. The first key to the mystery must be there. True, the whole case had been studied thoroughly, but perhaps not thoroughly enough.

Yes, he must reexamine the jailbreak, and do it personally. He must review all the information on the case himself, seek more, and probe every possible angle. In case Amy failed to help them, it would be all he had to go on.

The more Sartain thought about it, the more convinced he became that the Berlin jailbreak had something to do with Carlos's present plans. He regretted not having given it more attention at the time. After all, that was what he had set out to investigate before he was recruited by Atkins, before he had joined the Triple C. Carlos was in Berlin . . . and Fusako . . . why? And where were the women now? All, with the exception of Erika Küzler, who had been caught and reincarcerated, had disappeared. Why? Perhaps Erika should be more carefully interrogated. Maybe she knew something, maybe she'd talk now, maybe she'd make a slip.

At least Jim's appearance in the States confirmed beyond any doubt that Carlos was indeed planning to strike here, and soon. Maybe something else would correlate. Yes, they must review the case. It should be the task force's first priority. Linda must not have died for nothing after all.

With that final thought he left his office and headed toward the conference room.

"Just imagine, Helga," Dr. Baumann sighed as they sat in her living room, "less than one month from now we'll be together forever. And rich, very rich."

"*Ja, ja,*" she tried to match his enthusiasm, "very rich!"

He sighed happily again, a dreamy look in his eyes. "You know," he whispered, "I always wanted to go to Brazil. To see the carnival in Rio. I wish I were younger though. I would have loved to samba in the streets with you."

"Don't worry," she winked at him, "you will. With the plastic surgery and the full head of dark black hair, you'll look at least ten years younger. Trust me."

Pleased, he asked tenderly, "What about you, Helga? What will you look like?"

"Oh, it's a surprise," she responded mysteriously. "I may look younger, or I may look older. You'll just have to wait and see . . . Perhaps, if you are a good boy, you will have the old Helga back. Remember what I used to look like ten years ago when we first met?"

He nodded wistfully. "How could I forget? You were the most attractive," he began a reverie, but then snapped back. "But I like you even better now. Truly."

"You big liar," she kidded him.

"No, no. Truly. I swear. You're so much more exciting now, so much more of a woman. In fact, if there was no need, I'd rather that you stay the same."

"We'll see," she said, pretending to be mollified. "I told you, it's a surprise."

"There are a lot of Germans in Brazil," he mused on a different subject. "It will be a nice change from this godforsaken place."

"*Ja, ja,* there will be plenty of them there," she replied, wanting to add, those are the ones in particular we should keep away from. But what was the point in saying it? They weren't going to Brazil anyway. Especially Baumann. He was going nowhere. So why not let him be as happy and hopeful as he wishes to be?

"Yes," she said, "we'll feel right at home there. Everything is taken care of. Believe me, you'll love Brazil."

"I'll love it, Helga," he said sincerely, "because you'll be there. I think I could be happy anywhere with you."

She loathed him when he talked like that, even more than when he crawled on all fours, panting in pain and delight, saliva dripping from his ugly mouth.

She had to keep reminding herself that at least she hadn't needed to resort to blackmail or coercion. Karl had cooperated voluntarily all along, from the first time that he provided her with the general, seemingly harmless information about the nuclear plants, to the present, when he willingly became part of the intricate plot. Surely she had pictures and tapes that could ruin his career and marriage; but as it turned out, pressure was not necessary. Her spell over him proved to be sufficient, and it made things so much easier.

Helga thumbed through the photocopies in front of her again. They contained, in detail, the security arrangements at the Braidwood plant.

"Was it very difficult to get these?" she asked appreciatively.

Baumann shrugged. "Not really. Not much more than the rest."

"Well, the boss will be absolutely delighted," she said. "And now, since this was the last thing we needed, you'll be entitled to the bonus. You've made it, Karl, you've delivered it all, and on time. I must admit, I'm very, very proud of you."

She wondered what his reaction would be if he knew that "the boss" was no other than Carlos and that the attack on the nuclear plants was to be carried out by Terror International. He believed it was to be the work of a group of disgruntled German revolutionaries out to make money, lots of money. It was to be their last act, and then they would disperse and live happily ever after on the proceeds. She had agreed to live the rest of her life with him. He never felt the need to know more.

"I already have my bonus," he said. "You."

"Of course," she teased him, "me. And my share . . ."

"You know that's not true," he protested, playing along. "I don't even know what your share is."

"It's not as much as yours, but it's big enough."

"How big?"

"Half a million dollars."

"*Mein Gott!*" he exclaimed. "Along with my bonus, we'll have between us a million and a half dollars!"

She nodded.

"Brazil, here we come!" he burst out cheerfully in English, affecting an American accent.

"*Ja. Ja.* Here we come," she repeated, feigning enthusiasm again. Yet all she could think about was Brigitte. They would be together soon. Oh, how she missed her, longed for her. That had been the most difficult part of her mission. Oh, Brigitte, she thought, it will be so good to be with you again, to be able to love you again.

And as Karl began to undress, she considered that the most perfect way of doing away with him at the end would be to whip him to death as he screamed for more, more, and more.

A wry smile crossed her lips as it struck her that, in fact, if he knew he had to die, that would probably be how he would choose to go—under her whip, relishing it to the last, final stroke.

CHAPTER THIRTY-THREE

"SOMEHOW, I have a definite feeling that Helga is our key here," Sartain said as he refilled Tara's wineglass with the Windsor Pinot Noir. He had learned she liked the California wine the last time they had dinner at his place, before her trip to Israel.

"Why Helga?" she asked, raising her glass to sniff the fresh bouquet.

"Going over Erika's latest interrogation," he explained as he poured himself some wine also, "Verner and I discovered that Helga was the only one who was really supposed to be freed. Apparently the other three became part of the escape only after she refused to leave without them."

Sartain cut a slice of juicy sirloin. "If you also take into account the fact that she was the only low-ranking, nonimportant terrorist on the Entebbe list, and that Carlos chose to ignore her explicit disobedience, it becomes very clear that they needed her badly."

Tara studied him curiously. "Do you know why?" she finally asked.

"For the big operation, I suppose. I can't see it any other way. That's why I believe she may be the key to the whole thing." He paused, staring into her eyes. "I wouldn't be at all surprised if that's exactly what Linda discovered when she was in Berlin."

Tara thought for a long moment about what he had just said. "But why Helga? I can't see why they would need her that badly."

"I don't know, Tara. I wish I did. Apparently for something she's very skilled at. Though I can't find any indication of what it must be."

"Where is she then?"

Sartain shrugged his shoulders. "I don't know. That's part of it.

She has totally disappeared since her escape. Now the other two, as you know from the Mossad report, were spotted in Aden the other day. A strange coincidence . . ." He sipped on his wine. "But no one, and I mean no one, seems to know where our Ms. Helga Denz is. She has not been seen again. But I can tell you one thing, she is not dead. And wherever she is, and whatever she is doing at the moment, I guarantee you, it has a lot to do with what Carlos is busy planning for us."

"But what is so special about Helga?" Tara queried again. "What in . . . Moses' name, can she do that others, who were more available, can't?"

Sartain raised his hands to convey his own bafflement. "I don't know. I don't understand it either. All I know is that Carlos didn't go to all this trouble for romantic reasons. Incidentally, according to some of the inmates at Lehrter, she was crazy about Brigitte. And it seems that it was because of Brigitte that Helga refused to escape alone."

"A lesbian?" Tara sounded somewhat surprised, recalling that the first descriptive line in Helga's Mossad file was that she was Ralf Demmer's girl friend, and that it was he who had introduced her to the terrorist movement.

The professor raised his eyebrows and shrugged, "Perhaps bisexual. Anyway there seems to be a few other things about her that we don't know. I asked Verner to seek the help of the Verfassungsschutz in fully investigating her past. I impressed upon him that the most obscure detail in her background could turn out to be immensely significant. I asked him to omit nothing, even if it meant a thousand-page report."

Sartain paused and smiled for the first time. "I told him I am relying on the good old German thoroughness in this case."

Tara smiled too. She could visualize the new German permanent representative practically clicking his heels together before rushing to demonstrate superior German efficiency. Well at least some of them are on our side now, she couldn't help but think.

Sartain changed the subject. "How is the sirloin this time?" he asked. It was the third time Tara had eaten at his place, and it was the third time he had served steak.

"I told you, I love it. You don't seem to believe me, but I swear, if there was any meal that I missed while I was gone, it was eating one of your juicy steaks, right here, at this table, listening to Bach, surrounded"—she swept the room with her eyes—"surrounded by all these books and personal mementos . . . conversing freely with the most brilliant—"

"Okay, Okay," Sartain interrupted, feigning modesty. "But I warn you, this and soft-boiled eggs are just about the only thing I know how to make."

"You don't have to apologize," Tara said. "Just tell me, what's your secret recipe?"

"For the soft-boiled eggs?"

She laughed. "The steak, you smart ass."

"Never!"

"Never? Why not?"

"Because if I told you, you wouldn't have any reason to come back here."

"Sure," she chuckled, "I'll cook it right in my room in Kibbutz Madison." She reached for her wineglass and emptied it. It was her third.

Sartain examined her closely as he poured more wine. She had never drunk that much before in his presence. She looks ravishing tonight, he thought as he toasted her and emptied his own glass. Her long raven hair was stylishly and very flatteringly pulled behind one ear. Her light taupe dress accentuated her tanned olive skin and her lithe figure.

"With your looks . . . with your *charm*," he quickly corrected himself, "I'll bet you could persuade the chef himself to bring his oven and cook in your room."

"Thank you," she said with a dazzling, seductive smile, one he had never seen before. "You realize of course, Herr Professor," she said, her smile becoming all the more provocative, "that that is the first compliment you've ever given me."

"Certainly not," he protested. "I—"

Her eyes teasing, she nodded. "It's true," she said. "You have never before commented on my looks, what I wear, or anything else. Perhaps you haven't noticed . . . but first and foremost, I am a woman. And women, Sam, love compliments, no matter how independent we seem . . ."

She was amused by his manifest embarrassment. She had caught him off guard.

And she was right. He never had complimented her nor expressed his appreciative thoughts. He cleared his throat. "Incidentally," he said, his countenance sober as he pointed to the salad bowl, "I love this salad of yours."

Tara burst out laughing. It was a genuinely cheerful laugh which filled him with happiness.

"No, truly," he said, maintaining the same solemn expression. "How the devil do you manage to slice these vegetables, particularly the tomatoes, into such tiny slices. And that lemon-based dressing you make . . . You know, when Steve was here the other week, I tried to make it for him, just as you taught me. I told him beforehand that he was in for a special treat, a true Israeli salad. Well, what can I tell you? It just wasn't the same, didn't look the same and surely didn't taste the same. Thank God the rest of the dinner was so utterly delicious." He chewed his meat, deadpan.

"Oh really? What did you cook for him?"

"Steak!" he laughed loudly. "What did you think?"

The music ended, so he rose to replace the records. "Any preference?" he asked, his face still beaming.

"I leave it up to you," she said. "Unless you have some good guitar music."

He thought for a moment. "I have an excellent album by Mario Parodi. It's mostly Liszt, Schumann, and Chopin. Would you like to hear it?"

Tara nodded. "Sounds perfect."

As he searched his vast collection for the album, she gazed at him meditatively. He seemed fatigued, despite his cheerful mood. She noted the markedly lined brow, the puffed eyes, indicating both weariness and worriedness, and for good reason. Yet it was apparent that he was happy to be with her, and that she made him relax, if only temporarily.

A warm glow spread over her, and she knew it was not just the wine. She would have loved to touch him tenderly, to smooth his brow with her fingertips, to let his head rest on her lap. She desired to make him happy, eternally happy. She had missed him. Much, much more than she had expected. He had become part of her life in a way she had never anticipated. Once again her heated conversation with Echad, last week in Tel Aviv, crept into her thoughts.

Echad had been clearly unhappy about the intimacy of her continued relationship with Sartain.

"Do you sleep with him?" he threw out bluntly.

"It's none of your damn business," she had responded angrily, taken aback by his uncalled-for impudence.

"Oh, yes it is." His eyes filled with ire. They sought confrontation. "It very much is. May I remind you, my honorable lady, that you are not just working for Kafir Inc., that there is much more at stake here than the question of your virtue."

She fought for control. "Well, if you insist on knowing, I don't."

Obviously relieved, Echad said, placating, "Please don't misunderstand me, Atara, I meant no offense, but—"

She didn't quite know what made her interrupt him to retort cruelly, "But I didn't say I wouldn't want to." Perhaps it was the fact that he chose to call her by her full Hebrew name, Atara. She hardly ever used it, even in Israel, and never abroad. Perhaps she was oversensitive to the insinuation it carried.

"Would you?" he asked, unable to mask the pained expression on his face.

She stared at her boss and long-time friend. The truth was that she had wanted to badly. Yet, she responded quite differently.

"I don't know," she murmured. "What do you have against him anyway?" It was a question she knew the answer to.

"To begin with," he said, "I don't buy his plan. I don't believe Carlos will fall for it. Secondly I don't like his attitude, as if he can really read Carlos's mind. Granted, he is clever and has guessed right in a number of instances, but all this business about thinking like a terrorist . . ." Echad shook his head in disdain. "Coming from him, with his liberal opinions, with his sympathies for the Palestinians, I sometimes don't know how to read him. And frankly I don't quite know if I can trust him. Add to that the fact that he joined the Triple C immediately after his fiancée was murdered . . ."

Echad paused and looked at her pointedly, as if to tell her that she too had not fooled him, that he knew very well why she had really joined the Mossad and that he didn't like this collusion between two vengeance seekers. "And it doesn't add much to his credibility in my eyes. If it wasn't for Fred Atkins . . ." He let the thought conclude itself. "Anyway all I can tell you is that your professor had better prove himself soon, because I'm very quickly losing my patience."

Tara wanted to point out that he had contradicted himself but held her tongue.

"Okay," Echad said, his blue eyes steel cold. "You want to be chummy with him? Fine, be chummy with him. For all I care, you can even go to bed with him. Just do me one personal favor. Watch yourself. And none of this pillow talk, eh? Or better," he grinned sarcastically, "extract from him whatever you can, just keep your own mouth tightly shut."

Sartain sat down again. "How do you like it?" he asked.

"What?" she asked snapping to.

"The music."

Tara sipped on her wine and listened to the soothing guitar music wafting from the two large speakers on each side of the room, wondering whether she should tell him about the conversation with Echad. Impulsively she made up her mind.

Sartain listened quietly. Echad's disquiet over their intimate friendship neither surprised him nor particularly annoyed him. Mostly he was grateful for her candor and for her complete trust in him, which, considering her profession, he greatly valued.

"You have to excuse him," Tara said. "I believe he has been secretly in love with me for some years now, and I suspect that it's pure jealousy on his part. I'm sorry."

"Sorry? It is not for you to be sorry. Besides I can fully sympathize. Frankly," he smiled, "if I were he, I would have also forbade you to get too close to me."

Tara hesitated. "He thinks . . . he asked me if we sleep together."

"I see," Sartain raised his eyebrows. "What did you tell him?"

"I told him the truth, that we don't," she said quietly. But then, as if her words assumed a will of their own, she added, "I did tell him though, that I wish we did . . ."

There was a frozen silence as they stared into each other's eyes. At that moment there was no Echad, there was no Mossad, nor Triple C nor Carlos. There was only the two of them; even the music seemed to have suddenly faded away. It was now or never. There could be no vacillation, no more postponement, no turning back. The bridge had to be crossed now.

Silently, slowly, his eyes still fastened on hers, Sartain stood and walked to Tara's side of the table. She rose to meet him, his equal, yet now simply a woman who wanted him and wanted to be his. Before his mind could grasp the meaning of it all, he felt her body against him, warm, pliant, vulnerable. Only then did he realize how much he had wanted her, longed for the moment he could hold her in his arms, feel her heartbeats against his, her soft, sensual lips close on his. All his senses were in turmoil, exploding and drowning, engulfing and overwhelming him with almost unbearably sweet pain. In one flush he was being born, dying, and being reborn again.

Eternal moments later, when she led him to the bedroom and began to undress in the soft light of the bed-table lamp, Sartain gazed at her, immobile for a short time, as if hypnotized by the unfolding sensuous beauty. Unclothed, she had the perfect lissome grace of a dancer; slender waisted, with long, perfect legs and lusciously tight buttocks. At thirty-eight her skin was still smooth and her breasts firm, curving upward with delicate, dainty aureoles and short, dark nipples.

He began to undress himself.

"No," Tara protested. "Please wait."

Sartain stopped, puzzled.

"I'd like to do it," she said softly.

He nodded hesitantly, but somehow it seemed only right.

Naked, looking like some mystical goddess, she approached him. Gently she unbuttoned his shirt. As she let it drop to the carpet, her hands, lightly, delicately followed the pronounced musculature of his shoulders and arms.

"I love your body," she whispered.

He moved to take her in his arms.

"No," she said, "not yet. Please."

Unused to such passivity, he let his arms drop to his side.

She pulled him gently toward the bed and, sitting on its edge, bent down and removed his shoes and socks. A shudder went up his spine when she began to unzip his trousers. But he didn't move, not even when she removed his briefs. She traced the muscular curves of his strong legs, down, and then up again, but he kept still as if in a trance, his body detached from his brain, wholly submitting to her desires.

When her lips suddenly sought his manhood, he wanted to say no, to protest that he didn't want it this way, not yet, that he wanted first to feel her full body against him, that he wanted to kiss her again. But he surrendered, quiet and still, a prisoner of the irresistible sensual pleasure pulsating in his groin, a willing captive to her own act of submission.

His hands finally reached to touch her head, and he began very tenderly to stroke her soft, flowing hair. Suddenly, however, he could not discern in his reverie whose hair it was that he fondled, Tara's or Linda's. He twitched involuntarily, his back stiffening.

Tara lifted her head and looked up. There were tears in her eyes. "I haven't done . . . It's been years since . . . I thought I would never want to do this with any other man," she whispered.

He shut his eyes, nodding. He understood, and his heart went out to her. He bent down, and holding her face very gently between his palms, he kissed her wet eyes.

"I love you, Sam," she whispered as they lay down on the bed.

"I love you too, Tara. With all my heart."

But when they made love, wildly, desperately, he was haunted by recurring images of Linda. And when he finally climaxed, he screamed, as never before, to unload both the unbearable pleasure and the tormenting guilt.

Lying still in each other's arms, their hearts slowly resuming their normal beat, she suddenly pushed herself away to face him. "You thought about Linda, didn't you?" she whispered.

He wanted to lie, to deny it, to spare her the agonizing truth, but he couldn't. Silently, sadly, he nodded.

She shut her eyes, which were dry now, and took a deep breath. "I thought about Aaron," she whispered with equal sadness when she opened them again. "You were both Aaron and yourself . . . it was . . . as if I was making love to both of you at the same time. I'm sorry. I'm truly sorry."

God Almighty save us! he wanted to shout, grasping what she said. It was not just the two of us who made love. He felt squeamish.

Reading his mind, Tara nodded soberly. "It was all four of us, all in one bed together."

Sartain studied her gloomy face for a long moment. "You didn't reach . . ." he began, but didn't finish.

She shook her head, a bitter smile twisting the corners of her mouth. "I couldn't, Sam, I'm sorry. I wanted to very much, but I just couldn't. I guess I didn't realize how guilty I still feel, we both feel, that they are dead, and we are alive, and in love . . ."

CHAPTER THIRTY-FOUR

"**N**O," said Verner, a slender, fair, sharp-featured man with a slight German accent, "there is nothing to indicate that Helga has ever been to the United States." He searched through the pile of colored cards on his desk and pulled a yellow one. "We haven't fed these into the computer yet, but it shows here that she had been to England, to France, to Switzerland, the Netherlands, Italy, Lebanon, and Southern Yemen. But there is absolutely nothing here about the United States, or Canada, or even Latin America."

"So far as you know," Sartain suggested.

Verner, a taciturn man who weighed his words carefully, only shrugged.

"Have you checked with Immigration and Naturalization here?"

"Certainly. Nothing." The German, who held a master's degree from Harvard in criminology, wanted to add something about the inefficiency of American bureaucracy but refrained. "So unless she entered illegally," he continued instead, "we have to assume that she has never been here."

"What about associating with Americans back in Germany?"

Verner pulled a batch of blue cards and glanced through them. He shook his head. "No, nothing that we've managed to uncover. No American military personnel, nothing. Nothing to indicate that she even corresponded with Americans or ever knew any." He paused at one of the cards. "It says here that her English is quite good, though. She got high marks in it in secondary school where she demonstrated an aptitude for languages. And according to an old girl friend here, she managed pretty well with it during her visit to London."

"London?"

"*Ja*, once when she was twenty-one and again when she was twenty-three, as a tourist. The first time for five days; the second, for two weeks. That trip included Brighton and Bristol."

"That's it?"

Verner nodded.

"I see," Sartain said, sighing in disappointment. So far there seemed to be not a single lead as to why Carlos would need Helga, let alone need her badly enough to spring her from prison. Once more, he began to question the wisdom of the entire investigation, to wonder if they were not merely chasing wind. Perhaps Atkins is right after all, he pondered. Perhaps they should give it another try with Jim Anders. But that would be tantamount to a death sentence for both Anders and Amy.

"Have you exhausted all your resources?" he asked the German.

"No. There are still a number of people we haven't been able to talk to, and there are certain periods in her life which haven't been thoroughly investigated. Do you think we should proceed with the investigation?"

"Definitely. I told you at—"

The telephone on Verner's desk rang. "Excuse me," he said, picking it up.

Verner listened for a few seconds. "Yes, he's here." He handed the receiver to the professor sitting across the desk. "It's for you," he said. "It's Lucy."

"Thank you," Sartain reached for it. "Yes, Lucy, what is it?"

"You've a call on the D.C. number," she said. "It's Ivy."

"Ivy?" Sartain sat bolt upright, his face lit with surprise and excitement. The German watched him curiously. He had never seen the professor react in such a way.

"Are you certain it's Ivy?"

"Yes, Dr. Sartain, I am sure." There was a twinge of irritation in her voice which the professor was far too agitated to notice.

"Put her through, immediately!" he ordered.

"Yes, sir!"

Sartain covered the mouthpiece. "It's Amy," he whispered excitedly.

The German's eyes opened wide. "Amy Lahr?"

The professor nodded, regaining composure.

"Mr. Samuels?" He recognized Amy's voice.

"Yes, Ivy. It's me. It's good to hear your voice, believe me. How are you? Where are you calling from?"

"I'm okay, so far. I don't have much time to talk though. I'm calling from a restaurant in San Antonio. Luckily there is a pay phone in the ladies' room. I'm not alone, almost never alone, if you know what I mean."

"I understand. Is there anything you can tell me? Anything?" He sounded more anxious than he wanted to.

"Not really. I'm sorry. I don't even know where we're heading from here, although I gather that our final destination is Washington, D.C. But I'm not certain. The two Palestinians who are with me don't seem to know either. I'll have to call you again when I know more. How is . . . Jody?"

"You know about him, then?"

"Yes, I've heard. Is he okay?"

"Yes, yes, he's fine. Don't worry about him, he's in good hands. But Ivy, now that he's out of the picture, everything depends on you. Everything. You must get me something to go on." Again he sounded more desperate than he had intended.

"I'll do my best. Give him my love. I'm sorry, but I've got to hang up now. I'll contact you as soon as I know anything. Goodbye." The line went dead.

Several minutes later both Sartain and Verner were conferring with Atkins at his office. At first the Triple C chief was clearly elated by the news. The fact that Amy Lahr had surfaced safely in Texas seemed to have greatly increased their chances of preempting Carlos's scheme after all. No more was there doubt in his mind that Carlos planned a major strike in the U.S., and soon. Obviously Jim's capture had not altered the Jackal's plans, at least not his determination to move against a yet unidentifiable target within the United States.

Yet Atkins was clearly disappointed and distressed to hear that Amy was as yet unable to provide them with any substantial information.

"How do you think she crossed the border?" he questioned Sartain.

"She didn't say. But since she is in San Antonio, chances are she came from Mexico, by land."

"Thank God our friends at the Bureau didn't botch it up this time," Atkins muttered. "At least she is here."

Both the professor and Verner nodded their agreement.

Atkins, preoccupied, repeated, "Well at least she is here, and we know it's the Capital. She didn't mention any dates, did—"

"We don't, Fred," Sartain interrupted.

"I beg your pardon?"

"We don't know it's the Capital. At least, we don't know that for sure. All she said was that she thought Washington, D.C. was their final destination, but she was in no way certain. And as for dates, she didn't mention any. I still suspect, though, that it's going to be July Fourth. In fact I'm becoming more and more convinced of it. Of course, the twenty-seventh of June is still a possibility."

Atkins frowned. "You're only guessing again, Sam. A 'hunch,' as you call it." There was a tinge of vexation in his voice. "The way I see it, we know practically nothing at this point, except that Carlos is planning to strike some time in the near future. But where, when, and how? We don't seem to know. Do you agree?"

Sartain nodded reluctantly. The German, who had never witnessed a confrontation between the Triple C chief and the professor, maintained his grim façade despite his amusement. He too had been secretly annoyed at times with the professor's "hunches." He already had the Verfassungsschutz laboring around the clock, with no results, over the "hunch" about Helga. Life is not a novel, he mused. Not everything winds up a piece in a puzzle.

"Well then," Atkins cleared his throat, "if Ms. Lahr doesn't seem to know anything, perhaps the two Palestinians do. Have you considered the possibility of apprehending them for the purpose of interrogation. That shouldn't be too hard; we do know after all that they are in San Antonio, and I can issue the Red Alert . . . Or at least, we can have them put under tight surveillance until—"

"Sir," Sartain cut him short again, intending the formal address to counteract his forthcoming opposition. "Amy clearly indicated that she very much doubts the Palestinians are aware of their final destination, let alone of their specific targets or the date of the attack. I also do not recommend that we engage in any surveillance at this point. If they become the least suspicious that they're being followed, it will be all over, and we'll lose the only chance we have to find out what Carlos's target is. Anyway, worse comes to worst, and Amy cannot reach us in time, she will try to sabotage their action on the spot. Even at the risk of her own life."

"You really believe she'll do it?" Atkins asked both doubtfully and hopefully.

"If she is in a position to, I believe she will. But more importantly, I believe that we must give her more time. Let's not jeopardize her mission yet."

Atkins remained silent for a long moment, absorbed. He swiveled his high-backed chair and stared unseeing out the window, pondering the risks. When he finally turned back, he asked, "What about Helga? Have you come up with anything there?"

Sartain stirred uneasily and motioned to Verner to reply.

"So far, Mr. Atkins, nothing. Not a clue."

"I see," the Triple C chief remarked somberly. "Well, are you still proceeding with it?"

Verner turned toward Sartain.

"Yes we are," the professor responded for him. "I haven't given up on it yet."

"Verner," Atkins said abruptly, "would you please excuse us. There are a number of things I would like to discuss with Dr. Sartain alone."

"Certainly," the German obliged and rose from his chair. "I'll be in my office if either of you needs me."

Left alone, Atkins turned to Sartain. "I want to believe," he said in a more placid tone, "that Amy Lahr will help us preempt Carlos's strike. But, Sam, I have to be prepared for the worst. This morning I received the Japanese response to our informal protest against their six-million-dollar ransom payment and the release of those six imprisoned Red Army terrorists.

"Do you know what they told us?" Atkins asked rhetorically. "They told us that people who live in glass houses should not throw stones. They told us, in so many words, to shove it up the appropriate orifice. And can you really blame them?"

Not really, Sartain thought, not with the history of one American concession after another to terrorist demands. The Japanese had a point, even though he too was infuriated by their total capitulation. Worse, he strongly suspected that it was Fusako Shigenobu who masterminded the last week's hijacking of the

JAL jetliner, and that both the money and the freed gunmen would go to augment the forces of Carlos and Terror International. No wonder Atkins was in such a foul mood.

Atkins stood up and began to pace behind his desk. "Well," he continued, "I am determined to stand my ground this time. If somehow we manage to frustrate Carlos's plans beforehand, fine. If not, I'll do everything in my power to make sure that we don't capitulate to his demands, even if it means loss of lives. We cannot continue to surrender to blackmail and extortion the way we've been doing." He punched his right fist into his left palm.

"You and I know, Sam, that all capitulation does is to encourage further terrorist acts. And in the long run, many more lives will be lost. It's about time that the American people begin to understand that this increased terrorist activity is tantamount to a war. Granted, it's a different kind of war, but it's still a war, and you just can't hope to win a war unless you're prepared to make sacrifices."

Atkins stopped pacing and leaned forward on his desk. "Do you agree with me, Sam, or do I sound like some raving right-winger? I want to hear it from you, 'a liberal professor.' And forget for a minute your own personal reasons and . . . that you owe me one . . ."

Sartain looked up at him. "I agree with you, Fred. I—"

"Then you'll back me up on it, all the way?" Atkins challenged without letting him finish, his eyes riveting the professor.

Sartain squirmed. "If it comes to it, Fred, I will. I still very much hope, however, that Amy will be able to save us from making such a . . . decision." It was one decision, which in the face of the anticipated nonconventional, perhaps nuclear blackmail, he wanted to have no part in.

"I very much hope so too," Atkins said somberly. "Though sooner or later, one way or another. I am afraid we'll have to make such a choice."

An uneasy feeling of premonition crept over the professor as he left Atkins's office. Tara, I wish you were here, he thought wistfully. Right now. He hadn't seen her since the night they first made love; a night which left them both with ambivalent and conflicting feelings.

He had talked to her only once afterward, over the phone. It had been brief, businesslike, just before she left for New York. But he conversed with her often in his mind, like he had done a million times with Linda. Tara had become an integral part of his psyche, an invisible friend who was always there to share his thoughts, his feelings, and particularly his frustrations. He wished very much, however, that she were there right now in the flesh.

Well, he sighed as he entered his office, at least she'll be back the thirteenth for my birthday. That's only two days away. My last? he wondered morbidly, yet the prospect of that reality caused him no real anxiety. Perhaps he was resigned.

Sheik Ali-Abdel-el-Rahman-Abdel-el-Aziz-el-Husseini-el-Saud's Boeing 727 descended over the Nevada desert, and, under the expert hands of the two British pilots, made a perfect landing at McCarran International. The jet—which had been converted the previous year at the Los Angeles facilities of Airsearch Aviation into a double-decker aerial palace to the tune of three million dollars—taxied smoothly to the Hughes terminal which serviced Las Vegas's fleet of private planes. Few of them were as luxurious as the portable penthouse of the modern-age Croesus from the oil-soaked Arabian peninsula.

At the terminal the two standby customs and passport officers greeted the disembarking sheik and his entourage—including four veiled women. Eager to please, the passport control men oozed broad smiles, bowing enthusiastically as they waved the party on to the waiting limousines.

Once inside the Mercedes 600, Carlos and Lattore, disbelieving the ease with which they and their deadly luggage were allowed into the country, sighed in relief. Only now did Carlos fully comprehend the sheik's repeated assurances that looking Arab was more than sufficient; they didn't have to masquerade as concubines in order to gain safe and anonymous entry into the United States.

How could Husseini-el-Saud know that by denying the Venezuelan terrorist the opportunity to disguise himself as a veiled Arab female, he had deprived him of a great pleasure. But Carlos had not insisted; all too familiar with the Arab attitude toward the "inferior" sex, he knew it could stigmatize his virile image. He did promise himself one thing, however. If anything went wrong, the sheik would be the first one to ascend to Allah's promised Heavenly Kingdom.

It took the five-car motorcade barely fifteen minutes to reach

Las Vegas Boulevard—"the strip." They turned into the notoriously ostentatious driveway at Caesar's Palace, complete with its reflecting pools, color fountains, and overblown replicas of Greek and Roman statues. The welcoming smiles here were even more toothy than at the airport. Bellmen well remembered the hundred-dollar tips of the sheik's last visit. They were ready to do battle for the privilege of serving him and his entourage.

Rage, who had driven to Las Vegas the day before and installed herself at one of the small motels on the outskirts of town, arrived at Carlos's luxurious hotel suite shortly after he had checked in.

When Lattore let her in, and she looked around her, she gasped, "Jesus!"

"Allah!" Carlos corrected humorously as he walked into the huge two-story parlor from the adjacent bedroom.

"Hey man," she said with one of her rare smiles, "this is obscene. And as they shook hands, she continued to survey the gilded, chandeliered parlor of the Apollo Suite with a mixture of awe and disgust.

"How much do you pay for this . . . place?" Rage asked as Carlos led her past the giant TV screen and the white baby grand to the saloon-sized bar.

"I don't," he said, offering her one of the barstools. "And neither does the sheik. It's all free, including the liquor . . . What would you like to have?"

"Vodka."

"Straight?"

"Straight."

"Very Russian," Carlos remarked as he searched for the best brand among the large selection of bottles behind him. "Would you like Manuel to order some caviar?"

"You're too much," she said, amused. "No. I wouldn't. But tell me, how come all this is free? Or are you putting me on?"

Carlos handed her the drink, and pouring himself some chilled champagne, he shot a questioning glance at Lattore. The Uruguayan terrorist, who had been sitting quietly all this time on one of the white sofas, shook his head.

Turning his attention back to Rage, Carlos responded, "No, I'm not kidding. This is one of the 'fantasy suites,' as the hotel calls them, and they're reserved, free of any charge, for the high rollers. Since our friend, the sheik, had been known to lose, or sometimes win, in excess of one million dollars a day . . ." He paused to toast her with his glass. ". . . it's no wonder they are willing to provide him with a string of these suites, for him and his guests, whenever he comes to town. Incidentally, if you think this is something, you should see His Highness's penthouse suite."

"Thank you, but I don't think I could stand it," she said humorlessly.

"Don't be so quick to judge," he continued to tease. He wished she had a better sense of humor, that she could fully appreciate the irony of the whole thing. Besides where was it written that the revolution can never be enjoyed?

"Come on," Carlos persisted, leaving the bar. "Let me show you one of the bedrooms. I think you'll get a kick out of this one."

Lattore, who continued to sit silently, smiled thinly as he watched the Jackal leading the American revolutionary into his bedroom.

The oval room had a large round bed, with a shell-like headboard at its center. And as Carlos pulled open the white, gauzy draperies which enclosed the bed, Rage could see the large circular mirror above it. She shook her head. She shook it again at the sight of the Jacuzzi with the illuminated round mirror above it.

Carlos couldn't help but wonder at this point what Rage would be like in bed. He subtly examined her lips. He had always prided himself on the fact that he could accurately tell if a woman was a good lover just by the shape and size of her lips.

Very mediocre, he concluded in this case, relieved in a way that their dealings would not be distracted by his sexual appetite.

"Are you much of a gambler?" Rage asked as they reentered the parlor.

"You mean here, in Vegas?" Carlos asked as he sat down by Lattore. "No, not really. I don't like the odds against me. The only way I would gamble here," he smiled teasingly, "would be to stick up one of these places. But then I might get into trouble with the Mob . . . and *them*, I fear."

He burst out laughing and patted his old friend on the knee. "Right, Manuel?"

The Uruguayan nodded, even though he didn't exactly know

who "the Mob" was. It didn't matter; he knew it was only a joke. The Jackal feared no one.

When they finally got down to business, Carlos presented the American woman with a list of things he needed for the big operation, mostly arms and explosives. Rage puzzled over his request for two complete sets of diving gear. Carlos quickly explained, not going into detail, that he needed it for the diversionary attack on the Potomac boat. He wanted it to be ready at the Washington hideout prior to June 27.

"It will be there," she assured him. "But tell me one thing, what the hell is a DPV?"

"Oh, I'm sorry. It's short for diver propulsion vehicle. Frogmen use it to get to their objectives."

"I see. But where do I get it? Isn't it strictly navy equipment?"

"No. You should be able to buy it at any large outlet for marine gear. If possible, I would like you to get me the Farralon, the MK-five or the MK-six."

She wrote it down. "How expensive is it?"

Carlos shrugged. "Not expensive at all, a couple of grand. Incidentally I brought you the dough." He enjoyed using the American vernacular which he had acquired while living with his mother in Florida. His accent was only slightly off when he put his mind to it. Languages, after all, had always been his forte.

Carlos excused himself and walked into his bedroom. When he returned a couple of minutes later, he carried a leather briefcase. He placed it on the marble cocktail table in front of Rage.

"Do you want it in cash or chips?" he kidded, unlocking the case.

Rage stared appreciatively at the neat stacks of hundred-dollar bills inside the briefcase.

"There is two hundred fifty thousand dollars here," Carlos said matter-of-factly. "Is that enough?"

Rage nodded.

He couldn't resist teasing her again. "You can buy yourself a nice piece of real estate in Beverly Hills with that."

"Not anymore," she answered him, this time in kind. "Not with such small change."

"Oh well," he laughed. "There is much more where this came from. We're better bankrolled now after we hijacked that Japanese plane."

She glanced at him curiously. "I thought the Algerians confiscated the money," she said. "At least, that's what had been reported by the press here."

A crafty grin crossed his lips. "Now, now, my dear. Since when do you believe the media?"

"All right, all right, smart ass. What happened?"

"Fifty, fifty . . . That's what happened. We reached a compromise—three million to them and three million to us. Not a bad deal, considering we also gained the freedom of six additional comrades. And, by the way, since we're talking about manpower, how many people can you provide us with?"

"How many do you need?"

"I'm figuring on using a dozen at each plant. We have eighteen of our own, so we'll need eighteen more. Do you have them?"

"I have fifteen now that I can count on. I'm pretty sure I can come up with another three who are as reliable. But what about the boat? Don't you need any of our comrades for that operation?"

He shook his head. "No, I don't. The boat hijacking, you see, will be carried out to the bitter end, so as to assure the success of the main event. It will be mounted by a specially selected suicide team whose aim will be to convince your government that we mean business, that I shall not hesitate to carry out my threats if our demands are not fully met.

"There will be no bargaining there," Carlos continued, his expression and voice hardening so suddenly it seemed there was a different person in the room. "It's all or nothing, and this time we are not going to fall for any of their delaying tactics. Our willingness to die for our cause will be demonstrated beyond the slightest doubt. In fact . . ." He stopped himself abruptly, and changed the subject.

He had been about to say: In fact our brave comrades will have no choice in the matter.

CHAPTER THIRTY-FIVE

IT was a balmy June evening; the breeze was soft, soothing, and surprisingly enough for D.C., fresh and unpolluted. Sartain, who stepped first out the door, paused and took a deep breath, attempting to clear his lungs from the heavy cigarette smoke inside the pub, and somewhat less successfully, his head from the four dry martinis he had drunk on an empty stomach.

As he and Atkins strolled leisurely toward the open parking lot, his tie already loosened, Sartain removed his jacket and tossed it over his shoulder, holding it with one finger by the loop. In his other hand he carried the small unwrapped box which contained his birthday gift from Fred, an expensive Meerschaum pipe.

"You really shouldn't have, Fred," he said again. "At least you could have let me pay for the drinks."

Atkins, who had had a few himself, slapped Sartain merrily on his shoulder. "On my birthday, pal, you can pay for as many as you want."

"When is it?"

"What?"

"Your birthday, I don't know when your birthday is."

"Oh, it's on October ninth. And don't get any ideas, pal. I never celebrate it. I'm too much of an *alte kacker*, as the Jews say, for that."

"Jesus!" Sartain exclaimed.

"What?" Atkins stopped and turned toward him.

"I'm surrounded by Libras," he laughed.

Atkins raised his eyebrows. "What the hell are you talking about, Sam?"

"Don't you see?" He shoved him good-naturedly. "Carlos is a

Libra. Steve is a Libra. And now, I find out that you are a Libra too. I wonder what Linda would have said about it . . ."

"Linda?"

"Never mind," he said as they resumed their amble toward Atkins's car. "It's a long story. Not really worth repeating."

"How is Steve, by the way?" Atkins asked.

"He's fine. He has a new girl friend."

"Another one?"

"Uh-huh. This time a few years older than he. An attorney, working for the government. I haven't met her yet. Anyway I gave him the choice of joining us here for drinks or going to dinner with me and Tara, and bring his girl friend. Now are you sure you don't want to change your mind and come along?"

Atkins pulled the keys out of his pocket as they approached his car. "I told you, Sam, we really would love to. But with Bev's sister in town, we've got other obligations. We'll—"

"You two! Get into this car, quick!" the tall, rangy gunman barked as he jumped out of the blue Grand Prix parked next to Atkins's station wagon.

And before the startled Atkins and Sartain had time to react, the gunman's shorter, broad-shouldered accomplice emerged from the other door, covering them from behind with a sawed-off shotgun.

Both assailants were blacks, as was the driver of the four-door sedan, and they all wore dark, impenetrable sunglasses, giving them a mean, threatening look.

"Do what you told, man, or you're dead," the broad-shouldered one hissed, ramming the double-barreled muzzle into Sartain's back as the professor momentarily considered resisting.

Sartain was shoved into the front passenger seat while Atkins was sandwiched between the two gunmen in the back seat.

"Now don't contemplate no tricks," the broad-shouldered one ordered from the back, the cold metal of his gun pressing against Sartain's neck.

"Easy, brother, easy," the tall one, who seemed to be the leader, said to the driver as he backed out of the parking space with a heavy lurch. "Keep it cool, man. No one saw nothing. Just drive it easy and smooth. We don't want no pigs on our trail . . . As for you, *Professor*, you keep it cool too, and you may live to see the sun rise again."

Sartain could not see the cruel, sarcastic grin which crossed their abductor's dark face, but he could feel its meaning in every bone.

As the blue sedan cruised east on M Street, out of Georgetown, Sartain cursed his own stupidity. Had it not been for the heavy drinking, he and Fred most probably would have been wary of the three blacks in the blue car next to theirs. But would it have made any difference? He was not armed. Was Atkins? He didn't see them frisk him.

Sartain wanted to turn his head to catch a glimpse of the Triple C chief. But as soon as he tried, he felt the gun's muzzle against his left cheek.

"I wouldn't," the voice behind him advised.

He froze. But his mind raced now, cleared of any alcoholic fog. They must know who we are, he considered. But why did they let me know that they knew? Why did they call me "professor"?

"Who are you? What do you—"

"Keep your trap shut, man!" the tall one barked angrily. "I didn't hear no one givin' you no permission to talk. Just keep your arms folded in front of your chest. That's it, my man. And shut up!"

Did they work for Carlos? Sartain searched his brain. Are they the same gunmen who assassinated Colonel Navon? Didn't the Bureau suspect it had been American blacks who did the killing? If they were the same ones, then both he and Atkins were doomed.

I must get away before they reach their destination, or I'm a dead man, the urgent realization flashed through his mind. There was no fear, only a determination that it was not yet time for him to die, not on his birthday, not before he accomplished what he set out to do.

The car continued east on K Street toward Mount Vernon Square, the grimly silent, scar-faced driver keeping it carefully within the speed limit, making sure they didn't attract any undue attention.

Sartain examined him from the corner of his eye, unable to tell where he kept his gun, though certain that he too was armed. He looked back at the road, contemplating escape. He must get out of the car when it slowed down, he decided. But not when it stopped at a light or he would be a sitting duck. If he could only manage to divert the attention of the gunmen for a couple of seconds, he could quickly open the door and roll out before any of them had a chance to take good aim. He knew he was bound to get hurt, if not from bullets, then from the fall itself. But it was better than being executed in cold blood. And he was convinced that fate awaited him.

Linda flashed through his mind. Is this how she was kidnapped? Fury at that thought suddenly surged within him.

Cool it, he told himself, like the man said.

Reassessing his predicament, Sartain noted that the lock on his door had been pressed down. That complicated his plan. That one extra second needed to unlock it could cost him his life.

Just then the car stopped abruptly for a jaywalking pedestrian. Sartain used the jolt to inconspicuously place himself as close to the door as possible. Keeping his head erect and staring straight ahead, his left hand sought the safety button under the cover of his folded right arm.

His fingers found the button. Yes, he thought, grateful that no one had noticed, it can be done. And it had better be done on a busy street, or I'm done for.

They circled Mount Vernon Square and entered New York Avenue, heading northeast. The sun had set; inside the car the darkness made the gunmen feel more secure. The chance was even more remote now that anyone would suspect anything fishy about the innocuous blue sedan.

The professor, too, welcomed the darkness; it enhanced his chances of succeeding. If only he could take Fred with him. But that was impossible. At least, if he survived his attempt, he could summon immediate help. And if he died, there would still be the chance that the commotion would help Fred's chances.

It was when they approached the Fourth Street intersection that Sartain saw the white police car cruising toward them from the opposite direction.

This was the opportunity he needed. It was now or never. He felt no fear, even though he knew the slightest mistake would cost him his life. I love you, Linda, his mind whispered soundlessly. Forgive me, Tara.

"Watch out! Police!" Sartain screamed as his left hand lifted the safety button and his right opened the door. He thrust himself against it and let himself roll out.

As he hit the asphalt, desperately trying to cover his head with his arms, he felt a sharp pain penetrate his body. Surprisingly, however, he didn't hear shots. His first thought was that they were drowned out by the screeching of the van which came to a halt a mere foot away from his sprawled body.

Dazed, and with great effort, he turned his head to see the blue sedan speed away, its open door being pulled shut as it made a sharp left turn into New Jersey Avenue. The police car made a sharp U-turn, sirens wailing, and stopped only a few feet away from him, then zoomed off after the fast-disappearing Grand Prix.

A circle of blurred faces peered down at him curiously.

"You can consider yourself lucky, Professor," the doctor at Freeman's Hospital emergency clinic said as he finished examining the X rays. "I can detect no major injury. However, in addition to the sprained left ankle, you have a slightly chipped bone. I would like to apply a soft cast there."

"Can't you just use an Ace bandage?" Sartain asked.

"I will for the sprained wrist, but I would prefer—"

"I would very much prefer, Doctor," Sartain interrupted, "unless it's absolutely necessary, that you do the same for my ankle." And in order not to sound overly rude, he quickly explained, "It's very important that I be able to move as freely as possible."

The prematurely bald young physician shrugged in concession. "It's your ankle . . ."

"Thank you. I appreciate it. Now what about the pain in my chest? Did you detect anything there?"

"I was just getting to that," the medic said with measured patience as he picked up one of the X rays and reexamined it against the light box. "You seem to have a couple of slightly fractured ribs. Again, nothing serious, and in this case, a rib belt will do. It will be painful for a few weeks, especially when you twist or bend, but I'll prescribe a pain-killer, and that should help. All things considered, you are a lucky man to take such a fall and end up with nothing more serious."

"When can I get out of here then?" Sartain asked as he raised himself on the examining table, biting his lips against the sharp pain in his chest. He glanced at his watch. It was eight minutes after ten. He had been there for close to two hours.

"Just as soon as I wrap you up. I must warn you, though, that what you need most, if you want these injuries to heal properly, is lots of rest. And make sure you don't strain—"

There was a polite knock on the door, and the policeman stationed outside peered in. "Excuse me, Doc," he said, "but this guy's son is here."

Sartain looked up at the physician. "Is it all right for him to come in? I have some very important things to discuss with him."

"Certainly," the accommodating MD said, nodding his approval to the cop. "I have to locate a rib belt anyway."

Steve, dressed for dinner, entered as the physician left. "How are you, Dad?" he inquired with much concern.

Sartain forced a reassuring smile. "I'm fine. The doctor says I should consider myself very fortunate." Seeing his son glance apprehensively at the X rays on the table, he added, "He detected no serious injury, just a sprained ankle, a sprained wrist, and a slightly fractured rib. No internal damage. In short, nothing to write home about."

"Thank God," Steve said, relieved.

". . . and my old army parachute training," the professor added sardonically. "Now tell me, did you find Tara?"

Steve shook his head. "No, Dad, I'm sorry. I just don't know where she disappeared to. I stopped by your place, but it doesn't look like she's been there."

"What about the hotel?"

"Well, it's sort of strange. The first time I called, they said she wasn't in. When I checked with them a second time, they tried to tell me that she was not registered there at all."

"Did you use the name I gave you?"

"Of course. But they insisted they had no one by either name. It was only after I drove there and talked to the manager that he admitted she had checked out shortly before I made my second call."

"Checked out?" Sartain was astounded. He changed position to ease the pain in his chest. He had only pretended to swallow the pain-killing pills after the doctor told him they might make him dizzy.

"Perhaps she already heard about the kidnapping and is just being extra cautious," he said, more to himself than to Steve, trying to stem his mounting anxiety.

"Most probably. She might—"

Steve was interrupted by another knock on the door. Mike, the police sergeant who had first questioned the professor, walked in.

"Any news?" Sartain asked apprehensively. "Have they still got Mr. Atkins?"

"Well, they're still barricaded in that apartment on Jackson Street," the bulldog-faced sergeant responded. "But we have established telephone contact."

"And?" Sartain raised himself to a full sitting position despite the piercing pain.

"And we know now who they are and what they want. Are you okay?" he asked, noticing the agonized expression on the professor's face.

"I am fine. Go on, please."

"Well apparently they are members of the Hanafi Muslim sect—"

"The Hanafis?" Steve couldn't contain his surprise. "You mean the same . . ."

"Yes, the same group that pulled the March raid on the B'nai B'rith offices and the District Building. Well, now they want the release of Khaalis and the eleven gunmen who took part in those assaults."

Sartain was stunned; when he had pondered their kidnapping, he never suspected his assailants to be Hanafi Black Muslims. He had been convinced that Terror International had a hand in it. Unless . . . unless Carlos had managed somehow to hire the Hanafis for his own purposes. Could he be that effective?

"Do they know who their hostage is?" he asked the police officer.

"Yes." Mike nodded emphatically. "Very much so. They keep referring to him as the 'head honcho,' and they certainly know his value . . ."

"Do you think Mr. Atkins told them who he is?" Steve interjected.

"No. I don't believe so. I think they knew beforehand."

"Probably so," the professor agreed. "They knew who I was,

all right. And they must have followed us all the way from Langley to the Dutch Inn."

"Yes," Mike confirmed. "They do seem to know who you are too. In fact," he cleared his throat and added uneasily, "they asked about you . . ."

The professor looked at him searchingly. "What do you mean, they asked about me?"

"Well," the sergeant was clearly embarrassed, "they wanted to know how you were doing and . . . and they wished you a quick and happy recovery and . . . a Happy Birthday."

Sartain exchanged a quick, meaningful look with his son. "The sons of bitches!" he cursed in a low, loathing voice. "A Happy Birthday, ah?"

Just then the doctor reentered the room, the rib belt and a few rolled elastic bandages in hand.

Mike greeted him with a nod and turned back to Sartain. "Anyway," he continued, "the place is surrounded by police and SWAT teams. We'll try and wait them out before we make any concessions. Now the SWAT captain is here, and he'd like to ask you a few questions, Professor, about the three men. He thinks it'll be useful to his team." He turned to the doctor. "Is that all right with you, sir?"

The physician glanced at Sartain.

"It's okay," the professor said. "Let him in. Just get me out of here as soon as possible."

CHAPTER THIRTY-SIX

THE gang of wild-eyed, machete-wielding blacks closed in on him. There was no place to run; he was trapped in the cul-de-sac. If only he had a gun, he thought desperately, he could take some of them with him. Where is his gun? He shook his head and tried to remember but couldn't. He was perspiring heavily. Someone was behind him, shaking him and whispering, "Those who live by the gun, die by the gun." And then the voice said something about Tara which he failed to catch, but he knew it was important, very important . . .

"What? What?" he mumbled groggily, opening his eyes.

"Dad, Tara is on the phone," Steve was bending over his bed, shaking him. "She says it's very important."

Sartain was still dazed, straining for consciousness, the taste of death still lingering in his mouth. "What? What time is it?"

"It's five o'clock."

"Five o'clock?!"

"Yes, Dad, it's five o'clock in the morning. I guess between the codeine and the sleeping pills you were under too deep to hear the phone."

A sharp pain pierced Sartain's rib cage as he tried to lift himself from the bed. It swiftly recalled the incredible events of the previous night.

Steve, clad only in his shorts and half-asleep himself, handed Sartain the telephone. "I'll hang up the extension," he said as he walked out of his father's bedroom.

Sartain brought the receiver to his ear. "Tara?"

"Yes, Sam. Are you okay? Are you badly hurt?"

"I'm fine. They wouldn't have sent me home if I wasn't. But I've been worried about you. Where've you been? We've been looking for you all over the place. Where are you now?"

"I'm in New York—"

"In New York? Are you okay?"

"Yes, I am. I'm calling from my apartment."

"Why didn't you let me know you were going back?" There was a tinge of reproach in his voice. With everything else, not knowing where she was had caused him enormous concern.

"I tried," she said. "I . . . well, it's a long story, but there was an attempt to kidnap me, or . . . harm me. I don't know."

"What? Who?" And he bit his lower lip to muffle the cry of pain that he almost let out when he sat up too abruptly. It felt as if someone drove a long, sharp needle into his lungs.

"I don't know," she said. "Perhaps the same people who took you and Atkins."

"So you know about Fred." He found himself a comfortable position in the bed. "But tell me first what happened to you. When did it happen? Where?"

"Around seven thirty, right after I left the hotel to go to your place as we'd agreed. I noticed that we were being followed by a blue car with two black guys in—"

"A Grand Prix?" he interrupted.

"What?"

"The make of the car. Was it a Grand Prix?"

"I don't think so." She thought a moment. "No. It was an old Cadillac. Why?"

"Forget it. It's just that the car we were kidnapped in was also blue, and it was a Grand Prix. I'm sorry, please go on."

"Anyway, once I realized we were being followed, I told the cabbie I would give him a fifty-dollar tip if he managed to lose them. It took him a good fifteen minutes, but he finally did. I called our Mossad emergency number from a diner, and two security men came to pick me up. They checked me out of the hotel—I didn't want to take any chances—and drove me to New York. I did try to call you before we left, but there was no answer. Then when we were outside Baltimore, we heard about the kidnapping on the car radio. But we still didn't know it was you and Fred Atkins they got. Are you sure you're not badly hurt?"

"Yes. Only a cracked rib and a twisted ankle. Can't even feel it. When did you find out?"

"Only when I got to my apartment, just before one o'clock,

when I called Tel Aviv. I tried to reach you at home again, but there was still no answer."

"I was with the SWAT team outside the building where they're holding Fred. I got back only around two."

"I know. But I only just found that out. How is Atkins? I understand there is a new noon deadline."

"Well he's alive, and so far that's what counts. The negotiating team believes that further extension of the deadline can be extracted from them. There is a willingness to meet at least part of their demands, such as safe departure for them out of the country. I hope it will be sufficient. Unless . . . unless they're somehow linked to Terror International, and then I'm afraid it will be a totally different ball game. If they are, I don't know how they got into this unless they were bought outright. God knows Carlos doesn't lack money, not with the six million they've just managed to extort from the Japanese. Do you think it was Hanafis who tried to get you?"

"I don't know, Sam. But I . . . I am leaving."

"What do you mean you're leaving? Leaving where?"

"Leaving for Israel, on the morning flight. In a few hours."

There was an awkward silence on both sides of the line. Then Tara added apologetically. "These are the Mossad's specific orders, Sam, and there is nothing I can do about it. They are extremely apprehensive about my safety, now that my cover seems to be blown. So, at least until the dust settles, I am ordered back. I don't know if they intend to send a replacement."

"I don't care about a replacement," Sartain could hardly contain his sudden fury. The pain in both his chest and ankle increased. "I want *you* here. I need *you* here, not some goddamn replacement. Don't you see the time has come? We have only three weeks at the most before Carlos will strike."

"Please, Sam, not on the phone."

"I don't give a damn!" he barked in anger. "If the son of a bitch has my phone tapped too, then he is omnipotent and we are doomed anyway. I ask you, beg you, to reconsider your decision."

"I am sorry, Sam, but I can't. I cannot disobey orders. You know that, and—" she stopped abruptly.

"And what?"

"And . . . I shouldn't tell you this, Sam, but the Mossad, that is,

Echad, trusts you now even less the way you've managed to escape the Hanafis."

"What?"

"I'm sorry, I knew I should never have told you."

Sartain's voice, however, was now composed as he asked: "And you, Tara? What about you? Do you trust me?"

"I love you, Sam."

"That was not the question. Do you trust me?"

"Of course I do. I couldn't love you if I didn't. But, Sam, listen. I tend to agree with Echad that there has to be some sort of a security leak within the Triple C. Maybe it's crazy, and I hate making him 'omnipotent,' but I can't help but feel that it's the Jackal who is behind these abductions, and that he's trying to stop you and Atkins. Which must mean that you are on the right track after all."

"If you really believe that, how can you go back to Israel?"

"I told you, Sam. I have no choice. If I don't, I'll be summarily sacked. And then what good am I to you? Believe me, I have argued, but they won't listen. It kills me to leave you at a time like this. I know what Fred means to you, and I pray he'll be all right. Do you think he will?"

"I don't know, Tara. I have a bad premonition. If I never see you again, just remember—"

"Please don't talk like that, Sam. You will see me again. I am not giving you up."

"But you're leaving . . ."

"I have to. But whatever happens, I'll be back. It's a promise. I love you, Sam. I love you as . . . I never loved anyone before. *Shalom.*"

"*Shalom,*" he muttered bitterly when the line went dead, knowing the Hebrew word meant not only "good-bye" but also "peace." But there was no peace, neither in his mind nor in his heart. Without Tara and without Fred, he felt alone, as lonely as he had ever been.

He lay still staring vacantly at the ceiling, emotionally paralyzed, when the phone suddenly rang again.

Not daring to hope, he half-heartedly picked up the receiver. "Sam?" He heard her distinct voice, and his heart leaped with renewed optimism.

"Sam, how could I be so forgetful? Your birthday . . . I still have your present with me. I'll make sure it is mailed to you before I leave. So Happy Birthday, Sam. And one more thing. I shouldn't have said "*shalom*," I should've said "*lehitraot*," which means 'see you.' So again, Happy Birthday, my love, and I'll see you soon."

"*Shalom*," the professor mumbled again as he hung up, feeling even lonelier than before.

"Are you okay, Dad? Is everything all right?" Steve asked as he came back into the bedroom.

Sartain nodded, forcing a smile. "Yes, Steve, I'm fine. Thank you." And thank God, he thought, that at least I have you with me.

"We don't need your fuckin' filthy food nor anything else, you dig?" the leader, whom Atkins had heard the other two call Abdul, shouted into the telephone. "We've got enough ammo to blow a thousand of your motherfucker asses. So you listen to me, you dick head. No! No! You listen to me! Don't you try to bargain with me no more. Don't take me for no fool. I ain't taking no more of your shit, man! Either you put the brothers on a plane by tomorrow noon, or I swear by Allah, the head of your chief honcho here is going to roll . . . right out of the fuckin' window."

The raving Hanafi leader was about to hang up when he changed his mind and spoke once more into the mouthpiece, "And don't you ask me for no more new deadlines, shitbrains. There won't be any!" He slammed the receiver down.

"Goddamn motherfuckers!" he cursed as he turned toward the Triple C chief, who was sitting on the floor, his back against the wall, hands tied behind his back.

"If these mothers don't deliver, man, if they try to play games again, you're dead, man, you hear? You're dead!" To emphasize his words, he pulled a machete from the leather scabbard hanging from the heavy steel chain about his hips. He waved it menacingly in front of Atkins's face.

The Triple C chief, however, did not so much as blink. He glared back into the black man's wild eyes with cold contempt. He had made his decision, and he was without fear.

One thing was certain, Atkins reflected when the still fuming Hanafi left the room to consult with his comrades about the new deadline extension, the third floor tenement apartment was well stocked with canned food which seemed as if it could last them for at least a couple of months. In the other room he had seen literally hundreds of soft-drink cans. "Just in case the pigs turn off the water," they had smugly told him. There were no spirits though; and they went out of their way to expound on the fact that as devout Muslims they were forbidden to drink alcohol. But, they assured him, the killing of infidels like him would assure them a place in heaven.

His abductors had definitely prepared themselves well in advance. Besides the large quantities of food, weapons, and ammunition, the windows were painted over and shielded from sniper fire. There was no question that this abduction was no last-minute thing.

Fred was glad that Sam managed to get away. It made it so much easier for him to make his decision. In the few confused seconds that followed Sartain's daring escape, he too had looked back and seen Sartain roll on the road. And when he saw him lift his head, he knew he was alive.

Like Sartain, he too expected the gunmen to open fire and was surprised they didn't. At least the broad-shouldered man with the shotgun, the one they called Ali, had ample time and opportunity to do it. Perhaps he was waiting for orders from Abdul, the apparent leader. But they never came. Perhaps they were afraid to attract attention, hoping that the two officers in the squad car would not give chase if they didn't fire. One way or another, Atkins thought, Sam was alive, one hell of a man, and he was free to make the decision for himself.

From the moment they were taken at the parking lot, the only choice he had began to slowly form in his mind. If he wavered at first, it was primarily because he didn't feel he had the right to sacrifice Sam's life. Moreover he felt that at least one of them had to survive to face the Jackal. Of course there was also Bev. But Bev would surely understand, as she always did. If he could only see her once more and tell her how much he loved her, if he could only explain to her in person. But she would understand, better than anyone, that he really had no choice, that he would have had to resign otherwise—since he would have never been able to stand up to them anymore. She would surely realize that he couldn't preach what he didn't practice. Amazing, he thought, it was as if they had heard the exchange between him and Sartain in his office a few days before and decided to put him to the test.

Could it really be? he asked himself. Could it be that the Triple C headquarters had been bugged. He couldn't help but think of the increasingly frequent talk at Langley about a "mole" within the Company's highest ranks. And what about the way they knew exactly where to find the two of them?

And then the troubling thought which he had been trying hard to keep buried in the deepest levels of his brain surfaced again. Could it be Sartain himself?

No! his mind shouted the thought down. How could he even think that? And what about Linda? Damn the Jackal! He had even managed to get him to cast doubt on the one person he had the greatest trust in, and admiration for. Yes, surely Carlos was behind the kidnap. The Venezuelan was toying with him, putting him to the test.

The loud telephone ring jolted him and brought his captors back into the room.

"What the fuck they want now?" Abdul muttered angrily as he walked over to the phone. "Yes?" he barked into the receiver.

Atkins watched and listened carefully but could only deduce the full exchange.

"Why can't you do it by noon? . . . Well, 'trying' is not good enough for me, man . . . Well, you'll just have to try harder. I told you I don't believe you, and I don't trust you . . . No, man, I don't buy it. You can't tell me any of my brothers refuse to be free. They'll have to tell me that themselves . . . You damn right . . . No! By tomorrow noon. I warned you, no more new deadlines. Okay. Five o'clock, but that's absolutely final!" He slammed down the receiver.

"What's happening now, brother?" the broad-shouldered one inquired.

"I'm telling you, these cocksuckers don't take us seriously enough," he responded as he leered threateningly at Atkins. "Now they claim that some of our brothers refuse to come out. Can you believe that shit? Well, you heard what I told him, let me hear it from their own mouth. Otherwise I don't buy it. I don't buy it at all. He said only Hamid and Latif are willing to go, and he'll see if he can arrange for the others to talk to me personally by five o'clock tomorrow."

"What do you think?" Ali asked. "Do you think these mothers will let us go, or do you think it's just a trick?"

Abdul shook his head. "I don't know, brother, I don't know. But I'll tell you one thing. I see anything fishy," he motioned toward the Triple C chief, "and this motherfucker's head is goin' to roll."

"Sir," Atkins interjected politely.

"What d'you want?"

"If you let me talk to them, maybe I can convince them. I'm afraid they may do something stupid. I don't like the sound of it at all. I have a feeling they may doubt your determination to kill me if they don't deliver. Perhaps if you let me talk to them, I can warn them against doing anything foolish."

"You want to do that?" Abdul asked somewhat incredulous.

"Yes, I have no desire whatsoever to die because of some bastards like you. I—"

"Hey, watch your language, you goddamn honkey cocksucker!" Abdul moved forward, his hand on the machete's grip.

"I am just being honest."

"I bet you are! Getting a little scared of losing your head, ah?"

Atkins nodded silently.

Abdul reflected for a moment. He turned toward his comrades. "What do you think?"

Ali shrugged his wide shoulders. "I don't know, brother. You're the leader, you decide."

"What about you?" he asked the scar-faced, reticent driver.

"What do we have to lose? The motherfucker wants to weep a little, let him."

"Okay, Abdul," the leader said to his namesake. "Untie him." He turned to Ali. "Cover him," he ordered. "I trust this one even less than the other."

Atkins stood up, rubbing his wrists to help circulate the blood in his numb hands. Abdul began dialing.

He was about to hand the Triple C chief the receiver when he suddenly changed his mind and hung up. A cunning smile formed at the corners of his thin mouth.

Atkins was perplexed.

"I have a better idea," he said and turned toward the driver. "Abdul bring me the bullhorn from the other room."

"You want me to talk through the bullhorn?" Atkins asked.

"Yeah, that's exactly what I want you to do," Abdul said, still smiling. "Let them see you, let them take a good look at you. Let the media see and hear you too. Maybe your wife and children are there, and your professor pal . . . yeah, I think you should talk to all of them. Let them all hear what the chief honcho has to say."

Atkins shrugged in compliance. The other two, getting the point, grinned at each other.

Leading him toward the window, ordering Ali to open it carefully and take cover, Abdul added snidely, "A tear or two won't hurt, ah?"

Halting by the wall next to the open window, Abdul brought the bullhorn to his lips and yelled, "You pigs out there, your chief honcho here wants to say something to you. He'll come to the window to speak, so hold your fire."

Atkins took the bullhorn and moved slowly toward the window. The guardrail rose just above his navel.

When he looked, he could detect some of the SWAT snipers crouching behind protective shelters, weapons targeted on the open window.

Then he heard the amplified voice of someone he couldn't identify. "Are you okay, Mr. Atkins?"

"I'm fine," he said weakly. He looked straight down. He estimated a fall of almost forty feet to the pavement below. No wonder they let him approach the window unrestrained.

"Is there anything we can do for you?" he heard the same voice ask from across the street.

"Yes!" he shouted into the bullhorn. "Don't make any concessions! Never capitulate! An end must be put to this plague of madness!" His amplified voice thundered and echoed through the street. "And if it must start with me, so be it. Enough is enough!"

"You motherfucker, you . . ." Abdul cursed as he lunged for Atkins to pull him away from the window.

With all the ferocity he could muster, Atkins swung and smashed the bullhorn into the Hanafi's face. The sound of amplified crushed bone could be heard throughout the street below.

Before the other two could fully comprehend what had gone wrong, before they had a chance to reach him, Atkins leaped over the window ledge and silently dived to his death.

CHAPTER THIRTY-SEVEN

SARTAIN sighed in despair and pushed away the foot-high pile of paper on his desk. He rubbed his tired, blood-shot eyes and cursed softly as he emptied his third cup of coffee. It was ten o'clock in the morning, June 27, and he had already been in his Triple C office for almost five hours, an hour more than he had slept the night before.

For the past few days, after Amy failed to make contact, Sartain, still suffering discomfort in his chest and ankle, had reimmersed himself in the grueling task of combing through the thousands of pages of intelligence dossiers, background studies, and other reports gathered by the TF-3 staff. He insisted on personally reviewing every detail in a last-ditch effort to find some significant clue as to what Carlos's intentions might be. Thus far it had all been to no avail.

Even without concrete proof Sartain was still convinced that Carlos would strike on July 4—if not on June 27—and that the attack would be monstrously spectacular. But where and how? There were just too many possibilities, too many vulnerable targets. He had tried to compile a list, but when it climbed toward five hundred prime targets without exhausting all the possibilities, he gave up. It only confirmed his argument that such a static, defensive strategy would not work. "Besides," he had been told by Watson, the new Triple C chief, "who in their right mind could be convinced to implement tough security measures by July Fourth, just because of a professor's unsubstantiated hunch?"

Now that Amy had disappeared without a trace, Sartain felt guilt pangs for having failed to heed Atkins's suggestion that she, and her two companions, be tracked down in San Antonio and placed under surveillance.

Poor Fred, Sartain reflected, and the tragic, hideous afternoon, twelve days before, flashed through his mind again in all its horrible detail. He had arrived just before Atkins's ultimate sacrifice, watched him dive to his death, unable to turn his head away until the body smashed hard against the pavement.

If he had deluded himself before that he had grown immune to emotional pain and sorrow, he realized how wrong he was. It seemed as if the potential for man's suffering was infinite.

Ignoring the fierce fire exchange which erupted following Atkins's suicidal fall, Sartain dashed, game-legged, toward the sprawled body. But there was nothing he could do, and Atkins died in his arms, well before anyone else could reach them.

"The Jackal . . ." Fred's final, almost incomprehensible words came, as blood streamed from both corners of his mouth, streaking his beard with red. "Get the Jackal." He tried to say something more, but it was too much for him. He closed his eyes for the last time. Later Sartain told Bev that he had asked for her forgiveness, knowing she would understand. It was not a lie, he explained to Steve. That was probably what Atkins had really tried to tell him.

Despite his fury and desire for revenge, Sartain wanted to take the Hanafi gunmen alive. He knew that they were only foot soldiers of no real consequence, but there was still a possibility that they could have provided him with some information, certain clues as to what the Jackal was up to. The SWAT snipers, however, reacted automatically. No longer concerned with the safety of a hostage, they released the frustration of the long, tedious hours of waiting in a spontaneous fusillade.

Two of the Hanafis perished in the ensuing gunfire. The third, the leader, died of his injuries a few hours later at Friedman's Hospital, having never regained consciousness.

The day after Atkins's death, Sartain received a telegram from Israel:

> Deeply grieved over our friend's death. Wish I could be with you. Have courage. Love you.
>
> Tara.

But there had been nothing else since. Not a letter, not a telephone call, not a single word.

Sartain agonized over Tara's silence. She knew how much he missed her, he told himself, how much he needed her. Why then didn't she write or phone? Or was she unable to? And if so, why? And why had there been no replacement? What was going on within the mysterious confines of the Mossad? Had the Triple C been that stigmatized in Echad's eyes? Or was it only he himself?

The trouble was, Sartain reflected bitterly, that Watson had been less than helpful. He knew the Triple C chief must have had contact with Echad. Something was going on, the professor concluded, and to complicate his life even more, Roger Watson was definitely no friend.

From their first meeting, after Watson took over Fred's position, it became apparent that the new chief was no fan of the professor's. Nor did Sartain harbor excessive respect toward the rather pompous, yet not strikingly brilliant civil servant. Watson, who had been the head of the State Department's Office for Combatting Terrorism, now wore two hats as the chief of both the OCT and the Triple C, reporting directly to the National Security Council.

The morning following their first meeting, Watson summoned Sartain to his office, Fred's old office, to express in his best officialese what amounted to displeasure over the way the TF-3 had been handling the Carlos case. He was "chagrined" that Ms. Amy Lahr had not been placed under immediate surveillance in San Antonio. Furthermore he would "never have authorized, let alone, condoned, such a felonious scheme involving two such dangerous outlaws, to begin with."

To top it all Watson stated in his "unprejudiced opinion" that the Hanafi incident had nothing to do with Ilich Ramirez Sanchez and further insinuated that the Triple C under his predecessor seemed to have been obsessed to the point of paranoia with the Jackal . . .

There was a sharp knock at the door, mercifully halting Sartain's train of thought. It was Verner, who entered the "cage" with a toothy smile.

"You look tired, Professor," he greeted the professor cheerfully. For some reason his clipped accent was particularly grating to Sartain's sensibilities this morning.

Sartain stared at him pointedly. "Is that what you came here to tell me?"

"No, I came to tell you that I have here something which may be of considerable interest to you." He handed Sartain a manila folder.

Sartain opened it and looked at the long telex sheets.

"It's still in German," Verner apologized. "I've just received it, but I thought you'd want to know about it before I take the time to translate. I can tell you what it's about."

Sartain, whose German was only fair, nodded.

The German unfolded the metal chair and sat on it cross-legged. "One of Helga's former girl friends was questioned yesterday by our people in Stuttgart. She had been away until then, in Los Angeles."

Sartain straightened up in his chair. "Los Angeles?"

"Yes, but that really has nothing to do with it."

"I'm sorry, it's just that . . . go on, please."

"Christina Rauch, the person in question, was a close girl friend of Helga's when they both lived in Stuttgart back in 1970. She claims that Helga confided to her that she had had a rather bizarre sexual relationship with an older man before she moved to town. Helga was vague about the affair, but Christina seems to remember that the man's first name was Karl.

"Karl?"

Verner nodded.

"And the last name?" There was anxiousness in Sartain's voice.

"According to Christina, Helga never mentioned it. She knows very little about the man, but she does remember Helga remarking that her 'weirdo' was a nuclear scientist . . ."

"A nuclear scientist?" Sartain practically jumped out of the chair, but the pain in his ankle brought him back to his seat. "Where? Damn it, Verner, that must be it! This is the link we've been looking for!" He calmed himself. "What else does she know? Does she know where he worked at the time? Anything else about him or their relationship?"

Verner shook his head. "I told you, she knows very little. That seems to be all she was able to remember. She doesn't know where he was from, where Helga met him, how long their relationship lasted, or anything else. She suspects that no one else does either. Apparently Helga was tight-lipped about it, for rather obvious reasons."

"Well, then," Sartain couldn't hide his disappointment, "keep interrogating her. Maybe she will remember more. But in the meantime, for God's sake, compile a list of all the nuclear scientists in Germany whose first name is Karl. How many can there be after all? Ten? Twenty? Thirty? And then start investigating them, questioning them. It shouldn't take more than two or three days, should it?"

Verner looked doubtful. "I wish it were that easy, Dr. Sartain. You don't really believe that any of them will readily admit to having any relationship, let alone sexual, with a young woman who has become by now a well-known fugitive terrorist? We have a full-fledged democracy in Germany now, you know, just like here. It's going to be extremely difficult, if not totally impossible, to interrogate such respected scientists, most of them probably happily married, just because some travel agent alleges that she thinks she remembers that someone with the first name of Karl had an affair with Miss Denz . . ."

"What do you mean, 'she thinks she remembers'?"

"Well, apparently she is not totally sure his name was Karl. It sounded right to her, but she couldn't say it with certainty."

"Well, put her under hypnosis!" the professor exploded. "And maybe in the process she'll come up with more information."

"If she agrees, Professor. She might very well refuse, and—"

"I know, I know," Sartain muttered impatiently. "West Germany is a democracy. Offer to pay her, then. It's important enough. And if the Federal Republic doesn't wish to pay, then we'll pick up the tab . . . Damn it, I'll pay, from my own pocket. Is that good enough?"

"How much are you willing to pay?"

"I don't know. Offer her a thousand marks, two thousand . . . and if that's not enough, offer her more, three thousand, five thousand, whatever it takes, damn it."

"Five thousand? From your own pocket?"

Sartain's agitation had visibly reached the boiling point.

"Please don't take it out on me, Dr. Sartain," Verner placated. "I have to go by the rules. We had a fascist dictatorship in our country not so long ago, as you well remember. People are extremely sensitive back home when it comes to such things."

"Okay, okay, but let's start rolling. All we have is seven days, at the most, and—"

The telephone buzz cut him short.

Sartain picked up the receiver and listened silently for a couple of minutes, his expression draining from anger to resigned defeat. When he finally hung up, he stared at Verner and said simply, "We don't now. Not anymore."

"We don't what?"

"We don't have seven days anymore. Terror International has just taken over a tourist boat on the Potomac with three hundred people on board."

CHAPTER THIRTY-EIGHT

"I really didn't think twice," the young man responded to Watson's question. "The moment I heard that unmistakable Arab accent shouting, 'This is Commando Buddha, and we've taken over the boat'. . ."

"Boudia," Sartain corrected patiently.

The young man shrugged. "Buddha, Boudia, I don't know . . . Who is he, anyway?"

"Never mind now," Watson interrupted. "Just go on, please."

"Well, anyway, as I said, I was leaning against the rail, my back to the water, when I heard the voice and saw these two swarthy-looking characters pulling what looked to me like submachine guns out of their backpacks. I didn't wait around to see what happened. I dived into the river. It was automatic."

Sartain watched the animated youth with a mixture of curiosity and immediate liking. He looked to be almost Steve's age with a dark, sharp-featured face and the physique of a wrestler. Below his thick head of curly black fuzz were two small, deep-set eyes which bespoke an alert intelligence. A Northwestern University student, he was the only one known to have successfully escaped the hijacked catamaran.

"Besides the two under the companionway, can you tell us how many more gunmen were involved in the assault?" one of the police officers asked.

The student, whose name was David Gerber, shook his head. "How could I? I was on the lower weather deck at the time, on the port side. And as I told you, the moment I heard the word 'takeover,' and saw those Arab-looking fellows pull out their guns, I was already climbing the rail." He hesitated for a second, debating whether he should say what he was about to admit. "I didn't even look for my buddy. He'd gone to buy himself a hot dog at the snack bar . . . He's not Jewish though," he added quickly, defensively, "so I guess he has less to worry about than I would have. I hope so."

"What happened then?" Watson took over the questioning again, looking every inch a prep-school headmaster.

"I dived headfirst. You can't see sh—, I'm sorry, anything in that water. I swam under and as far away from the boat as I could, until I thought my lungs were going to explode. And when I came up, the bastards were shooting at me. I ducked again, and I tell you, if I didn't know it was impossible, I could swear I lasted for a whole five minutes. When I had to surface, I came up just enough to expose my face. The boat was already a few hundred yards down the river. Thank God I was smart enough to swim in the opposite direction." He smiled, embarrassed. "You always wonder what you'd do in that kind of situation. You know . . . if you'd get yourself out safe, or panic."

Watson ploughed right through Gerber's soul searching. "Had you or your friend noticed anything suspicious when you boarded the boat, before the takeover took place?"

"No, not really. To be honest," he grinned, "me and my buddy . . . well, we had our eyes on these two chicks. So no, I didn't notice anything out of the ordinary until I saw these two Arabs pull out their weapons. I tell you," he shook his head, "I sure do hope they'll be okay."

"Who?" Watson asked.

"The chicks. They were really something. The one I liked was—" he stopped in mid-sentence, noting the frown on the face of the Triple C chief. Sartain cleared his throat to prevent a chuckle from escaping.

"So in other words, Mr. Gerber," Watson said reproachfully, "you can't really tell us anything more, anything which can be helpful to us. Am I right?"

The young man wrinkled his brow in concentration, distressed at not being able to be more useful.

"Do you think, David," Sartain broke in, "you would be able to identify the two men if we showed you some snapshots?"

David's face brightened. "I believe so, sir," he said gratefully. "Particularly one of them. I don't think I could forget that mean a face. Boy, was he ugly!"

"Thank you, Mr. Gerber," Watson said, ever formal. "You can go now."

The young man nodded and left the room.

Sartain looked at his watch. It was already one o'clock in the afternoon. They should hear from the terrorists soon, he thought. As he had learned when he arrived at the Harbor Patrol building which now housed the makeshift task force assigned to the *Fraternity* hijack, the catamaran's hijackers had indicated on the VHF radio-telephone that they would make their demands known by that time.

And indeed just then the radio officer walked in. He handed Watson a couple of large blue cards. "This is the list of demands. We just got 'em, sir."

Watson studied the cards silently. Everyone else in the room waited, in silent suspense, watching his face for a sign.

The Triple C chief cleared his throat. "They demand, in return for the lives of the two hundred eighty-nine hostages—two hundred eighty-four passengers and five crew members—nine point nine million dollars. Half of it to be in German currency." He stopped.

There was almost an audible sigh of relief among the dozen people in the room. Money was the least the terrorists could have asked for. Money was no problem, and the sum, though excessive, was not preposterous.

"Nine point nine million? Why not ten million?" the FBI man was perplexed.

"German currency?" the army liaison officer asked. "Why German currency? I thought they were A-rabs."

"They're a multinational group," Sartain corrected the young, crew-cut colonel. "But that's not the point. If I read them right, they are trying to humiliate us, to tell us American dollars are no longer dependable. As for the odd figure, well, it's probably just a product of Carlos's perverse sense of humor."

"I believe the professor is right in this case," Watson agreed, though not without a purposeful stress on the last three words. "Some of the other demands display the same kind of psychological twist. Their second demand, however, is the release of all the imprisoned, and I quote, 'freedom fighters, whose rights had been so wantonly denied by the cowardly, treacherous raid of the Zionist forces in Entebbe.' "

"No names, sir?"

"Not included," Watson replied and cast a questioning look at the radio officer.

"There weren't any, sir," the man responded. "All that has been communicated is on the cards."

"Well then, we're talking about a total of fifty-three captured terrorists," the professor offered. "Forty in Israel"—he couldn't help but think of Tara, remembering that one of those on the Israeli list was the Japanese Kojo Okamoto—"six in Germany, five in Kenya, one in Switzerland, and one in France. Actually," he corrected himself, "it's only five from Germany now, as one of them, a woman, has managed to escape."

Sartain remembered something else. "There is one more thing. The five in Kenya—two Germans and three Palestinians who had tried to shoot down an El Al Boeing at Nairobi Airport with SAM-seven missiles—are now imprisoned in Israel. So, with the exception of seven, all of them are in Israeli hands. And you know as well as I that it would be close to impossible to extract such concessions from the Israeli government."

"Particularly if we concede to the hijackers' next demand," Watson concurred. "They want the President to make a public statement supporting the legitimate rights of the Palestinian people."

"Do they outline exactly what they want him to say?" Sartain asked.

Watson shook his head.

"Well, unless they ask for something more specific, like support for the establishment of a Palestinian state, the President can reiterate some of his earlier statements. Still," Sartain shrugged, "it will amount to an unprecedented political capitulation. What else do the bastards want? We might as well hear it all and then discuss it."

"Thank you," Watson said pointedly. "They also want us to lower the flags at all the federal buildings in memory of their 'revolutionary comrades' who perished at Entebbe. And they demand that Israel agree to financially compensate Uganda for the damage it endured during that attack. Finally, when all the above demands have been met, they want a Hercules C-one thirty to fly them out of National Airport to a destination of their choice."

"A Hercules C-one thirty?" the air force colonel was astonished.

"It's just one more symbolic act," Sartain explained. "After all, those were the planes the Israelis used in their raid on Entebbe."

"For which we now are having to pay," Watson remarked acidly.

The comment did not escape Sartain. How could he say such an unfair, idiotic thing? the professor thought to himself. Seeking to avoid an open confrontation with his nominal superior, however, he remained silent. How different this man was from Fred, he mused bitterly. It was almost as if they had eliminated Atkins to assure the appointment of such an ass. How ironic it was that Watson was now in charge of this case. It had been the Triple C report, submitted by Atkins, which anticipated a major, unprecedented retaliation for Entebbe on most probably July 4 . . . and which Watson had pooh-poohed.

"What about a deadline?" someone asked.

"They gave us until tomorrow noon," Watson replied. "If we fail to meet their demands, they threaten to blow up the boat and kill everyone aboard."

"This is utterly ridiculous," said the Bureau man. "That's less than twenty-four hours. Even if we wanted to, we couldn't comply in such a short time. No way."

"That's the whole point," Watson stated smugly. "They're bluffing. Don't you think they know there is no way we can fulfill their demands by then? They know they'll have to negotiate. They already expect they'll have to extend the deadline. They are not fools. This is just their opening bid. We, on our part, will begin the process of watering down their demands. We'll bargain, give in somewhat here and there, but primarily, wait them out. So, if we don't do anything rash, maintain a firm, yet flexible profile, in the end I'm certain we'll be able to secure the safe release of all the hostages."

"I'm not so sure," Sartain said flatly.

"You're not so sure about what?" Watson snapped, his face coloring.

"I'm not sure the usual tactics are going to work in this case. I'm afraid they have no intention of backing down on their demands. This operation has been in the works for a long time, and I suspect they mean what they say." He paused to let what he said sink in. "I believe we should give immediate consideration to the military options available to us."

"Hear, hear!" Sartain had the vocal support of the young army colonel.

If it annoyed the State Department man, he tried his best not to show it. "It's much too dangerous, too risky," the bureaucrat responded. "Too many lives are involved, lives of women and children, and the hijackers are in much too superior a position, strategically, for us to even contemplate such an option."

"Where exactly are they now?" the SWAT commander, who had arrived late, asked.

"They have anchored at a point between National Airport and Bolling Air Force Base," Watson repeated the information, pointing to a red pin on the large grid map behind him. "The Potomac is almost a mile wide here, and, as you can see, they are now practically in the center of the river, about fifteen hundred feet south of Hains Point. They couldn't have chosen a better spot."

"Sir," the air force colonel broke in, "I was just thinking. The professor here has mentioned these guys have attempted to use Russian heat-seeking ground-to-air missiles before. As you may know, these SAM-sevens are portable and can be fired from the shoulder. What if the terrorists on the boat are in possession of such missiles? They could try to shoot down a plane landing at National, or for that matter any of our planes landing or taking off from Bolling . . ."

"I've thought about it already," Watson replied calmly. "First there is no evidence that they carried such equipment onto the boat. That would have been much too conspicuous. Don't forget, the missiles are about five feet long. Secondly, even if they had them, I don't see any logical reason for them to use them before the deadline. Why should they? However, if you wish, you are free to recommend the diversion of your Bolling flights to Andrews Air Force Base. As for National, I prefer, at least until the time of the deadline, not to disrupt the air traffic and create unnecessary panic."

Sartain wanted to say something but remained silent. In essence he agreed with the Triple C chief; his misgivings were still with the other matter.

Watson consulted his watch. "I'll be meeting shortly with a special session of the NSC to report the situation. It will really be up to them to decide what concessions, if any, are to be made, and how to approach the other governments involved."

Preparing to leave, Watson added authoritatively, "I shall meet you all again at fifteen thirty at the Anacostia Naval Air Station, in the new command post which is being set up for us there. In the meantime Dr. Sartain," he motioned in the direction of the professor, "will brief you on the background of this Abu Sherif, who so far seems to be in command of the hijack. He'll also report to you on the nature of the group we are faced with. He's our top expert on this subject, and to give credit where credit is due, he anticipated such an assault, although," he added pointedly, "his scenario was a bit more dramatic than this one, and not to happen until July Fourth . . ."

With that backhanded compliment, Watson excused himself, handing his briefcase to his State Department assistant. At the door he paused to straighten his tie and smooth his hair, bracing himself for the onslaught of the media mob outside the Harbor Patrol building.

The sun began its final descent across the Potomac River, as Sartain peered one last time at the white and red catamaran— now renamed *Entebbe* by the new breed of sea pirates who commandeered it. Through the tall second-floor window he had a clear unobstructed view of the hijacked boat anchored less than a mile away. In contrast to the unfolding drama aboard it, the vessel, gleaming softly in the last sunrays, rested peacefully on the calm water of the wide river.

Sartain sighed and lay the field glasses on the sill. Still slightly limping, he walked to the large mahogany table which served as his desk at the Anacostia Officers' Club, now transformed into the headquarters of the multinational task force which handled the *Fraternity* hijack.

He shook his head and sighed again as he sat down to reexamine the dozens of enlarged color photographs spread atop his desk. They had been taken that afternoon by special telescopic cameras set up on both banks of the river for the purpose of identifying the terrorists on the boat.

If they could identify the exact makeup of the group, Watson had thought, they might be able to judge the strength of their threats and the measure of their determination to carry them out.

So far six men and two women could be distinguished with some degree of certainty as part of the hijacking team. Though they were dressed no differently than any of the passengers, they all carried weapons—either Kalashnikovs or what seemed to be

MP40 submachine guns. Two of them had been positively identified by the Northwestern University student as the men he saw
pulling guns from their backpacks under the companionway. It
was the clothes they were wearing, as much as the rather blurred
faces on the pictures, which helped him recognize them.

In fact none of the faces on the pictures was particularly clear,
since almost all of the photographs were taken while the terrorists were in motion, when they ventured briefly out of the cabins.
In addition, even though their faces were unmasked, most of
them wore some sort of headgear which helped distinguish them
from one another, but complicated their identification by those
on shore.

Sartain was convinced, as were the rest of the members of the
task force, that there were more than eight gunmen involved in
the hijacking of the boat. He figured there must be another half
dozen of them whom the cameras had not yet managed to capture. Who they were, or how many, was anyone's guess. Was
Carlos really on board, as the media widely and loudly claimed?
There was no concrete evidence. Was Fusako Shigenobu there?
And what about Amy? Where was Amy? Of the eight whose
snapshots he had, only four were positively identified, and neither the Jackal, nor Fusako, nor Amy was among them.

Yet they had definitely identified Abu Sherif, the former Black
September deputy chief of operations who defected to the rival
PFLP and became one of Dr. Wadi Haddad's closest associates.
He was, in fact, the only one on board the hijacked catamaran to
reveal his identity in his communications with them over the
VHF radio. He claimed to be the leader of the operation, "the
captain of the boat." Sartain questioned that he would make
such a claim if indeed the Jackal was on board.

The second man—pointed by the student as the one with the
unforgettable face—was Mustafa Saka, known to Sartain as a
member of the Turkish People's Liberation Army who was
sought for the brutal murder of the Israeli consul general in
Istanbul. The professor's earlier research had already associated
him with the Jackal's inner circle.

The third was Ahmad Hashem, a Palestinian and long-time
PFLP gunman who worked with Boudia in Europe even before
Carlos's appearance on the scene.

The fourth was Samia Khaled, a gorgeous PFLP member who
had adopted the first name of Wadi Haddad's wife, and the last

name of the most notorious Palestinian female hijacker, Leila Khaled, who allegedly had been the doctor's mistress in the late 1960s. As for Samia Khaled herself, it was whispered that when Carlos stayed in Baghdad, he would spend far more time in her apartment than at his own place. Even from the grainy photographs on his desk, Sartain could easily understand why.

He needed a Mossad expert to help him identify the other four, Sartain brooded. Curiously enough, at least from the pictures, they too all looked Middle Eastern. They could be Latins, he allowed, but even then, where were the Japanese and the Germans on whom Carlos had relied on so much in the past? If this was the Jackal's big operation, and he was secretly on the boat, why then such a heavy concentration of Arabs, even more than at the Entebbe hijacking?

Something was not right, something didn't quite jell, Sartain puzzled. Yes, he could definitely use the help of a Mossad man, or . . . a woman . . . But Watson seemed reluctant to seek direct Israeli involvement. He had rejected Sartain's suggestion that they fly someone in from Tel Aviv. Not yet anyway, he told the professor. It was obvious that the Triple C chief wanted no interference in making his own decisions as to how to handle the hijacking.

"Any more progress, Professor?" Watson's metallic voice halted Sartain's thoughts.

Sartain winced. How different this man was from Fred. He shook his head in answer.

"Neither here," Watson admitted, almost proudly, loud enough for everyone else in the room to hear. "They have refused our offer of food and medical supplies."

"The sons of bitches!" someone uttered in dismay.

"Well, it was kind of expected," Watson said calmly to the group as he stood by Sartain's desk. "After all, they do seem to have enough food in the galley to last them at least through tomorrow. They also claim that no one was seriously wounded in the takeover."

"Are they going to keep these poor souls tied to the rail through the night?" Sartain asked, referring to the fact that a dozen or so hostages had been handcuffed to the outer deck railings on each side of the boat to provide a shield against sniper fire.

Watson pulled up a chair and sat with an air of reassurance.

"At first," he said matter-of-factly, "Abu Sherif raved that those hostages were Jews and that that was the very least that would happen to them if we didn't comply with the demands. But when I told him our main concern is the safety of the hostages, he mellowed down a bit and promised to replace those tied to the rail every four to six hours. He's sounding tough, but not totally irrational, which is somewhat encouraging."

The professor was anything but reassured. The more he contemplated it—the scale of the attack, the apparent exclusion of nationalities other than Middle Eastern, the absence of Carlos, Fusako, Helga, and the disappearance of Amy—the more he became convinced that something far more sinister lurked behind the boat's hijack.

"I still believe," Sartain said grimly, glaring directly into Watson's eyes, "that we should discuss more seriously the military option and prepare for it."

Watson glared back. "If you are suggesting an assault on the boat, Dr. Sartain, by a . . . SWAT team, marines, or whatever . . . forget it."

He waved his hand impatiently when the professor tried to interject, continuing, "Abu Sherif just gave us the exact composition of the hostage group. Of the one hundred and seventy-two Americans on board, one hundred and fourteen are women and children; of the non-Americans, sixty-seven are women and children. The figures corroborate our earlier estimates, and, incidentally, we have already been approached by a number of envoys who demand that we exercise utmost caution in handling the case, to insure the safety of their nationals on the boat." His countenance hardened. "Abu Sherif warned us that the boat is wired with explosives. One bullet, he says, and the whole thing blows up."

Sartain was dubious. "That's exactly what they claimed at Entebbe, where it could have been easily done, and it turned out to be nothing but a ploy. We can't just assume they're telling the truth."

"Nor can we afford not to," Watson retorted. "I am not going to risk it."

"Then what are you going to do? You know they won't accept what the NSC authorized us to offer them. There is just no way—"

Watson cut him short. "I don't know that, not yet. Besides the whole point is to continue to negotiate, to continue to bargain, water down their demands, erode their confidence, wait them out. But one thing for sure: I am not going to mount a direct assault on the boat. I will not sacrifice the lives of all those women and children. I believe time is on our side, and the more time they spend with the hostages, the less likely they are to carry out their threats. Statistically, in most cases, that's how it has worked out in the past. We'll give in a little, they'll give in a little, and somehow we'll resolve it without the loss of innocent lives."

Before Sartain had a chance to argue his case further, Watson stood and walked away.

CHAPTER THIRTY-NINE

THE river lazily lapped at the hull, and the ropes creaked amiably as the wind moved low, swollen rain clouds across the dark sky. Inside the closed cabin of the twenty-seven footer berthed at the Second Street Marina, Carlos in a wet suit, examined his and Lattore's diving gear. The Sherwood aluminum tanks, the regulators, the depth gauges, the rectangular Perivision masks, the Tenka lights, the Fara-fins, the knives, the luminescent compasses, the weight belts, and the Rolex diving watches: all seemed to be in order.

"Where are the backpacks?" he asked the American.

"Oh, sorry. Here they are," responded the muscular youth, whom they knew only as Mike. He opened one of the compartments under the forward bunk and pulled out two plastic and stainless-steel packs.

The Jackal checked them. Like the rest of the equipment he had ordered from Rage, the Healthways' Scubapacks were brand new and of the finest quality. Money, after all, was no problem. In fact the American equipment seemed to be of better quality than the Italian brands with which they had trained in Algeria.

As Mike helped Manuel adjust his gear, Carlos fit two nylon-wrapped packages, which he had brought with him, onto the backpacks.

"It's okay," he told Mike, when the latter offered his help. "I can manage. I'd rather do it myself. It has to be done in a certain way. You just go on helping Charlie."

The American complied good-naturedly.

Carlos was pleased. He liked this discreet young man, who, though obviously curious, never once—not during their drive to the marina, nor on the sailboat—asked any unnecessary questions. Mike proved to be attentive, skilled in what they needed, efficient, and, not of least importance, quiet. Excellent, Carlos thought. If the other Americans Rage would provide for the assault on the nuclear plants were of the same caliber, he would be content.

While Mike treated the two of them with deference, there was nothing to indicate that he was aware of who "Victor" and "Charlie" were. Nor did he convey any sign that he knew the true purpose of their little jaunt underwater to the *Entebbe*. If he suspected at any time what the nature of the deadly packages were, he never showed it. Carlos wondered what the American would report to Rage but concluded that it didn't really matter. Unconfirmed suspicions were of no interest to him. In the end only he and Lattore would know what had really happened. Perhaps, he mused, smiling inwardly, when it was all over, at the appropriate moment, just before he reached climax, he would whisper the secret in Fusako's ear . . .

"When do you want to leave, Victor?" Lattore, who was almost ready, asked.

Carlos consulted his Rolex. "At one o'clock. Exactly seventeen minutes."

Manuel nodded. Mike, synchronizing his watch to theirs, asked, "When do you think you'll be back?"

Carlos studied the Farralon's five-foot driver propulsion vehicle on the decking beside him as he calculated his answer. The DVP could pull them under the water at three miles per hour. That meant it would take them about twenty minutes to reach the catamaran, which was approximately a mile away. They would need another twenty minutes to plant the two mines, and then twenty minutes more to return.

"I can't tell you exactly," Carlos, alias Victor, replied, "but it will be at least an hour. If all goes according to plan, we should be back here not much later than two o'clock."

"How long do you want me to wait for you then? And what happens if you fail to come back?" the American asked matter-of-factly.

Carlos contemplated the question. What happens if they fail to come back? The thought had never occurred to him, and it was not just superstition. He should be more cautious. No one is totally invincible. And yet, if he did fail to come back, who gave a shit what happened? It would be all over anyway, and it would be the professor who would win the last round. Après mois, le déluge . . . Mme. de Pompadour was so right.

"Wait for us until the first light," he said. "If we fail to return by then, report back to Rage. She'll know what to do," he lied.

Just as Carlos was about to put on his hood and mask, he heard the first raindrops land on the cabin's fiber-glass roof. He grinned happily, blessing his added good fortune.

Once they were ready, Mike opened the hatch and helped them out onto the wet cockpit. It was still only drizzling outside, but the scent of the approaching storm permeated the air. Mike made a silent sign about it, to which they nodded their under-standing. And before he helped them slip into the dark water, he spit on his palm and patted them each on the head for good luck. Once they were in the water, he lowered the seventy-pound DPV to them.

It was exactly two o'clock when the two South American ter-rorists started the DPV's engine and began their underwater voyage. Only forty-five minutes later, two of the most sophisti-cated, remote-control Russian mines—the improved, extrapow-erful TM46—were securely fastened to the inner sides of the catamaran's twin hulls. Above neither captors nor hostages heard or felt anything out of the ordinary.

Each of the thirty-pound mines was attached at a spot fifty feet from the bow of the hundred-and-three-foot long boat and two feet below water level. Thus both mines were only a few feet away from where most of the plastic charges smuggled aboard the catamaran had been dutifully set by the unsuspecting hi-jackers, just as the Jackal had specifically instructed them to do.

Half an hour later, as Mike helped the two fatigued but elated frogmen out of the water, a lightning bolt touched shore. Deaf-ening thunder rolled, announcing a powerful deluge.

On the catamaran Abu Sherif ordered all of his twelve gunmen awakened and to their posts. He feared the Americans might try to take advantage of the storm to mount a surprise attack on the boat. The Palestinian would never know that it was the Jackal, his own comrade, who only moments before, had united and sealed the fate of all those aboard the doomed catamaran.

By late morning the rain had diminished; there were breaks in the clouds to the south. At eleven forty-five, fifteen minutes before the noon deadline, Watson reestablished radio contact with the hijacked catamaran, requesting to speak with Abu Sherif.

When the Palestinian confirmed his presence on the line, Watson wasted no time. "We can't meet all your demands," he said. "Even if we wanted to, there is no way we could do it. You yourself must realize that your requirements are not only exorbitant but also unrealistic, just impossible to fulfill."

"Are you telling me then, that you are rejecting our offer to spare the lives of our hostages?" Abu Sherif asked. Even over the radio one could not mistake the threatening tone in his voice.

"Well, not necessarily," Watson responded quickly but as calmly as he could. "All I am saying is that we cannot meet *all* your demands."

"Don't play games with me, Mr. Watson. I want to know exactly what you mean. You do not have much time."

Watson cleared his throat, then spoke slowly. "We fully realize that, sir. Time is definitely of the essence here. The decision, however, is by no means in my power alone to make. Our top decision makers are involved and, as you surely realize, the matter does not pertain only to us. It involves other governments, over which we have no control. At the same time great efforts are being made to find a way out of this mutual predicament which we confront. And we are willing to meet you halfway. I'm sincerely convinced that you will find our offer most generous and very satisfactory."

Watson paused, wiping the perspiration from his forehead. He cast a nervous glance at the two consulting psychiatrists next to him.

They both nodded reassuringly. So far, he was doing all right.

"I'm still waiting to hear your so-called generous offer, Mr. Watson," Abu Sherif replied icily.

The two psychiatrists nodded, prodding Watson to continue.

"To begin with, Mr. Abu Sherif, we are willing to pay you, in exchange for the safe release of all passengers and crew, the sum of *five million dollars.*" He paused after dramatically emphasizing the figure.

"Go on," the Palestinian said, unimpressed. "I am listening."

"Secondly we're willing to provide you with a plane, the Hercules C-one thirty if you so choose, to fly you and your men to a destination of your choice. But—only you and your men."

"Is that it?" Abu Sherif inquired when Watson failed to continue. "Or do you have anything more to add before I give you my answer?"

Watson's brow wrinkled. He pressed his thin lips tightly together. The unnerving suspense was shared by all those present in the communications room. Some stared apprehensively at the large clock on the wall. There were only five minutes left to the noon deadline.

"You must understand, sir, that with regard to the . . . prisoners, whose release you've asked for," Watson hesitantly began, "there is nothing that we can do. After all they are not in our hands. The same goes for your demands that Israel compensate Uganda. I am sure you are well aware of their unswerving position, and again we are helpless to . . . help you here. However, to demonstrate our willingness to meet you halfway, we are prepared to lower the flags at all American federal institutions in return for the immediate release of all women and children aboard the *Fraternity*."

"The *Entebbe*," Abu Sherif corrected.

"The *Entebbe*," Watson obliged, not minding at all to concede on such an issue. The psychiatrists offered encouraging smiles.

"Don't you think you forgot something, Mr. Watson?" Abu Sherif asked, rather solicitously.

Sartain, standing at the far side of the room, felt a slight shudder go through his spine. The contemptuous sarcasm of the Palestinian was all too obvious to him. He knew that Abu Sherif was playing a cruel game with Watson.

Watson, however, felt encouraged by the Arab's response. He knew exactly what Abu Sherif had in mind. The senior psychiatrist clenched his fist to signal an agreed-upon change of tactics. Watson proceeded in a firmer, more aggressive tone of voice. "Your demand for a political statement by the President, sir, is totally out of the question. Even if the President were willing to make such a statement, it would be meaningless if extracted under coercion. As you may well know, the President, at his own initiative, has already expressed support for the legitimate rights of your people. Support, which I am afraid, your present action seriously threatens to undermine. The question then remains, do you wish to achieve some concrete results for your people, or are you merely seeking to humiliate our highest office? If the latter is the case, you will leave us no choice but to adamantly resist your actions."

Total silence befell the room when Watson finished. The clock's two hands were only a minute away from joining at the apex.

Abu Sherif did not respond.

"Sir?" Watson finally tried.

"The question is," the Palestinian's voice startled them, "whether you are willing to meet our demands or bear the full consequences? The question is, *sir*, yes or no?"

The hitherto seemingly calm psychiatrists began to look worried.

"Mr. Abu Sherif," Watson protested, "there is no way we can meet all your demands. I have tried to explain that to you. But give us more time, and we'll see what we can do. Set free at least some of the women and children, as an act of goodwill, and I can guarantee that we'll do our utmost to narrow the gap between us. I trust, for example, that we'll be able to come up with the . . . full ransom if you do make such a humanitarian gesture. I . . . I can also promise you that we will do our best to persuade both France and Switzerland to release your . . . imprisoned comrades. They are not completely unreceptive to the idea. But we need more time, much more time." There was no mistaking the supplication in Watson's voice. "In the meantime I beg you to release these innocent women and children who have done your people and your cause no harm whatsoever."

Once again there was an unbearable silence in the room as Abu Sherif took his time to respond. It was already three minutes past the deadline.

"I will give you another twelve hours," the Palestinian terrorist finally said to a collective sigh of relief.

"It's very generous of you, sir, but I'll need more time than that," Watson persisted, taking his chances. "At least another twenty-four hours. You are, after all, demanding a lot from us. And then can I assume that you will free some of the women and children?"

"Now you listen to me!" Abu Sherif's voice thundered through the radio. "There will be no release of women and children! We are not going to repeat the mistake we made at Entebbe!"

Practically everyone in the room knew he was referring to the fact that the freed non-Jewish hostages at Entebbe were debriefed—some of them under voluntary hypnosis—by Israeli intelligence officers, and that it was the information extracted from them which finally assured the success of the raid.

"I'll give you your twenty-four hours," the Palestinian continued, "but there will be no more extensions. And if you fail to fulfill my demands by then, so help me Allah, I shall start executing twenty of the passengers each hour."

There was the hint of smile on Watson's face when the radio contact had been broken off. "He will come around at the end," he asserted. The two psychiatrists nodded their agreement. "Now that he has started bending, he'll bend more. Hopefully, all the way." Some people in the room shook hands.

Only Sartain—who managed that morning to identify two more of the hijackers, both Arabs—left the room in a funk. He sensed that Abu Sherif had no intention of giving in on anything. He still could not rid himself of the feeling that an impending disaster loomed behind the hijacking of the boat. If anything, that premonition was only reinforced during the exchange over the radio. He had twenty-four hours—at the most—to act. That did not give him much time.

"I am deeply grieved at Fred Atkins's death," Colton said with apparent sincerity. "He was a remarkable man, a unique man, and it's . . . a great loss to the Agency and to the country as a whole."

Sure, Sartain thought bitterly, one more star on the marble wall in the main hall. But what about the message he was trying to convey through his death? "My hope is that he didn't die in vain," he explained, "that we've learned something from his courageous act, from his ultimate sacrifice."

The CIA director studied the rugged-looking professor sitting across the desk from him very carefully, as he had done with his file when he agreed to this highly irregular meeting at Sartain's urgent request. There was no question that the professor was going over the head of his direct superior, that such a request should have ordinarily been submitted through regular channels, that is, through the Triple C chief. But the professor had invoked Fred Atkins's memory when he called, and Colton, who knew Atkins had been not only Sartain's boss but also a close friend, felt the moral obligation to at least listen to what the man had to say. And besides . . . Colton still resented the appointment of a Foggy Bottom man to head the Triple C, reporting directly to the NSC. In fact he was rather pissed off about the whole thing.

Now this professor-turned-spook or spook-turned-professor—who, according to Watson, had made some serious error of judgment, but who had also evidently predicted the Entebbe retaliation and its timing—was trying to tell him, in so many words, that Watson was about to make some grave mistakes in his handling of the hijack and that he suspected the whole thing to be nothing but a diversionary ploy by Carlos.

"What do you actually think will happen when this deadline is over?" Colton asked.

"I am convinced, that when we fail to meet *all* their demands by tomorrow noon," Sartain consulted his watch, "that is, twenty hours from now, they will start executing the hostages just as they threatened to do. When that happens, we will be faced with one of two equally distasteful alternatives: either we totally succumb to their demands, meaning an unprecedented capitulation with God knows what kind of consequences—and by then twenty, forty, maybe even sixty of the hostages will be already dead anyway; or we mount a hasty attack on the boat—again after some of the hostages have already been executed. The result of such a daylight assault, lacking the element of surprise, would be catastrophic.

"On the other hand," Sartain continued as he glanced at the plaque which read BE BRIEF, BE BLUNT, BE GONE, "if we take the initiative and attack them by surprise before the deadline, chances are we'll lose some people—most probably about the same number who would be executed anyway—but we will save the rest. The reason I had to see you was to express my conviction that we have no choice but to take our chances now, or people will die anyway, perhaps many more, and in vain."

Sartain paused, but when Colton remained silent, he added, "And I am not even speaking of the untold number of people who will perish in future terrorist attacks if once again we show indecisiveness and demonstrate our unwillingness to fight back, even in the face of the most outrageously provocative blackmail."

There was a buzz on the intercom. Colton pressed the button. "Yes?" he said.

Edna's voice came through the speakerphone, "Mr. Reiley wants to talk to you, sir."

"I can't right now. I'll have to talk to him later, sometime tomorrow. And Edna, unless it's an emergency, see to it please that we are not interrupted." He switched off the machine.

"Now," Colton turned back to Sartain, "how do you suggest we go about mounting such an assault on the boat, and who exactly would you recommend for such an operation? You know SWAT can't do it, not an attack on a boat in mid-river. The marines? Not unless we want to kill everyone on board. So who? the army Rangers?" There was contempt in his voice. "Sure, I know the L-Force has been receiving antiterrorist training, but I also know they've been spending most of the time fighting urban terrorism in the swamps, feeding on snakes and lizards." He shook his head and rolled up his eyes. "Now that ain't going to save us any lives."

Sartain knew exactly what Colton was talking about. He was all too aware of the losing battle Atkins had fought to establish a specially trained and equipped American counterterrorist force along the lines of Israel's Headquarters Reconnaissance Regiment, or Germany's Group Nine, or the British Special Air Squadrons. But it was to no avail. Sartain recalled Atkins's bitterness over the U.S. reticence to prepare for crisis until a major catastrophe occurs. He also remembered how, during the Hanafi Muslims' siege, the Washington police who were to attack the District building if the negotiations failed, were issued their M-16 machine guns for the first time that day. They were to jump by night from hovering helicopters onto the building's roof. They had never jumped from helicopters before, let alone at night. The helicopters were not to be flown by the Washington police, and the radios in the helicopters didn't net with those of the police.

"How about the SEALs?" Sartain suggested. "We can bring them here from Norfolk in no time. They can operate both under and above water and are well equipped with special weapons. At the moment I bet they are the best-trained professional strike team in the entire armed forces. They would be perfect for such an operation."

The professor could be right, Colton reflected. The SEALs, the elite group of navy commandos, won their acronym because they were trained to sneak soundlessly on the enemy by sea, air, or land. Like the navy's UDTs they started with underwater demolition training but then continued through jump school and advanced training in special warfare and weapons.

"Yes, they may do," Colton granted thoughtfully. "They probably would be more effective with their K-bar knives than . . . How many are there at Norfolk?"

"I already checked," Sartain answered quickly. "There are fewer than three hundred of them in the whole navy, but half of them are at Norfolk. It's more than we need."

Emboldened by Colton's seeming receptiveness now, the professor hammered on. "They should attack exactly two hours before dawn. That's when the hijackers' alertness is apt to be at its lowest ebb. We should assure Abu Sherif tonight that we are planning to meet all his demands. The Israelis, in fact, should be persuaded to call an advertised special meeting of their Cabinet to, supposedly, discuss the concessions, and we should spread the word about mounting pressures on them." Sartain paused and explained, "It will all contribute to making the terrorists less watchful, less vigilant. For the SEALs' raid itself we'll have to use a lot of noise. I was thinking about using the British numb grenades, but it won't work here . . ." He paused thoughtfully and then continued excitedly. "I've got it. Jet fighter planes . . . from Andrews Air Force Base . . . diving low suddenly over the boat. Yes, that's it, and just as they sweep very low over it, creating a deafening roar, the SEALs will attack the catamaran, having reached it underwater. This is what I would recommend to the NSC."

The director caressed his chin thoughtfully with one hand, tapping absentmindedly on the desk with the other. Finally, clasping both hands together, he peered directly into the professor's eyes. "What do you estimate to be the number of casualties?"

Sartain had expected the question. "There is no way of telling exactly. Not in an operation such as this. If we go by the ratio at Entebbe, where two out of the one hundred hostages were killed during the equally complex raid, then we should expect six of those held hostage on the boat to lose their lives."

Sartain hated to talk about human casualties as numbers, but he knew he had no alternative. If the director was to persuade the NSC to see it his way, these sort of statistics were vital. "If we multiply it by a factor of three," he continued, "to allow for a less successful operation, we are still talking about less than twenty civilian casualties—the number of hostages who we can expect will be executed anyway the very first hour after the deadline is over."

"What are the chances that it will be less than ten people?"

Sartain sighed, shaking his head. "I don't know. I don't really know. However, from what I've learned about the SEALs' level of performance so far, and if the element of surprise is on our side, then I believe it's very possible."

"In other words, with some luck, we may save ninety-seven percent or even ninety-eight percent of the hostages?" Colton was obviously preparing his case.

Sartain nodded. "Yes, sir. With some luck, we may."

"If the SEALs don't blow it."

"They won't, sir. And they don't have to fly three thousand miles into enemy territory to rescue the hostages either."

"I understand," the director said solemnly and then paused to weigh the plan in his mind for a long silent moment.

"If the decision was totally up to you, Dr. Sartain," he finally asked, "could you make it in clear conscience?"

It was Sartain now who kept the director waiting for a long moment before responding. "Yes, sir, I could," he said at last. "Sadly, but in clear conscience. I just don't see any other alternative. I believe that acting before the end of the deadline will save many more lives both in the short and the long run. I am also convinced that if Fred Atkins were alive now, he would recommend, in his capacity as the Triple C chief, the very same thing."

"I believe you are right, Dr. Sartain. I believe he would. In fact he did recommend it—with his own life."

CHAPTER FORTY

UNLIKE the previous stormy night the dark velvet sky was without a cloud and literally sprinkled with stars that seemed within reach. Carlos, who had been awake since two A.M., when he replaced Lattore in the boat's cockpit, let his mind drift as he lay on the floor gazing up at the sparkling heavens. Since early adolescence he had been fascinated by the riddles of the universe: its vastness, its origin, the enigma of no beginning or end, the meaning of life on this less than minuscule planet, the significance, or insignificance, of it all.

Did Abu Sherif or Wadi Haddad or anyone among his illustrious colleagues even begin to think about such matters? Those narrow-minded "great revolutionaries." No way! Not even Fusako. The only one perhaps was Boudia, his late mentor, and even then, never really on a conscious level and not in such depth. And his victims, those so-called "innocent" casualties, did they ever gaze at the stars and sense the meaninglessness of their lives? If they did, Carlos chuckled, they might even perhaps be grateful to him for giving their death a purpose, a meaning that far surpassed their mundane existence.

"The Philosopher King," Carlos whispered to the stars, that's what he really was . . . or at least the only true Philosopher Terrorist alive. He grinned to himself in the darkness. The sobriquet appealed to him. It was at least as good as the "Jackal," which was not of his own making anyway. He could visualize the headlines: THE PHILOSOPHER TERRORIST STRIKES AGAIN; THE PHILOSOPHER TERRORIST BLOWS UP BOAT WITH HUNDREDS ABOARD; THE PHILOSOPHER TERRORIST . . .

He shook his head. Now that he kept repeating it in his mind, he didn't like it so much. Made him sound too soft, swishy, like some damn Mahatma Gandhi queer. He'd have to settle for the Jackal until the press came up with a better name.

There was a slight noise coming from the cabin below. Carlos listened, but it didn't repeat itself. Manuel must have stirred in his sleep.

What did Manuel think about when he stared up at the sky during his watch, the Jackal wondered now. The origin of the universe? The meaning of life? He laughed softly, amused. Most probably about the last bottle of tequila he consumed or the last woman he slept with or some other banal thing. Thank God, though. All he needed was for his men to start philosophizing . . .

Besides, am I really a true philosopher? Carlos questioned himself frankly. Obviously not. What was he then? He shrugged. Under different circumstances, with his brain, he would have probably become a professor himself. But a professor of what? Politics? Languages? No. One does not have to become a professor to excel in those fields. He would have become a true scientist, a professor of astronomy or . . . nuclear physics. Yeah, nuclear physics . . .

He giggled softly at the irony. He had definitely grown to like science. He admired its exact logic, its precision, its reliability and applicability. At the same time there were no limits to where one could go with a scientific theory. Take for example Einstein's theory of relativity, he thought. It was so mind boggling and yet so . . . refreshing, so absolutely superior to all the religious and Marxist junk. But it's too late now, he sighed. Still, at least he was Number One in his field, even if . . .

He was struck with an amusing thought. Perhaps one of his demands should be an honorary doctorate from Harvard or Princeton or the University of Chicago. Yeah, a Ph.D. in nuclear terrorism.

He chuckled again and consulted his watch. It was already three o'clock. In less than half an hour he would wake Manuel. Sunrise came at five forty-six, and he was told to anticipate the action to begin approximately two hours before then.

Forty-five minutes later, waiting for the combined air-marine assault on the catamaran to materialize, Carlos and Lattore trained their binoculars first on the water around it and then on both riverbanks. But there was no trace of the military activity which they were told would be under way. The scene couldn't seem more quiet and serene. Only a few lights shone from the boat's cabins, and no movement could be detected on board.

It was four o'clock when Carlos had begun to question the accuracy of the information he had received, but his alert ears picked up the first sound of the approaching jets. Within a few seconds the distant buzz turned into ear-splitting thunder as the Phantoms, in succeeding waves of two, swept perilously low over the catamaran, then roared upward again with a deafening boom.

Lattore glanced questioningly at Carlos.

The Jackal nodded, hastily crossed himself, and depressed the handle of the sonar-operated remote-control ignition fuse whose main extension was immersed in the water below the sailboat.

He counted: "One, two, three, fou—" The thundering explosion, triggered by the two mines they had planted on the catamaran, rivaled even the roar of the jet fighters. It was immediately followed by the chattering of heavy gunfire.

"Bye-bye, Ibrahim Abu Sherif," Carlos muttered sarcastically; the content smile on his lips now clearly visible in the light of the burning catamaran.

And now to the big one, he thought. On to the dissertation itself.

The Triple C chief could barely control his fury. "Your unconscionable act of insubordination, my career, the director's career, which you've irrevocably damaged . . . all these are insignificant matters compared to this!" He pointed an accusing finger at the newspapers on his desk. Their headlines screamed the terrible news about the disastrous assault on the hijacked boat.

Sartain was all too painfully aware of the tragic outcome of his recommendations to Colton. Ninty-eight hostages were killed, most of them women and children. In addition eleven SEALs perished in the attack, more than were lost during the entire Vietnam War. Those terrorists who survived the blast were killed in the ensuing hand-to-hand battle. None remained who could provide them with information about the planning, execution, and the true purpose of the hijacking.

Sartain's analysis and predictions had proven to be deadly erroneous: from the look of it the hijackers not only had managed to smuggle aboard the catamaran far more explosives than he had expected, but they also were sufficiently alert at that predawn hour to detonate them at the very first sign of attack. To add hurtful insult to injury, Watson accused the professor of having been mercilessly duped by Amy Lahr, whose body had been recovered from the sunken boat and who must have taken part in its hijacking.

What troubled the professor at the moment, however, was the fact that there was no trace of Carlos, Fusako, Helga, or any of the non-Arab members of the Jackal's inner circle. Either they miraculously managed to survive the assault on the boat, or, as he suspected, never took part physically in the hijacking. The whole thing was nothing but a diversionary ploy, Sartain concluded. Thus the Arabs—for whom he knew the Jackal harbored little love—seemed to have been sacrificed in the interest of something much larger in scale, and far more ominous, than the hijacking of a tour boat.

Sartain realized that now there was little point in appealing to Watson to see it his way, yet too much was at stake not to try. "I take full responsibility for going above your head to encourage the SEALs' raid on the boat," he said gravely. "I can never find words to express my grief over the loss of life. I . . . I shall have to live with it for the rest of my life. But, at the same time, Mr. Watson, I can't but reiterate my conviction that the hijacking of the boat is merely the tip of a monstrous iceberg. I am certain now that it was Carlos's way of diverting our attention from a far more devilish scheme which I fear he is planning to coincide with our Independence Day."

There was contempt in Watson's cold gray eyes. Forsaking his usual composure, he lashed out. "You don't give up, do you? You and your paranoia . . . your obsession with that Carlos which has already cost us so many lives. You and your personal vendetta . . ." He shook his head in manifest disgust before continuing. "You just don't comprehend, do you? Well then, I shall have to make it crystal clear to you. Your advice, your so-called expertise, is not wanted here anymore. What I do want is your resignation. I *demand* your immediate, unconditional resignation. Not tomorrow, not this afternoon, but right now! Or . . . you can consider yourself fired as of this very moment."

Without waiting for Sartain to react, he handed him an already typed sheet. "Read it, if you wish," he said. "But you must sign it now, in my presence."

When Sartain expressionlessly signed the request for immediate resignation on personal grounds, Watson added, not without malice, "My secretary will accompany you to your office so that you can vacate it immediately and take with you only what are clearly your personal belongings."

Sartain nodded and stood up. But before leaving the room, swallowing his pride, he tried one last time. "What about the Helga Denz investigation?" he asked in a subdued voice. "You must pursue it. It has to be the key to—" He stopped in mid-sentence when the Triple C chief shut his eyes in pronounced exasperation and disgust.

"Of course we will, Professor," Watson responded venomously. "Right after we bury all these people, all these women and children. We will go looking for your Helga . . . Good-bye, Professor."

The CIA director did not return Sartain's calls, but the following evening the professor did manage to reach the German permanent representative at his unlisted home number.

Verner was surprisingly accommodating. In his heart the German sympathized with his American colleague. He secretly nursed the conviction that if the Bundesgrenzschatz's Group Nine had carried out the raid on the boat, they would have been far more successful in preventing the detonation of the explosives, thus saving many more lives and vindicating the professor.

The American commandos, he thought to himself, SEALs or no SEALs, were inadequately prepared for an operation involving civilian hostages, which required very special skills. He saw the case as an American repetition of the fiasco at the Munich Olympics. There was no question in his mind that if Germany had had in 1972 a federal force similar to the present Group Nine, the ambush of the Black September terrorists at Fürstenfeldbruck air base would not have been bungled as it was by the inexperienced, poorly trained and ill-equipped Bavarian police. It had been, after all, that failure to rescue the Israeli athletes which led to the creation of Group Nine.

Verner was also annoyed that the Americans—either for political reasons having to do with the nature of the hijackers' demands or merely for reasons of national prestige—had not sought the assistance of his government, nor that of the Israelis, nor the British in planning and carrying out their preemptive attack on the boat. Wasn't that the purpose of the Triple C in the first place? Why was he wasting his time in Washington, D.C., if there was no need for him to coordinate precisely such a joint action?

Thus, in a confidential report to Bonn, Verner had already insinuated that Roger Watson was far less inclined toward real multinational cooperation in combating terrorism than Atkins had been. The simple fact that the new chief coordinator was wearing two hats at the same time, the report implied, showed less than a one-hundred-percent commitment to the Triple C.

Now, as Verner listened to the professor, the same questions troubled him too: where indeed was Carlos? Where were the rest of the members of Terror International's inner circle? It was disturbing that the different intelligence services had failed to locate them in the last month or so. Usually, while unable to lay their hands on the terrorists in their Middle Eastern and East European sanctuaries, the operatives would at least spot some of them occasionally, and through combined efforts, their headquarters would manage to keep some track of the terrorists' whereabouts. Now, however, these terrorists seemed to have disappeared from the face of the earth. And they could not have all drowned in the Potomac River. The professor was right, something was definitely going on.

"Of course I'm keeping the Helga investigation alive," Verner encouraged. He knew the displeasure this conversation would cause Watson if the Triple C chief ever found out he had talked to the dismissed professor. Well, he smiled to himself, it would be one way of finding out if his telephone was bugged.

"Is there any new information? Anything at all?" the professor pressed.

"As you know, we have discovered so far a total of twenty-six scientists with the first name of Karl, or Carl with a C. Of these, only three, in terms of age, location, etcetera, seem to be a possibility. One is a Dr. Karl Wessel who works at the atomic research center in Jüblich. Another is Karl Pohle who is with ALKEM, a nuclear fuels firm. He is in Frankfurt. The third is Dr. Carl Sturm, who works for Interatom in Köln. Each of them has been placed under tight surveillance, and if anything is found to warrant their interrogation, we'll proceed without the slightest delay."

"I see," the professor said, not disguising his disappointment. "You realize we may not have much time. Three or four days at the most."

"We are doing our best, Dr. Sartain. The moment we find something concrete to go on, I promise I'll be in touch immediately. I still greatly value your advice, professor, and I'll do my best to keep you in the picture."

"Thank you. I appreciate it."

"*Auf Wiedersehen,*" Verner said and hung up.

It would have taken a seer to make any connection between the young couple who moved into an old house in Morris, Illinois, on July 1, and another, who moved on the same day into a small, nondescript home in Joliet, twenty miles away. And no one would suspect that the friends who helped them unload were, like the two innocent-looking couples, devoted members of the most radical movement in the United States or that many of the sealed boxes which were carried down to the two basements contained arms—including a few deadly bazookas—ammunition and explosives. Joliet was chosen over Seneca and Braidwood because the latter, although closer to the nuclear plants, were too "small town" to allow such a move to go unnoticed.

In Chicago, on the very same day, three men and one woman checked into a South Lake Shore Drive motel. No one took them to be anything more than ordinary German tourists traveling by Volkswagen van from coast to coast. By the same token one would have had to be an extremely suspecting person to find anything out of the ordinary when the four Germans were visited, at their two adjoining rooms, by three young Americans. After all, the tall, rail-thin German had already mentioned to the desk clerk that he had acquired his fluent English while attending the University of California at Berkeley a couple of years back. The young American visitors could have easily been old school friends.

Further north in Chicago, again on the very same day, a young woman with red-orange close-cropped hair and lots of dark makeup received in her apartment off Division Street two out-of-town male visitors. The way she looked now, even her friends would have a hard time recognizing her as Rage. And the one neighbor who saw her overnight guests didn't think it peculiar that the dyke upstairs had guys visiting her. Anyone could tell instantly, by the way Carlos and Lattore dressed and walked, that those guys were screaming fags.

And, finally, no one thought anything of it when Dr. Karl Baumann offered, although it was not his turn, to supervise the night shift on the two consecutive nights of July 3 and July 4. Baumann had always been considered by his fellow workers at the Dresden Nuclear Power Plant to be a kind, generous man, and someone would have to be out of his mind to doubt his true motive. As the German who became a naturalized American citizen explained himself, not that July 4 was less important or less meaningful to him, it was just that it was one way of trying to repay native Americans for their most gracious, openarmed hospitality.

CHAPTER FORTY-ONE

STEVE, playing black, moved his king's bishop deliberately slow. "Check!" he announced triumphantly.

The professor hadn't been paying much attention to the checkered board, but now he forced himself to concentrate on his next move. It didn't take him long to realize that he had little choice but to suffer a disadvantageous castling. He knew such a move would dangerously expose his queen, but there wasn't much else he could do. Steve had him cleverly trapped.

Sartain crossed his two chessmen, noting the glee in his son's eyes. Steve, as his father had figured he would do, couldn't wait to sacrifice a rook and a pawn in order to capture the white queen, a move which gave him a decisive edge.

The truth was that the dispirited professor didn't care. He had only agreed to play with his son, after they had shared a takeout dinner, to distract his mind from the depressing knowledge that it was July 3, and that he had failed miserably.

Indeed, he concluded, in the real-life chess match with the Jackal, he was about to be royally checkmated. He expected Carlos to make his inevitable move any time after the clock struck midnight. The tragedy was, that it was by no means he alone who would be the loser.

Personal loss he had learned to accept. As Fred had done, he would gladly sacrifice his own life to save others. What distressed him most was the premonition that the real victims of his clumsy, craftless game strategy would be hundreds, perhaps thousands, or even hundreds of thousands of innocent people.

The telephone rang. He picked up the receiver to hear Verner's agitated voice on the other end.

"Professor!" the German exclaimed, not taking time for the usual salutations. "I think we have got him!"

Sartain felt his heart begin to pound wildly. "Carlos?" he asked, afraid to believe.

"Carlos? . . . No, not Carlos. The nuclear scientist, Helga's friend, the missing link. His name is Karl Baumann."

"Karl Baumann?"

"Yes. Dr. Karl Baumann."

"And you've got him? Does he admit anything? Where is he?"

There was a brief pause on the other end of the line. Steve, noting his father's excitement, rose from the table at the other side of the living room and joined him.

"We . . . do not exactly have him yet," Verner corrected himself apologetically. "But I am almost convinced he is the man we have been looking for. You see, my colleagues back home were making the mistake of looking only for scientists who are presently employed in the nuclear industry there. Anyway, after my urgent appeal for a more intensive investigation, they came across a reference, mind you, only a reference to a certain Dr. Karl Baumann who eight years ago used to work at the Biblis nuclear reactor near Stuttgart." Verner paused to let the information sink in.

"Now listen to this," the German permanent representative continued dramatically. "Baumann's file at the plant, they discovered, has mysteriously disappeared. No one knows when it happened. It could have been some time ago or just recently. There do not seem to be any records of him at the plant. Nothing! Not his former address, family background, education, work history . . . nothing. Luckily a few of the veteran workers at the plant seem to recall a rumor that he ended up in the United States, although they have not seen or heard from him since he left eight years ago."

"So he's here now, in the U.S?" Sartain was impatiently trying to get to the point.

"Well, that is what his former co-workers believe. And since we did not come across his name before in our survey of the German nuclear industry, unless he changed his profession, it does make sense. Incidentally he would be in his late forties now. He was single at the time, supposedly a quiet, reserved man who never talked about his private life. So far as we can see, he could very well be the man Helga was involved with. It fits."

"It sure as hell does," Sartain agreed. "The disappearance of the file alone . . . Any indication of where he could be? Did he ever mention family ties in the States? Places he wanted to visit? Scientists here he admired? Anything?"

"So far, we cannot find anything. If he is here, he could be anywhere."

"What about Immigration? Or . . . the NRC, or ERDA? Maybe they have something on him. Maybe he's working here at some plant, or laboratory, or something." Sartain's growing frustration was unmistakable. He exchanged a quick, meaningful look with his son who was trying hard to follow the telephone conversation. It would have been easier for Steve to pick up the extension in the study or the bedroom. He knew his father kept no secrets from him and that he wouldn't have minded. But Verner might have been unnerved if he knew someone else was listening in on the conversation.

"I am planning to check all those possibilities," Verner answered. "If he is working here and became a citizen, he might even be working for the military. But anyway, I can not do a thing before your holiday is over. Right now there is no one I can talk to. All the offices are closed for the Fourth. And really, I have nothing concrete in my hands, only speculation . . . And I would not dare to approach Watson on this to request the Red Alert. Not at this point. I do not think I could convince him yet. And I know you could not. So we will have to wait until the morning of July fifth."

"July fifth? Listen, Verner, you know we can not wait! By then it will be too late!"

"I hope not."

"What about Germany, then?" Sartain's mind searched for a way to speed up the process. "There is no holiday there. Why can't you proceed with the investigation there? There must be something on him somewhere. Your equivalent of the NRC . . . what do you call it?"

"Das Reaktor Sicherheit Kommission."

"Whatever . . . city records, his school, your immigration office, something. After all, wherever he went, he must have needed some references. Somewhere there must be someone who knows where he is."

"That is precisely what we will continue to do. Do not forget, it is only just after two in the morning there now. Do not worry, Professor, we will find him. It is only a matter of time now."

"You're damn right it's only a matter of time, but time is surely not on our side."

"Dr. Sartain, I am sorry." There was a tinge of irritation in Verner's voice. "But as much as I want to, there is nothing I can do right now. I shall call you first thing in the morning, immediately after I talk to Bonn. Good night."

"Good night," Sartain mumbled dejectedly and hung up.

He filled Steve in on the details of his conversation with Verner, and Steve also argued that there was nothing his father could do but wait. So they returned to the table to resume their game.

But Sartain paid scant attention to the chess board. He kept hashing and rehashing what the German had just told him.

There was little doubt in his mind that Karl Baumann, wherever he was, was the man they had been looking for—Helga's mysterious lover. There was just too much coincidence for it to be otherwise. If only they had found out about him earlier. If only, if . . . "Ifs" were not going to help him, he chided himself bitterly. The fact was, they hadn't. And yet he could not accept Verner's and Steve's reasoning that there was nothing to do but sit and wait. There must be something he could do with the new information. But what? Damn it, what?

Sartain moved his knight instinctively to protect his king. He glanced at the small digital clock on one of his overburdened bookshelves, a gift from the first student whose Ph.D. dissertation he had helped supervise. The time was nine twenty-five.

It was then that his eyes fell on the bottle next to the clock. Although it no longer contained the tap water, it was the very same one-pint bottle, still labeled "nitroglycerin," which he had smuggled, back in 1974, into the Dresden Nuclear Power Plant.

Seeing the bottle triggered the memory of Linda's first visit to his house in Washington and her curiosity about the odd memento. Later, when they were moving some of his things to the house in Tiburon, she had objected to shipping this personal memento there. It was not a question of the bottle's aesthetic virtues, she had argued. It was just too tangible a reminder of the false sense of security under which they lived. How right she was, he thought bitterly.

Her last words rang afresh in his ears: "You've been right all along, Sam. It's even bigger and more horrifying than what you predicted."

The retrospection suddenly sparked a new thought in the professor's mind which made him almost jump from his chair. There are seventy-two of them altogether, he thought. So what if he had to spend the rest of the night calling? It was better than sitting idle and helpless, hoping for the best. If he managed to reach fifteen plants each hour, which was not at all unfeasible, he could reach the last one in less than five hours.

Better start immediately, he thought. And I might as well start with the Dresden Nuclear plant, and see how it works . . .

"Excuse me," Sartain said and abruptly rose from the table, heading for the telephone.

"Sure," Steve, who seemed thoroughly engrossed in planning his next move, muttered. In spite of the fact that his father had lost a queen and had paid minimal attention to the game, Steve still found it difficult to force his father's king into a cul-de-sac for more than just a stalemate.

Sartain picked up the receiver and dialed zero. "Can you tell me how to reach information at Morris, Illinois?" he asked when the operator got on the line.

"Can you spell it please?"

"M-O-R-R-I-S."

"You dial the area code first," she said after a brief pause, "which is eight, one, five, and then the number five, five, five, one, two, one, two."

He dialed and asked for the number of the Dresden Nuclear Power Plant.

"Dad, what are you doing?" Steve asked curiously as he walked over. "Why are you calling the Dresden nuclear plant?"

"The number is eight, one, five, four, nine, nine, two, nine, two, zero," Sartain heard the operator as he hushed his perplexed son with a finger to his mouth.

"I don't know exactly what I'm doing," he said as he hung up and began dialing the number given him, "but at least I'm doing something. I refuse to sit here all night with my arms folded, waiting for Carlos to make his move. These nuclear plants surely don't shut down for the holiday, so if necessary I'll call each one of them myself and find out if by any chance a certain Dr. Karl Baumann happens to work there . . . ."

"Are you kidding?"

"No. I'm certainly not. Shush!" Sartain said as the phone was picked up at the other end. "Is this the Dresden Nuclear Power Plant?" he asked.

"Yes, it is," a male voice responded. "What can I do for you, sir?"

"I . . . I would like to speak with Dr. Karl Baumann, please."

"Who may I tell him is calling?"

Sartain couldn't believe his own ears.

"Who may I tell him is calling?" the man repeated.

"You mean he's there . . . right now?" Sartain still had difficulty believing it. He glanced at the clock. It was nine thirty-three, eight thirty-three Illinois time.

"He's in the control room. He's in charge tonight. Is this long distance? I can't hear you too—"

Sartain hung up, his hand, for the very first time in his life, trembling uncontrollably.

"Steve!" Sartain called after his son, who had left the room during the telephone conversation. "Steve, did you hear that? Baumann is at Dresden, right now, at the control room! Steve? Where the hell are you?"

"I'm here! I'm coming!" Steve called back from the hallway.

"I must call Verner immediately," Sartain exclaimed. He raised the receiver and was about to dial when he heard Steve's voice command him: "Put down the phone, Dad! You're not calling anyone!"

"What on earth . . . ?" Sartain turned to face his son.

Steve stood by the living room door. His hand held a pistol, trained at Sartain. He motioned to his father to move away from the telephone.

"What the hell are you doing, son?" Sartain had recaptured his voice. "Are you out of your mind? Don't you understand? I've got to call Verner and warn him that the sons of bitches are about to take over the Dresden plant. I—" He stopped in mid-sentence as the meaning of his son's act began to dawn on him.

Steve nodded, a smirk on his face. "You're only partially right, Father. Don't exclude the La Salle and Braidwood plants . . . When midnight comes, we are going to take over all three of them. The whole goddamn complex. Now please let go of the phone and sit in that armchair over there."

"We?" Sartain gasped in disbelief, retreating toward the chair.

"What do you mean by 'we'? Are you trying to tell me that you—" His brain would not allow his mouth to form the words.

"Yes, Father," Steve responded, unflinching under Sartain's hard, accusing stare. "I am in on it, if that's what you're asking. Or shall we say, I'm part of it? You see, there's a lot about me that you don't know. For example, you are looking at one of the founding fathers of the New World Liberation Front. And it was through me, two years ago, when one of Carlos's top men was at Berkeley, that a contact was established with Commando Boudia. You might say, then, that for two years now I've been a full-fledged member of what you call Terror International. You might also say that I am a great fan and admirer of Carlos, who I've had the privilege of meeting, though regrettably only once."

He paused and smiled defiantly at his father's speechless shock. His eyes fell on the chess board where their game was left still incomplete. There was no draw here, he thought.

"In fact," Steve continued, "and God knows that I've been waiting to tell you for some time now, your book . . . our book . . . although quite accurate in some of its details, is also full of errors and misconceptions. Particularly about the man himself, whom you definitely have failed to either understand or appreciate."

"You . . . my own son . . . and Carlos . . . are partners in this . . . horror?" Sartain asked, still incredulous. In the depth of his soul he hoped he was only a victim of another nightmare. His eyes searched the room feverishly for some sign that he was dreaming.

Steve, reading his mind, laughed contemptuously, "You're not dreaming, Dad. This whole thing is as real as it can be. I have been providing Carlos with extremely critical information. For example, Jim and Amy. Those two never had a chance . . ."

Sartain closed his eyes in unbearable pain. He didn't want to hear anymore. Horribly, it all began to fall into place: the mysterious tip that led to Jim's arrest, Amy's failure to contact him, and her presence on the boat, the hijackers' unexpected preparedness in those predawn hours . . . The Jackal had been toying with him all along, making a total mockery of him, always one step ahead of him because—the thought made his stomach turn —because his own son, his own flesh and blood, had stuck a knife in his back. And now he was turning it, slowly, over and over again.

He opened his eyes and stared at Steve's strangely radiant face, trying to comprehend. "How could you betray me like this, son. Why? Why?"

Steve shook his head. "It's not I who betrayed you, Father, as much as you've betrayed me . . . and yourself. It's you who have turned your back on your own convictions, who became a hypocrite, a reactionary, who joined the establishment to suppress the revolution, to preserve the status quo."

The professor tried to say something, to protest, but Steve immediately shut him up, waving the gun angrily.

"Don't interrupt me," he warned. "You want to know why? Then listen! You call Carlos and the rest of us terrorists, anarchists, misfits who are bent on violence. But tell me, dear Father, in what other way can one bring about change in this age of superpower parity, of nuclear hegemony, of institutionalized and legitimized suppression? What other avenue is left?

"And let me remind you also, that throughout history changes have taken place primarily through wars, revolutions, uprisings, rebellions, and other forms of violence. That's how progress occurs. And always at the cost of human lives, often the lives of 'innocent victims,' as you're so fond of referring to them. But now, suddenly, when more than one-third of this planet's population is still starving and living in subhuman conditions, not only national boundaries have assumed a certain divine sanctity, but the developed nations have become committed to resisting any kind of real change. A new, world-wide establishment has emerged which is dedicated to the preservation of the present state of affairs and is determined to use its power to eternalize the status quo between the haves and the have-nots.

"Tell me then, Professor Sartain," Steve challenged, sarcastically, "as a 'liberal,' as one who truly cares, what choice do we 'terrorists' have, other than to resort to violence, if we are to bring about change?"

"But you are wrong, son. Not only do you exaggerate the so-called worldwide conspiratorial commitment to a status quo . . ." Sartain paused to weigh his words carefully so as not to antagonize his son. Much too much depended now on how he handled this confrontation. If it were only his life that was involved, he would have thrown in the towel, even perhaps welcomed death in the face of this final blow. But he knew he must try to avert the impending disaster.

"But there are ongoing changes," he continued, "perhaps not as drastic, or dramatic, as one wishes them to be, but yet meaningful. I truly believe that it is a totally one-sided view of history which claims that there cannot be progress without violence, without the killing and maiming of . . . yes, son, of innocent people. Like those poor people who perished on the boat." Sartain realized by the expression on Steve's face that it had been a mistake to make that reference. But before his son could interrupt, he pushed on.

"There must be a way to effect change in this nuclear age without resorting to violent means, Steve, or we are all doomed. And besides, what kind of changes do you think you can bring about through hit-and-run terrorism? Without the support of the people, of a mass movement, you are fish without water, as Mao himself so rightly stated."

Sartain quickly glanced at the digital clock. It was a few minutes to ten. Not much time left, but as long as he could keep talking, as long as he remained unbound, there was still hope. God! All three nuclear plants . . .

No! He must remain calm. He must concentrate on only one thing at a time. He must be in complete control of all his senses.

"All you'll achieve, son, is to provide the establishment with the law-and-order justification to arrest the sort of change you are seeking, to strengthen and reinforce the status quo. You embark on nuclear, or any other kind of nonconventional terrorism, and you can write off freedom and write in legitimized tyranny for decades to come, perhaps forever. You embark on such a doomed road, and all you'll succeed in doing is to unleash a massive wave of fear and terror. You'll provoke an unprecedented backlash of reactionism which will destroy not only you but whatever is left of our democratic institutions and personal freedoms. Can't you see that, son? Can't you see it?"

Steve shook his head. "All I can see is fear. Fear in the heart of the man who taught me to believe one way, and then expects me to behave differently. No, Father, Carlos is right. He's perhaps one of the last genuine revolutionaries left, a free man who fears no one and who is willing to challenge any form of institutionalized oppression, be it imperialism, capitalism, Zionism, or what stands today for communism. He works for no one but the people. He—"

"The people?"

"Yes, the people. You yourself, in your book, have described how, throughout Latin America, he's admired and considered to be another Simón Bolívar, how he's viewed as a Third World man, who single-handedly challenged Yankee and European supremacy, a man who stood up to and outwitted both the Americans and the Russians. You yourself know that he's fast becoming a new symbol for effective individual protest at a time when such a thing has all but been eradicated."

"But in what way? And at what price? He's evil, Steve, evil beyond redemption. He doesn't care about the people. All he cares about is fulfilling his urge for violence, his . . . He's a dangerous, depraved man who enjoys killing with his own two hands. How can you be so blind, son?"

"A violent man? Hear, hear, who is talking, my esteemed father? What about Lebanon, Father? What about the Druzes, your two revolutionary friends whom you killed in cold blood? Don't you preach to me about violence, about evil."

Sartain's instinctive reaction was to attempt to justify his own actions of years ago. "I had no choice . . . ," he stammered, "it was to save lives . . . I—"

Steve's cruel, mocking laugh cut him short. "Lives? Sure . . . the lives of the invading marines. Admit it, Father, you betrayed your friends. You murdered two innocent men with your own hands to aid an imperialist invasion while masquerading as a liberal, sympathetic American. Admit it, Father. Admit it!"

The entire episode, which had tortured Sartain's conscience for almost twenty years, again flashed through his mind.

It was June of 1958 when sunbathers on Beirut's sparkling beaches were startled by wave after wave of grim-faced marines, rifles poised for action, emerging from the calm blue water. It had been a surprise move by the American Sixth Fleet to bolster Christian President Kamil Chamoun's pro-Western regime, which was threatened by leftist Moslems supported by the Russian-backed President Nasser of Egypt.

Sartain, who was teaching at the time at the American University in Beirut, was also in the clandestine employ of the NSA. Then, as in later years, he reported to Fred Atkins who was then based in Athens. Displaying leftist sympathies, the young, brilliant, virile American professor had gained an introduction to Kamal Jumblatt through some mutual Druze friends. The leftist

Jumblatt was the fierce, yet intellectually sophisticated leader of the martial Druzes, who under his unchallenged leadership allied themselves with the anti-Chamoun forces.

Sartain, exploiting their growing friendship and mutual respect, managed to convince Jumblatt to tolerate the marine invasion, arguing that if it were unopposed, it would be limited and brief—which indeed it turned out to be. The marines spent large sums of money, mixed easily with the Lebanese, and departed after three months without firing a single shot.

There was, however, one unknown hitch which developed a few days after the landing, when the situation was still tense and volatile and could have gone either way. Two of Sartain's Druze friends uncovered, due in part to his own negligence, that he was an NSA operative.

A bitter confrontation took place, and when the professor realized that there was no other way to prevent them from disclosing his true identity to Kamal Jumblatt—thus perhaps not only undermining the uneasy truce and sparking an armed confrontation with the marines but also precipitating a full-scale civil war —he felt he had no choice but to eliminate them. And so he did.

Sartain had kept the whole painful incident to himself, never divulging what really happened to anyone, not even to Atkins. It was a dreadful secret which tormented him all his days. Linda was the only person to whom he finally, the night before she left for Berlin, dared unload his guilty conscience.

Linda! . . . a terrible thought crushed against his brain.

"How do you know about Lebanon?" the ashen-faced Sartain asked, dreading the answer.

Steve shrugged in affected indifference. "I just know. What difference does it make?"

"It makes a difference to me!" Sartain's voice was filled with rage. "There was only one person who knew about it, and that was Linda. Is that how you found out? Did you set her up? Were you also behind her murder? Answer me! Were you?"

Steve met his father's wild, accusing eyes. "We suspected that she was working for Mossad . . . which we found was not the case. But, by that time, it was too late. She had managed to uncover too many things about the plan." He shrugged again. "I guess she was just too good an investigative reporter for her own sake. It became necessary to eliminate her. It was during her interrogation, when she was drugged, that she told us about Lebanon."

Sartain's body went numb, and his mind began to cloud. He fought it desperately. He heard his own faint questioning: "Luana? Did you?"

Steve nodded grimly. "I had to. She found out about Linda. She went into hysterics and threatened to tell you. I just couldn't take the chance."

"You killed Luana, with your own hands?"

"I had to. Just like you did, I guess. I had no choice."

"And Atkins? . . . and Tara?" Sartain forced himself out of the paralyzing weakness which still captured him. "It was you then who provided the information?"

Steve nodded again. His grip on the gun tightened as he noted the expression on his father's face change from pained sorrow to wakening determination. "But you were safe all along. I had an understanding with Carlos that you were not to be harmed. That's why you managed to escape alive from the Hanafis."

"Why, though? Why spare me?"

"Because you are my father, and in spite of everything . . . I love you."

Once more Sartain had to convince himself that the whole thing was not a distorted, atrocious nightmare, a cruel joke of his imagination, a haunting product of his inner guilt. He was discovering that hate for one's adversary, of which he was now deprived, could be a soothing medicine, indeed a panacea. And yet Steve's response offered him a ray of hope. If his son was indeed so reluctant to have him die, there was a chance that he could still do something, that he could somehow prevent the holocaust which threatened the lives of many thousands, if not millions, of people. His own life mattered less to him as each moment ticked by.

Jaws tight with cold determination, Sartain stood up and walked toward the telephone.

Steve, taken aback, retreated a couple of steps waving his gun. "Stop!" he yelled. "What the hell do you think you're doing?"

"I'm going to get us out of this mess," the professor responded with outward calm as he picked up the receiver.

"Have you gone crazy? Put it down or I'll shoot!"

Sartain ignored the warning and proceeded to dial.

"Dad, I mean it!"

Sartain continued to dial.

He heard the shot before he felt the pain and saw the blood streaming from his right forearm.

The single bullet, however, had only grazed the flesh. Instinctively, Sartain covered the wound with his other hand.

There was a wild look in Steve's eyes as he kept the 9-mm gun pointed at his father. "I warned you, Dad, don't try me. If I have to, I won't hesitate. I'll shoot again. Don't test me."

The blood dripped through Sartain's fingers, creating a sizable stain on the carpet. Fighting the pain, he contemplated his next move. Somehow he must disarm his son.

Staring at the wound, Steve said grimly, "We'll have to dress it. Do you have any bandages in the house?"

The professor nodded. "In my bedroom," he said, hoping Steve did not know where he kept his guns. I may have to shoot my own son if necessary, he told himself, fearing he wouldn't be able to. Yet, he must be prepared to do it if there was no other way. Too many lives were involved, too much was at stake. He was suddenly consumed with a terrible feeling of déjà vu.

"Okay, you walk, slowly, ahead of me there," Steve said, motioning wih his head toward the door at the right which led to the main hallway, across which was his father's bedroom. The other door, to the left, closer to Sartain, connected the living room with the study. "My gun will be aimed at your back at all times. So please, don't try me again, because I won't hesitate—"

The sound of footsteps coming from the main hallway stopped him.

"Sam?" the familiar female voice called. "Sam? Are you home?"

Sartain, as shocked as his son, wanted to scream and warn her, but before he could, she was already at the door, gaping in disbelief at the sight of Steve aiming the gun at his bleeding father.

"Sam!" Tara cried. "What's happening here?" She began moving toward him.

"Stop right there!" Steve ordered, threatening her with the gun.

Tara froze midway between him and the professor.

"Well, now. What a surprise," Steve mocked. "Ms. Tara Kafir herself . . . all the way from Tel Aviv . . . Coming in without knocking just because she has a key. Well, well, what do you know, I got two love birds with one stone."

"Sam, what's going on?" Tara turned to the professor. After the initial shock of seeing her so unexpectedly, he was puzzled now by her strange, uncharacteristically naïve behavior.

"I'll tell you what's going on," Steve said. "I—"

"Drop your gun!" a heavily accented male voice commanded from the hallway. A hand holding a gun appeared from behind the door frame.

"Drop it, now!" another husky voice ordered from the door leading to the study.

Momentarily panicked, Steve didn't know where to aim his gun.

"Please do as they say, Steve," urged Tara, who assumed her normal, controlled demeanor. "They are Mossad agents. They will not miss."

Steve, lowering the gun to his side, pretended to obey. But then he suddenly ducked, training the gun on Tara. "You treacherous bitch! You will—"

"No!" Sartain, who saw what was coming, shouted, throwing himself at his son.

As he knocked Steve to the ground, shots rang through the room. Only one of them was fired from Steve's gun. The slug missed Tara's head by an inch. The other four shots came from the Mossad agents' Berretas, and they all found their target.

"No!" Sartain shouted again as he crouched over Steve's body, his blood mixing with that of his son's. "Oh my God! No!"

Although she had led Sartain to believe otherwise, Tara had never left for Israel after her attempted abduction. Echad had become so suspicious of the professor after that incident that he forced his top agent to choose between being recalled to Tel Aviv and reassigned or agreeing to go temporarily underground and place her lover under surveillance.

While Tara had never really lost her trust in Sartain, she had to concede that increasingly peculiar things were going on around him: Linda's death, the assassination of Colonel Navon and his immediate replacement by the professor, Luana's murder, the kidnapping and suicide of Atkins, and finally Sartain's miraculous escape. No matter how she looked at it, and even if on the surface it all seemed unrelated, there were simply too many mysterious, violent deaths surrounding Sam. And when one added to those events Jim's arrest, Amy's disappearance, and the last straw, the attempt to kidnap Tara herself on the way to Sartain's house, she had to admit that there were enough suspicious circumstances to warrant a close, undercover investigation of the man she loved. This, in spite of the fact that her female intuition, which didn't count much in Echad's eyes, told her that Sartain could be trusted.

Thus Sartain's Nineteenth Street townhouse had been placed under surveillance by Mossad agents the day after his last conversation with Tara. Two days later, when the professor was at his Triple C office, highly sophisticated, concealed microphones, the size of tiny buttons, were planted throughout the house. The telephone was bugged as well.

Mindful of Sartain's conviction that Carlos would strike on July 4, Tara had left her Washington hideout on the evening of July 3 and joined the Mossad agents who were monitoring Sartain's house from an apartment across the street. Her heart, too, skipped, when after listening in on Verner's call, she heard the man at the Dresden Nuclear Power Plant confirm Dr. Karl Baumann's presence there. Like Sartain, she put two and two together and was about to sound the alarm when she was shocked by Steve's action.

With mounting incredulity Tara and the Mossad agents listened to the son's confession and the confrontation with his father. It carried clearly through the bugging devices.

It was only after they heard the shot that Tara, terrified for Sartain's safety, decided not to wait any longer and moved to intercede.

Seeking, however, to minimize the danger to the professor from his trigger-happy son, who she feared would shoot him if he heard someone enter the living room, she put on the theatrics of innocently calling for Sam and then being stunned by what she witnessed. The scheme allowed the two Mossad agents to sneak into the house behind her and assume cover positions.

Her orders to the two operatives had been clear and specific: "If the bastard tries anything, shoot to kill!" She couldn't help but feel that, considering what Steve had done, it was not only better for his father, but for him too, if he were dead.

Ironically Dr. Karl Baumann was apprehended by a combined force of federal agents and local police at exactly five minutes to midnight, Eastern time.

It was only later discovered that the premature arrest of the German scientist, at the Dresden plant's control room, constituted a very grave error. It apparently had allowed all the terrorists who were to take part in the assault on the three nuclear facilities to escape the trap which had been set for them by beefed-up security forces at the plants. It was only the following day that Baumann disclosed under interrogation that he was supposed to have signaled the green light for the attack by a coded phone call to Helga at 23:00, Central time.

The raid itself, which was to start at 00:15 on July 4, was to be preceded by the delivery, at midnight, of a few cases of champagne to the gate of the Dresden plant. The champagne was Baumann's July 4 gift to the other night-shift workers. They were to be delivered, he had told the security guards at the gate, by two German friends visiting him. Baumann, in fact, had never before laid eyes on his so-called buddies who were to gun down the security detail at the gate to begin the operation.

As had been agreed beforehand between Baumann and Helga, if he failed to place the phone call, it meant that something went wrong and that the whole operation would have to be either postponed to the following night—if he called an hour later—or canceled altogether.

Baumann, though willing to cooperate once he thought Helga was out of danger, couldn't really tell his interrogators much. He was genuinely surprised to hear that the notorious Carlos was behind the entire plot. But his only regrets seemed to be that he would probably never see Helga again, and that he would not be able to make use of the Portuguese he had been studiously learning on his own.

Shortly after one o'clock in the morning of July 4 the telephone rang at Sartain's home. Tara, who had stayed with the shaken, grieving professor after Steve's body was removed, answered it.

"Is Steve Sartain there, by any chance?" a male voice with a slight accent asked.

"No," Tara responded curtly.

"Do you know where I can reach him? It's important."

"Who are you, please?"

"My name is Victor, Victor Manzano. I'm a good friend of his,